EVIL IN MIND

A DCI DANNY FLINT BOOK

TREVOR NEGUS

Revised Edition 2021
INKUBATOR BOOKS

www.inkubatorbooks.com

First published as "The Coal Killer" by Trevor Negus (2017)

PROLOGUE

Newstead Colliery Village, Nottinghamshire 1970

The scruffy blonde boy sat on the dusty concrete floor of the yard behind the terraced house, where he lived with his elderly grandparents. He was wondering what to do. It was the last week of the school summer holidays, and he was totally bored, having already exhausted every fun thing there was to do.

He was wearing a dirty Leeds United football shirt and red shorts that didn't match the shirt. He had black plimsolls on with no socks. His dirty feet felt uncomfortable, sweating in the heat.

Lethargically, he dragged himself to his feet and kicked the deflated football that sat on the concrete of the yard.

The ball scuffed noisily across the floor and landed in the corner; it was useless.

Ignoring the ball, the boy slouched over to the small brick outbuilding in the corner of the yard. Opening the door, he found the cool darkness appealing after sitting in the baking hot sun.

LOOKING on the shelves in the small shed, his eyes latched onto a magnifying glass. Taking the magnifying glass, he stepped back out into the sunshine. Scanning the concrete, he soon spotted movement.

Over by the back door of the house, he spotted a column of ants.

He wore a serious expression as he used the magnifying glass to focus the sun's rays on the line of ants that were purposefully marching across the yard.

Suddenly, he felt enthused again. He was now an alien from Mars, circling planet Earth in his spaceship. The magnifying glass became the spaceship's death ray, wiping out whole populations below.

He grinned as the ants popped, fried alive by the sun's rays.

Eventually, after twenty minutes, he bored of the game. After surveying the rows of burned ants – now twisted into macabre shapes – with a satisfied grin, he slouched down into the corner of the yard.

The boy looked along the row of brick-built terraced houses.

The once-red bricks had become discoloured over time and were now almost black. The mortar in between the bricks had been stained by decades of smoke, soot and grime. The grey slates on the roof shimmered in the bright sunlight, and the boy could see the heat haze bouncing off the tiles.

The houses had been built just after the turn of the century to house miners working at the local coal mine. Every house was identical, traditional two-up, two-down terraces. They were known locally as the Newstead Rows.

All the backyards were small, with an outbuilding in one

corner and an outside toilet in the other. The wooden fences separating the yards were only three feet high. Standing up, the boy looked over the fences at the different coloured clothes on the washing lines.

It was roasting hot with a very gentle breeze, a perfect wash day.

Squatting down on the concrete, the boy began thinking about the local grammar school, where he was due to start next week. He wasn't looking forward to it. He didn't make friends easily and was worried by tales of vicious bullying he had heard.

It came as no surprise to the boy's doting grandmother that he had sailed through his eleven plus exam; she was always quick to point out, to anyone who would listen, that her grandson was a 'gifted child'.

Gifted he might have been; strange he was.

The boy had no friends. He was happiest when left with his head buried in a book. He was considered to be a bookworm and a swot by the other kids in the village. Adult neighbours considered him to be plain weird with his aloof and sullen attitude.

Six months ago, just prior to his eleventh birthday, a group of neighbours had rounded on the boy, accusing him of harming their children's pets. Two rabbits and a cat had gone missing from nearby gardens. The adored pets were later found mutilated after being throttled by wire nooses.

His grandmother had vehemently defended the boy. She had quickly lied to the group of neighbours, saying her grandson had spent the last two days at home, ill in bed with a cold.

The gathering of angry neighbours didn't bother involving the local police, as there was no hard proof of the boy's involvement. The boy had smirked at the neighbours from behind his grandmother's back.

He really couldn't understand what all the fuss was about.

The cat had scratched his hand; surely it was only fair that he made it suffer. The rabbits were plain stupid and deserved to be tormented.

Killing the pets was the thing he had enjoyed most through the entire boring holidays.

In her heart, his grandmother knew the boy was odd, but she felt it was her duty to protect him after the harsh start in life he had endured.

The boy had never known his own father. His mother had only just turned seventeen when she fell pregnant following a brief affair with a foreign businessman.

The young woman had become infatuated with the tall blonde Norwegian whom she met while working as a chambermaid at the Royal Hotel in Nottingham. The Norwegian businessman had used her for casual sex, then as soon as his business in the city was completed, immediately returned to Oslo. He had gone, leaving no message for the young chambermaid, and without a moment's hesitation. He had also left her very pregnant.

Shortly after his third birthday, the boy's mother left the family home in Newstead, to start a new life on the east coast, working at a holiday camp near Great Yarmouth.

It had been an easy decision for her to leave behind a son she had never really wanted. It was then left to the grandparents to raise the boy.

The boy never asked after his mother, and his grandmother did her best to provide everything he needed, within the meagre budget they lived on.

The sun was getting hotter now, and the boy was being plagued by a troublesome wasp that continually flew around his face.

He moved nearer to the outbuilding as it created the only small parcel of shade in the yard. He didn't want to sit inside, as the smell of creosote and old paint tins gave him a headache. The back door to the house itself was locked, and both grandparents were out at the shops.

The grandfather now insisted that the boy was not to be left alone in the house, after he had caught him smoking his cigarettes.

Before going out to the shops, his grandparents had left strict instructions with the boy, ordering him not to stray from the yard. They knew that relations with some of the neighbours were still quite raw and strained.

Suddenly, he heard a door bang a few houses along the street. He immediately stood up, and looking over the fence, he saw his neighbour, Mrs Daines, coming out of her back gate, pulling on the arm of her young son, Billy.

The family had only moved into the terrace about three months before, and she didn't yet know many of her new neighbours. Since the family had arrived in Newstead, the only person she had spent any time chatting to was the boy's grandmother.

The harassed-looking young mum was now dragging Billy along by his arm.

'Come along, Billy. I haven't got time for any of your nonsense today.'

The small boy said nothing; he just dragged along behind her like a dead weight.

Mrs Daines walked up to the boy's gate.

'Hello, Jimmy, is your grandma home?'

'No, she's at the shops with my grandad.'

'Are they going to be home soon?'

'I reckon so. They've been gone a couple of hours already, so I don't think they'll be long. Why?'

Mrs Daines looked worried; she shifted her weight from one foot to the other before taking a deep breath.

'Jimmy, could you do me a huge favour and watch young Billy for a while, just until your grandma gets home? My hubby's had an accident at the pit. I've got to go and meet him at the hospital over in Mansfield, and I don't want to drag Billy down there as well.'

The boy looked over the gate at young Billy, who was now sitting cross-legged at the feet of his harassed mother.

The youngster looked even more bored than he felt himself.

Billy Daines was about seven years old, a short, plump child with a mop of unruly red hair. He was also an only child, and his parents doted on him, dressing him immaculately. Today was no different, the young boy was dressed in a blue-and-white-striped T-shirt, matching blue shorts, blue sandals and white ankle socks.

With a broad smile on his face, the boy opened the gate to the yard.

'No problem. I'll watch Billy. It'll be fun.'

Mrs Daines eased her young son into the yard, and the boy closed the gate.

As she walked hurriedly away, the young mother looked back over her shoulder and shouted, 'Don't go wandering off, Billy! Be good for Jimmy and do what he tells you.'

Both boys played in the yard for about half an hour before once again boredom set in. There was only so much to do in such a small space with no toys. Even frying the ants soon became tedious.

The boy suddenly stood up, turned to Billy and said excitedly, 'Shall we go for an adventure, Billy? There's a small pond just over the fields. I saw a huge pike in there the other day. Do you want to see it?'

'What's a pike?'

'A pike's a massive fish with huge teeth. It can eat other fish and even ducklings. It's amazing, Billy.'

'Okay,' said Billy, his eyes widening at the thought of meeting this monster fish.

The boys then left the haven of the yard and set off walking through the maze of terraced houses. The terraces were criss-crossed with narrow alleyways, which ran in front of tiny postage-stamp front gardens and rear yards. The boy knew the alleyways like the back of his hand.

The boys walked quickly through the Rows, eventually passing Newstead Miners Welfare and crossing the disused railway line.

Billy whined as his podgy little legs struggled to keep pace.

'How far do we have to walk, Jimmy?'

'It's not far now, Billy, we're nearly there.'

Having crossed the overgrown railway tracks, the boys walked into a field of nearly ripe wheat that was almost the same height as Billy.

The youngster was getting agitated because of the heat and the dust from the high wheat.

He pulled back against the older boy's grip and said, 'I'm tired. I want to go back.'

The boy bent down so he was looking straight into Billy's eyes.

'Look, Billy. Do you see those bushes and trees over there? That's where the pond is, come on.'

The older boy gripped Billy's hand tighter and began to pull him along behind him.

The youngster protested, 'Okay, I'm coming. There's no need to drag me.'

The boys reached the bushes, and sure enough, there was a small pond. It was completely surrounded by vegetation and couldn't be seen from the fields. It was a small irrigation pond that had been dug years before by a farmer who had previously owned the land. He had raised a few cattle on the land and needed a source of water.

The field hadn't been used to raise cattle for over twenty years; everything was now geared towards raising crops. It was difficult for the current farmer to plough right to the edge of the pond, and that was the reason the bushes and small trees had flourished.

'Come on! Come and see the big fish.'

Billy looked apprehensive. He spluttered, 'I don't want to, Jimmy. I'm frightened of the pike. You said it's got huge teeth; will it eat me?'

The older boy smiled kindly. 'Don't be daft, Billy; of course it won't eat you. You're way too big, but if you're lucky, you might see it grab a smaller fish and eat that.'

Feeling a little bolder, Billy grinned and walked through the bushes until he stood right at the side of the pond.

'Where is it?' he said.

'You've got to look a little closer.'

Billy edged ever closer to the water's edge until he was on his knees, bending right over the dark brackish water.

'I still can't see it.'

Suddenly, the boy grabbed Billy by his shoulders and rammed his face down into the water.

The youngster twisted his body frantically, trying to escape the older boy's grip. All Billy succeeded in doing was to twist over, so he was lying on his back in the water with the older boy standing astride him.

The water in the pond was quite shallow near the edge, but was still up to the knees of the older boy, who slowly exerted more pressure on the youngster's shoulders, forcing his face down under the water.

Billy started to scream, but clamped his mouth and eyes shut as his head was forced under the brackish water.

The boy held Billy just below the surface of the water until, suddenly, he saw the child's eyes open. There was a panicked expression on the youngster's face. The older boy was fascinated and stared into Billy's terrified eyes. As the seconds passed, he watched closely as the expression in the youngster's eyes went from panicked to pleading to nothing.

After several minutes, there was nothing in the eyes except a blank lifeless stare.

The boy suddenly realised that everywhere was now deathly quiet. The frantic splashing that had been made by Billy's arms and legs had now stopped.

The youngster was lifeless and floppy.

The boy slowly stood up and finally released his grip on Billy's shoulders.

He remained standing astride the dead boy, who was now lying just below the surface of the dirty brown water. He peered intently into the water and saw tiny bubbles escaping from the nostrils and partially open mouth.

After a couple of minutes, he stepped out of the pond and looked at the drowned child lying just under the surface of the water.

He didn't know what he felt.

It was a toxic mixture of excitement, fear and pleasure. He had no idea why he'd drowned the child. It just felt right. When he had looked into the youngster's eyes, the boy had known it was something he had to do.

But now, his brain was going into overdrive. He felt panicked, and his breathing was shallow.

He sat down in his wet clothes on the bank of the pond to think.

A bright green dragonfly skimmed across the surface of the pond, and birds had started to sing in the bushes around him.

Life had resumed its normal course.

After a few minutes everything became clear. He knew what he had to do. He turned his back on the pond and walked out from the bushes, back into the harsh sunlight. He stopped and began forcing himself to cry. Eventually there were real tears streaming down his face, carving track marks in the dusty grime caked on his cheeks.

Then he began to run as fast as he could, back towards Newstead Village.

He smashed his way through the high ripening wheat and sped over the railway line until he could see the Miners Welfare. As he raced towards the Welfare, he saw a group of four men standing outside drinking beer, chatting and smoking.

The boy ran straight up to them, shouting for help at the top of his voice.

One of the younger men in the group intercepted the shouting boy and said, 'Calm down, lad. What's up? You're soaking wet, what's tha' been doing?'

Breathless from his sprint, the boy tried to speak between sobs.

'It's young Billy Daines. I'm supposed to be looking after him, but he ran off! He's fallen into the Farmers Pond, and I can't get him out!'

One of the men bent down to the anguished boy, put his hand on his shoulder and said, 'Stay here with George. We'll go and see what's happened.'

The three younger men threw down their cigarettes and ran off in the direction of the Farmers Pond. The older miner who had stayed with the boy took a long pull on his cigarette and quaffed a mouthful of cold beer.

'Don't thee worry, lad; it'll be alright. You're not to blame. Have you tried to get him out? Is that why your clothes are wet?'

The boy sobbed and nodded.

'He wasn't moving. There's something wrong with Billy, I know there is.'

'There, there, lad, it's not your fault. You tried to get him out,' said the old man gently, trying to comfort the boy.

'Aren't you young Jimmy Wade? Brian Wade's grandson?' the old miner asked.

The boy nodded again.

'Come on then, Jimmy, I'll walk you back to your house. I know it's hot, but you need to get out of those wet clothes.'

Just as they were about to set off, one of the men came sprinting back towards the Welfare.

He shouted to the older miner standing with the boy.

'It looks bad, George; I reckon the kid's drowned. We've got him out of the pond. I need to call the police and an ambulance.'

The young miner ran inside to call the emergency services.

The boy standing with George started to sob even harder.

'Don't worry, lad, I've already told you it's not your fault. It was an accident. You tried to get him out. Stop crying now, lad. You're only a kid yourself. You did your best. Come on, let's get you home to your granddad's house.'

The old miner put his gnarled, bony hand on the shoulder of the boy, and together they walked through the Newstead Rows back to his grandparents' house.

As they walked, the old miner didn't see the sparkle in the boy's eyes or the sly smirk spreading slowly across his mouth.

1

Mansfield Woodhouse – March 1984

Jimmy Wade was getting ready for his first shift of the week. He was on early turn at the colliery, and his alarm clock had gone off just after four thirty that morning. It had been a real struggle to drag himself out of bed; he'd been awake most of the night studying for the exam he hoped would see him through to getting his deputy's papers. It was his ambition to be a deputy at Warsop Main Colliery by the time he was twenty-five years of age.

Wade had entered the mining industry straight from leaving school, much to the dismay of his teachers, who wanted him to further his education at university. After the death of his devoted grandmother, just before he left school in 1975, he'd made the decision to leave education and start work so he could earn a wage and look after his elderly grandfather, whose health was also failing.

The other reason that helped him make the decision not to pursue further education was the realisation, at around fourteen years of age, that he was different from the rest of the pupils at his school.

It wasn't just that he was different from the other pupils. Jimmy knew he was different from everybody.

Ever since the incident from his childhood at the Farmers Pond in Newstead, when young Billy Daines was drowned, he had fought hard to suppress the emotions he felt on a daily basis.

The involvement of the police and subsequent coroner's enquiry into the boy's drowning had taken its toll on him. So many times he had wanted to try to explain to the police and the coroner that it wasn't an accident, and that it wasn't wrong either, as what had happened at the pond just came naturally to him.

Eventually, after the coroner's inquest ruled that the death was an accidental drowning, Mr and Mrs Daines left the village. They couldn't accept that their beautiful little red-haired child had been snatched from them. Mr Daines never believed the verdict of accidental death, and prior to him leaving the village, he twice made allegations to the police that Jimmy Wade was responsible for his son's death. On each occasion, the police made brief enquiries, then decided that no blame could be apportioned to the boy.

The grieving parents left the village to move back to the Kent coalfields, and over time, sentiments in the village settled down again. The incident at the pond was generally forgotten.

Some of the neighbours in the village continued to point the finger at Jimmy, refusing to rule out that he had some sinister involvement in the youngster's death.

It was this constant mudslinging that began to affect his grandmother's health. As a child, he noticed how she dramatically lost weight and developed a constant, stuttering cough.

Even when doctors diagnosed that his grandmother was

suffering from lung cancer, he still believed the real reason she became so ill was because of the poisonous gossips in that small-minded village. After her death, he lost all interest in school and left at the first opportunity. He immediately applied for a job in the thriving coal industry and was accepted into the training centre for mining near Bevercotes village.

He enjoyed working at the mine. It helped to give him the cloak of normality and invisibility that he craved. He knew some people regarded him as strange, even weird, and he tried hard to blend in as normal. As soon as he was down the pit, and once the dust and grime had settled on his face, he knew that in his work clothes and helmet, he looked the same as everyone else.

Fourteen years had passed since Billy Daines had died at the pond. In that time Jimmy Wade matured into a strong, good-looking man, over six feet tall with golden blonde hair and piercing blue eyes, a reminder of his Nordic genes. As he grew into manhood, women were drawn to him, and he had a confident attitude, which women generally found alluring. There were several girlfriends, but they all found him impossible to get close to.

Physically, he was a brilliant lover, but icy cold with it.

Passion was not within him; he could make love energetically, but to him, it was like running an eight-hundred-metre race. It was purely physical exertion to him; there was no emotion. Eventually, all the women he dated grew tired of this, and although they said the sex was great, they wanted more.

They were looking for someone to love them, and the only person Jimmy truly loved other than his grandmother was himself.

His grandfather died just before Christmas in 1982 after suffering briefly from pneumonia; he had succumbed to the deadly illness very quickly. In November, he developed an irritating cough and quickly lost his appetite. He was taken into hospital on 3 December and died two weeks later.

The old man, ignoring his wayward daughter, left Jimmy everything. The house in Newstead and his beloved pristine Ford Cortina car.

Jimmy had passed his driving test in 1980 but had never owned a car. Now he could drive this beautiful, if dated, car. His grandfather had always lavished time on the vehicle, and it was literally in mint condition. It was only ever taken out from under the protective covers when the weather was fine. As a result, the mileage on the car was next to nothing.

With the passing of his grandfather, there was nothing to keep Jimmy in Newstead anymore. He had come to despise the village and the people in it for the way they had ostracised his grandmother.

He immediately sold his grandfather's terraced house in Newstead and purchased a fairly new three-bedroom, semi-detached house with attached garage on Marples Avenue at Mansfield Woodhouse in May 1983.

He had been living alone in the house on Marples Avenue for just under a year now. He liked the smart tree-lined street with its well-kept manicured gardens.

He had lavished time and money on the house and the garden, and it was now a very smart house in a lovely quiet neighbourhood. He also respected his neighbours for the way they kept themselves to themselves.

He was very well paid as a face worker at Warsop Main Colliery, so he was able to decorate the house well inside and out. He had more than enough money to buy a brand-new car, but he insisted on driving the dark green Ford Cortina that was his grandfather's legacy to him.

All in all, life was good for Jimmy Wade.

The only problem for Jimmy was that over the last three months, long-suppressed feelings and urges were once again pushing their way to the surface, and they were extremely disturbing to him.

They didn't manifest themselves as manic voices in his head urging him to kill, or as messages from God telling him to purge the unclean from the earth.

The urges he felt came to him in a very strange manner. He would find himself looking directly into people's eyes, staring, unblinking, at them. He knew something inside him was making a calculated assessment, asking the same question silently in his head: 'Is this the one?'

The last time he'd felt urges this strong was the day he had stared into young Billy Daines's eyes.

Jimmy knew already that he was losing the battle to keep the feelings and urges in check, and that it was only a matter of time before he would need to placate them.

Today, as he ate his breakfast and got ready for work, he felt in control. He switched on the small television in his kitchen. The news was dominated once again by the president of the National Union of Mineworkers, Arthur Scargill, stating he would call a national strike by the end of the week unless he received assurances from the conservative Prime Minister Margaret Thatcher that the programme for pit closures would be reassessed.

Listening to the news report, he was disturbed when he heard Scargill insisting that this Tory government, and Margaret Thatcher in particular, were hell-bent on destroying the coal industry of Great Britain.

Jimmy had always believed that a job in the coal business was a job for life.

Scargill continued to rant into the camera, pointing angrily with his index finger. He was standing outside one of the pits destined for closure in the Yorkshire coalfield. Heavy on the rhetoric, he claimed the pit closure would not only mean the death of the industry in that area, but also the demise of the close-knit community that relied on the mine for employment.

Jimmy quickly bored of Scargill's impassioned rhetoric and switched off the television. They might close a few uneconomic pits up in Yorkshire, but Jimmy felt strongly that the cuts wouldn't impact the more profitable Nottinghamshire pits. He grabbed his black reefer coat and made his way out of the house.

He started up the Cortina and began the short drive along the main A60 road into Warsop, finally turning into the large car park of Warsop Main Colliery.

During the drive, his thoughts were concentrated on the television news bulletin. The impending strike was sure to be the main topic of conversation again at work. It had been for weeks. He knew that most of his colleagues were reluctant to strike. They all knew the financial hardship it would bring to their families. Nottinghamshire Collieries were some of the best in the country, producing the most coal, and more importantly, the best coal to fire power stations.

Not many of his colleagues truly believed the vitriolic, working-class-struggle rhetoric coming from Scargill and Mick McGahey, the leader of the Scottish miners – the idea that the whole industry was at risk from Thatcher and her Tory government. There were some who believed Scargill was speaking the truth. There had been several heated arguments about the merits of a strike; the division was already starting to show.

Jimmy personally thought that a few unprofitable pits, probably in Yorkshire, would close, and that would be it, business as usual.

He was worried about a strike, though. If the union called a national work stoppage, there would be enormous pressure across all the coalfields to comply. The division between men used to working together would get wider, and families would be deeply affected. Brother against brother, father against son. The strike, if and when it came, would only be bad news.

With these thoughts racing around his head, he walked

into the busy pit canteen, where he drank a mug of strong tea while chatting with workmates.

Finishing his tea, he walked into the clean-side locker room and stripped off completely, hanging his clothes in the locker. He glanced around him at his now-naked colleagues. It never ceased to amaze him how unfit and fat some of them were. Jimmy, although slim, was naturally very muscular and strong. He couldn't help but strut a little as he walked naked past the huge communal showers towards the dirty-side locker room.

He got dressed into the grey vest and pants supplied by the mine, and then slipped on football shorts and socks before putting on the orange overalls, heavy boots and leather work belt. Finally, he removed the dirty, coal-stained helmet from the locker.

Once dressed, he followed other miners into the Deployment Office, where an overman informed him and the other miners where they would be working that shift. While waiting in the queue, he joined in the talk of the impending strike with his workmates. Once again, there were varied opinions that were expressed strongly, each man trying to impress that his opinion was the correct one.

Jimmy ignored the arguments and made his way to the lamp cabin, where he obtained his lamp and the large battery, which clipped onto his belt. The man in the cabin then issued him with a self-rescuer, which he also clipped onto his belt. Finally, he was given two brass tags stamped with a number.

The queue of miners then made their way slowly down to the cage. Jimmy stepped into the cage after handing over one of the brass tags to the banksman. As always, he stepped over to the far side of the cage.

He always liked to stand in the same place if he could.

As he waited for the cage to fill up, he looked to his right and saw that the man standing alongside him was sixty-four-year-old Albie Jones.

Albie was a short man, his dirty orange overalls were open to the waist, and his huge belly was straining to burst out of the grimy vest he was wearing.

Jimmy smiled and said, 'How do, Albie? There can't be many more of these rides left for you, old lad?'

In a broad Welsh accent, Albie replied, 'No, boy, finished next week, I have. Ready to put my feet up, me!' He laughed.

Another voice chimed in, 'If Scargill has his way, boyo, you'll be finished sooner than that.'

This comment was met with mutterings of agreement and disapproval in equal measure.

Albie said, at the top of his booming Welsh voice, 'Just do what the union tells you and you'll be fine. You can't trust this Thatcher woman, boys. She'll have all your jobs if she gets her way.'

Jimmy found himself staring into the old Welshman's watery blue eyes.

The realisation hit Jimmy like a hammer blow.

This was it; he had found him. Albie Jones was to be the next one. Instantly he knew what he had to do. The eyes were telling him it was the old man's destiny.

Jimmy quickly turned away to avoid staring into the old man's eyes, but it was too late. The fate of Albie Jones was already sealed.

With a small jerk, the cage began its rapid descent. Seconds later, they were plummeting down towards the pit bottom.

Jimmy knew that this part of the descent was always one of silence as hard men said silent prayers to themselves. There aren't many jobs where even the mere process of getting to work was death-defying. One flaw in the machinery was all it would take for the entire cage to send all the men crashing to their deaths at the bottom of the shaft. This brief silence was always quickly filled with general chat and laughter as the men hurtled towards their day's work underground.

All too soon, the men were emerging from the cage, out into the relatively wide area of the gate at the pit bottom.

Jimmy was soon setting off along the gate with the other miners, making the long walk to the coal face.

As they walked along the loader gate, they passed the freshly hewn coal hurtling past on the automated belts. One of the first lessons learned at the mine was to keep well clear of these belts. In an instant, an inattentive man could be dragged onto the rollers and crushed. Many a collier had lost his job for jumping on the belt to hitch a ride instead of walking.

Jimmy found himself walking directly behind old Albie.

'You working at the face today, Albie?' he asked.

'Nah, lad, my time hewing coal with the machinery at the face has long since passed. I'm on a button just up here a way.'

Being 'on the button' was one of the loneliest jobs at the pit. It was monitoring a button to stop the belt. Basically, if instructed by the men working on the face, you pressed the button and stopped the belt. Except this never, in actuality, happened.

At certain parts along the loader gate, the belt would reach a junction where the coal would drop from one belt onto another. If the debris or dust got too great around the working parts of the belt, it would need to be cleaned off to prevent a jam. This was also the responsibility of the button man.

By rights, the belt should be stopped and the covers taken off for the working parts to be cleaned. This invariably never happened; instead, the working parts were always cleaned while the belts were moving. Every time the belt stopped, it meant cutting coal on the face had to stop, too, and that meant a loss of money for the face workers.

So, in reality, the hardest thing about being the button man was staying awake in the darkness.

As they walked along the loader gate, Albie said, 'I don't mind the button now, Jimmy. It's about all I'm good for.' He chuckled and raised his voice so everyone could hear: 'While you boys are all sweating your bollocks off, I'll be sitting with my helmet off and my feet up, reading the paper!'

The deputy in charge of the men, Dave Smedley, shouted back to Albie, 'You'd better not let me catch you reading the bloody paper, Jones, and keep your fucking helmet on! Some of the cover tins that prevent minor roof falls in that area have slipped, and we haven't had time to send a haulage team in to fix them yet. There's been a couple of large chunks down from the walls and the roof already. If one of them hits you on the head, you're gonna need more than a Disprin, old lad.'

The men reached the location of Albie's button.

Albie settled down for his battle against boredom while the rest of the miners continued on the remaining three-hundred-yard walk to the face.

After three hours working at the coal face, Jimmy sought out the deputy.

'Sorry, Dave. I've got a problem, mate. I've got the biggest load of muck in my left eye. It doesn't matter what I do, I can't fucking shift it. I reckon I need to get to the medical centre, topside, and get it flushed out properly.'

'Fucking hell, Jimmy! We're just about to bang a new stint in. I can't afford to take anyone off the face to take you back to the pit bottom. It's gonna have to wait, I'm afraid. Just wash the fucker out.'

'I've tried that already, Dave; nothing I'm doing is shifting it. I don't need anyone to walk me back. I'll be fine. I can see okay out of my right eye. If I don't get it cleaned out properly, it's just gonna end up scratching my eyeball, and then I'll be forced off work for a week or two.'

It was against best practice for an injured man to take himself out of the pit, and Jimmy knew this.

'Bloody hell, Jimmy, you pick your moments. All right, I'll walk with you the first hundred yards or so, and then you can just fuck off out of it. But if any of this lot asks you later, I walked you all the way to the pit bottom, got it?'

'Yeah, got it. Cheers, mate.'

They immediately set off, walking past the stage loader and continuing along the loader gate. After a hundred yards or so, Dave said, 'Off you go then, Wade, and remember what I said: I walked you all the way to the pit bottom, got it?'

'No problem, Dave. I'll be fine, thanks.'

Jimmy now set off alone along the loader gate back to where they had left Albie Jones earlier. There was a bend just before the junction where Albie was. Jimmy could now see the glow from Albie's lamp.

He reached up and dimmed his own lamp before covering it with a hessian rag from his pocket. This made the beam from his lamp barely visible.

As he rounded the bend, he could see the old man sitting on the floor, facing away from him, leaning sideways against one of the rings. Sure enough, he had taken his helmet off, and his legs were stretched out in front of him. Jimmy walked silently until he stood directly behind the old man, so close he could see the long, rhythmic breathing of the man as his chest rose and fell slowly.

Albie Jones was asleep.

Jimmy quickly looked around, and in the light cast from Albie's lamp on the floor, he saw a large rock below the belt. He knelt down and, with some effort, removed the huge rock from its resting place. Carrying the rock in both hands, he crept silently behind the old man once again. Albie was still dozing, and his mouth was wide open. He could have been snoring loudly, but any noise was drowned out by the clatter of the coal-filled belt rushing past.

Using all his strength, Jimmy raised the large rock high above his head before bringing it down with tremendous force straight onto the top of the old man's head.

He saw instantly that the head injury was catastrophic.

Albie's head had split wide apart, and he could literally see brain below the huge crack in his balding head, blood starting to pour out of the massive wound.

It was obvious the old man had been killed instantly. A red frothy mucus was bubbling from his mouth and his nostrils.

Taking the oily rag from his lamp, he turned it up to full beam and surveyed the scene of the carnage properly.

Nobody would survive a head wound of such devastation, especially not an old man. The force of the blow had caused Albie to roll sideways out into the middle of the loader gate. He was now on his back, and his lifeless eyes were wide open and staring up at the roof of the gate. The life force had gone; the eyes were blank, expressionless. The bright blue eyes that had sparkled in life were now dull.

Once again, he felt that familiar mixture of excitement and achievement. He noted this time there was no fear, just a real sense of release and a feeling that was almost pleasure. He only regretted that he had not been able to see the life force leave the eyes. He knew it was a special moment to watch and enjoy.

Staging the large rock carefully at the side of the body, Jimmy removed two more cover tins directly above where Albie now lay, sliding them down the side of the gate. Satisfied the scene was set correctly, he made his way along the gate, eventually arriving at the pit bottom.

Once at the pit bottom, he used the telephone to contact the banksman and arranged to be taken in the cage back to the surface as a medical emergency. After a twenty-minute wait, he was once again topside. He made his way directly to the medical centre, where the muck and grime he had rubbed into his left eye was washed out.

The accident book was filled in by the attending nurse, and Jimmy knew by the time Albie was discovered, he would already be at home.

After undressing, he checked his overalls and boots for

any spatters of blood. He then showered and got changed before having a cup of tea and a cheese roll in the canteen.

As he drove home, he found himself smiling. He was acutely aware now that his destiny was not to suppress the urges, but to act on them when he knew it was right.

He had killed again, and this time, he felt fulfilled and totally at peace.

2

Mansfield Woodhouse – March 1984

The banging on his front door was getting more insistent.

'All right, I'm coming,' yelled Jimmy.

Getting to the front door, he paused. It was nearly eleven o'clock at night.

'Who is it?' he shouted.

'It's me, Dave Smedley! Open the door. I need to talk to you now!'

Jimmy had a small rush of panic, but composing himself quickly, he opened the door to the pit deputy.

'What the fuck's the matter, Dave? Don't tell me there's a problem about me coming out of the pit today? Has old Albie fucking blabbed, mate?'

'It's not that, but I have come about Albie, yes. What was he like when you walked past him on the gate?'

'He was like Albie always is. He was sitting with his feet up, whistling, when I went by. He offered to walk me to the pit bottom. He was surprised you'd let me come out alone, but said he'd seen it a thousand times. I told him he'd better stay on his button. Why? What's he said?'

'He hasn't said anything; he's fucking dead, Jimmy!'

'What do you mean he's dead? He's retiring next week! What the fuck happened?'

'Oh, believe me, he's dead alright. It must've been sometime after you went by; the roof came in and smashed his head in. The silly bastard had ignored what I told him and had taken his helmet off. Was his helmet on when you saw him?'

'I reckon it was, yeah. Who found him?'

'Some of the haulage lads. They put a call topside, saying there'd been a large roof fall and that a number of the cover tins had slipped out of place, leaving the roof exposed, and that it was too dangerous for them to recover his body.'

'Fucking hell, they called out the Mines Rescue team?'

'Yes, they fucking did. The shit has well and truly hit the fan. Did you say he did have his helmet on?'

'I'm pretty sure he was wearing it, yeah.'

'Thank fuck for that. I told the Inspectorate boys that he was fine when I walked back from taking you to the pit bottom, and that when we went past him, he was wearing his helmet. You've got to stick to that when they come asking you at work tomorrow; otherwise we'll both be in the shit. You for walking out alone and me for letting you. Sorry to bother you so late tonight, but I thought I'd better let you know what's happened.'

'That's okay.'

'How's the eye now?'

'It's fine. I'll be back at work in the morning, if I wake up, that is, after getting no sleep.'

With a grin at Dave, he opened the front door.

Dave took the hint and left, saying, 'Alright, Jimmy, see you at work tomorrow. Just stick to the story when they talk to you, and we'll both be fine.'

'No problem.' He chuckled.

He closed the front door and let a smile develop across his face. It was great when a plan came together, he thought.

As Dave Smedley walked back to his car, he was troubled. Why had Wade immediately assumed it was Albie Jones he had come to see him about?

He also noticed that there hadn't been a shred of sympathy offered by Wade when he told him that Jones was dead.

It all felt a bit strange.

Smedley got in his car and started the engine. As he drove the car away, he pondered whether to tell the truth, tell the Inspectorate that Wade had walked from the face to the pit bottom alone and that he was the last person to see Albie Jones alive, not him.

'Fuck it!' he said aloud. There was nothing he could say that would change anything. Albie Jones would still be dead. All he would achieve by speaking out was losing his deputy status and a massive drop in his take-home pay.

He would stick to the story.

3

Mansfield – March 1984

The week he had taken as annual leave had passed way too quickly, and for Detective Inspector Danny Flint that meant another seven days of shifts at Mansfield Police Station, dealing with whatever crimes the people of the North Nottinghamshire market town could throw at him.

Danny was just under six feet tall and broad shouldered. Even though he was now nearly forty, he was still slim and extremely fit.

His short black hair was just starting to grey a little at the temples.

Danny had always taken pride in his appearance, wearing smart suits and ties.

Today was no different. As he carefully tied a smart Windsor knot in his tie, he thought about the consequences of a strike by the National Union of Mineworkers.

There was a strange atmosphere and palpable tension

around the town as all the talk of a long-drawn-out strike by the miners became more and more likely.

The implications of such an action by the union would be felt strongly by the town.

Mansfield was a town surrounded by coal mines.

The vast majority of men in the town and the surrounding areas were employed by British Coal. The local economy relied heavily on the income generated and spent by those mineworkers.

Danny also knew that in any strike action, there would be some who would follow the union doctrine and come out on strike, and others who would defy the union and continue to work.

In this area, that would mean pitting neighbour against neighbour, even family member against family member.

It would be a recipe for conflict on a grand scale.

Danny was well aware that if and when the strike did happen, it would herald an extremely busy time for the police.

The transistor radio in his kitchen was on as he ate breakfast and got ready for work. He shook his head in dismay as he listened to the latest updates on the news.

Once again, Arthur Scargill was doing his best to rally the miners to hold a national strike, citing the fact that the livelihood of every working miner in the land was at risk if they did not stand up to pit closures now.

Danny sighed as he listened to the arguments put forward by the union's charismatic, firebrand leader. It looked a done deal that a strike of some description was coming.

He thought to himself how easy it would have been for him to have followed his own father down the mine. He still had an uncle working at Thoresby Colliery in nearby Ollerton.

A life underground had never appealed to Danny, and after leaving school, he had worked for a couple of years in one of the local furniture stores, helping out with deliveries.

He had joined the police force quite late, but had been in

his current post as the detective inspector at Mansfield CID for the last three years.

DANNY HAD TAKEN the decision to accept the promotion even though, at the time, his marriage had been struggling. Following his promotion to detective inspector and the added workload and hours that came with that role, inevitably his marriage had broken down. Following a messy divorce, Danny had moved back to live with his mother, Jean, and his father, Frank, in his childhood home at High Oakham in Mansfield. Moving back to his parents' house had only ever been intended as a short-term arrangement. First, he had needed to stay on to help his father cope with his ailing mother. Then, after his mother had passed away, he stayed to help his father, whose own health had suffered as a result of his wife's illness.

His father, Frank, although still working at nearby Silverhill Colliery just outside Sutton in Ashfield, suffered badly from depression and needed constant assistance with the running of the house.

THE ONLY CONSTANTS in Danny's life were his work and his love of football. Even though he was now approaching his forties, he still regularly played in a game of five-a-side football with some of the younger lads from the uniform section.

His real enjoyment was accompanying his father to watch the local team, Mansfield Town, at their Field Mill ground, a short ten-minute walk from his father's house.

It was the one time his father could forget his troubles and lose the black dog depression that plagued his life. Win, lose or draw, it didn't matter to his father. He was happy just watching his beloved Mansfield Town play football.

Switching the radio off, Danny grabbed his coat.

He decided to make the fifteen-minute walk into work today rather than take the car. It wasn't raining, and Danny found that the walk in to the police station helped to focus his mind on the day's work ahead.

It was still dark when he left the house.

The walk into town was an easy one: downhill all the way from the house on Garth Road to the police station.

It was a foggy morning and there was a cold chill in the air; there wasn't another soul about.

As he walked down the hill in the quiet darkness, with the mist swirling in front of him, the town took on a foreboding look. He sensed a feeling of real menace lurking below the surface, but pulling his coat a little tighter into his neck, he shrugged off the feeling as being just one of returning-to-work blues.

Arriving at the station, he made his way into the CID office. The first person he saw was his friend and colleague, Detective Sergeant Rob Buxton.

Rob Buxton had joined his team two years ago after transferring to Nottinghamshire from South Yorkshire upon promotion to detective sergeant.

He arrived with glowing references, not always the case with transferees.

Rob had settled in quickly and easily overcame the petty resentments some of the other detectives already in the office felt. A few of them had also applied for the vacancy for detective sergeant, but Rob quickly got them onside by his demeanour and attitude to hard work. It didn't take long for the other applicants to accept that he hadn't taken their job.

Rob's wife was local to the Mansfield area, and this was the reason he had applied for the transfer, so his wife could be nearer her family.

He was an enthusiastic character always willing to help, a very fit and tough-looking man who, in his youth, had suffered a badly broken nose playing schoolboy rugby.

The battered face together with the shaved head gave him the look of a squat, powerful boxer, which he often used to his advantage. The truth was very different: He was a doting father and husband and would spend every minute the job allowed with his young family.

This was something that Danny himself envied a little. The ease with which Rob achieved that work-life balance staggered him.

'Good morning, boss. Had a good holiday?'

'Yes, thanks, Rob, raring to go now, though. Not!'

Both men laughed.

'Let me grab a brew, Rob, then you can brief me on what's been happening. I'd better catch up on what I've missed last week.'

'No problem. I'll go and check today's teleprinter messages to make sure nothing else has come in since I left yesterday.'

Danny walked into his small office and took off his coat, hanging it on a peg at the back of the door. His office was a small room added onto the large open-plan office used by the rest of the CID.

As well as DS Buxton, there were four other detective constables working the office at that time, with a further detective sergeant and three other detective constables working the late shift.

Danny tried to split himself between the two shifts as much as possible, but tended to work more with Rob Buxton and his team.

He walked back into the main office and made himself a mug of coffee from the small area set aside to make hot drinks.

Taking the steaming hot coffee, he then returned to his office and sat down heavily in the chair behind his old dark wood desk, placing the mug onto his Mansfield Town coaster.

He picked up the first report from the pile that sat in the

in-tray and started to read. He was still reading the first paragraph of the report when someone entered the room.

Expecting to see Rob Buxton, Danny was surprised to see Superintendent Ken Jackson standing there. The senior officer was unshaven and dressed in civilian clothes.

He looked like he had just got up.

Danny said, 'Bloody hell, boss, it's not seven o'clock yet! What the hell are you doing here?'

'Don't worry, Danny, once I've spoken to you, I'm going home for some more shut-eye. I wanted to give you this heads-up in person rather than over the phone.'

'Christ, I don't like the sound of that. Grab a seat; what's so urgent that it's dragged you here at this time of day?'

'You've obviously been watching the news about the miners' strike. Well, we got word last night that it's definitely happening. It's starting tomorrow night. The government are going ahead with the pit closures up in Yorkshire as scheduled, and Scargill will call a national strike straight away, no doubt starting at midnight tomorrow.'

'I thought they were going to hold a ballot first?' said Danny.

'No, they're not, and that's the rub. Our information suggests that some of the Notts miners are claiming the call for them to strike without a ballot is not in the union rules, and are refusing to join the call to strike.'

Danny let out a slow whistle. 'Jesus, the shit will really hit the fan if the only mines not on strike are here in Notts. We'll have pickets descending from everywhere. They'll cause mayhem.'

Jackson continued, 'It's not a given, by any means, that none of the Notts miners will strike. Initially, at least, I would expect that the vast majority of mines in this area will be brought to a standstill.'

'But that won't stop British Coal trying to get the stockpiles of coal from the pits to the power stations,' said Danny.

'Exactly right, and with that in mind, the chief constable has ordered that we ready all Police Support Units, even the emergency ones.'

The reason for the face-to-face meeting now became apparent to Danny.

'You're taking my staff for fucking PSU duty, aren't you!'

'I've no choice! This order has come from the top – the very top in London. Our chief constable has no say in this whatsoever. The political masters at the Home Office are calling the shots here.'

'What staff are you leaving me with?'

'As well as yourself, you'll have one detective sergeant and two detective constables.'

'You're joking, Ken! How am I supposed to run a viable Criminal Investigation Department with those numbers? It's impossible for the size of the area we cover.'

'Like I said, this is already a done deal. I've not come here for a debate.'

Sighing heavily and leaning back in his chair, Danny said, 'Do I at least get to choose my own staff?'

'They've sort of selected themselves, really. DS Buxton, DC Andy Wills and DC Rachel Moore are the only officers who aren't PSU trained. I'm sorry, Danny. Obviously, we'll monitor it constantly. If your men aren't needed on this fucking strike, they'll be back with you straight away. Oh, one other thing: There's no limit on overtime. Work whatever hours you have to; it will get paid. That little gem has also come direct from the Home Office.'

'Marvellous, the four of us will be like zombies within four weeks. I know it's not down to you, Ken, and I do appreciate you getting up to tell me face to face. I'd better start ringing around to let them all know.'

'Sorry, I rang them all last night as soon as I knew what was happening. The only person I didn't speak to was Detective Sergeant Buxton.'

At that very moment, Rob tapped on the door, carrying a large bundle of papers.

The superintendent opened the door, allowing Rob to enter the office. 'Did I hear my name being used in vain, sir?' he said, with a smile.

Ignoring the comment and the smile, Jackson turned back to Danny and said, 'Your other two detectives will be here for eight o'clock; I'm off home now. Any problems, and you know where to reach me.'

'Yeah, thanks, sir,' said Danny as the superintendent closed the door.

'What have I missed, boss? Are we getting more staff?'

Danny grimaced. 'You couldn't be more wrong, my little Yorkshire friend.'

Pointing at the other chair in the office, Danny indicated for Rob to sit down. He then relayed the conversation he'd just had with the superintendent.

'Bloody hell, I'd better give my missus a quick ring and tell her to expect me when she sees me.'

He smiled and added, 'I tell you one thing, boss, the Yorkshireman in me is loving the overtime bit. Might get that holiday to the Algarve yet.'

'I thought you might like the sound of that. Anyway, down to business, Rob. Is there anything startling on the briefing sheet this morning?'

Rob let a grim smile play across his features and said, 'Looks like this one's down to you and me now, then, boss. There was a death underground at Warsop Main Colliery last night. A sixty-four-year-old miner was killed after a roof fall.

'Silly bugger had taken his helmet off, according to the Mines Rescue Team that brought him out. The Mines Inspectorate turned out with the MRT and did all the necessary underground. Photos of the scene will be coming over later. There were no suspicious circumstances, so no police officers were requested to go underground to the scene. Apparently, the deceased was alone, watching a button for the conveyor belt, when part of the roof came down. It says there'd already been a number of roof falls logged at that location. They've asked that the police attend the post-mortem first thing this morning, to confirm no foul play and to provide the evidence of the injuries that caused the death once they have been identified, ready for the coroner's inquest.'

'Marvellous.' Danny sighed. 'This day just keeps getting better. What time's the PM scheduled for?'

'It says here, Mansfield Mortuary at a quarter to eight this morning.'

'Okay, Rob, we'll finish this drink and get down there. Leave a note on the briefing board for Rachel and Andy telling them where we are, and saying not to go out. Tell them there'll be a meeting at eleven o'clock back here. If we're going to be able to function as a credible CID office with just the four of us, we need to get organised and fast.'

4

Wembley, North London – March 1984

'For God's sake, woman, will you give it a bloody rest!'

The voice belonged to Mick Reynolds, who at thirty-eight years of age was totally sick of his life – well, his married life anyway.

Reynolds was an ugly man, short and squat with a large nose and bad skin. His teeth were uncared for and rotting. His black hair was chopped short in no apparent style, and he had a permanent five o'clock shadow.

He had married Rita late in life when he was thirty-four. The last four years had been a living hell. He'd regretted the marriage almost from the first week they had lived together.

His wife never missed an opportunity to slag him off. It was either his lack of ambition to attain a promotion at work, his lack of handyman skills, or – most cutting of all – his lack of prowess in bed.

Throughout his life, Mick Reynolds had always struggled

with the opposite sex. Unfortunately, Mick wasn't blessed down below. His penis was very small, and he could rarely raise or sustain an erection.

When they first got together, his lack of sexual prowess didn't seem to trouble Rita, who seemed far more interested in the material things in life. At the time they met, she was living in a very small bedsit in one of the roughest parts of the East End. The area was frequented by prostitutes and criminals. Quite understandably, she had jumped at the chance to live with Mick in his relatively new and spacious three-bedroom, semi-detached house in suburban Wembley, about half a mile from the famous football stadium.

Mick was a hardworking man with a responsible job that paid well and had the prospect of a very good pension. Whether Rita went out to work or not, there was always plenty of money to spend.

As the months of virtually no sex of any kind turned into years, Rita blatantly embarked on a series of squalid affairs that really rubbed Mick's nose in it. As well as deliberately flaunting her own promiscuity with a string of different men, Rita never missed an opportunity to ridicule him for his lack of prowess in satisfying her needs.

As a result, the couple now lived virtually separate lives.

Mick had grown to physically loathe his wife and constantly dreamed how much better his life would be if Rita weren't in it. He constantly fantasised about killing her, replaying various plots and schemes over and over in his mind, both during the day and at night. Especially at night, as he lay awake in bed and Rita snored loudly next to him.

Mick had never laid a finger on a woman in his life, but recently he found himself getting the urge to physically assault her, to shut that poisonous mouth for one second so he could get some peace and quiet.

Finally, after his last shouted plea, Rita had finally stopped goading him.

The front door of the house slammed shut, and he heard her tarty heels clipping up the front path of his house.

'At last,' he breathed to himself.

It was getting on for eight o'clock at night. Mick knew if he hurried, he would still be able to get there before he started work at ten o'clock.

'Bloody nights again already!' he mumbled to himself.

He grabbed his bomber jacket and lunch box, and after switching the lights off in the house, he walked through the interior door that led to the garage.

He switched on the light in the garage and smiled as he saw his pride and joy, a very new Ford Sierra.

Mick opened the garage door, then drove the car out of the garage onto the sloping drive. He quickly jumped out of the car, closed the garage door and locked it.

Getting back into the car, he smiled and revved the powerful engine.

He really did love his car.

One of the only good things about Rita was that she had failed her driving test. The last thing he needed was the expense of buying the bitch her own car.

When Rita had stormed out of the house earlier, he had no idea where she was going. Now, as he drove his car away from the house, he found himself wishing she would fall under the knife or hammer of some sadistic serial killer.

'If only!' he muttered aloud before switching on the cassette player in the car.

As he listened to Depeche Mode belting out their latest track, he replayed the brutal slaughter of his wife over and over again in his mind.

A quick drive across town, and fifteen minutes later he was cruising slowly along one of the roads in a well-known red-light district near the centre of London. The cassette player in the car was now switched off.

Mick knew this place like the back of his hand; for the

past two years, he had sought company with various working girls who were only too pleased to lavish him with a bit of false admiration and sexual fulfilment in exchange for cash. The women were happy to exchange sexual favours for his money so they could get the next fix of whatever drug they were abusing.

As he drove slowly along the dimly lit road, he saw a young girl standing alone, leaning backwards against the large wall.

The young prostitute had long, straggly blonde hair, which was wet and plastered to her head due to the very fine drizzle that was falling. She was wearing a plastic-looking pink top that was left open, revealing a tight white vest covering her ample breasts. Her short skirt was fake leather and more like a belt. The whole look was finished off with white plastic knee-length boots.

She was hard-faced with dark-rimmed eyes and looked about twenty-five years old.

The woman was not the type he would normally choose to go with, but the cold and the drizzle had kept most of the working girls off the street.

He parked the car at the side of the road, thirty yards away from where the prostitute was standing. He let the wipers move the drizzle from the screen and squinted, trying to get a better look at her. As the blades moved silently from side to side, displacing the water on the windscreen, he could momentarily see her features clearly; then the drizzle on the screen distorted them again.

He remained in the car, watching her like that for five minutes.

'God, she looks rough!' he grumbled.

However rough she looked, Mick was desperate for some relief. He checked his mirrors for other vehicles that could be the vice squad before driving his car along the road until he was directly in line with the woman leaning on the wall.

As soon as he stopped the car, the prostitute heaved herself away from the wall and sauntered over, swaying her large hips in an exaggerated sexy walk.

As the prostitute walked towards the car, Mick leaned over and wound down the passenger window. She leaned in the open window of the Sierra, and as she did so, her ample breasts, accidentally on purpose, spilled out of the vest top, and Mick was treated to a free full frontal.

'All right, darling,' she said breathily before fluttering her false eyelashes and adding, 'Are you gonna let this girl spend some time out of the rain?'

'How much for a hand job?' Mick said abruptly.

'Blimey, you don't mess about, do you, mate? Hand relief's ten quid; full relief's thirty. Either way, you're wearing a condom. No arguments; I don't want my new clothes messed up.'

'Okay, get in,' stammered a now breathless Mick.

The car door opened, and the woman got in.

The car was immediately filled with the smell of her cheap perfume and cigarettes. He glanced over and saw that she had made no attempt to put her breasts back inside her vest top. They were big, far bigger than Rita's. The cold wet weather had made her nipples erect.

Staring at her breasts, Mick could feel himself getting aroused already.

The prostitute pointed along the dark road. 'Just drive straight on for about a hundred yards; there's an alleyway on the left. Pull in there, and we won't be disturbed.'

Mick did as he was asked, and a minute later was sitting in the car with the prostitute in almost complete darkness.

The only sound was that of the steadily falling rain drumming on the car roof. The passenger window of the car was still open.

Mick reached over and wound the window back up, brushing his hand against the prostitute's large fleshy breasts as he did so. He felt himself shudder as he felt her bare skin against his hand.

As he leant over to wind the window back up, she breathed into his ear.

'What can I do for you, love?'

'Hand relief. Here's your tenner,' he stammered as he passed her the note.

Without a word, the prostitute reached for the zip on his trousers. She swiftly slid open the fly, then unfastened his belt and undid the button of his trousers. She then yanked them down slightly and moved his boxer shorts to one side.

His pitifully small penis was already erect, and he could feel himself nearing a climax. The woman quickly removed a foil packet from her pink cagoule pocket. She tore open the packet and expertly flicked the condom onto his diminutive manhood. It was just in time; he ejaculated with a loud groan.

The prostitute giggled.

'Jesus Christ in a hand cart! That didn't take long, did it, mate!'

Mick could feel a rage building within him that he'd never felt before.

He quickly removed the now-full condom and adjusted his clothing. He opened the driver's side window and threw out the condom before finally doing himself up.

He looked at the prostitute and hissed menacingly, 'What do you mean by that, darling?'

Still feeling buoyed by her easy ten pounds and unaware of any possible danger, she smiled and said, 'I didn't mean anything by it, ducks. It's just that little Peter seemed anxious to get everything off his chest, so to speak.'

She smiled a nervous smile.

Mick glared at her.

'What did you call my cock?' he said in a low menacing whisper.

She giggled nervously. 'Little Peter. Let's face it, he ain't exactly Big John, is he, darling!'

Mick smashed his fist straight into the woman's face, causing her nose to explode in a torrent of blood and mucus. The punch was so hard it smacked the woman's head back onto the passenger door window.

'Fucking 'ell, you lunatic, you've smashed my nose. Let me out of this fucking car!' she screamed.

Mick reached across and opened the car door. He forcefully pushed the prostitute out of the car, sending her sprawling across the wet pavement.

Desperate to get away from a further assault, she shuffled back from the car. Her short skirt rode up, exposing her buttocks; they felt cold and wet on the rain-soaked pavement. Blood dripped from her damaged nose onto her still-exposed breasts. She whimpered as she dragged herself over the rough pavement, further away from the car.

Mick slammed the door. Leaving the car lights off, he reversed quickly out of the alleyway.

Try as she might, the dazed prostitute could not make out the registration number of the car. Very slowly, she clambered to her feet and staggered off further down the alley, away from the direction the car had sped off in.

'Fucking nutter!' she screamed.

MICK REYNOLDS DROVE four hundred yards in the darkness before he risked putting the cars lights on.

'Damn, that felt good!' he shouted.

As he drove, he switched the car stereo back on.

The loud reggae beat of a UB40 hit thumped out, increasing his euphoric state. He felt exhilarated, and his hands drummed on the steering wheel in time to the music.

When he had punched the tart, it was Rita's face he had

seen. Now he imagined repeating that punch over and over again until he couldn't recognise Rita's poisonous features.

He looked at himself in the rear-view mirror. He was smiling like a Cheshire cat.

A short ten-minute drive later and Mick arrived at work. He parked his car and walked into the old building. He went straight into the locker room to get his kit.

Some of his colleagues were already there, getting changed. As he took off his jacket, one of them looked across at him with a worried expression.

'What you staring at?' asked Mick in an indignant tone.

'Are you alright, Mick? You've got blood on your hand and the cuff of your shirt.'

Feeling a moment of panic, Mick looked down and saw that his hand was indeed covered in the blood of the prostitute.

Regaining his composure, he quickly said, 'It's nothing. There was a dog in the road that had been hit by a car; it was stone dead, but a bit of a mess. I dragged it away from the middle of the road into the gutter. It was dark, and I didn't realise there was blood on my hand. Get yourself into the briefing room. I'll give my hands a quick wash, then come and brief you for the night shift.'

Police Sergeant Mick Reynolds then walked calmly off to the gents' toilets to wash the blood of the prostitute from his hands.

He had just finished washing off the blood when the duty inspector walked in.

'How's it going, Mick? I'm glad I've caught you before you start the briefing. We have had a request for at least twenty Police Support Units to travel as mutual aid to the Nottinghamshire force this week. This coal miners' strike that's been threatening all over the news has started. The Notts force are expecting the shit to hit the fan big time. You go and sort out the guys who make up your PSU, and I'll brief the remainder of your shift. Once you and your men have got all your gear together, just stand by in the canteen. As soon as transport has been arranged, you will be on your way up to Nottinghamshire.'

'Will do, sir.'

'Are you alright?' the duty inspector said. 'You look a bit flushed, you know ... red in the face.'

'I'm fine, sir. Actually, I've never felt better. I'm just loving life at the moment,' he replied, grinning broadly.

5

Mansfield – March 1984

Having finished their coffees, Danny and Rob headed for the public mortuary. The building was only a short five-minute walk from the police station.

From outside, it looked like a small bungalow that was surrounded on three sides by high walls. A driveway led to the rear of the building, where there was double-door access for vehicles to deposit the recently deceased.

The two detectives headed for the front door of the building and were met by a very tall, skinny man. Stewart Henson had been the coroner's officer since he retired from the force two and a half years ago.

Stewart had been a police officer for thirty years before adopting the role of coroner's officer. He spent most of his day either at the mortuary assisting the pathologists, or in his small office at Mansfield Police Station, helping officers prepare files for an inquest.

He was well liked by all the cops, uniform and plainclothes alike, as he was always helpful and brought a respectful joviality to an unpleasant but very necessary part of police work.

Unbeknown to Stewart, he was affectionately known by some of the younger constables as Dr Death.

Stewart opened the door for Danny and Rob. 'Good morning, gents, sorry for the early start, but Professor Haynes is the on-call pathologist today. He's got a full workload starting at Newark from ten o'clock today. He'll be here shortly. Do you want to see what we've got?'

'Okay, Stew, lead on,' said Danny.

Walking through a couple of doors, the three men passed the public viewing area, where loved ones had the awful task of identifying their next of kin. Through one more door, and the detectives were standing in the large room where the post-mortem examinations were carried out.

There were two stainless-steel benches in the centre of the room.

On one side of the room were rows of floor-to-ceiling drawers where the dead were kept under refrigeration. On the other side wall were further drawers where the dead would be kept in a state of deep freeze. These were only used when the police couldn't release a body for burial or cremation due to ongoing criminal investigations.

Along the wall, opposite the door they had entered by, were long benches that had various sinks and scales, as well as all the tools used by the pathologists.

Underneath these benches were cupboards that contained the green surgical suits, masks and overshoes used by pathologists and police officers alike to protect their clothes.

The room was stark white and brightly lit, smelling strongly of disinfectant.

Lying on one of the stainless-steel benches was the naked body of Albie Jones.

'Here we are, then, gents,' said Stewart. 'This is the body of Albert Jones, otherwise known as Albie, born 30 March 1919. He was identified last night by his wife and daughter-in-law.'

He continued, 'Mr Jones was brought here by the Mines Rescue Team, who extracted his body from Warsop Main Colliery late yesterday evening. His body was found on the loader gate between the pit bottom and the Harley Face. He was found by the afternoon shift haulage team as they went into the pit to relieve the morning shift. It would appear on face value to be an accident, pure and simple. He was found lying on his back next to a large chunk of the roof, with this massive head wound. His helmet had been placed to one side of the gate, as though he'd removed it himself.'

Danny and Rob both leaned forward to inspect the massive wound.

'Jesus!' exclaimed Rob. 'That must've been a large piece of the roof to cause that mess.'

'I can't help you with that, Rob,' said Stewart. 'I haven't seen the photos they took of the scene yet.'

A doorbell that sounded like it should be fitted in a house rang twice, abruptly disturbing the silence.

'That bloody doorbell! I must get it changed. Every time it goes off, it jars right through me. It's totally inappropriate!' exclaimed Stewart.

'That'll be the prof, gents. We can get started shortly,' he added before leaving the room.

The two detectives remained in the room, examining the head wound on the body of Albie Jones.

It was Rob who broke the silence. 'This is all a bit weird, boss. When I was a DC up in South Yorkshire, I went to a couple of pit deaths that had happened down the mine near Dinnington. One of them was a roof fall – well, two roof falls to be precise. The first fall had been enough to knock the helmet off the guy, and the second, more devastating one killed the man. He had very severe trauma to his head, but it looked nothing like this. Mr Jones looks like he's literally had his head smashed in.'

'I know what you mean, Rob. It looks like his head has been hit with tremendous force. We'll know better shortly, once the professor does his stuff.'

Professor Gerard Haynes entered the room and offered a perfunctory greeting to the detectives before saying, 'Right, let's get straight on, shall we? I've got a busy day ahead.'

The professor, a Home Office pathologist, looked every inch his title. He was in his late fifties, quite overweight and wearing an ill-fitting suit. He had grey receding hair and wore spectacles that sat on the very tip of his large florid nose.

He quickly removed his jacket and put on a green protective gown, overshoes and gloves, finally adding a face mask similar to that worn by surgeons. This was the cue for the detectives and Stewart to also get into protective gowns.

As this was not a criminal investigation yet, neither of the officers would be carrying out the evidence-gathering that would be required in a murder case. They were there purely to observe at this stage and to note anything out of the ordinary, or anything that the pathologist identified as a probable cause of death, ready for the coroner's inquest.

With a flourish of his arms that was almost theatrical, the professor said in a loud voice, 'Right, gents, let's begin, shall we?'

The professor started at the massive head wound and instructed Stewart to take photographs as he progressed. The scalp was peeled away to reveal the glistening bone of the skull, which glared white under the harsh lights.

There was a huge crack in the skull that led from a point at the top of the head, both forward down as far as the bridge of the nose and back as far as the top of the spinal cord.

The skull appeared almost cleaved in two, as though it had been struck by some medieval weapon such as a battleaxe or a claymore sword. When the full extent of the injury was apparent, and the grey matter of the brain was visible below the split, the professor spoke: 'Well, that's as plain as a pikestaff for cause of death. Jot this down, please, Stewart: "Massive injury to the cranium, causing numerous heavy bleeds to the underlying brain tissue." I've kept it in laymen's terms for you gents, but basically, this wound is the primary cause of death and is consistent with being hit by a heavy piece of rock from above.'

The professor was in full flow now and continued rapidly. 'Close examination of the area around the wound reveals traces of mineral content that, when analysed, I suspect will match the offending piece of rock.'

Turning to the two detectives, the professor said, 'Gentlemen, there really is no need for you to stay and watch the rest of the examination. Stewart and I can finish up here. I will contact you if I find anything abnormal with the toxicology or bloods. Any questions?'

Rob immediately spoke up. 'Just one question, sir ... how come the wound and the fracture of the skull itself are so huge? I've seen a head injury from a rock fall at the pit before that was fatal, and it looked nothing like this one.'

'Was the victim of the rock fall you saw a younger man, Detective?'

'Yes, sir, he was. As I recall, he was only in his late twenties.'

The professor took a deep breath and pointed at the skull of Albie Jones before continuing in a voice similar to that of a schoolteacher talking to a particularly slow child. 'As the body ages, the bone structures become weaker, density lessens, and bones become brittle. We are all familiar with the elderly falling in the wintertime on snow and ice and easily breaking their limbs. Arms, legs, even hips on occasion. This is down to the bones weakening. The same thing happens to the numerous bones of the skull. It would appear that this is the case here. I've taken samples of the skull bone, and I fully expect them to show that lack of density. To make a comparison, that rock hitting this poor man's skull would have been like hitting a boiled egg with a spoon. Any other questions?'

As both detectives shook their heads, he continued, 'Thank you for attending this morning, gentlemen, but I can't see anything here that would lead me to believe any sort of foul play has occurred.'

Danny spoke up: 'Okay, Professor Haynes, thank you. I look forward to reading your report in full.'

Both detectives stepped out of the room, followed by Stewart.

As they got out of the robes, Danny said, 'I know he's the pathologist, Stewart, but something about that wound doesn't look right to me. Make sure he's thorough with the rest of the exam, will you? And let me have his report as soon as possible. Thanks, mate.'

Stewart nodded before returning to the grisly task of the remainder of the post-mortem.

Danny and Rob walked slowly back to the police station, both deep in thought.

'What are you thinking, boss?' asked Rob.

'I was just wondering how easy it would be to kill somebody down the mine and make it look like an accident. I'm not happy with this, but everything points to it being just an accident.'

'I know one thing, boss,' said Rob seriously, pausing before continuing. 'I won't be having a boiled egg for my breakfast any time soon!'

'Idiot!' Danny laughed as both men walked through the large double doors of the police station.

6

Mansfield – March 31, 1984

It had been just over two weeks since Arthur Scargill had called upon the National Union of Mineworkers to begin a national strike.

As predicted by the experts, the strike hadn't been accepted right across the coalfield. The dissent was mainly in Nottinghamshire, where some miners felt they had been railroaded into striking without having a ballot on exactly what they, the Notts Miners, wanted. Scargill maintained an intransigent stance that no ballot was necessary. He claimed that his mandate to call a national strike came when he had been elected leader of the National Union of Mineworkers.

The moderate leaders in the Nottinghamshire branch of the union had tried to reason with Scargill that the timing for action was wrong. Summer was just around the corner, and the stockpiles of coal at the power stations had never been so huge.

It was obvious to all parties that any strike would be a

very long drawn-out affair. It was also obvious, except maybe to Scargill, that the government – and Margaret Thatcher in particular – had shrewdly chosen her time to make a stand against the miners' union and the power she believed that union wielded.

The Prime Minister had been instrumental in the appointment of John McGregor to oversee the running of British Coal during the strike. John McGregor had previously fought a long battle with United States coal miners and won. In the process, he'd decimated that country's once-proud coal industry, laying waste to large once-prosperous communities.

Arthur Scargill, meanwhile, was constant in his message that pit closures were happening now and that miners were already losing their jobs; his mantra was that the time to fight for the industry was now.

It was becoming clear that hard times were coming to the small market town of Mansfield, which had always been so reliant on the coal industry to prosper.

It was now two weeks since Danny had been instructed to run his CID office on a skeleton crew for the duration of the strike. Most of his staff had been deployed to Police Support Units, to contain flying pickets that were regularly coming into the area from South Yorkshire and other coalfields in order to make the strike solid nationally.

It had taken that two weeks for him and his small team of DS Rob Buxton and Detective Constables Andy Wills and Rachel Moore to make the skeleton crew staffing levels viable.

Danny felt he was fortunate in so much as the two detectives who remained in the office were both serious grafters.

DC Andy Wills was a smart-dressed individual, wearing dark suits that were cut well. He was always well-groomed and was in every way an immaculate man.

Andy was a very intelligent man and an extremely competent detective with a strong work ethic. He was also very ambitious.

Danny knew that in normal times Andy would be a certainty for promotion to sergeant. Unfortunately for Andy, these were far from normal times.

At the beginning of the strike, Danny sat Andy down and spoke to him one to one, asking him to put aside his personal ambition for the duration of the strike, and to concentrate solely on the job of maintaining CID cover for the division.

To his credit, there had been no argument from Andy. He totally understood the situation they were all in.

The other detective who remained in the office was Detective Constable Rachel Moore. She had her own different reasons to excel in the police service generally, as well as in the CID.

Rachel was twenty-nine years old. Having joined in 1974, she now had just under ten years' service in the police force.

She had witnessed first-hand, and often been the subject of, the outrageous bigotry and sexism that had been rife throughout the service at that time.

From the outset, the shift she was assigned to at Hyson Green made it obvious that they didn't welcome her. Rachel was the only woman on the shift and put up with sexism and harassment on an almost daily basis. In spite of this pressure, she kept her head down and worked hard and easily completed her two-year probation.

On the day she completed her probation, she immediately applied for a transfer to Mansfield Police Station to continue her career.

The reason for the transfer request was simple: She knew other female officers already working at Mansfield Police Station, who assured her that, although still an issue, sexism and favouritism there was nothing like on the scale of the police stations in Nottingham city.

Rachel was successful in her transfer request, and after

arriving at Mansfield, she had shown that she was a hard-working and competent police officer.

It came as no surprise to anyone that her subsequent application to join the CID was successful, and she had remained at Mansfield to start her career on the CID.

That had been two years ago, and Rachel was now an experienced detective.

What Rachel had not been aware of at the time was the fact Danny Flint had been instrumental in getting her the posting at Mansfield. He had watched Rachel work and admired her drive and tenacity. He was also aware that there were no female detectives at the police station, a situation that needed addressing.

Rachel was a single woman who lived alone in Mansfield. Now approaching her thirtieth birthday, she was an attractive woman with long chestnut brown hair and dark brown eyes. A keep-fit fanatic, she was very slim and toned but curvaceous at the same time. Although admired by many of her work colleagues, she had made the decision early in her career never to date a fellow officer.

Danny was now extremely pleased he had pushed for Rachel to remain at Mansfield. Since the start of the strike, her work rate had been phenomenal.

Since 12 March, the first day of the strike, Rachel had systematically gone through three-quarters of the other detectives' outstanding workload and, through her efforts, effectively cleared the decks.

She had regularly worked between twelve to fourteen hours a day to achieve this.

Andy Wills, meanwhile, cleared the remaining quarter of the outstanding workload and, together with Detective Sergeant Buxton, took on all the new work that came into the office.

Danny now felt encouraged that with this small but very enthusiastic team he would be able to provide a suitable CID response to most situations. However, he knew this would only be the case as long as a major enquiry necessitating large amounts of manpower didn't materialise.

If that happened, the shit really would hit the fan.

Providing adequate cover meant working long hours, but they were all committed to doing just that.

Now they were on top of the existing workload, Danny decided that every one of the team would have at least one day off a week. Obviously, these days would need to be staggered, and must be flexible and subject to work commitments.

The team were overjoyed to know that through their hard work they were now in line to spend some time at home with their families – and, weather permitting, Rachel would get to spend a day out in the fresh air.

It was now eight o'clock at night. The detectives had all been at work since eight that morning.

Danny came out of his office, carrying his coat, and said, 'I reckon that's enough for today, folks. What say we all adjourn to the Railway pub next door. It's my round. I just want to say thank you for the way you've grafted over the last two and a half weeks. I know it's not been easy. I never thought as a detective inspector I would find myself interviewing and charging a shoplifter, but these are the times we're living in, folks.'

He smiled, saying, 'Now, who fancies a quick beer before home?'

They all chorused, 'Just the one, boss,' before laughing and heading out the door to the Railway.

The pub was literally fifty yards from the front door of the police station and had always been frequented by officers just finishing their shifts.

Recently the police had opened their own social club upstairs in the station. This tended to be used more by the uniform officers, and since the strike began, it was full most evenings with various foreign-force PSUs who had just finished policing pickets for the day.

Inside the Railway pub, the lounge bar was small and very cosy, with a welcoming open fire burning.

It was a typical mining town pub with prints of local mine headstocks and pictures depicting old miners with ponies down the mine. There were genuine grimy and battered Davy lamps swinging from the ceiling. Ancient horse brasses were nailed to the dark wooden beams, a constant pall of blue smoke emanated from the taproom, and there was the smell of stale, spilt beer.

The team all sat in one corner of the lounge bar. There were no other patrons there, and inevitably, after the first few sips of their drinks, the conversation turned to police work.

Danny turned to Rob. 'Now we're a bit more on top of the workload, I'd like to take a closer look at the circumstances surrounding the death of that miner over at Warsop Colliery.'

'You mean Albert Jones?'

'Yes, that's the man. I know Andy's rostered for his day off tomorrow, but if you can look after the office in the morning, I'd like to take Rachel to the Mines Rescue Station at Woodhouse and do some digging. It's the coroner's inquest next week, and from everything I've seen so far, a verdict of accidental death will be the outcome. Something about the magnitude of that man's injuries just doesn't seem right to me. I heard what the professor said to you, and his explanation was very plausible, but if only for my own peace of mind, I want to dig a little deeper.'

'I can look after the office; if anything major comes in, I'll contact you by radio. For what it's worth, as you know, I had the same gut feeling about that job. We should always follow our gut, right?'

'Dead right. Cheers, Rob.'

Raising his glass to the small team of detectives, Danny said, 'Okay, folks, listen in. I don't know how long this bloody strike's going to last, but what I do know is this: We're a team that's willing to graft and work long hours, and there's nothing we can't handle if we continue to pull as a group. I just wanted to say thanks, everybody, I really appreciate your efforts. Cheers!'

The glasses clinked to a chorus of cheers.

Twenty minutes later, Danny was making the short walk back up the hill to his father's house.

As he walked, his head was full of thoughts.

Tomorrow heralded the start of April. With a bit of luck, this strike wouldn't last long; normality would return.

It was dark, but the sky was clear with a stunning full moon. The brightness of the moon matched his mood as he walked briskly up the hill.

He felt happier than he had at any time in the last few weeks.

If Danny had known of the challenges that lay ahead, he might not have been so confident, nor felt so cheery.

7

Cuckney Crossroads, Nottinghamshire – April 1, 1984

Sergeant Mick Reynolds was totally pissed off. He had been in the Nottinghamshire coalfields on strike duty for three weeks now, and he couldn't wait to get home for a week off, even if that meant going home to his nagging bitch of a wife.

The duties were onerous, long and mind-numbingly boring.

It was just after four in the morning, and as usual, his Police Support Unit were sitting at the Cuckney crossroads, ready to intercept pickets travelling down from Yorkshire.

Cuckney was a tiny village situated on the main A60 road between Mansfield and Worksop, and from this particular crossroads, striking miners could make their way into the small towns of Warsop, Mansfield or Ollerton to picket any one of several pits.

The intelligence at the briefing that morning was that large numbers of striking miners were expected to be travelling to

Ollerton Colliery to stage a mass picket. It wasn't hard to understand why.

The only people going down Ollerton pit at the moment were deputies carrying out essential maintenance and safety work. However, fleets of lorries were still going in and out, carrying more coal to swell the already huge stockpiles of coal at the nearby power stations dotted along the River Trent.

Mick wondered how they were getting the intelligence on the pickets' intended targets. However it was gained, it was usually extremely accurate.

'Come on, lads, I want three volunteers to get out of the van for the first hour. I'll swap it about after that. Any takers?' said the sergeant.

The ten officers sitting in the back of the unmarked Ford Transit made no effort to stir, and certainly no volunteers were forthcoming. After three weeks of grinding boredom, they were all just looking forward to a week off.

'Okay, Jackson, Miller and Venables, out you get! You're up for the first hour.'

Loud grumblings came from within the van.

Sergeant Reynolds rounded sharply and snarled towards the rear of the van, 'Look, I don't want any of your shit! Just grab a Maxpax coffee and get out, ready to stop any motors that turn up. You know the score: Any car with more than two blokes in, turn 'em around. It's easy money, for fuck's sake. You've all earned a small fortune doing this shit, so stop fucking moaning!'

Slowly the three selected officers put on their helmets, gloves and coats; then, after grabbing a hot drink, they went and stood in a little group at the centre of the crossroads.

It had been a very cold night with a clear sky, and from his front seat in the van, Mick could see the clouds of breath coming from the three men, who were stamping their feet on the frosted tarmac and waving their arms to try to stay warm in the freezing cold air.

'Maybe I'll change it after half an hour,' Mick said quietly to himself.

Nobody else in the van was listening; the rest of the lads were already nodding off back to sleep. Only the driver of the van, sitting next to the sergeant, remained alert and awake.

'What do you reckon, Ken, shall I change it every half hour?'

'Nah, Skip, it's too much pissing about. They ain't gonna freeze to death, are they?'

At that moment, a single vehicle's headlights could be seen approaching from the direction of Worksop.

Mick wound the front passenger window down. 'Heads up, lads; here come our first customers!'

One of the cops stepped into the road, switching his torch on and raising his right arm in the air, signalling for the approaching vehicle to stop.

The vehicle, a red Vauxhall Viva, came to a gentle stop in front of the officer, who then stepped around to speak to the driver. The other two officers took up a position in front of the car.

Mick listened to the conversation from the front seat of the Transit.

The driver of the Vauxhall wound down the window on the car and said, 'What's up, mate? Why've you stopped me?'

The car contained two other occupants, both men in their thirties.

The young constable who had stopped the car, leaned forward and said robotically, 'I believe you're striking miners who have the intention of unlawfully picketing premises that aren't your usual place of employment. Please turn the vehicle around and go back where you came from.'

'No, owd lad, you've got it all wrong. Us lads in here, we all work at Ollerton pit. We're on the day shift,' one of the men in the back seat of the car said in a broad South Yorkshire accent.

The comment was accompanied with sniggers and chuckling from the back of the car.

One of the other officers standing in front of the car, a big burly man in his forties, now approached the driver's open window and said loudly, 'Listen to me, you dickhead, there isn't an early shift at that mine this morning. Do yourselves a favour and fuck off back to whichever northern shithole you've just crawled out of, before we nick the lot of ya!'

The chuckling in the car stopped.

Mick heard a voice from within the Viva say, 'Come on, lads, it's not worth getting nicked for. You know what these Met coppers are like, bastards the lot of them. We'll try to find another way through.'

Good luck with that, thought Mick. He knew there were intercepts like this on all the roads leading to Ollerton.

He shouted over to the three officers, 'Well done, lads! They'll be on their little CB radio now, telling the rest of the fuckers travelling down not to try to go through Cuckney, as them horrible Metropolitan Police fuckers are there, miserable cockney bastards the lot of 'em.'

'Oi, Sarge, I'm from fucking Lancashire me,' shouted one of the men.

'Well, that's alright, son, it's like the War of the Roses for you, innit? You hate Yorkies more than us, don't ya!'

'What's the War of the Roses, Sarge?'

'Never mind. Get another hot drink down ya!'

Mick had only been involved in similar boring duties to this ever since he had arrived with his PSU serial on the night of 12 March. Rushing out to various intercepts early doors, trying to turn around pickets as they travelled in.

At the very first briefing, they had been told that their actions were perfectly legal. If any miners refused to turn around, they were to be arrested for police obstruction. Mick hadn't been convinced, but briefed his men accordingly anyway.

. . .

FROM THAT FIRST NIGHT, Mick and his PSU had been billeted in an old disused army base called Proteus Camp just outside the small town of Ollerton.

They were sleeping in dormitory-like Nissen huts; conditions were Spartan, to say the least. Meals were provided at the camp by outside caterers. The food was basic, but it was hot, and there was plenty of it.

Nobody moaned about the conditions too much, as they were being paid handsomely. Because they were, in effect, living away from home on a permanent basis, there were all sorts of allowances they could claim on top of the huge overtime payments.

The main issue was the boredom. There was nothing to occupy the men when they weren't working. They had been instructed that under no circumstances were they to stray away from the army base when they were off duty. Anybody caught drinking in any of the pubs at nearby towns would be disciplined and sent directly back to their own force.

As well as serials from the Metropolitan Police, there were others from as far afield as Hampshire, Essex and Kent all staying at Proteus Camp.

All the Metropolitan Police officers had initially travelled to Nottinghamshire in double-decker buses. After a briefing at the police headquarters, they were deployed in hired Ford Transits as individual Police Support Units, each with its own radio call sign.

For the first week, each PSU had a local Nottinghamshire officer on board as a guide. After that, they'd been expected to know the area a little better for themselves.

Luckily for Mick, his driver, Ken, had spent quite a bit of time holidaying with his family in the area a couple of years before the strike, so he knew the area reasonably well.

. . .

SITTING BORED in the van now, Mick rejoiced in the fact that at three o'clock that afternoon, they would all be going home for a week. He couldn't wait. He was excited about the prospect of visiting the red-light area again. With the hours of boredom, his mind had constantly returned to the last time he was there. How he had taught that mouthy little whore a lesson. He had relived the moment over and over again.

When he thought about that punch landing so hard in her face, the feelings he experienced were almost electric. The fact that it was his wife's face he saw every time the punch landed only intensified the feelings. Every time he thought about the assault, he could feel himself getting sexually aroused.

At first, he had felt a little shameful about experiencing those kinds of feelings over an assault, but over the four weeks, he had come to embrace them and had often masturbated when recalling the assault.

He knew that as soon as the nagging from his bitch of a wife got too much, he would take himself off to the whores, and one of them would get it, big style.

Breaking through his thoughts, he heard Ken's voice at the side of him, 'Time to change over, Sarge.'

'Alright, three more of ya, out ya get. I ain't bothered who it is; look lively.'

As three more men clambered out the back of the Transit, he looked at his watch, not long to wait now.

He would soon be back in London, with one of the whores.

His thin lips formed a cruel smile just thinking about that prospect.

8

Mines Rescue Station, Mansfield Woodhouse – April 1, 1984

'Yeah, I remember poor old Albie Jones. It was all so sad; he was into his last week of work after spending a lifetime at that pit, and then goes and does something so stupid.'

The voice belonged to Ray Machin, the leader of the Mines Rescue team that had recovered the body of Albie Jones from Warsop Main Colliery.

'Do you mind if we come in and have a chat about the recovery of Albie from the mine? You know, what you found when you first got there, that sort of thing?' Rachel Moore asked.

Rachel was standing with DI Danny Flint outside the large red-brick building that housed the two Mines Rescue vehicles.

The imposing building stood in between the towns of Mansfield and Mansfield Woodhouse. The building was regarded almost with reverence by the people of both towns, in much the same way as the buildings that house lifeboats at fishing villages on the coast are.

The people of the towns understood that the men who worked there, and the equipment housed there, could one day be saving the life of a loved one deep underground.

The Mines Rescue Team were quite rightly regarded as heroes of their community.

'Yes, of course we can have a chat; both of you come in out of the cold. It's half past nine now, and I've got to hold a drill at eleven. Will that be long enough to go through everything?'

Danny replied, 'Thanks, Mr Machin, that should be plenty of time. We just want to go over a few things. I've read the report you provided to the Mines inspectors, and I've seen their photos. It's just a couple of things that are nagging at me.'

'No problem, Inspector. Everyone here calls me Ray, so feel free to do the same.'

Ray Machin showed the detectives into a classroom that doubled as his office.

'I'll grab us all a brew, and then we can get started. Will tea be alright? We don't drink much coffee here, I'm afraid. We're all tea monsters.'

'Perfect,' said Danny.

Within minutes, Machin had returned carrying three large mugs of builders' tea, strong and very sweet.

'Right, fire away, Inspector! What do you want to know?'

'Firstly, who moved the lump of rock that killed Albie? I've noticed on the pictures taken at the scene that it was lying near to his right shoulder when he was found. Where was the rock taken after you got Albie out of there?'

'It was chucked under the belt; it will still be there, as far as I know.'

'Who actually moved it?'

'I did, as it happens. I'm always the last person at the

scene. I like to make sure no equipment has been left lying about. I always make a final check, that sort of thing. Well, I saw that the rock was still in the middle of the gate, so I shifted it under the belt.'

'This might sound a strange question, but how heavy was it?'

'Yeah, that does sound strange. It was fairly heavy; it was quite a big chunk of rock. I could manage it pretty well on my own, though, thinking about it.'

This time, it was Rachel who spoke: 'Obviously, Ray, we've nowhere near as much experience as you have when it comes to witnessing various injuries down the mine. You must have seen quite a few roof falls in your time and the damage they cause?'

'I have, lass. Far too many for my liking, I'm afraid.'

'My point is, you saw the injury to Albie. Do you think that piece of rock falling from the height of the roof at that part of the gate was big enough and heavy enough to cause that injury?'

'I couldn't say for certain, Detective. I've seen some awful injuries down the pit, but Albie's was one of the worst. The human head's a very fragile thing next to rock. If only he'd been wearing his helmet, he'd still be alive and enjoying his retirement.'

Danny said, 'I've only one more question. Could you have lifted that piece of rock right above your head?'

'It would have taken some effort, but yeah, I reckon I could have done. Am I missing something here? Do you people suspect some sort of foul play?'

'Not at this time. Everything's pointing to Albie's death being a tragic accident. Like you say, if only he'd been wearing his helmet. Thanks for your time, Ray, and for the brew. Talk to you soon.'

'No problem, Inspector; any time.'

The two detectives left the Rescue Station. Walking back

to the car, Danny said, 'Rachel, will you drop me back at the station? I'm going to pick up another car so we can split up. We need to save a bit of time in case anything else comes in. I want us to see both the deputy in charge and the miner who was injured on the day Albie died. I'll visit the deputy, and you can nip and see the injured miner. I think his name's James Wade.'

9

Mansfield Woodhouse – April 1, 1984

Rachel Moore parked the CID car directly outside the smart semi-detached house on Marples Avenue. She glanced down at the report on the passenger seat, checking the address.

"Mr James Wade, 56 Marples Avenue, lives alone," she muttered to herself. She noted there was no vehicle on the drive.

The house was typical for the street and the area. It had been built sometime in the late fifties, early sixties and was obviously very well looked after. It had freshly painted guttering and drainpipes, and all the windows had new double glazing. The front garden was very well kept, and the grass was short and well cared for.

As she got out of her car, she thought she saw movement at one of the upstairs windows. *Good,* she thought, *he's in. I can have a quick chat with him and get this enquiry put to bed.*

Rachel walked up the slight incline of the driveway to the front door. Ignoring the doorbell, she knocked loudly on the door.

'Just a second!' a man's voice yelled from within.

Almost immediately, the door swung open. Standing in the doorway was a very good-looking man, around six feet tall with quite short, well-kept blonde hair. He had the most piercing blue eyes she had ever seen, and was dressed casually in Levi's jeans and a blue-and-white check Ben Sherman shirt.

Rachel took a breath and said, 'I'm looking for Mr James Wade?'

'That's me, and you are?'

Raising her police warrant card for him to see, she said, 'Sorry, Mr Wade, my name's Detective Constable Rachel Moore. I need a moment of your time, please. There's a few questions I need to ask about the accident at Warsop Main Colliery when Albie Jones died.'

Without a flicker of emotion, Wade said, 'I thought that had all been sorted. Why do the police need to ask me questions? I've already said everything I know about the matter to the Mines Inspectorate.'

Rachel noted there was an attitude to James Wade. It wasn't quite animosity, more like antipathy. It was as if it was all too much of an effort to speak to her.

She pressed on: 'Do you mind if I come in? It won't take long, I promise you.'

Suddenly, Wade's entire manner changed. It was like a switch had been turned on. 'Of course, Detective Moore, where are my manners? My grandmother would be spinning in her grave, me leaving you on the doorstep like that. Come in out of the cold, please.'

He gestured for her to follow him and showed her into the lounge.

When Rachel followed him into the room, she saw that the

lounge was extremely tastefully decorated with a huge colour TV at one end of the room and a brand-new multi-change CD player at the other. The CD player had only just come onto the market, and Rachel could only guess at what they had both cost.

There was a tan-coloured leather three-piece suite that dominated the rest of the room.

Pointing to the sofa, he said, 'Take a seat, Detective. I was just making a coffee. Would you like a cup?'

Rachel sat down on the large sofa. She hadn't touched the builders' tea at the Mines Rescue Station and was actually gagging for a hot drink.

'Yes, please, Mr Wade. That would be lovely, thank you.'

'How do you take it?'

'Just milk, no sugar, thanks.'

A few minutes later he returned carrying two very nice earthenware coffee mugs.

Coasters were already on the walnut coffee table in front of the sofa. He carefully placed the hot drinks on them and then sat in one of the armchairs opposite her.

Rachel said, 'I'm sorry for the intrusion, and like I say, it's just a couple of questions. It won't take long.'

'No problem. I've got nothing planned today. And please call me Jimmy.'

Rachel was aware now just how large Wade's piercing blue eyes were. He was staring hard into her eyes; it was almost too intense.

She forced herself not to look away and said, 'On the day Albie was found dead, you were one of the last people to have seen him alive. What was your overall impression when you last saw him?'

'To be perfectly honest, Detective, I never really thought too much about old Albie.' He shrugged nonchalantly.

He finally looked away, glancing out of the window.

Rachel couldn't believe the relief she felt just because he

had turned to look away. She hadn't been aware of just how uncomfortable his piercing stare had become until he looked away.

He continued, 'I often saw Albie at the pit. He was like part of the fixtures and fittings. He'd worked there for ever, I think. He was a good bloke, always friendly.'

Rachel noted there was no warmth to anything Wade said, no depth of feeling at all. It was as if he knew he was expected to say these comments, so he just said them.

Just trotting out platitudes, she thought.

'Tell me about that particular day?' she said, taking a sip of her coffee.

'It was exactly the same as any other day down the pit, until I got a load of crap in my left eye. It happens all the time: You get muck and dust in your eyes, but you can usually shift it with water. On that day, one of the cutters flirted a bit of loose muck out that hit me straight in the face. I never even had time to shut my eyes. Well, try as I might, I couldn't get the muck out of my left eye. If you can't get it out, it can become a serious problem, as the grit can scratch your eyes and cause lasting damage.'

She found herself locked onto those piercing blue eyes again, starting to feel like a rabbit being circled by a predatory fox.

Glancing down towards her cup of coffee, she continued, 'Then what happened?'

'I went to the deputy in charge, Dave Smedley, and asked him if I could go topside to the medical centre to get sorted. He wasn't best pleased, as we were just starting a fresh stint on the face, but he appreciated the problem I had and walked with me from the coalface to the pit bottom. We passed Albie on his button on the way to the pit bottom. Nothing was said, only a quick "ayup", you know.'

'Was Albie wearing his helmet?'

'I reckon so. Thinking about it, he must have been. Otherwise Dave Smedley would have bollocked him, excuse my French, sorry.'

'So that's everything, is it, nothing else that comes to mind?'

'Yep, that's it, the whole kit and caboodle. Sorry if you've had a wasted trip, but at least the coffee's good, right?' He grinned.

Taking a large sip, Rachel said, 'Yes, the coffee's good, Mr Wade. Thank you for your time and the drink. Have you been notified to attend the Coroner's Court for the inquest next week?'

'No, I haven't. Do you think I'll have to go?'

'If you've not heard already, it's doubtful you'll be called at this late stage. Thanks again for the drink.'

Rachel stood up, smoothing down the skirt of her suit as she got up from the sofa.

He stood up and showed her to the front door.

'Have a good day, Detective!' he called after her as she walked down the sloping drive.

As she walked to the car, Rachel felt uneasy.

She couldn't fathom out why until she sat in the car. Just as she was about to switch the ignition on, she said aloud, 'That bastard was smirking at me.'

Half an hour later, back in the CID office, Rachel outlined the uneasy meeting she had experienced with James Wade to Danny.

'It's just a feeling, boss, nothing concrete. He just gave me the creeps, that's all. There you are, pure and simple: It's a woman thing. He was making me feel really on edge. It was like he thought me asking him questions was all a huge joke, a game. It felt like he was laughing at me.'

'Did he say anything incriminating, Rachel?'

'No, he didn't. He answered all my questions and was extremely polite.'

'Well, I couldn't verify his story with Dave Smedley. He's been seconded over to South Wales for the duration. They're short of deputies to do the safety work at their pits while the strike is on. They've both made statements for the coroner already, so I don't think there's anywhere else we can go with this. All the evidence suggests Albie's death was nothing more than a tragic accident. At the moment, there's not a shred of evidence to say it's anything other than that. No doubt the coroner will confirm it was just a pointless, tragic accident.'

Rachel shrugged her shoulders. She wasn't happy, but he was right: There was nothing else to be done, no other enquiries to follow. The inquest would reach a verdict of accidental death, and unless something new came to light, that would be that.

She wasn't easily spooked, but Rachel knew it would take her a long time to shake off the unnerving feeling she'd experienced when staring into James Wade's piercing blue eyes.

She shuddered involuntarily.

10

Mansfield Woodhouse – April 1, 1984

He had sat there motionless for over an hour. There wasn't a sound in the room. He could still see the half-empty coffee mug on the walnut table in front of the leather sofa. It was exactly where she had placed it before leaving.

Jimmy Wade had stared into the detective's dark brown eyes and realised that she was to be the next one.

Once she'd left the house, he had returned to the living room and sat quietly, trying to suppress the urges.

It was impossible; he couldn't even think about it. She was a police officer, a detective. It just wasn't worth the risk.

Try as he might, he couldn't remove the nagging voices in his head. Deep down, he knew they wouldn't be denied.

Finally, he stood up from the leather armchair and took both his own and the detective's coffee mug into the kitchen.

In the kitchen, he placed both mugs on the draining board next to the sink, ready to wash.

He picked up her mug and stared intently at the red lipstick ring on the rim. Very carefully, he put his lips directly over the faint red mark until there was the slightest tinge of red on his own lips.

He closed his eyes and licked his lips, tasting her lipstick.

As he vigorously washed the two mugs in the sink, he looked at his reflection in the glass of the kitchen window. In that moment he knew: It didn't matter that she was a detective, it didn't matter how long it took, he would find a way to have her.

He knew he had no choice and that it would happen. Detective Constable Rachel Moore was destined to die.

The eyes never lied. As soon as he stared into those deep, melancholy dark brown eyes, they had told him.

Her fate would be her release.

11

Wembley, London – April 7, 1984

It was sheer hell. Mick Reynolds had only been back six days, and Rita was being a complete cow.

It didn't matter what he did or said, she would criticise. It had been a welcome relief when his tart of a wife went out each evening to some sordid, illicit liaison.

Mick didn't give a toss anymore; he just wanted the disgusting woman out of his life for good, one way or the other.

He knew she was on too much of a good thing for her to ever consider leaving him. While ever she was living in his beautiful house sponging off him, she would never go anywhere.

No, he was going to have to deal with the problem of Rita a different way.

It wasn't even as though she was attractive in any way, shape or form. She was forty-something, short, plump and had hit every branch of the ugly tree on the way down from the top.

The hours of boredom up in Nottinghamshire had polarised Mick's thoughts. After tomorrow, he would be back up there for another four long weeks. He was going to use the time wisely and think of a way to be rid of Rita permanently.

He was a cop, for Christ's sake; he should know better than anybody how to work this problem out without spending the rest of his life behind bars for doing it.

All he could think about tonight, though, was to try to get some relief from the pent-up anger and frustration she had built up in him all week.

Tonight was his last opportunity; he was travelling back to Nottinghamshire at five o'clock tomorrow morning.

It was now eight o'clock in the evening. He knew that any time now, Rita would be going out to meet some sleazeball, and after drinking vodka and tonics all night, she would end up with her miniskirt hitched up around her waist as she got shagged behind some backstreet pub, somewhere down the East End.

God help the poor bastard who wants to shag the ugly cow, he thought.

Another painful hour ticked by; then suddenly he heard the telltale noise of the front door slamming. He looked out of the front window of his lounge and saw her tottering towards a waiting black cab.

He dismissed his earlier thought: *Tonight she'll be getting shagged behind some poncy wine bar up West.*

She disgusted him. He watched as she tottered along the path, ungainly on the five-inch heels, her fat legs bulging the black stockings in all the wrong places, the way-too-short skirt, and finally, the black shiny leather bomber jacket that looked a size too small and had ridden up over the rolls of fat at her midriff.

'Go on; hurry up and fuck off!' he said out loud.

As soon as the taxi pulled away from the kerb, he raced downstairs and picked up a small grip bag from the hallway.

He quickly opened the black holdall to make sure everything he needed was there.

There was a set of blue forensic overalls, a few pairs of forensic gloves and overshoes. He had taken these items from the exhibits store at work. Also in the grip bag was a roll of sticky brown gaffer tape, a plastic bag containing black plastic cable ties, a small pair of gardening shears, a Stanley knife and a claw hammer.

All the hand tools had been purchased earlier in the week from the local DIY store on Wembley High Street.

Picking the bag up, he walked into the garage to his midnight blue Ford Sierra.

Bending down at the front of the car, he used some black electricians' tape to change the number 3 to an 8 and the letter F to an E on the front registration plate. He then walked to the rear of the car and did the same to the rear plate.

It wasn't perfect, but unless somebody got a really close look, it would effectively change the registration number of the car.

Mick had been worried that the first tart he punched might have somehow clocked his car number, so tonight he was taking no chances.

If, as expected, he felt the same urges tonight, he wanted to be prepared and not run any unnecessary risks.

Mick felt ready and strangely excited about what he was setting off to do.

Tonight, in his mind at least, was the night he was going to rid himself of that disgusting bitch of a wife.

In reality, his intention was to pick up and badly assault – or worse – a prostitute off the street.

He drove for the fifteen or so minutes it took to reach the red-light area he preferred. Mick cruised up and down the roads slowly, looking for two things. Firstly, any sign of the vice squad. He knew a couple of the guys who worked on the squad, and he had made it his business to know exactly what vehicles they were currently using.

Secondly, he started searching the empty, desolate and dark streets for his prey.

The prostitute needed to be carefully chosen. She had to be small enough to be easily overpowered. He didn't want a big fat thing who would fight back and struggle.

She would also need to be young enough to still have that slight naivety that he needed to achieve his objective.

Mick had driven around the red-light area for a good ten minutes before he spotted her. She looked to be the perfect target.

Even better, she was standing alone on a stretch of the road where none of the other working girls were plying their trade.

There wasn't another person within two hundred yards of her. The stretch of road where she was standing was also particularly dark. The one working street light was very weak; the light it gave out was more of an ethereal glow.

Making one last check all around, he pulled his car slowly to the side of the road and stopped opposite the young girl.

He wound down the front passenger window and beckoned for the girl to come over to the car.

Slowly, almost hesitantly, the girl walked over.

Mick could see her better now, as the glow from the weak street light illuminated her face. The white light reflecting off her pale, drawn face gave her an almost ghostly appearance.

Her pale features were framed by long dark hair.

She looked to be young, in her late teens at most. She was wearing a short denim skirt, black patent-leather knee-length boots that looked scuffed and worn, and a short-sleeved black cotton blouse that was undone to her navel, exposing a black lacy bra that covered very small breasts.

It was a bitterly cold night, and the girl was shivering so

badly her lank, dark hair was wriggling at the bottom of her jawline like worms on a fishing line.

As she got closer, Mick saw the telltale signs of drug addiction. Her brown eyes were deep set and surrounded by dark rings. There were fresh sores on her face, and looking at her skinny white arms, he could see where she had recently injected.

'You looking for business, love?' she stuttered, her voice reflecting her shivering body.

Mick noticed the accent wasn't a London one.

'I might be, darling. How much for full sex?' he said.

Her eyes suddenly got bigger at the prospect of all the smack she was going to be able to buy with fifty large ones.

'Full sex is fifty quid, and I'll need the cash first.'

'No problem, get in.'

Mick reached over and opened the passenger door.

He gave her five ten-pound notes as soon as she got in. He watched as she stuffed the banknotes into the top of her right boot. He had no intention of having any kind of sex with this drugged-up slag, and he knew he would get the money back off her, all in good time.

He turned to her and said, 'Do you have anywhere you normally go?'

'No, I don't really know this area. I've only just come up to London. Go where you like, darling, so long as there aren't any vice coppers knocking about. I can't afford to get pinched again already.'

Mick started to drive off. *This is perfect,* he thought to himself.

Only just in town. No fucker will know who she is or where she's from, and the silly cow won't have a clue where I'm taking her.

Furtively, he glanced over at the girl now sitting in the passenger seat.

She looked as though a breath of wind would knock her

over. Looking closer, he could see that the girl had scored quite recently. She kept licking her lips, and her head was lolling from side to side.

She looked totally out of it.

Only one thing worried him, her comment about being pinched again. If this girl had come to the notice of the police before, that might cause him a problem. He let an evil smile play over his lips as he thought about the contents of the grip bag. He knew exactly how to overcome that little problem.

His excitement was mounting, and already he could feel familiar stirrings down below. He was glad he had prepared well and brought his grip bag along.

He picked up speed and drove quickly away from the red-light area.

In his mounting excitement, Mick had failed to spot the skinny red-haired youth with his ferret-like eyes and thick glasses, watching as he drove the girl away.

What the girl hadn't said was that she had only just arrived in London from Norwich with her junkie boyfriend. The only reason she was out on the street tonight was because he needed to score. She'd taken the last of their gear just before she came out onto the streets.

The skinny boyfriend got the broken pencil out of his pocket and scribbled down the car registration number on the scrap of paper she had given him.

He had done what she asked.

The girl always told him to write down the registration numbers of any cars she got into, just to be on the safe side.

He stepped back into the shadows and clutched his skinny arms tightly around himself.

He hoped she wouldn't be too long. He was already hanging, desperate for a fix.

With a low moan, the cold wind blew along the dark street, and he started to shiver again.

12

River Thames, London – April 8, 1984

The weak early morning sun shimmered softly on the chocolate brown waters of the River Thames as it flowed swiftly by. The river here was tidal, and at certain times of the day, the currents were fast.

The body of the naked woman was no more than ten feet from the water's edge and was lying on the top of the thick black mud. She had been left lying face up with her arms splayed out at odd angles. Her legs were crossed at the ankles, the right leg on top of the left.

It had been a police launch that first spotted the body lying on the mud at the side of the river. It was a lonely and desolate spot, and river traffic was light.

None of the tourist pleasure boats came to this part of the river.

At first glance, the sergeant on the police launch thought he was seeing a shop mannequin, but something about the position it was lying in made him squint through his binoculars to get a better look.

Only then did he realise it was the body of a young woman, and that the dark area around the head was congealed blood.

The sergeant had spent a lot of years on the launch and had seen countless victims of drowning in the fast-flowing river. He knew that the tide was still on the way out and would be for another hour; only then would the water start creeping back over the mud towards the body.

He estimated it would be around four and a half hours before the muddy river would claim the body.

He had immediately swung the launch over towards the bank to get a closer look. Once the boat was manoeuvred as close to the bank as possible, he could see the horrific injuries to the woman's head.

The sergeant could also see that the woman had not yet been in the river and had just been placed on the muddy bank. There was a scaffold board left lying across the mud down to the side of the body.

He immediately radioed in the sighting to the control room, then remained as close to the bank as possible to ensure nobody approached the body.

Following his radio message, the police quickly arrived in numbers to the scene. As he looked over towards the bank, the sergeant could now see two detectives as they squatted down next to the body.

Detective Inspector Glyn Johnson had arrived about five minutes ago.

He was the only black detective inspector in the Metropolitan Police, and this deprived area of London, south of the river, was his patch.

There were no upmarket penthouse flats or trendy wine bars near this part of the river.

This area was inhabited solely by criminals, whores and

junkies. It was the type of area decent, ordinary people went out of their way to avoid.

All large cities have them, sinkholes of desperation and criminality where the occupiers all have the same law-of-the-jungle mentality.

Glyn Johnson was now fast approaching forty-three years of age, and his short hair and goatee beard were starting to show flecks of grey. He was a tall, thin, athletic-looking man who would not have looked out of place on a basketball court.

He was now a widower, after his wife had lost a short battle with pancreatic cancer.

A stunned and shocked Glyn had been unable to grieve due to the speed everything had happened.

Just two days after he buried his wife, he had returned back to his job and thrown himself hard into his work. While ever he was totally engrossed in his work, he could ignore the feeling of despair and loneliness.

Eventually, he achieved an existence that was manageable: He went to work, did his job, and then returned home to his quiet house, to his memories and his thoughts about what might have been.

Now, on the riverbank, squatting over the body of another victim, he pondered over the way life was so indiscriminately unfair and brutal. Glyn Johnson had over twenty years' service and had dealt with more than his fair share of violent and suspicious deaths.

Glyn stood up and stretched; the sleeves of his suit had ridden up his long arms. He quickly smoothed them back down again.

As he glanced back up towards the bank, he could see that most of the buildings were falling down, and that there were no houses that appeared occupied within view.

He might get lucky and find that one of the derelict houses or disused warehouses was a squat where the occupiers weren't all selectively deaf, dumb and blind.

'What's the word, Craig?' he said, in his soft voice that still carried more than a hint of a Jamaican accent.

The other man squatting at the side of the dead woman stood up and spoke. 'She was discovered on the mud flats at around six o'clock this morning by the River Police. Sergeant Davies, on the launch, spotted her on the mud flats as he was patrolling upriver. He's still standing to off the bank.'

Glyn turned back towards the river and saw the sergeant standing on the deck of the launch.

'Make sure we get his statement as soon as possible. Advise control there's no longer any need for him to remain standing to in the boat. Everything's under control now.'

'Will do, guv'nor.'

Detective Sergeant Craig Fraser immediately got on the radio and relayed the order for the launch to stand down, and also to request the statement from Sergeant Davies.

'Do we have any other witnesses?'

'No, nothing so far, but it's early days.'

'Okay, soon as we can, I want search teams going through all the buildings up on the embankment. It's obvious she wasn't killed here; we might just get lucky and find where she was actually killed. God knows, we may even hit gold dust and find a witness.'

'I'm on it, guv,' the detective sergeant said, in his broad Scottish accent.

Craig Fraser had been a detective sergeant for four years and had been promoted onto Glyn Johnson's team in South London.

He knew how the detective inspector ran his operations and prided himself on taking steps under his own initiative.

Born and raised in the Gorbals area of Glasgow, Fraser was hard as teak. He was a short, powerful man with a face that looked as if it had been carved from granite.

He was a similar age to Glyn Johnson, and the two men were close friends as well as colleagues.

'I've got two full search teams on the way, to start going through the derelict properties, and I've also blagged the uniform inspector to send me whatever uniform staff he can spare. They can start talking to anyone who turns up.'

'Thanks, Craig, good work.'

Looking down at the scene once more, Glyn could see the long plank of wood, a disused scaffold board, that had been placed out over the mud down to the body.

'Looks like our killer used that to bring the body down onto the mud.'

'Yes, guv, when I first got here, there were no footprints in the mud. The ones you see now around the body are ours and the Scenes of Crime officers. I've taped off the board. Scenes of Crime are going to drag the board up onto the flat in a couple of minutes and will be having a close look at it. They've already photographed everything here in situ, and they've taken photographs of the girl as well, including the wrists and what's left of the face. It looks like she's been bound and gagged at some stage. You see the cuts into her wrists; they reckon something like plastic cable ties. There's residue around the damaged mouth that looks like adhesive. They've taken swabs, but their educated guess is gaffer tape.'

'Okay, Craig, make sure that information's passed on to the search teams. The killer obviously removed the ties and the tape before dumping her here. He may have got careless and left them behind where he killed her.'

Glyn looked down at the mangled remains of the young woman and said, 'You know the score, Craig, it's imperative that we identify this woman as soon as possible. Once you've finished up here, I want you to concentrate solely on that. I want three detectives working specifically on her identification. Fingerprints may help us out, but in the meantime, get them trawling through any missing persons reports that come in. I'll deal with the post-mortem side of things. I'll take DC

Briggs with me; he's had plenty of experience doing the exhibits job.'

He paused and looked down at the pitiful sight of the naked woman.

There really was no dignity in death, he thought to himself.

'How long before the river becomes an issue here?'

'Sergeant Davies reckons we've got until ten thirty at the latest to have either finished here or get swept into the river.'

Glyn glanced at his wristwatch. The time was fast approaching seven fifty.

Plenty of time left to do what needed to be done.

'Can we expect the arrival of the Home Office pathologist any time soon? Or am I going to have to organise a fucking tent to cover this poor woman up? Before all the gawkers come out to have a stare!'

The Jamaican accent became more pronounced as his temper frayed a little.

'Speak of the Devil, guv; she's here now.'

Walking down the boating ramp towards the stinking mud was a slim attractive woman in her mid to late thirties, wearing a white forensic suit and carrying a holdall that held the equipment she would need.

'Who the fuck's this? Where's Jock McArdle?'

'Retired a month ago, guv. Don't you ever read memos?'

'Not if I can help it,' he growled.

Craig indicated for the woman approaching to follow the footmarks they had made previously through the thick mud. The mud was black and had the same consistency as molasses; the smell was a cross between rotten fish and vegetables. Eventually, the slim woman reached where the two detectives were standing ankle-deep in the glutinous mud.

Craig said, 'Guv'nor, this is Emily Cook, our new Home Office pathologist. Ms Cook, this is …'

She finished the sentence for him: 'This is Detective

Inspector Glyn Johnson. We haven't met, but I've heard a lot about you.'

She held out a small gloved hand.

Her accent was like cut glass; it was obvious she hailed from the Home Counties. Surrey, guessed Glyn, probably around Virginia Water.

'All bad, I expect?' he said, reaching over and gently shaking the proffered hand.

'Quite the contrary, actually. Now what do we have here? Any idea who she is?'

'Other than a young woman who probably sold her body, abused Class A controlled drugs, and ended up getting her face smashed to a pulp and being dumped at the side of the river in the largest city in the country, without anyone seeing or hearing a thing ... No, not a clue.'

Smiling, she said, 'It seems that everything I've heard about your succinct manner sounds about right. Okay, Detective Inspector, you're obviously looking at a murder enquiry. I'll do the necessary here, quick as I can before the tide becomes an issue, and then arrange to get the poor woman back to my office for the post-mortem. See you at St Barnabas hospital mortuary in a couple of hours. Shall we say ten o'clock?'

Glyn nodded curtly. 'Okay, Ms Cook, I'll see you up at St Barny's at ten.'

With that, she turned and started the procedures to gather any evidence possible from the scene.

Leaving Craig with the pathologist, Glyn walked slowly through the mud and up the slope to his waiting car.

This was all he needed on a Monday morning.

As he quickly removed the mud-covered wellington boots, he glanced over his shoulder at the new pathologist now going busily about her business. All he could see was the blonde hair tied back in a ponytail above the white suit.

Emily Cook. He liked her already.

13

St Barnabas Hospital Mortuary, London – April 8, 1984

'Hello again, Inspector,' said Emily Cook as Glyn walked into the mortuary examination room. Lagging behind was DC Briggs, who was weighed down with a large bag full of various size exhibit bags and labels.

He would use these to bag up various items for evidence as the examination progressed.

The examination room was large and had four stainless-steel bench tables in the centre of the room; each bench was fitted with an independent sluice system. One wall was made up of floor-to-ceiling refrigerated drawers that were the temporary home of the recently deceased.

The walls were all covered by large white porcelain tiles, and the floor was a lime green linoleum. There was an almost overpowering smell that was a mixture of disinfectant and formaldehyde. It was one of those smells that, once experienced, stays with you for the rest of your life.

In front of them, lying on one of the stainless-steel examination tables, was the naked body of the white female, still covered in the stinking mud and debris of the riverbank.

Emily Cook was standing on the other side of the bench, already wearing a white protective suit and mask.

'Good morning again, Ms Cook, shall we make a start?' Glyn said.

She began the post-mortem examination by taking samples of the mud and debris that covered various parts of the woman's body. These samples were carefully bagged and labelled by DC Briggs.

After this was done, a preliminary visual examination was carried out, with photographs being taken every step of the way.

Once this had been completed and notes made, the post-mortem proper began.

Fifty-five minutes later, Emily Cook stepped away from the cadaver. Pulling her mask away from her face, she spoke directly to Glyn. 'The woman was obviously a drug abuser; there are numerous injection sites on both arms and even on the lower legs and feet. I've taken bloods, so this may give us some idea of her drug of choice, but from her general physical appearance, most likely it'll be heroin.'

She continued, 'As far as identification goes, you may be in some difficulty. Dental records are going to be useless, as the damage to her face – and in particular her mouth – is devastating. Her lower jaw's been completely smashed and so have all of the upper teeth. I don't know if you noticed this at the riverbank, Inspector, but whoever did this paid particular attention to the woman's hands. Because her hands were bunched into fists, it was only when I got her back here that I noticed that every finger and both her thumbs have been severed with a sharp instrument. Probably a small set of pruning shears or suchlike. The palms of both hands have also been damaged beyond all recognition with numerous slash marks across each one until the inside of the hand has been reduced to a latticework of destroyed flapping skin. What I can tell you is that, interestingly, all the damage to the face, jaws and hands was carried out after she died. She wasn't tortured. It looks to me like her killer's somebody who's very aware of how the identification process works.'

Glyn stroked his goatee beard thoughtfully. 'I read recently about a case where they'd recreated a bloke's face from a skull. Is there any way of carrying out some sort of facial recognition from this skull?'

He continued, 'It's vital for the enquiry that we have something to work with to identify this girl.'

'My old professor at Bristol University is a leading expert on facial recognition and mapping. The best he could do would be to give you a visual likeness of how this woman looked in life, but it's only ever an approximate likeness. It would be especially so in this case, because of the massive damage to the facial bones around the eye sockets and the extensive damage to the lower jaw.'

'That would at least be something. How soon could you speak to your professor? I need to know from him if it's feasible to do, and more importantly, how soon could he get a likeness to us?'

'You're in luck. I've arranged for him to come up to London tomorrow to have lunch and take in a show with me. I can ask him to examine her for you. I'm sure he'll oblige. It's not something he has the opportunity of doing very often.'

'Thank you, Ms Cook, that would be very helpful,' he said, smiling broadly.

Old Jock would never have sorted that out so fast, he thought. Chalk up one for the new girl.

Emily Cook smiled back before saying, 'The only other identifying feature I can find is a very small tattoo on the heel of her right foot. The killer probably missed it because it's so small and in such an unusual place. It's a picture of a small blue cartoon rabbit with a date below. The date is 12/07/83. I can also tell you this woman has recently gone full term with a pregnancy, and this date may have something to do with that. I've got plenty of photographs of the tattoo.'

Glyn leaned forward to look closely at the small blue mark on the woman's heel. 'That's fantastic news. This date's going to be personal to someone. Somebody out there will know someone who has that tattoo. If we can match it to a facial likeness, we might be in business.'

Emily continued her summation: 'The cause of death was a massive brain haemorrhage caused by several major blows to the head with a blunt object. My guess is a hammer with a rounded head. Some of the fractures, as you've seen for yourself, have a pronounced round depression at the centre that are consistent with that type of implement.'

With a worried expression, she continued, 'I know I've only been here just over a month, but I think this case has some very strange implications.'

'In what way, Ms Cook?'

'Well, the injuries are consistent with an attack carried out in a rage: too much force used, etc. But then, after the frenzied attack, the killer displays a great deal of control, an ordered mind. This is shown by the damage that was all caused post-mortem to try to avoid identification. All the research that's been done on offender profiling points to either one or the other, rage or order. It's strange to find the two together. The worrying thing for me is that the ordered side of the individual responsible displays all the traits of somebody who will definitely kill again.'

'Bloody marvellous! What you're telling me is that we have a potential serial killer on our hands.'

'I'm afraid so.'

'Great, that's all we need!'

'I'll get my full report to you as soon as I can, and I'll call you after I've seen the professor about the facial recognition.'

'After what you've just told me, the sooner the better, please.'

Glyn walked out of the mortuary and made his way through the maze of hospital corridors back to the car park. He walked briskly, his long legs striding out. His face was set in a mask of concentration. It was only a couple of years ago when Peter Sutcliffe, a lorry driver from Bradford, had led the West Yorkshire Police a merry dance all over Leeds and other northern cities, killing thirteen women and being dubbed 'The Yorkshire Ripper' by the press before he was caught.

It was every detective's worst nightmare: a killer on the loose, targeting total strangers for no other reason than the uncontrollable urge to kill.

Glyn walked to the large hospital car park and found his car.

Gunning the motor, he raced away from the car park. He realised he didn't have much time. This monster needed to be caught before he murdered another young woman and the press were thinking of a new name for the latest serial killer.

14

Mansfield Town Centre, Nottinghamshire – April 10, 1984

Jimmy Wade had been waiting patiently for over an hour. He had parked his car towards the back of the large car park normally used by the clients and staff of a large solicitor's firm.

The car park was poorly lit, and there were large trees around the edges. More importantly, it was located directly opposite the entrance to the police station car park.

It was well after ten o'clock at night, and he had expected her to be finished over an hour ago.

Earlier that day, he'd been on the same street, waiting for her to arrive at work. He'd been standing outside an estate agent's, pretending to look at properties for sale. The agent's window was just down the road from the police station. Jimmy had watched as she arrived just before nine o'clock that morning. He'd kept the hood of his parka coat up and thrust his hands deep into the coat pockets.

Rachel Moore had driven straight past him in a small red

Mini Cooper. He'd walked slowly up the road and watched her as she parked her car.

He had spent the rest of the day either driving slowly past the station in his car or walking past to see if the red Mini was still there.

Once it reached nine o'clock at night, he knew she had been at work for over twelve hours, and he took the decision to park up and wait for her to drive her red Mini out of the car park.

Jimmy chose the darkest area of the car park, where he knew there was very little chance of anyone seeing him waiting in his car.

His Ford Cortina was a dark green colour and was almost invisible in this poor light.

As he was out on strike at the moment, he had plenty of time on his hands.

He was seriously pissed off about his situation. He felt as though he had been forced into joining the strike. He was worried, as he had large bills to pay.

Most of the nice things in his house were being paid for on hire purchase, and there was a small mortgage to find every month, not to mention the usual utility bills.

He'd been sitting pretty before the strike – money in the bank and everything he wanted.

The bills weren't a struggle for him while ever he was earning.

Jimmy knew that by the beginning of July, his savings would run out. By then he either went back to work as a scab or he lost his house.

The choice really was that simple.

The strike didn't look like it would be over by then, not a chance.

Jimmy knew a lot of other miners who were in the same position as himself. He heard them moaning on about having no money, usually as they downed another pint and smoked another cigarette in the local Miners Welfare.

Jimmy had cut down his smoking to just five cigarettes a day and had stopped drinking alcohol altogether in an attempt to save money.

When he'd ordered an orange squash to drink in the Welfare, the other blokes had taken the piss out of him mercilessly.

Well, they could all fuck off, and Scargill could fuck right off too.

There was no way he was going to lose his house because of that Yorkshire twat.

Suddenly car headlights being switched on in the police car park snapped him away from his thoughts. Instinctively he slunk lower down in his car seat. Two cars were coming out at the same time. The first car was a white Datsun and was being driven by a stocky-looking bloke with a bald head. This car turned right out of the car park and was quickly followed by the red Mini Cooper turning left out of the car park.

Jimmy was surprised to see there was somebody in the front passenger seat, and that person was obviously a man.

As the Mini pulled away from the car park, he followed, at first with his car's headlights off.

Once on the road, he switched the lights on and maintained a discreet distance from the car in front.

Jimmy followed the Mini out of the town centre until it turned right onto Garth Road.

He watched as the brake lights on the Mini lit up and the vehicle slowed to a stop.

He drove straight by and parked up further along the road. In the rear-view mirror, he saw the passenger get out and wave before walking up a driveway.

She must have been dropping him off, he thought. He made a mental note to try to find out who the mystery man was who lived there.

He let the Mini drive past him quite a way before again pulling out from the kerb and following the vehicle.

This time he followed the Mini to a block of flats called Bateman Court.

Again, he stopped his vehicle some distance away and watched as Rachel Moore parked up and then walked to the block of flats.

Bateman Court was only a small block that held four flats. Two on the ground floor and two on the first floor.

It was quite late, and the entire block was in darkness.

All he had to do was wait to see which lights came on. A minute later, the lights in the left-hand flat on the first floor came on.

'Bollocks!' he said aloud. He had been hoping she lived in one of the ground-floor flats.

At least he knew where she lived now.

All he had to do now was carry on watching both her and the flat. He'd soon ascertain everything he needed to know about her life and who else, if anybody, featured in it.

He needed to gather as much information as he could about her. Only then would he be in a position to formulate a successful plan that would ultimately result in the death of Rachel Moore.

15

Peckham, London – April 10, 1984

Two days had gone quickly by since the young woman's body had been discovered on the riverbank, and Glyn Johnson was no closer to identifying her. The three detectives guided by DS Fraser had certainly put the hours in trying to find out who she was, but to no avail.

They had trawled through hundreds of missing persons' reports, looking for anyone who came close to the description of the dead girl. After hours of painstaking work, they had drawn a blank.

Every enquiry they tried resulted in nothing. The frustration was mounting.

Acting on Glyn's orders, the detectives visited each hospital in the Greater London area and researched the records for every infant born on 12 September 1983. After completing that mammoth task, they then set about the painstaking task of tracing every mother.

This enquiry alone required a further two detectives being added to the team.

Glyn knew it was a long shot. The woman could have given birth at home or, more likely, outside the London area. He had to try something though. Without an early identification of the victim, he knew the trail to the killer would rapidly go cold.

The only piece of good news was that Professor Mason from Bristol University, at the request of Emily Cook, had spent the last two days carefully and skilfully creating a facial mould from the reconstructed bones of the dead girl's face. Professor Mason had worked long into the night without rest, and promised Glyn that a preliminary image of the dead girl's face would be ready before the end of the day.

Glyn didn't care how preliminary it was; he wanted to get the face and the tattoo out there.

He was confident that someone out there would know who she was.

Suddenly he was disturbed in his thinking by an urgent knocking on his office door. 'Come in!' he bellowed.

A very young and very nervous policewoman timidly opened the door.

'Sir, control room thought you'd want to know one of the search teams just radioed in. They've found cable ties and blood on the floor of a derelict property on Wharf Road. It's about a hundred yards from the riverbank where the woman was found.'

'I bloody knew it!' he yelled as he jumped from behind his desk.

Grabbing his coat, he shouted, 'Craig, have you got a motor?'

Craig Fraser appeared immediately from the general office. 'Yes, guv'nor.'

'Come on, then, Wharf Road sharpish. I reckon there's a good chance they've found our fucking murder scene!'

'That's great, guv! I'll make sure Scenes of Crime are travelling too.'

TWENTY FRUSTRATING MINUTES LATER, after ploughing through the beginning of the rush-hour traffic, they were finally approaching the derelict building on Wharf Road.

The building was a disused warehouse with a row of small offices on the ground floor and large open-plan storage areas on the other three floors. It had fallen into disrepair after the company that owned it went bust in the late seventies. It was now a haven for junkies to shoot up in, and a place for prostitutes to bring their punters.

There was one of the distinctive plain white Ford Transit vans that were used by the Tactical Support Group parked outside the main entrance.

Standing by the side of the van were a sergeant and eight officers, drinking coffee from paper cups.

Seeing the CID car approaching, the young sergeant threw his hot drink onto the ground and walked towards the car.

As the two detectives got out, the TSG sergeant spoke: 'DI Johnson?'

'Yeah, Skip, that's me. What've you got?' said Glyn evenly.

'We'd only just started on this building, guv'nor, when one of my lads shouted up on the radio and told me he'd found something in one of the front ground-floor rooms. It's a proper shithole in there, the light ain't the best, but he's adamant there are plastic cable ties and brown tape on the floor and what looks like plenty of blood. As soon as he told me what he'd found, I pulled the rest of the lads out of the building. I've left him in there guarding the interior door leading to the small room where he's made the discovery. I've also instructed him to start and maintain a log of the scene. He's a good lad who knows the crack; he hasn't touched a thing. I hope you don't mind, guv'nor, but I've already set things in motion. There's a Scenes of Crime team already en route.'

'That's great work, Skipper; tell your lads I appreciate it. It's no fun crawling around in these shitholes, with all the dirty needles and crap everywhere. You've done a professional job, and I'll be having a word with your guv'nor. What's the lad's name inside?'

'It's Tom Kane, guv.'

With that, Glyn and Craig grabbed overshoes and an overall each from the boot of the car. As they quickly donned the protective clothing, Glyn looked over his shoulder back towards the fast-flowing river. Less than a hundred yards away he could see the part of the riverbank where the young woman had been dumped.

Finally, after putting gloves on, both men made their way into the decrepit building.

The stench of stale urine and faeces hit them as soon as they walked into the filthy building.

The door led onto a dark corridor. Glyn took a small Mini Maglite torch from his pocket and shone it along the passageway. The beam from the torch picked out the young constable standing five yards away. . He was outside one of the rooms that must have previously been an admin office when the building was part of a thriving business.

Picking their way carefully through the excrement, condoms and used needles that littered the floor, the detectives made their way to the officer. 'You must be Tom Kane,' said Glyn.

'PC Tom Kane, yes, sir. Can I have your names and ranks for the log?'

He opened his pocketbook to note the names and the time.

Craig spoke quietly in his guttural Scottish accent. 'Aye, laddie, you can. I'm Detective Sergeant Fraser, and this man here is Detective Inspector Johnson. The time is now fourteen minutes past four.'

Glyn put a reassuring hand on Tom Kane's shoulder and said, 'Well done, son, you've followed the book to the letter. I want you to point out to me exactly where you've been and what you've touched.'

PC Kane stepped sideways to allow Glyn line of sight into the dirty room littered with rubbish and a small pile of broken-up furniture.

He said, 'I took one step inside the room; then I stopped to let my eyes get adjusted to the gloom before going any further. Once I could see properly, I moved that piece of newspaper there.'

He indicated a screwed-up sheet of old newspaper before continuing. 'Directly underneath the sheet of old newspaper were two black plastic cable ties like we'd been briefed about. They'd both been used and had been snipped in half. I straight away stepped back out of the room and radioed my skipper to tell him what I'd found. While I waited for him to come in, I stayed here at the door, looking around the room. Over there in the corner is what looks like screwed-up brown gaffer tape, and that stain on the floor, just there, looks like old dried blood to me, guv.'

'Well done, son; good stuff. I want you to tell the Scenes of Crime people exactly what you've told me when they get here,' said Glyn with a smile.

The two detectives retraced their steps and made their way back out of the building.

Only once they were back outside in the daylight did they realise just how dark and gloomy it was inside the building.

Both men breathed in deeply, trying to get the stench of the building out of their noses.

'Finally, a break!' exclaimed Glyn.

He continued, 'Any other day and that young lad would've trampled over everything before he even saw it.

He's got the makings of being a bloody good copper. Craig, make sure he gets commended to his guv'nor for today. The professionalism he's shown today could prove vital.'

'Will do, guv'nor. Scenes of Crime are here now; I'll go back in with them.'

The TSG sergeant approached Glyn, saying, 'Guv'nor, your office has been on the radio looking for you. Apparently, the item you've been waiting for is now ready at St Barnabas Hospital Mortuary.'

'Thanks, Skip, well done today. Your team are a credit to you. Good work.'

'Thanks, guv'nor; we do try.' The sergeant grinned.

As soon as Craig had finished pointing out the room and the items on the floor to the Scenes of Crime officers, he rejoined Glyn, who was standing at the side of the CID car.

As both men removed the protective overalls and overshoes, Glyn grinned at Craig, saying, 'Finally, we're getting somewhere, Craig. I've just had notification that Professor Mason has finished his work, and the image of the dead girl's face is ready at the mortuary. Let's get over there and see what she looked like in life, shall we?'

As the two men left the riverside, Glyn said evenly, 'Craig, I want this woman's face in every newspaper, on every TV channel and on every cell block wall in every London nick. Someone, somewhere, will know who she is. I still want your team to keep working on the hospital enquiries. You never know that might just turn something up. All we need now is to get lucky and for that bastard to have left us some little scrap of forensic evidence in that shithole back there. We're getting closer, Craig, we're getting closer.'

'Aye, guv'nor, I reckon we just might be at that.'

16

Proteus Army Camp, Ollerton, Nottinghamshire – April 28, 1984

Mick Reynolds was in a foul mood. He'd already bollocked two of his men for next to nothing, and was now sitting in the front of the Transit van, seething. He glanced at his watch; it was still only seven thirty in the morning. He let out an audible groan and sat back in the seat.

His PSU had started their shift at three thirty that morning and travelled to Cuckney crossroads again for more intercept duty. They had been relieved at seven o'clock and were now back at Proteus Camp for food. Mick couldn't be arsed to eat yet another greasy fry-up, so he stayed in the van while his men went to eat.

He now sat quietly in the van, alone in the darkness with his thoughts.

It was the last week in April, and Mick knew he still had two more weeks of picket line duty before he could get another week back home, away from this Godforsaken shithole.

It was also three weeks since he had picked up and killed the young prostitute in London.

Some days, he still couldn't quite believe what he'd been capable of that night. He was confident that he'd committed the perfect murder; surely they would've come for him by now if he'd slipped up.

The days he'd spent since with his PSU on intercept duty were just a blur. He knew he was just going through the motions. Every shift, every day, every week was the same mixture of mind-blowing boredom.

A couple of times earlier in the day, Ken, the driver of the PSU van, had asked him if he was all right. 'You seemed a million miles away there, Sarge,' he had commented.

Now, as he sat alone in the quiet of the van, his mind drifted off, replaying the moment he had killed the girl over and over again.

That joyous moment when she first got into his car and he knew that once and for all he was going to shut her up.

Whenever he replayed the killing in his mind, it was always the face of his wife, Rita, he saw, not the dishevelled junkie prostitute he had actually killed.

At the precise moment of the killing, he found himself in the grip of the deepest rage he had ever experienced.

It had been the single most intense moment of his life.

He had driven her off in his car and parked up in a dark unlit corner of the red-light area. Before she could do or say anything, he had punched her once hard in the face, knocking her unconscious.

It was then an easy task to wrap the plastic cable ties around her puny wrists so tight that her wrists had bled a little.

He'd wrapped the gaffer tape three times around her head, covering only her mouth, leaving her nostrils clear so she didn't suffocate.

He had forced her down into the footwell of the front passenger seat so nobody could see her while he made the short drive over to the derelict buildings next to the Thames embankment, not far from Peckham, south of the river.

She had started to come around again when he was nearly at the derelict buildings and began to snuffle under the gagging brown tape.

He had ignored her pitiful muffled pleadings and parked up close to the side of one of the buildings. He then got out of the car and stepped into the shadows, where he quickly donned a full forensic suit, overshoes and gloves. He picked up his small grip bag and placed it in a room a little way along the dark corridor inside the disgusting building.

He quickly checked the other rooms in the building. He didn't want to risk being disturbed by some addict looking to score their next fix, or by another prostitute with a punter.

Satisfied the building was empty, he had returned to his car and dragged the young girl from the footwell. She weighed nothing, and he carried her quickly into the building before dropping her roughly onto the floor of the same room he had left his grip bag.

Once inside the room, he had quickly ripped off her clothes and stuffed them into a bin liner that he took out of the grip bag.

He closed his eyes as he sat in the van, replaying the actual murder. A cruel smile crept across his face as he recalled how he had made the girl sit naked on the filthy, disgusting floor in the pitch dark. He shuddered involuntarily as he remembered her making the whining noise beneath the suffocating gaffer tape.

He recalled everything in vivid detail.

The noise she was making had eventually got on his nerves, and once again he had reached into the grip bag, this time grabbing the heavy ball-peen hammer. He then walked behind the woman and half-closed his eyes.

His head had been filled with the sound of Rita's voice nagging him again, taking the piss out of his manhood again, ridiculing him again.

Suddenly, something inside him snapped, and he started to rain down blow after blow on the prostitute's head.

Mercifully, she was probably dead or at least unconscious after the first blow. He had continued to rain down blow after blow until he felt physically exhausted and was gasping for breath.

Finally, he had stopped and surveyed the scene of carnage.

There was blood everywhere. The forensic suit was covered in the prostitute's blood, and his gloved hands were glistening.

Quickly, he had regained his composure and began to think rationally again.

He could not allow the police to identify the girl, so he had put on a further pair of gloves over the blood-soaked ones and grabbed the shears from the bag. Painstakingly, he cut off each of the fingers and thumbs from the dead girl's hands, placing the severed digits into a plastic bag.

He had then used the Stanley knife to slice up the palms of her hands before snipping off the cable ties.

He had then removed the gaffer tape from around her mouth and placed it in the corner near the cable ties. He had then systematically smashed her lower jaw and teeth with the hammer. Finally, he had stuffed all the tools back into the grip bag, and, after checking the coast was clear, he had furtively walked out of the building.

He walked down to the path at the side of the river.

The moonlight was dancing on the dark water as it raced by. He saw the blood on his forensic suit; in the moonlight it was black, like molasses.

From the path, he had surveyed the bank down to the water's edge; it was thick glutinous mud.

Mick had known that he needed to get the body down to

the water's edge so the tide would wash it away before anybody discovered it in the morning.

At the side of the building he had seen a long abandoned scaffold board propped against the outside wall.

He placed the scaffold board out over the cloying mud down to the water's edge.

The board fell about ten feet short of the flowing river.

He recalled cursing silently for not researching the times of the tide. He could only hope the tide would rise enough to dispose of the body downstream before it was seen.

Ensuring there was still nobody about, he had returned to the building and picked the woman's body up, carrying her out of the building and down to the river.

He had carried her along the board and dumped her on her back on top of the stinking mud.

He had then tiptoed back along the board to the bank, making sure he left no marks on the soft mud.

Standing at the side of his car, he had then removed the overshoes, forensic suit and gloves before dumping them all in a bin liner. The bin liner then went in the grip bag.

He had then driven back over the river, back to his house at Wembley.

By the time he had arrived home, Rita had still not returned home from her sordid night out, so he had taken out the bin liner containing the prostitute's clothes and the forensic clothing that was heavily bloodstained from the grip bag.

He left the bloodstained tools, the unused cable ties and the roll of gaffer tape in the bag in the boot of his car.

He had then quickly showered before getting changed into his police uniform.

It had been nearly two o'clock in the morning when he had finally packed all the kit he would need for the deployment to Nottinghamshire into his large black PSU bag.

At the bottom of the PSU bag, he had stuffed the plastic

bin liner full of the bloodstained clothes. He knew he would be able to dispose of all the items in the incinerator at Proteus Army Camp when he got there.

Finally, he'd put the kettle on and made himself a cup of tea. He sat in his lounge, sipping tea, while he waited patiently for the police transport to pick him up.

Now, alone in the van, he was smiling broadly at the memories of that night.

Suddenly, his recollection of those momentous events was brought to an end; the silence was shattered by his men returning to the PSU van.

'Bloody hell, Mick, you've missed a belting fry up there!'

He just grunted a reply to the comment.

Mick couldn't wait to get back down to London. Another fourteen days of this shit was really going to drag. He was desperate to get back home because he'd finally come to a decision. The next time he killed, it really would be Rita who would die. He had proved to himself now that he could kill and also, more importantly, that he could get away with it.

The only thing he needed to concentrate on was how to dispose of Rita's dead body.

17

Peckham, London – May 3, 1984

The skinny, red-haired junkie was literally starving. His jaundiced skin was stretched taut across his skeletal face. The blue eyes were sunk deep into dark-rimmed sockets. Only that morning, one of his back teeth had fallen out for no apparent reason.

It was now almost four weeks since he had watched his girlfriend drive off in that posh motor. He was now very weak and felt slightly dizzy. He'd been existing on meagre scraps of food that he managed to scavenge while wandering the streets.

The rich geezer who owned the car she got into must have set her up very nicely for her not to come back to him.

He was angry but not surprised. Deep down he knew that she would do anything for money or another hit of heroin.

He allowed his mind to drift, and saw an image of his girlfriend in some posh pad, living the high life, eating, drinking, getting as much smack as she wanted and all the time getting fucked by the bastard in the posh motor.

He grew angry at the thought of her living the dream, while he'd been reduced to robbing bins at the back of shitty restaurants just to survive, nicking anything he could get his hands on just to get his next bag of heroin.

Lee Skipton had just turned nineteen. He first became addicted to heroin when he was seventeen.

It had been easy to drift into drugs back home in Norwich. There was fuck all else to do in the town. There were no jobs anywhere. It was a simple choice for everyone: the dole or the dole.

It was a proper dump.

He first met Jenny Taylor in Norwich town centre just before Christmas last year. He'd watched her, spellbound, as she went round the various shops in the precinct. He could tell she had no money, and it was obvious she was out on the rob, but she looked fantastic. There was an air of confidence about her.

He watched her go into Miss Selfridge and stick two tops up her baggy jumper before sauntering out of the shop.

She had made it look so fucking easy; it was like she was daring the security guards in the shop to stop her. He was totally captivated and continued to follow her around the shopping precinct like a lost puppy.

He had followed her, watching her every move for over half an hour, until suddenly she turned around and walked straight up to him. 'What's your fucking game! Are you a perv or something?' she yelled.

'I'm sorry, but you make this robbing shit look so easy.'

They had both laughed before she said, 'Come on, then, copper knob, I'll show you how it's done! We can both go shopping!'

He had then spent the next two hours with her being

taught the finer points of shoplifting – most importantly how to get away with it.

They had been together ever since, moving from one squat to the next, scraping enough money together to feed each other's drug habit and get enough food to live on.

Since they had been together, there were two occasions when times had been so rough, when neither of them had any money, that she'd taken the decision to sell her body to get enough cash to score.

Lee knew she hated doing it, and he never asked her or tried to force her into prostitution.

The second time she went on the streets soliciting in the red-light area of Norwich, she was arrested by the vice squad. As it was her first arrest, she was given a caution.

The vice squad cops made it clear to her that if they caught her again, she'd be charged and taken to court. The cops set up a meeting between the girl and a social worker, but she skipped the meeting.

It had been her idea to get a fresh start and to travel up to London. It had taken them from January to the middle of March to scrape enough money together for the two National Coach fares.

From the minute they arrived in London, everything went to rat shit. Far from being the fresh start they hoped for, very quickly they found themselves in a shithole of a squat not far from the coach station, with no money.

There were no jobs going, they had nowhere to live, and everything was twice as expensive. The area they were in was full of prostitutes and pimps. In no time at all, the little money they'd managed to bring with them from Norwich had been spent on their habit. The night she went missing, she had taken their last deal bag of heroin. He was left hanging and desperate to score. As he rattled around the squat, suffering, she made the decision to go out on the street to try to make some money.

In their desperation, they had left the filthy squat together. They didn't want any trouble, so they picked a stretch of the road where none of the other prostitutes were out plying their trade. She had only been on the street for half an hour when he saw the dark blue car pull up. It was an almost brand-new Ford Sierra.

The one thing Lee Skipton knew about was cars. He had stolen enough in his joyriding days. Squinting through his glasses, he scribbled the registration number of the Sierra onto the scrap of paper he carried in his pocket. He always did this in case there was a problem and the punter got nasty.

It never occurred to him now that the punter had got nasty; he just assumed his girl had not returned because she had got a better offer.

Now, as he slouched listlessly along Peckham High Road, he caught a glimpse of his reflection in a shop window.

He barely recognised himself. He looked as white as a ghost, his mop of red hair was unkempt and unwashed, his blue Adidas track suit bottoms and his maroon hooded fleece top were hanging off his skinny frame, and both were filthy dirty. His training shoes were worn down and dirty, and one of the laces was missing.

He looked like a tramp.

Suddenly, the hunger pangs hit home again. He desperately needed something to eat.

Lee slipped off the busy street and into a small convenience store. As he walked inside, he saw the burly Asian shopkeeper glaring in his direction from the far end of the shop. He quickly ducked behind the shelving so he was out of his sight. In front of him was a chiller cabinet full of food. There were pies, cakes, sandwiches and cartons of milk.

Quickly he grabbed a carton of milk, a couple of pies and a couple of packs of sandwiches, stuffing them beneath his baggy fleece top. With the food stashed, he immediately turned and made for the door.

Suddenly, he could see the shopkeeper bearing down on him. Panicking, he ran, but as soon as he went through the door, he stumbled over the unlaced training shoe, going down hard on the pavement. The carton of milk and the food scattered noisily all over the ground.

He was grabbed roughly from behind and pulled to his feet. 'You filthy bloody bastard! I'm sick of you tramps trying to rob me. I'm calling the police right now!'

Desperately, he tried to plead with the shopkeeper not to involve the police, and that he had only taken the food because he was starving.

'Shut your bloody mouth before I shut it for you! You're not getting away with it this time!' the shopkeeper raged.

He felt himself being manhandled back into the shop. He was dragged behind the counter and locked in a stock cupboard full of empty boxes and old magazines.

From inside the cupboard, he could hear the muffled angry tones of the shopkeeper as he spoke to the police. 'Please send someone straight away; I've caught a thief and I want him arrested.'

In the dark of the cupboard, Lee Skipton started to sob. He knew he was a petty criminal, but until now he had never been caught. When he went joyriding with his mates and drove stolen cars, he'd always dumped the cars without drama. Even though he regularly stole whatever he could to pay for his drugs, up until now he'd never been caught. If it weren't for that poxy training shoe, he wouldn't have been caught today.

Finally, after what seemed an eternity, the cupboard door was yanked open. In the bright shop lights, Lee could see two police officers.

One of them grabbed his arm and pulled him roughly out of the cupboard while the other one pinched his own nostrils between his index finger and thumb.

'Fucking hell, what's that smell?' the cop said.

'When was the last time you had a wash, son?' the other one asked, more out of disgust than pity.

The officer turned to the shopkeeper, who was holding open a carrier bag that contained the milk, pies and sandwiches that Skipton had tried to steal. 'Not exactly the great train robbery, is it, Mr Patel?' he said quietly.

'I don't care, Officer. I'm sick of these bastards coming in here every day robbing me. I want him arrested.'

Lee Skipton finally found his voice: 'I've never been in this shithole of a shop before, you lying Paki cunt!'

It was the worst thing he could have said. Suddenly, he felt his skinny arms being twisted behind his back by the nearest policeman, and the cold steel handcuffs going on his wrists. He heard the noise of the ratchet on the cuffs as they secured his wrists.

'Come on, mouth, you're coming down the nick, you gobby piece of shit!' said the cop.

The officer turned to the shopkeeper. 'I'll be back to get your statement later, Mr Patel, once we've got this little toerag banged up down the station, okay?'

'Yes, Constable, thank you very much. See you later.'

Once in the police car, the officer said, 'You had to open your big mouth, didn't you, ginge? If you hadn't started with the abuse, we could have talked old Manny around and just given you a bollocking!'

'I'm sorry,' Lee Skipton stammered before saying quietly, 'What time is it, please?'

'Just coming up to seven o'clock at night. Why, have you got somewhere to go?'

Both the officers laughed.

In the back of the car, Lee could feel the metal of the handcuffs biting into his bony wrists. He looked out of the car window and said quietly to himself, 'I wish I'd never come to this fucking shithole.'

Ten minutes later, Lee and the two cops were all standing in the cell block at Peckham Police Station.

'What have we got, then, lads?' asked the desk sergeant.

'This ginger ninja was caught nicking food from Manny Patel's off-licence on the High Road. He's got no money on him and started getting abusive towards Manny when we were there, so he's been arrested for the theft of one carton of milk, two Ginsters steak pies and two packs of readymade egg and cress sandwiches. Total value £1.75.'

'You've heard all that, son; what have you got to say for yourself?' the sergeant asked Skipton.

Skipton stared past the sergeant, transfixed by the poster on the wall behind the desk.

'I know that girl on the poster. She's my girlfriend.'

'Yeah, course she is. Stop messing me about, old son.'

'I'm not messing you about. Seriously, that's my girlfriend, but something's wrong with her face.'

'Alright, son, we'll talk about that in a minute. For now, do you want a cup of tea and something to eat?'

'Yes, please.'

'That's it, son, you just keep remembering your manners while you're here and we'll get along fine. I'll get you sorted out, and then we can think about getting you out of here. Now where do you call home, son?' said the sergeant.

'I'm from Norwich.'

Patiently, the sergeant obtained Lee Skipton's personal details before putting him in a holding cell with a cup of tea and a sandwich.

The two officers went back to the shop to get a quick statement from Manny Patel.

As far as they were concerned, this job had police caution written all over it, and they didn't want to waste all night on it.

The sergeant glanced at the clock on the cell block wall. It was now almost a quarter to eight in the evening. He reached for the phone and dialled the control room. 'Would you call Detective Inspector Johnson at home for me, and tell him we may have struck lucky about the dead girl on the poster. I've got a scruffy little shit from Norwich in the cells who's been nicked for shoplifting. He's telling me that he only came to London recently with his girlfriend and that the woman on the poster is her.'

18

Peckham Police Station Cells – May 3, 1984

Glyn Johnson and Craig Fraser walked into the cell block just as the sergeant was administering a caution to Lee Skipton for the theft from shop.

The sergeant finished and said, 'Lee, these are the detectives I was telling you about. They want to talk to you about the woman on the poster.'

'No problem, thanks for the tea and the food, Sarge.'

The two detectives now approached Lee Skipton, and Glyn said, 'I'm Detective Inspector Johnson, and this is Detective Sergeant Fraser. Lee, how sure are you that you know the woman in this poster?' Glyn indicated the poster on the wall behind the custody desk.

'I'm pretty sure it's Jenny. There's something about her mouth that looks a bit different, though.'

'Can you see the photo of the tattoo at the bottom of the poster?' asked Craig.

'Jenny definitely has a tattoo on her heel. Can you get the

poster off the wall so I can see it properly? I should wear glasses, but I've smashed them. The poster looks a bit fuzzy from here.'

The sergeant leaned over and said, 'Here, have a look through these.' He passed over his own spectacles.

'Oh my God! That's Jenny's tattoo; that's the date her baby daughter was born, 12 July 1983. Why is her picture on a poster here? What's happened to her face?'

'You'd better come in here where we can talk properly, son,' said Craig.

The two detectives led Lee into an adjacent interview room.

Craig spoke first. 'Sit down, son. I want you to tell us everything you can about Jenny.'

'I want to know what's happened to her first. I haven't seen her for about four weeks. Ever since she went off in that bloody posh motor.'

Glyn leaned forward and spoke softly. 'Listen to me, Lee. What I've got to tell you isn't good news. Around four weeks ago, we found the woman in the poster. I'm sorry, Lee, but she was dead. She had been murdered. I'm sorry to have to tell you like this, but we really need your help to find out what happened to her.'

Lee Skipton visibly disintegrated before their eyes. He held his face in his hands, and his whole body trembled. When the reality of what he was being told registered, he let out a long anguished cry: 'No!'

He stammered, 'Why would anybody want to hurt my Jenny?'

Glyn looked into Skipton's eyes and said, 'Tell us about the last time you saw her. What happened?'

Lee took a breath between sobs and said, 'We were strapped for cash; we both have a habit, see. She'd just scored, but I was on my arse, desperate for gear. I was hanging. Jenny said she'd go out and earn a few quid. I knew she meant she'd get a punter and sell herself. I told her not to, that I would be okay until the morning. I knew we could get some cash from somewhere, even if it meant going on the rob in a few shops. Jenny wouldn't listen; she said I needed the gear straight away or I'd be really bad. We didn't really know the area, but had seen girls working the streets over at the railway station not far from Wembley Stadium.'

He started to sob again. Glyn coaxed him gently, 'What happened?'

'Jenny stood on the street away from the other girls, and I stood in a dark doorway, just looking out for her. We'd only been there about half an hour when this car cruised by and stopped. He only saw Jenny; he didn't see me.'

'What sort of car was it?'

'It was definitely a dark blue Ford Sierra; I know my cars.'

'Did you get a look at the driver?'

'No, it was too far away, I couldn't see him properly. I could tell it was a bloke, though, and he had dark hair.'

'What about the car? Can you tell us anything about that?'

Suddenly, Lee sat upright in his chair. 'I wrote the reg number down. I think I've still got it.'

Lee stood up and frantically started to go through the pockets of his scruffy jogging bottoms, finally pulling out a scrap of screwed-up paper.

He quickly flattened the paper out on the table.

He handed the scrap of paper to Glyn. 'B 628 EJH. Is that the car?' asked Glyn.

Skipton nodded.

Glyn handed the piece of paper to Craig and said, 'Check this on the PNC for the owner's details.'

Craig immediately left the room to make the enquiry on the Police National Computer.

Glyn turned to Lee and said, 'Thanks, Lee, I know this isn't easy for you, but I need you to tell me everything you can about Jenny. I want to know her full name, where she's from, her family. Anything you can think of, I want to know. Can you do that for me?'

Lee Skipton nodded and slowly told Glyn everything he knew about Jenny.

Her name was Jenny Taylor; she was nineteen years old and was from Norwich. There was no immediate family and she'd lived in care until her seventeenth birthday. She had either lived rough or slept in squats ever since. She was an addict who'd been on heroin from around the age of sixteen. He'd met her just before Christmas last year and had been with her ever since. The tattoo on her heel was to remind her of her daughter.

She had called her daughter Bunny.

He had no idea what the baby daughter's real name was, or who the father was.

Jenny's daughter had been born on 12 July 1983, but because of Jenny's habit, the baby was born addicted to heroin.

The Social Services had taken the baby girl into care straight away. Jenny knew that Bunny was put up for adoption, but didn't know who adopted her or even where the adoptive parents lived.

Jenny still had a social worker back in Norwich.

Craig came back into the interview room. 'Are you sure you've got this car number right, Lee?' he asked.

'Yeah, a hundred per cent. I know I was rattling, but I'm sure it's right.'

'What about your eyesight, laddie? You couldn't read the poster on the wall, could you?'

'I know that, but I still had my glasses when I wrote the number down. I only smashed them in the squat last week. I definitely wrote the number down right.' He started to sob again.

Glyn said softly, 'Okay, Lee, don't worry about the

number. I'm going to get somebody to come and write down everything you've told me, okay? Before you leave tonight, I want you to show the detective exactly where you were when Jenny got picked up in the car, okay? I'll arrange a bed for you at the local YMCA. Don't leave London without me telling you it's okay. Do you understand?'

'I've got no money to go anywhere.'

'I'll make sure you get fed at the YMCA, but don't go taking any smack in there, or you won't be able to stay. Do you understand?'

'Yeah, I know. One thing, Detective, when can I see Jenny?'

'We'll talk about that in the morning. I'll see you tomorrow.'

A detective policewoman came into the interview room to take the written statement from Lee.

Glyn and Craig walked out of the room.

'Okay, Craig, what's the problem with the car reg?' said Glyn.

'It comes back to a red Opel Kadett, Glyn, that's what's wrong with the fucking number!'

'Bollocks!' said Glyn under his breath. 'Look, first thing tomorrow, I want somebody at the PNC to be checking similar reg numbers to see if we can get a hit on a blue Ford Sierra. I want someone to track down this social worker in Norwich and get chapter and verse on Jenny Taylor. I also want full background checks done on Lee Skipton. I don't think for one second that he's our killer, but stranger things have happened.'

'Okay, boss, I'm on it. Are you ready for some more bad news?'

'Go on, what now?'

'I was speaking to Scenes of Crime before I left work earlier today. They've found absolutely nothing from the murder scene at the warehouse.'

'Nothing?'

'Not a fingerprint, not a fibre. The only thing they did find was a partial footprint in the blood on the floor.'

'Well, at least that's something,' said Glyn.

'It is something, but this is where it gets weird, guv. We didn't go in the room, did we? The footprint they've found is identical to somebody who's wearing forensic overshoes. Scenes of Crime have done some comparisons, and they think it's the same overshoes that are issued to the Metropolitan Police.'

'For fuck's sake!' muttered Glyn. 'Be back here at eight in the morning, Craig; we've got a lot to do tomorrow.'

'Okay, guv'nor, no problem,' said Craig, glancing at his watch.

It was just after two in the morning.

'I think you mean we've got a lot to do *today*, guv,' he muttered to himself.

19

Peckham, London – May 5, 1984

It had been two days since the dead woman found on the embankment was finally identified as Jenny Taylor, a young runaway from Norwich.

Glyn Johnson and Craig Fraser now sat in the Black Prince pub just off Peckham High Road, having a brainstorming session over a couple of pints.

It was something Glyn maintained was good practice. He liked to talk things through with Craig and get ideas from everyone working on a case, rather than try to think of everything himself.

When a case became bogged down or an enquiry was stalling through lack of evidence or witnesses, these discussions very often revealed new lines of enquiry.

Both Glyn and Craig sat nursing their almost-empty beer glasses. It was amazing what a change of venue and the relaxation of a couple of beers could do. Many a tough case had been solved inside the smoky rooms of the small cosy pub.

The Black Prince pub had the reputation of being a coppers' watering hole. There were several such establishments across London where ex-coppers were the licensees and police officers were the main or only customers. Just as villains had their favourite pubs, where past and future crimes were discussed and planned openly, so the police had their licensed haunts as well.

The Black Prince was a very small pub comprising a lounge bar and a smoke room or snug.

The landlord, Geoff Greer, was a large man, standing well over six feet four inches tall. He had been a Grenadier Guardsman before spending twenty years in the City of London Police. He had taken on the Black Prince public house upon retirement from the force. With Greer installed as landlord, the establishment quickly became known as a police pub.

Greer was now completely bald and, as a result, was known by the nickname of Curly, which secretly he rather liked. His only customers in the snug that afternoon were the two detectives. 'Same again, gents?' he asked from behind the bar.

'Yes, please, Curly, a pint of Guinness for me and a pale ale for Craig,' said Glyn.

The landlord pulled the two beers and brought them over to where they were sitting. Placing the beers on the table, he said, 'I won't disturb you, gents, just give me a shout through to the lounge if you need anything else.'

'Thanks, Curly.'

Glyn waited for the landlord to move out of earshot before continuing, 'Right, Craig, these are the facts we've established. Jenny Taylor, a heroin addict, left Norwich in company with her boyfriend, Lee Skipton, also a heroin addict, for a better life. She had no ties in Norwich; her family's all dead. She gave birth to a baby daughter, who was born an addict and was immediately taken into the care of the Social

Services. That child has subsequently been adopted. What's the news from the Norwich Social Services?'

Craig replied, 'We've identified her social worker as being a Ms Tracy Price. I sent two detectives over to Norwich to get chapter and verse. It would appear that Ms Price was saddened but not overly surprised when she was told of Jenny's death and the nature of it. She confirmed the story about the baby girl and told us that the child is now living with her adoptive parents up in Lanarkshire, Scotland. The adoptive parents have no knowledge of the child's birth mother other than the fact that she was a heroin addict who was forced to give the child up for adoption. As far as Ms Price was aware, there's been absolutely no contact between Jenny Taylor or Lee Skipton with the adoptive parents. Ms Price said that although Jenny had been saddened to give up her daughter, she soon got over it and moved on. Ms Price was also aware that Jenny was spending a lot of time with Lee Skipton. She saw Lee as a damaging influence in Jenny's life, purely down to the fact that they fuelled each other's addiction. Apart from that, he was harmless. It was Jenny who was the dominant one in their relationship.'

'Okay, I don't think we need to bring the adoptive parents in Scotland into the enquiry at this stage. Any more on Lee Skipton?'

'We've done all the background checks on Skipton. He's definitely not in the frame for her murder, guv. He's soft as a brush and harmless. I've let him return to Norwich, back to his parents' address. I asked the local police to check that it was a suitable address, and I've asked Lee to attend Norwich Police Station every day to sign on. He's not on bail for anything, but he agreed to do it anyway. I reckon we can rule him out other than as a witness. What do you think?'

'I'm happy with that. What about the car he claims he saw Jenny getting into?'

'We've no progress there, I'm afraid. A dark blue Ford

Sierra registered number B 628 EJH does not exist. That number was issued to a red Opel Kadett, and the owner of the car has been traced to an address in Kent. It's a Mrs Brenda Owthorpe, who lives in Deal. I've already sent two detectives down there, and they've seen the Opel Kadett with that plate on. Because Lee is so adamant that it was a Ford Sierra, it leads me to believe that he got the make of the car right, but it's being driven around on false plates.'

'It looks that way. How about the PNC checks on similar registration numbers?'

'They've tried numerous permutations of the number and not pulled one Ford Sierra. It literally is like looking for a needle in a haystack. The PNC have asked us to consider it a last resort as an enquiry, as it's so time consuming.'

'Okay, we are going to have to leave that in abeyance for the time being. What about our second scene, the room in the warehouse where the murder was committed?'

'Right, Scenes of Crime have confirmed that nothing of any evidential use was found at the murder scene apart from the footprint of the police-issue forensic overshoes. The cheeky mare in the Scenes of Crime department asked me again the other day if either of us two had walked into the room. I told her exactly what I thought of that comment. What's more interesting to me, guv, is what we didn't find at the scene.'

'What do you mean?'

'Well, our killer went to a lot of effort, painstakingly snipping off all the fingers and thumbs from our dead girl's hands, and then took the time and trouble to carefully remove all the body parts from the scene.'

'I think I know what you're driving at, Craig. Our killer's very forensically aware and is desperately trying to stall this enquiry by making it nigh on impossible for us to identify the dead girl. If we hadn't had a lucky break when Skipton saw the poster after his arrest, we would still be no further on. This business with the forensic suit really worries me though. I'm going to throw this out to you for a reaction: Do you think our killer could be a cop?'

'You know me, guv'nor, I never rule anything out. The lack of forensic evidence is certainly pointing us that way, but this bastard has a cold, calculating mind. Is this what he wants us to think? Or is it his first genuine mistake and we're on the right track?'

'Right, Craig, as I see it, these are the things we need to do right now. Firstly, I want you to arrange a full briefing for all vice squads working anywhere in the City. I want them all to be on the lookout for a dark blue Ford Sierra cruising their red-light areas. I want the numbers of such vehicles to be logged and the details passed to our incident room for tracing and follow-up enquiries. I don't want the drivers being stopped or spoken to by vice squad officers. I don't want this bastard being given a heads-up.'

He took a sip of his Guinness and continued, 'Secondly, I want you to draw up a list of all professions that may have some knowledge of the forensic procedures used by the police. Just off the top of my head, there's a couple I can think of – pathologists, criminology students – and I'm sure there's many more.'

'Okay, guv, no problem.'

'We can catch this nutter; we've just got to get right back to basics and do the painstaking time-consuming enquiries. I don't think he's going to make many mistakes, and I want him locked up before he has the chance to kill again.'

Both men sat in silence for five minutes, drinking their beer, before Craig spoke again. 'We can't afford to put all our eggs in one basket, guv'nor. I know everything's pointing you towards the killer being one of our own, but I can think of any number of people who would have that knowledge of forensics. Just because it's a police-issue forensic suit, that doesn't mean other organisations don't use the same type as we use. Prison service, hospitals.'

Glyn was thoughtful and took another long drink of his Guinness before saying, 'Check the suppliers of the forensic suits for any single orders. Our worst-case scenario is going to be some lone-wolf nutter who's taken the time to read all the literature on police techniques.'

Craig nodded his head and sighed deeply before saying, 'How do we go about catching one of our own, guv'nor?'

'There's no easy answer to that question. The same way we catch everyone else. We do the hard yards, the legwork, the painstaking, time-consuming enquiries. We sift through all the crap and then hope for that one little mistake, that single careless moment from them.'

Glyn drained the last of the Guinness from his glass and stood up.

'I'll get the beers in, Craig. I think a couple more pints, taxis home and back in tomorrow early doors. What do you reckon?'

'You do realise it's our scheduled rest day tomorrow, don't you, guv?'

'We need to get these enquiries moving, Craig. I'll be in tomorrow; are you okay to get in as well, or have you got stuff planned?'

'Nothing that won't keep. I'll be in at eight o'clock.'

20

Proteus Army Camp, Nottinghamshire – May 31, 1984

It was the last day of May, and more importantly, it was Mick Reynolds's last day in Nottinghamshire for two weeks.
The current tour of duty had really dragged by.
The shifts worked were long and unsociable. The off-duty time was mind-numbingly boring, with absolutely nothing to do.
All the officers on deployment were getting listless and irritable. Cases of assaults by the police on pickets were getting higher as tempers started to fray quicker.
The Metropolitan Police officers had all been informed earlier that morning that their next deployment would start on June 14. They were then instructed by their senior officer to take the next two weeks off work.
Mick Reynolds was overjoyed at the news. Like everyone else, he had become totally bored and disillusioned with the role they were performing. It was getting harder and harder to

maintain the morale of the constables in his Police Support Unit.

He was also excited that two weeks off work would give him plenty of time to plan getting rid of his loathsome wife, Rita. As he boarded the coach that would transport him and his officers back down to London, he mulled over what he needed to do when he eventually arrived back home in Wembley.

The first thing on his agenda was to meet up with an old friend. Mick had arranged to meet Sergeant Ted Smith over a pint at the local pub. This had been done under the guise of simply having a catch-up after being away up in Nottinghamshire for so long. The real reason for the meeting, though, was that Ted Smith was a sergeant on the vice squad, and Mick needed to know if there had been any updates on the enquiry into the prostitute he had killed.

The second thing he needed to do was finally put into practice what he'd spent weeks thinking about while he was bored shitless in Nottingham. It was finally time to get rid of the bitch he was married to. It had been a long time coming, but things were starting to form in his mind; he had finally worked out how he could be rid of her. There were a few things to sort out first, but that would only take a couple of days.

He continued making plans and refining ideas during the long journey back down the motorway.

21

Wembley, North London – May 31, 1984

Mick Reynolds was the last of his serial to be dropped off. Finally, the coach had pulled up outside his home in Wembley. The journey back to London had been horrendous, the M1 motorway like a car park with tailback after tailback of unmoving cars. When they had finally left the motorway, the North Circular had been no better.

He got off the coach, carrying his black PSU bag and a holdall containing his personal belongings. He yawned and stretched before he walked down his short sloping driveway. Dropping the two bags on the floor, he fumbled in his pockets for the keys to his house.

He opened the front door and shouted, 'Rita, I'm home!'

The house was silent; that was unusual. Normally, there would be at least a snarling acknowledgement of his presence, something like, "So fucking what!"

Today there was nothing, just a stony silence.

Leaving the bags in the hallway, Mick walked into the lounge. Nothing. From there he went upstairs, checking each bedroom and the bathroom. Realising that the house was empty, he checked his watch. It was still only four o'clock in the afternoon.

'Christ, she's started early,' he muttered to himself.

Finally, he walked into the kitchen to put the kettle on. Propped against the kettle was a white envelope. It had a single word written in black felt-tip pen on it: 'Mick'.

It had been deliberately left in the place where he was sure to find it almost as soon as he walked in. Normally, the first thing he'd do when he walked in was to put the kettle on and make himself a cup of tea.

He picked up the envelope, tearing it open quickly. He scanned the content of the short note that had been left inside the envelope.

MICK,
I got the chance to go to Benidorm for three weeks with the girls.
Back on 20th June.
Rita

ANGRILY, he screwed up the note and hurled it across the room. On any other day, her prolonged absence would have been met by him with joy and a feeling of relief.

Today was different. He had made plans, and now she had scuppered them again. He paced angrily around the kitchen. Back on the twentieth? Mick knew he'd be back in Nottingham by then.

'For fuck's sake!' he shouted out loud.

He filled the kettle and made himself a cup of tea with

milk and two sugars. Sipping his tea at the kitchen table, he began to slowly calm down.

This wouldn't change anything. It was merely a stay of execution. He smiled to himself at that thought. He liked the sound of the words 'her execution'.

He did feel frustrated, though; he needed a release. He felt a strong urge to drive straight to the red-light area, where he could pick up a whore and buy some relief.

Suddenly, he remembered he had arranged to meet Ted Smith that evening at the Eight Bells pub. He was in two minds whether to call Ted and put their meeting off until tomorrow night.

Finally, he decided his relief and the tart would have to wait. He would have a catch-up with Ted tonight. In fact, he would order a cab. He felt like getting pissed. Mick finished his tea and suddenly felt drained. He lay down on the settee in the lounge to have a nap and quickly drifted off to sleep.

He woke with a start and looked at his watch. It was just coming up to seven o'clock. He'd arranged to meet Ted at seven thirty. He grabbed the phone and ordered a minicab to pick him up at twenty past seven. He ran upstairs and quickly changed into jeans and a T-shirt before cleaning his teeth and combing his hair.

He grabbed his wallet and checked there was enough cash in it. The doorbell rang. Mick looked out of his bedroom window and could see the black cab waiting outside.

Ten minutes later he was walking into the Eight Bells pub on Wembley High Road. Already standing at the bar was a tall, skinny fortysomething man with a comb-over hairstyle Bobby Charlton would have been proud of. He was wearing wire-framed glasses and a camel-coloured Crombie-style coat over blue denims and oxblood Dr Martens boots.

Mick walked straight over. 'Hello, Ted, sorry I'm a bit late. What you having?'

He could see that Ted Smith was only about a quarter of

the way down his pint, but he knew exactly what would happen next.

Mick watched as Ted picked up his glass and drained the rest before belching loudly and saying, 'I'll have a pint of Harp, mate! Cheers!'

Ted might be a skinny fucker, but he drank like a fish. *Glad I booked a cab,* Mick thought. *This could get messy.*

Both men stood drinking at the bar for the next hour or so, talking over general things, like how the Spurs were faring as opposed to Arsenal. Eventually, after four more pints, the talk started to veer towards police work.

Moving from the bar with two more pints of lager, they sat in a booth. Ted was moaning, 'We've just been given a shitload more work to do.'

'What, on the vice squad? You lazy fuckers don't do any work.' Mick laughed.

'For your information, we do plenty, and on top of all that, we've now got to clock and write down a shitload of car numbers we see driving around the red-light areas. As if we haven't got enough to do already, pulling tarts and punters,' he moaned.

'Car numbers? What's that all about, then, Ted?' asked Mick.

'It's all to do with that young prossie who was murdered and dumped on the embankment over in Peckham. That fucking black DI over there wants us to note down the registration plate of every dark blue Ford Sierra we see driving through the red-light areas. Does he give a toss how many of them fucking motors there are? No, he doesn't. Waste of fucking time, if you ask me.'

Mick felt sick; he felt bile rising up his throat. 'Just nipping to the bog, mate.'

He stood up and rushed into the gents.

Pushing open a vacant cubicle door, he vomited into the toilet. The regurgitated lager burnt the back of his throat. He continued to dry retch. His stomach hurt, and his eyes were streaming; tears rolled down his face, caused by the strain of vomiting.

Finally, the retching stopped, and slowly he stood up.

He walked out of the cubicle to the sink and splashed cold water on his face. By the time he had dried his face on a paper towel and rinsed his mouth with a mouthful of cold water from the tap, he had composed himself.

He walked back out to join Ted, who by now had two more pints of lager sat on the table.

'Sorry about that! I needed a shit!'

Mick very gingerly took a sip of his lager and felt it burn down his throat as he swallowed it.

'Who's this dickhead that's got you running around, then?'

'It's that black detective inspector, you know the one; he's always trying to make a name for himself. It's fucking Johnston or Johnson, something like that. Whatever his name is, he's a proper pain in the arse.'

'But what's the point of it? I don't get it.'

'Are you thick or just pissed? It's bleeding obvious, innit? They've obviously linked a blue Ford Sierra to this murder, but they ain't got the number, have they, and now they want us to find it for them. Bloody wankers!'

For the second time that night, Mick was glad he had called a cab and not driven over in his Sierra. He was also extremely glad he had disguised his car number plate with the black electricians' tape.

'One for the road, then, Ted? I'm off on my holidays tomorrow, and don't want to be too late in bed tonight.'

'Fucking lightweight, it's only just gone ten o'clock. Go on then, mate, I'll have a Bell's whisky seeing as how you're paying.' He laughed before adding, 'Going anywhere nice on your jollies, pal?'

'Just down to Cornwall with the wife for a couple of

weeks. It's all been paid for by good old Arthur Scargill, the wanker!' He laughed and went to the bar to order the whiskies.

He'd decided there and then that his car would stay in the garage at home for the foreseeable future.

He would, at some stage, have to get rid of it, but for now he needed a bit of time to himself away from London.

A quick break seemed the perfect solution.

He would get the train down to Cornwall in the morning, then find a cosy little bed and breakfast down near the sea somewhere.

Thank fuck he'd decided to meet Ted first and not gone driving straight to the red-light area in his motor, he thought to himself.

He felt bile rise again in his throat, but this time he controlled the fear.

He turned to the busty barmaid. 'Two large Bell's, love,' he said.

She winked at him and laughed before saying, 'Good of you to notice, sweetheart. Now what do you want to drink?'

'Bell's whiskies, darling,' he growled.

The smile disappeared from her face. 'Alright, keep your hair on, you miserable sod.'

Fucking women, tarts all of them, he thought.

22

Mansfield, Nottinghamshire – June 3, 1984

Danny Flint had been in the office of Superintendent Ken Jackson for twenty minutes now, and the conversation was starting to get heated.
'Look, sir, I'm just about holding the lid on things here,' said an exasperated Danny. 'Unless you give me back some staff soon, the shit's really going to hit the fan. The team I've got have been working non-stop for three months solid now. They're working their arses off every shift, while hundreds of coppers, including the CID staff you took from me, are sitting around in vans, drinking Maxpax coffee, doing next to nothing. It just can't continue!'
'They're not sitting around in vans doing nothing, Danny. Every PSU is tasked separately each morning from the command centre in London. They take into account current intelligence and deploy the PSUs accordingly. You've seen for yourself in the last two weeks alone, we've had three occasions around Mansfield where mass pickets have got through

and caused mayhem. There's been hundreds of arrests already. The bottom line is, you're going to have to suck it up. That's all there is to it.'

'I'm sorry, sir, but that's not good enough. All it will take is for one major incident to come in, and we'll be well and truly screwed. All I'm asking for is a few more detectives to spread the load. Can't you get some from the City temporarily?'

'It's not my decision. I'm sorry.'

Jackson paused before continuing, 'Look, Danny, I'll make representation with the chief constable tomorrow. All the superintendents have been called to a meeting about the state of general policing across the county. I'll see what I can do, but my guess is, everyone attending that meeting will be saying the same thing. We all need more men back on the divisions. We're reliant on the goodwill of the special constables on the uniform side. It's dire everywhere.'

Danny was about to protest further when suddenly there was a loud urgent knocking on the door.

'Come in!' shouted Jackson.

DC Rachel Moore stuck her head around the door. 'Sorry to interrupt your meeting, sir, but there's an urgent telephone call for DI Flint.'

'The meeting's over anyway. I'll see what I can do, Danny. Go get your phone call.'

'Okay, sir, you know I wouldn't ask unless it was absolutely necessary.'

'I know.'

Danny then stepped out of the office. 'What's so flaming urgent, Rachel? I think I was finally getting somewhere. You know how desperate we are for more staff!'

'Sorry, boss, but the phone call is from your next-door neighbour, Rosemary. She told me she's called an ambulance for your dad.'

'What?' said a shocked Danny.

Danny was striding very quickly now, and Rachel was all but jogging alongside him just to keep up as he powered down the corridor back to the CID office.

'The neighbour said she'd popped round after hearing a thump and found your dad lying on the floor. She called an ambulance first and then our office for you.'

Bursting into the CID office, he shouted, 'Which phone?'

'My desk.'

He picked up the receiver. 'Hello, Rosemary, it's Danny. What's happened?'

'Thank God you're there! I heard a loud thump, so I went around to yours and banged on the door. When there was no reply, I looked in through the front room window. I could see your dad lying on the floor of the lounge. I rushed back home and got the key you gave me. I went straight in, but I couldn't rouse him, so I called for an ambulance.'

'Has the ambulance arrived yet?'

'It's just left; they're taking your dad up to King's Mill Hospital. The ambulance man told me he thought your dad had suffered a stroke, but they couldn't tell how bad yet. I'm so sorry, Danny.'

He could hear the old lady sobbing as she breathed out, desperately fighting to hold back tears. Rosemary had lived in the house next door ever since Danny was five years old.

She had been great friends with his mother right up until she passed away. Danny had given her a key to his dad's house so if ever there was an emergency while he was at work, she would be able to get in. He counted his blessings now that he had made that decision.

His voice was softer now, less urgent. 'Don't worry, Rosemary, none of this is your fault. You've been brilliant. You did exactly the right thing. Thank you so much, bless you. I'm going straight up to the hospital now; I'll call you when I know what's happening. Are you okay, Rosemary? Do you want me to send someone up there to be with you? You sound a bit shaky.'

'Could you do that, Danny? I'm trembling here. It was such a shock seeing your dad like that.'

Suddenly, the floodgates opened, and the muffled sobs turned to full-blown crying.

'Someone's on their way now, Rosemary. I'll send a policewoman to sit with you. I've got to go now.'

'Thank you, Danny,' the old lady said between sobs.

Danny put the phone down and turned to Rachel. 'Did you hear all that?'

'Yes, boss. You get going, and I'll arrange for a uniformed policewoman to go and stay with Rosemary. Don't forget to call from the hospital as soon as you know anything, boss.'

Danny was already out of the door.

23

King's Mill Hospital, Mansfield – June 3, 1984

Danny had driven like a man possessed to King's Mill Hospital.

It was only a five-minute drive from the police station to the hospital, which was located between the towns of Mansfield and Sutton in Ashfield.

He parked the CID car in the bays reserved for police vehicles directly outside the Casualty Department of the hospital and raced through the doors.

He ran straight up to the desk and shouted breathlessly, 'My father's Frank Flint. He's just been brought here by ambulance with a suspected stroke. Can you tell me where he is, please?'

The young woman on reception was calmness personified. 'Your father's being assessed by the doctor now. Take a seat, and she'll be out to see you shortly. I'll get a message to her that you're here, okay?'

'Thank you, I need to know what's happening as soon as you can, please.'

Danny was not normally this good at controlling the panic he felt whenever he was in a hospital, but he had seen first-hand the way that panic and fear over a sick relative can turn normally mild-mannered people into rude, aggressive and abusive morons.

He was determined he wasn't going to behave that way, and that he would wait patiently for news, but after five minutes of pacing up and down, he was losing his personal battle to remain calm. He returned to the reception desk. He stared hard at the young woman behind the counter, and his voice rose a little when he said, 'I need to know what's happening with my father. Right now!'

The receptionist was about to respond to his raised voice when Danny heard a door open behind him. 'Daniel Flint?'

He immediately spun around and saw the doctor who had called his name. She was about thirty-five years of age, very slim and petite, with long dark hair tied back in a ponytail. She was wearing the usual white coat and had a stethoscope hanging around her neck.

'I'm Danny Flint. How's my father?' he demanded urgently.

'Please follow me, Mr Flint,' she said. He noticed a London accent.

He followed her back through the door she had emerged from into a small private room.

Danny recognised the room; it was known as the relatives' room. It was where doctors and sometimes the police had to break the worst news imaginable to relatives of the badly injured or the deceased.

Danny suddenly felt dizzy. 'My dad, he's not dead, is he?' he stammered.

The doctor turned and said softly, 'No, Mr Flint, your father's not dead, but he's a very poorly man.'

He felt the waves of initial relief rush over him; then suddenly he felt very cold, his legs weakening.

Quickly, he sat down on one of the chairs.

'What's wrong with him?' he asked in a whisper.

The doctor sat down in the chair opposite and looked him directly in the eyes. 'My name's Dr Rhodes. I've been tending to your father since he was brought in about half an hour ago. Your father has had quite a serious stroke, a bleed on the brain. He's being prepped for theatre as we speak. We need to stop the bleeding first; then we can assess how much damage has been done. I'm not going to sit here and lie to you, Danny: At the moment, your father's critically ill. Once we've done the operation, we'll quickly be able to give you a better prognosis. First things first, we've got to get your father through the operation. Are there any questions you've got for me?'

Danny felt like he had been hit with a hammer. He could feel his heart pounding and the blood pulsating through his temples. He felt breathless, and his mouth was suddenly very dry. He heard himself saying, 'Are you doing the operation, Dr Rhodes?'

'No, I'm not a surgeon. The on-call neurosurgeon, Dr McCaffery, is already prepping in the operating theatre. I'll be here all night though, so if you need anything, just ask on reception for me. I'll keep coming back to inform you of any updates I get. You're welcome to stay in this room; nobody will disturb you here. There's a drinks machine outside the door, and the toilets are across the hall from the reception desk. I'm sorry the news isn't better, Danny.'

Danny stammered, 'Me too, Dr Rhodes, but thank you for everything you're doing.'

'I'll be back soon. Call me Sue, okay?'

'Okay, thanks, Sue.'

Danny constantly glanced at the clock on the wall, watching the hours tick slowly by.

They were undoubtedly the longest hours of his life; he

had sat there constantly running through all the different possible outcomes in his head.

Two hours had passed by before he suddenly remembered to call home and let Rosemary know what was happening. He wasn't surprised that Rachel Moore answered the phone. 'I'm so sorry, Rachel! Thank you so much for staying with her. How is she?'

'She's okay, boss, just a bit on tenterhooks not knowing what's happening.'

'The news isn't great. My dad's currently having an operation to stop a bleed on his brain. He's had a massive stroke. They won't know how bad the damage is until after the operation. Rachel, would you do me a huge favour, please? Take Rosemary home and make sure she's settled, then lock my place up for the night using her key. I think it's going to be a long night for me here. Thank you so much for staying with her today. I really appreciate it. I know you should've been home hours ago.'

'No problem, boss. We're a team. It's what we do.'

FOUR HOURS LATER, Danny again spoke with Dr Rhodes.

He was sitting in the relatives' room, sipping a strong coffee from the vending machine, when she came into the room with a beaming smile. 'Danny, it's good news. The neurosurgeon has managed to completely stop the bleed. Your father's come through the operation well and is doing fine. He's in the recovery room, and we've just taken him off the critical list. We're not going to be in a position to do any tests, to see how much damage has been done, for at least forty-eight hours.'

Danny felt an overwhelming sense of relief at the news.

'Danny, you look dreadful! Go home and get some rest. I'll be monitoring your father's progress throughout the night, and if there's any change, I'll let you know immediately. Where can I reach you?'

Danny gave her his home phone number and the number for the police station, saying, 'I'm the detective inspector at Mansfield Police Station, and just lately, because of this bloody strike, I've been living at work. So you'll probably find me there.'

'Ah yes, the miners' strike. We've had so many injuries to striking miners and officers coming through here lately. It's been madness.'

For the first time since he met her, Danny found himself looking closely at the doctor. She had the most beautiful dark brown eyes, and the most perfect white teeth. He could now see beyond the white coat and saw the woman, not the doctor. Sue Rhodes was not only kind and gentle, but she was also a very beautiful woman.

'Thank you so much, Sue, for taking care of my dad. I would've gone out of my mind in this room without your updates and moral support. So, thank you.'

She smiled and said, 'Well, I'm sure I'll be seeing much more of you, Inspector. I'm still going to be looking after your dad.'

'That's good to know, thanks. I think I prefer Danny to inspector.'

'Okay, Danny, go home, and I'll see you soon.'

A near-exhausted Danny then made the short drive home. His head was spinning. There was a strange mixture of emotions racing through him as he stopped the car outside his house. He was very worried about his father, but also excited about meeting Sue Rhodes.

24

Proteus Army Camp, Nottinghamshire – June 20, 1984

It was a beautiful June morning. The sun was out, and the temperature had risen steadily as the day wore on.

Sergeant Mick Reynolds was lying on his back, staring at the blue sky. There wasn't a cloud to be seen anywhere.

He was shirtless on the grass outside the dormitory hut he shared with the rest of his PSU serial. There had been no deployment that morning, and they had been instructed to remain at the disused army camp where they were based.

This order had been met with groans at three thirty that morning, as the men anticipated another boring day. As the day had gone on, though, and the sun had got hotter and hotter, the men were all glad of the day off; they were busy topping up their tans on yet another glorious June day.

A young constable from his PSU approached Mick and asked, 'Skipper, any objections if a couple of us nip into the town to get a few cold cans?'

'That'll be fine once your shift finishes at three o'clock. Just make sure you're wearing civvies; you know the rules.'

It was now two thirty in the afternoon.

'Okay, Skip. Do you want anything from the shop?'

'I could do with a tube of toothpaste. I've run out this morning. I'm not bothered which brand. I'll give you the dosh when you get back. Don't go upsetting the locals and getting yourself in the shit. I won't back you up if there's any trouble, understand?'

'Yes, Skip. Straight there and straight back; we'll keep our heads down. Are you sure you don't want a few cold beers bringing back?'

'Yeah, go on then. I could murder a cold beer, cheers.'

Mick was cautious about allowing his staff into the town, as there had been a couple of occasions recently when officers from PSUs billeted at Proteus Camp had been involved, while off duty, in scuffles and altercations with striking miners in the nearby towns of Ollerton and Edwinstowe.

The officers involved had been dealt with swiftly and were immediately sent back to their own force, where they had been subsequently charged under the discipline code.

Although strike duty was onerous, boring and sometimes dangerous, nobody wanted to get sent back to their own force. All officers deployed as mutual aid from foreign forces were earning a small fortune during the strike in overtime and allowances.

After his last period of leave back in London and his meeting with Ted Smith, Mick had been fretting about how he would be able to afford to get rid of his Sierra.

Thanks to Arthur Scargill and the strike, all the overtime he was now earning meant that problem had solved itself. He could now easily afford to scrap the Sierra and buy a brand-new one.

Scrapping the car was definitely the best option, with the least chance of the car ever being traced back to him. It was something he planned to do at the end of the strike. For now, the car was safely tucked up in the garage at his home in Wembley.

JUST AFTER BEING GIVEN the news that there would be no deployment for his PSU that day, Mick was taken to one side by the operations commander at Proteus, who informed him that his serial had been selected for a different role. This new duty would be to provide the daily escort for working miners going into Warsop Main Colliery, the ones who wanted to break the strike .

The new role would start next week. At the moment, there were only two miners willing to go into work at that particular colliery. They had been going into the mine in secret for over a week with no problems, but now the government were keen to make a big show of the fact that miners were starting to drift back into work.

There had been ugly scenes at one of the other collieries nearby when miners started to drift back to work. Pickets from the South Yorkshire coalfield had descended in droves, and the risk of violent confrontation was very high.

Mick relished the prospect of this new duty, although it would still mean a very early start, because there was the promise of plenty of action instead of the mind-blowing boredom of intercept duties, standing around at crossroads out in the countryside.

The real bonus was that he and his PSU would have an early finish every day. Another Police Support Unit would be used to escort the working miners out of the mine. They were expected to be on this duty for a minimum six-week period. This meant it would be very nearly the end of July before they got any time off back in London.

When Mick later briefed his PSU about the new role , the fact they wouldn't be stood down until almost the end of July was met by a loud chorus of cheers by the men – it meant yet another bumper payday heading their way.

Mick had been a bit more reluctant to celebrate.

All it meant to him was that Rita had achieved one more stay of execution. He had used the time spent in Cornwall well and had identified a number of locations where he could easily dispose of her body, safe in the knowledge that it would never be discovered. His favoured option was an abandoned tin mine he'd found near to an isolated stretch of rugged coastline, not far from Penzance.

The mine was boarded up with wriggly tin that could easily be moved. He'd ventured inside and was excited to find an abandoned shaft that was at least fifty feet deep.

He had thrown a couple of rocks in and could hear that the shaft was full of water. A correctly weighted body would sink to the bottom of the shaft and would never be found.

Mick found himself smiling at the prospect of rolling his wife into that disused tin mine in the very near future.

The next time he was home, he planned to buy a cheap Ford Escort van and scrap his Sierra. He would then use the van to dump his dead wife before selling it and buying a new Ford Sierra Cosworth.

Happy days.

25

Warsop Miners Welfare, Warsop, Notts – June 21, 1984

The main hall of Warsop Miners Welfare was used to hosting fun-filled, joyous activities. It was the heart and soul of the small mining community. In normal times, every Friday and Saturday evening the hall would be filled with men and women spending their hard-earned cash on beer and cigarettes while watching the entertainment or playing bingo. During the week, the hall would be used for all manner of community-based activities such as keep-fit classes and mother-and-toddler groups. It was even the venue for the annual vegetable and flower show.

These were not normal times, though. Ever since the start of the industrial dispute, the main hall had been taken over by the local strike committee. It was now being used on a daily basis to provide hot meals for families that were struggling to make ends meet.

It was the place where strategies were discussed about how to move the strike forward, and where various fundraising ideas were proposed. Even during these troubled times, the main hall was still usually a positive and upbeat place. The women who provided the hot food saw to that. Although the strike was hitting them hard, they were fiercely loyal to their men and to the cause.

Today was very different.

The mood in the hall was dark and sombre. It resembled a wake; there was a totally despondent air in the room. The large room was full of tough men cradling pints of beer in their big hands, taking small sips, making them last. Their heads were bowed, and there was a low rumble of murmurings as they talked quietly amongst themselves. A thick pall of acrid blue smoke from their cigarettes hung in the air.

The strike committee had called a general meeting and asked as many of the striking miners to attend as possible. The committee had then informed the gathered miners that the strike at their mine was about to be broken. Rumours were rife that a few individuals had decided to provide scab labour and go back to work.

The news was a devastating blow to the strikers and was met with anger and incredulity. The men knew that once the drift back to work started, it would only grow. In that tense, angry atmosphere, the men were slowly coming to terms with the fact that their months of sacrifice could soon count for nothing.

They would try to turn it around and get the strike solid again, but deep down, they all knew defeat was on the horizon. The mood in the hall had now turned from anger to an almost resigned despondency.

Jimmy Wade was sitting with two other men at a table next to the door that led into the reception area of the Welfare.

'Can you believe it, Jimmy? We've got fucking scabs at our pit,' said one of the men.

Jimmy replied, 'I think it's all bullshit, Stan. Nobody's seen anyone go in yet, have they?'

'I'm telling you, it's the thin end of the wedge. Once one scab sets foot through the gate, we're all fucked. All this shit will have been for nothing.'

Stan slowly shook his head, taking another sip of his beer.

What Stan didn't know was that Jimmy Wade had himself contacted British Coal the day before to make arrangements about going back to work. He'd stayed out for as long as he could, but his savings were now gone.

He had bills and a mortgage to pay if he wanted to keep his house. He was not about to let Arthur Scargill or any of his Yorkshire bully boys make him lose it.

As he looked around the Welfare now, at the despondent, broken faces of his colleagues, he was starting to harbour a few doubts. He knew that every man in the room was going through the same shit, not just him.

His thoughts were troubling.

Prime Minister Margaret Thatcher was a fucking cow and no mistake. She had deliberately orchestrated the strike to start when it did in March, knowing it would continue through the spring, summer and autumn, when demand for electricity was less.

She knew that the stockpiles of coal at the power stations were mountainous, and that she could count on a well-trained, almost paramilitary-style police force, the likes of which had never been seen before in the UK. The woman was an unfeeling cow; all this grief and hardship caused to entire communities just so she could achieve her own political ambitions.

Suddenly, the door to the Welfare burst open, shaking Wade from his personal thoughts. A group of a dozen or so large, burly men strode purposefully inside.

'Is this where t' scabs are drinking, then?' shouted the leader of the group in an accent that was unmistakably South Yorkshire.

Not getting any response, he continued, 'We've come

down here today, dodging t' filth on t' way, to impress on you men to stay strong and support t' fight. We've heard there are some here thinking of scabbing. I'm here to tell you, don't even think about it.'

A voice at the very front of the hall shouted back, 'Who do you think you are? There's no scabs here. It's bullies like you who've caused all this shit, you and that lunatic Scargill. The little ginger twat has danced to every note of that witch Thatcher's tune! So why don't you fuck off back to whatever part of South Yorkshire you've come from. Don't come in here like you own the place, giving these good men shit!'

A loud cheer went up from the gathered Warsop pitmen.

The Yorkshireman who had spoken out now held his massive tattooed arms up with his palms outspread in a sign of appeasement and shouted, 'I can't agree with you about brother Scargill, but it's good to hear you men are still up for t' fight, and there's still fire and passion in your bellies.'

Another cheer went up.

'We've travelled down today from Grimethorpe just to let you know you're not in this fight alone. If there are backsliders here who want to scab and shit on us all, we'll be down every day to stop them getting through t' gates of t' pit. We'll hunt the scabs down to their homes and burn them out, like rats out of a nest. Are we solid, brothers?'

More loud cheers.

Jimmy Wade had heard enough. Any feelings of pity he felt for his fellow miners had just evaporated listening to them cheering the moronic Yorkshire bastard. Who did he think he was, coming down here preaching that he was going to burn people out of their homes?

Jimmy Wade despised being told what he could and couldn't do; he hated being a follower, a sheep. He had always considered himself to be the wolf that selected and killed the weak in society. The loud-mouthed Yorkshireman had made his mind up for him. He was definitely going back to work on Monday. Fuck Scargill, fuck Thatcher and fuck being a scab. He would never be a scab.

He was Jimmy Wade.

He finished the rest of his pint and slipped out of the Welfare. He walked to his car, still seething at the loud-mouthed thug from Yorkshire. As he drove slowly home, he began to calm down, and his mind turned to other matters and to a certain project he had been busy with while he had time on his hands.

What to do about Detective Rachel Moore?

He knew everything about her now. She lived alone in a first-floor flat in Mansfield; she drove a red Mini Cooper. There was no significant man in her life. She worked at Mansfield Police Station, and it appeared that she was a workaholic, the hours she spent at that place. He knew it would be difficult to get close enough to do what he intended to do. And now that he intended to go back to work, the project would have to go on the back burner for a little while.

Even though he would now have less time to plan, he knew the outcome for her was inevitable.

Once he had selected his target, it was only ever a matter of time before they would die.

26

Peckham Police Station, London – June 21, 1984

Time had passed by in a blur since the meeting between Glyn Johnson and Craig Fraser at the Black Prince pub.

Glyn had used that meeting to try to hammer out a strategy to move the investigation into the brutal murder of Jenny Taylor forward.

His team of detectives had methodically carried out all enquiries into the purchasers of forensic suits.

On one occasion, the hopes of the enquiry team were significantly raised when they discovered an order for just two forensic suits. The detectives quickly traced the recipient of the order to a private address in Hackney.

Glyn immediately mobilised an arrest team to the address. The team made entry into the property within twenty minutes of being deployed, only to find it occupied by a transgender dominatrix who answered to the name of Trixie, but whose real name was Peter Geddes.

Geddes was detained and his address searched.

Detectives searching the property following the arrest of Geddes found that the basement of the house had been converted into a makeshift dungeon ready for use by his clients.

Geddes was interviewed at length and described in graphic detail to the interviewing officers how part of the experience for some clients was for him to dress up as a surgeon, who then prescribed and carried out all kinds of sadomasochistic treatments.

The two forensic suits had been ordered from the supplier so that Geddes could realistically play the part of the surgeon.

Both suits were seized and submitted for forensic examination. Although several traces of blood were found on the suits, none matched the blood group of Jenny Taylor.

Geddes was subsequently released on bail and the vice squad informed to keep an eye on his address as a potential brothel.

The team were getting hit with dead end after dead end, and the frustration was starting to show.

Glyn had pinned his hopes on finding the dark blue Ford Sierra described by Lee Skipton. He felt sure the killer would revisit the red-light areas.

Some of the vice squad officers were reluctant at first to log sightings of vehicles matching the description provided by Skipton. Glyn and Craig had personally visited each Vice Squad in the Metropolitan Police area to impress on them the importance of finding this car, and hopefully their killer, before he struck again.

Glyn's greatest fear was another murder happening soon after the first, which would mean the press whipping up a frenzy of sensationalist reporting about the emergence of another serial killer on the loose in London.

The last thing he wanted was another Yorkshire Ripper

scenario here in the capital. His hopes of a breakthrough had been boosted when a potential witness had been found.

A well-known prostitute, Selena James, had approached vice squad officers near Wembley and told them how she was picked up by a punter in his own car from the same area Jenny Taylor had been abducted.

The punter had suddenly turned nasty and punched her in the face before he kicked her out of his car.

She complained her nose had been smashed.

The vice squad detectives at first thought it was just a punter trying to get his jollies for nothing, but then the prostitute told them that he'd paid her before the assault happened. Their interest picked up even more when she told them the car was a dark-coloured Ford Sierra, either black or dark blue.

The vice squad detectives had taken the woman straight to the incident room, where she was interviewed for over two hours by Craig Fraser and a female detective from the enquiry team. Again, it turned out to be a major disappointment, the woman could remember next to nothing about the man who assaulted her. The description she gave the detectives was that he was a white man, late thirties to early forties, with short dark hair. He was generally smart, and she remembered that he was wearing dark trousers and boots that were well polished.

The description, for what it was worth, was circulated out to all stations of the Metropolitan Police, the City of London Police and the British Transport Police.

Craig, in his broad Scottish brogue, had commented acerbically, 'Aye, and that description could fit two-thirds of the Met.'

Glyn Johnson could feel the enquiry stalling again.

The only positive was that the killer hadn't struck again.

Yet.

27

King's Mill Hospital, Mansfield – June 24, 1984

Thoughts were racing through Danny Flint's head as he sat in the car park outside King's Mill Hospital. It had been three weeks since his father had suffered a massive stroke, and three weeks since he'd first encountered Dr Sue Rhodes. He still had no extra staff at work, and even with the best efforts of his small team, a backlog of outstanding cases was beginning to form. Danny made a mental note to again challenge Superintendent Jackson over the current staffing levels as soon as he got into work that morning.

All of these things were rushing in and out of his mind as he tried to clear his head before visiting his ailing father in the hospital.

Every morning since his father had suffered the stroke, Danny had made the short drive to the hospital to check on his condition before going into work. His father, Frank, was still on one of the high-dependency wards.

The stroke had been far more catastrophic than they had first hoped. As a result, Frank had completely lost the use of the right side of his body and the ability to speak – although there had been a very slight improvement in the latter, of late. Any words he attempted, though, were barely comprehensible.

There was also the problem of incontinence. Ever since the stroke, his father had lost control of his bladder and bowel movements.

Danny visited him twice every day. Once early in the morning, and then again last thing at night, work permitting.

Each morning, he went into the ward filled with hope and determination to get his father well enough to return home so he could look after him. Every evening, he left the hospital feeling desolate and desperately sad.

Danny was only too aware that the prognosis for any kind of full recovery wasn't good. He had a meeting scheduled with Dr Rhodes this morning, to discuss what would be the best thing for his father now that he was well enough to be moved from the hospital.

He made his way up to the ward and was surprised to see Sue Rhodes already standing at his father's bedside.

His father was fast asleep, and Sue put her index finger over her lips, signalling for Danny to approach quietly so as not to wake him.

She then stepped across to meet Danny and took his arm. 'I'm sorry, Danny, your father has had a very bad night. He's only just dropped off to sleep. Unfortunately, there'll be a lot of nights like this in the future. He's going to need twenty-four-hour care, and with the job you do, there's no way you're going to be able to provide that for him, even with the help of your lovely neighbour.'

'What are you saying?'

'I'm saying, in the kindest way I know how, to consider looking at the nursing home option. I know you're resistant to the idea, Danny. He's your father and you want to care for him; I do understand that. But this is about what's best for him, and also what you can achieve as a son.'

She tenderly gripped his forearm before continuing, 'I've got a day off tomorrow. Why don't you let me show you around some of the nursing homes in the area. There are some extremely good ones in the area that are run in a professional manner, with competent and friendly staff.'

Tears welled in Danny's eyes, and he felt a huge lump forming in his throat. He rubbed his eyes and swallowed hard before nodding slowly.

'Okay, Sue, my head's telling me that every word you're saying makes sense, but in my heart it's so hard to even think about my dad being in a home. It's possible I can get away from work for a few hours after ten o'clock tomorrow morning, so we can go and have a look. I can't promise it will change my mind, though,' he said shakily.

'That's alright; I'm not trying to force you into anything. I'll drive over in my car and pick you up from the front of the police station tomorrow morning at ten o'clock. Just come with me and have a look. I think you'll be surprised what's out there.'

'Thanks, Sue. Won't your husband mind you spending your day off with a strange man?'

'What made you think I had a husband, Danny?'

Danny could feel himself colouring up as he said quietly, 'I didn't see how you couldn't have a husband. You're a beautiful, intelligent woman, and I must admit that I noticed you weren't wearing any rings. Then I thought you must take them off when you're at work. I could see how they may get in the way when you're working.'

'Be careful, Detective, you'll have me blushing! I'll see you tomorrow.'

'Thanks, Sue. I really do appreciate everything you're doing for us. See you tomorrow.'

Danny smiled at her before sitting at his father's bedside and gently holding his hand. There was still half an hour before he had to be at work.

AT THE DOOR to the ward Sue paused, turning to look at Danny. She couldn't help but notice the thrill of excitement she felt about her appointment tomorrow morning with the dark, handsome detective. She'd noticed how quickly he had coloured up when she commented that she wasn't married.

Sue Rhodes was a very private person, and nobody who worked at King's Mill Hospital knew that she was a widow; her husband of two years had been killed while working overseas as a doctor for Médecins Sans Frontières.

It had taken her six months to get over the death of her husband and return to work.

She had sold the family home in Surrey and moved to Nottinghamshire for a fresh start. Somehow, working in emergency care again had made her feel closer to her husband.

It was the first time since the death of her husband that she had even considered feelings for another man. It felt strange, but also very natural.

In the tenderness the detective showed towards his sick father, Sue could see the same care and compassion that had first attracted her to her late husband.

She hoped the detective felt the same way about her.

Tomorrow couldn't come soon enough.

28

Mansfield Police Station, Notts – June 25, 1984

It was nearing eight o'clock in the morning when Danny drove his grey BMW saloon car into the car park at Mansfield Police Station. He'd spent nearly an hour at the hospital, as usual.

He knew the rest of his small team would be arriving at work around fifteen minutes later, and he wanted to give himself a little time to sort out anything that might have come in overnight. He found a bay towards the rear of the car park and parked up. Grabbing his jacket from the front passenger seat, he walked briskly into the building.

Sleep had not come to him easily last night. His mind had been racing. Even now, his head was filled with a strange sense of guilt over today's trip with Sue Rhodes to look at nursing homes for his father. The guilt was not because he was looking for a nursing home. He'd already decided that was the right course of action and the best thing to do for his father. Danny felt uneasy because he realised that he was actually looking forward to spending some of the day with Dr Sue Rhodes.

He hadn't experienced these feelings about a woman since his divorce a few years back.

He'd been out for drinks or meals on a couple of occasions with different women, but had always known deep down that they were just one-off dates and that nothing would ever come of them.

This felt completely different, though. He just hoped that the doctor felt the same way, or all these feelings would come crashing down.

He walked into the main CID office and sat at one of the desks. Danny had long since abandoned his own small office. With only four in the team, it felt aloof and somehow wrong to be sitting away from the staff who had worked so hard over the last four months.

He checked the teleprinter messages and was relieved to find there was nothing urgent that would need their attention immediately. Next, he made a telephone call to the cells and asked the sergeant in charge if there were any prisoners detained overnight who would require CID officers to interview and process.

Again, he felt an unexplained wave of relief wash over him when the sergeant said, 'No, boss, nobody's been locked up overnight that the CID need to look at. There's only one daft lad who broke into a shed and tried to nick some tools, but it's a job that one of the uniform lads can deal with easy enough.'

'Thanks, Mike, I appreciate that. If anything comes in later, all four of us are working today, so ring the office if we're needed, okay?'

'Will do, boss.'

Gradually the team drifted in. First in was Rob, quickly followed by Andy and Rachel.

'Aye, aye! Coming in together like that, people will start to talk,' said Rob, laughing.

Rachel quickly retorted, 'Only if they're small-minded, jealous individuals with a particularly brutalised nose, Sarge!'

Rob laughed out loud. 'Harsh, Miss Moore, very harsh!'

At a quarter to ten, the office phone rang.

It was the front desk sergeant: 'Sir, there's a woman by the name of Susan Rhodes at the counter, says she's got an appointment to see you this morning.'

'Thanks, Jack, I'm on my way.'

Danny put the phone down, turned to Rob and said, 'Rob, I'm going out for a few hours. It's to do with my father. I'm trying to find a nursing home that will be able to look after him when he gets out of hospital. I've got my pager if you need me urgently, okay?'

'No problem, boss, everything's under control here. I'll see you later. Good luck! I hope you find somewhere nice for your dad. '

When Danny arrived at the front desk, he was surprised how different Sue looked. He'd only ever seen her in a work environment at the hospital, dressed in the baggy white doctor's coat and with her hair tied back off her face.

He always thought she looked good at the hospital dressed like that, but today she looked stunning.

Her dark brown hair was untied and fell loosely over her shoulders, framing her face. She was wearing a clinging mustard yellow T-shirt tucked into a pair of tight-fitting blue denim jeans. Danny could now see that under that baggy white doctor's coat, Sue had an amazing hourglass figure.

Danny realised he was staring and quickly said, 'Sorry, Sue, but you look so different.'

She smiled and said, 'No problem, Danny. Are you still okay to go?'

'I'll need to be back around two o'clock this afternoon,

but I've left my sergeant in charge, and I've got my pager, so yeah, I guess I'm good to go.'

As they walked out of the police station to her midnight blue Triumph Stag, she said, 'I hope you don't think I'm pushing you too hard, but this will be the best thing for your father, and for you in the long run. Trust me.'

He smiled. 'Trust me, I'm a doctor. Where have I heard that before?'

She smiled back. 'Very funny, Inspector.'

AS SHE DROVE her car away from the police station, she said, 'The first place I want to show you is over at Pleasley, not far from here. It's probably the best in this area for specialist twenty-four-hour care. It's a wonderful nursing home, but it's not cheap. I think you'll see what I mean when we get there.'

'It's not about the money. I want my father to be looked after, but I want him to be happy as well. Pleasley sounds good. I was worried they'd all be miles away. What's the name of this place?'

'It's imaginatively called the Pleasley Vale Specialist Care Centre.'

He watched her closely as she drove. As they spoke, she would often smile, revealing those perfect white teeth, and causing the faintest of laughter lines to crease around her dark brown eyes.

Danny felt almost mesmerised by that beautiful smile.

29

Secret location near Warsop, Notts – June 25, 1984

The disused quarry had been well chosen for its clandestine purpose.

It was set well back from the access road, and both the run-down office buildings and the deep overgrown quarry itself were not visible from the road. It was also surrounded by high, well-maintained fences that had originally been put in place to keep inquisitive children and teenagers out.

Danvers & Son Stone Quarry had not been a working quarry for over five years, and the office buildings at the heart of it had fallen into a bad state of disrepair.

However, the large iron gates at the only entrance to the quarry had been recently fitted with a large brand-new padlock. The location of the quarry was a fifteen-minute car journey from Warsop town centre. Most of the inhabitants of that town had forgotten the quarry's very existence.

It was now nearing four thirty in the morning, and two

unmarked Ford Transit vans were being driven at speed along the quiet country lane towards the quarry entrance.

In between the two navy blue Ford Transit vans was a private taxi.

The taxi contained the driver and three passengers. The driver and two of the passengers had made this journey every day, Monday to Friday, for the last two weeks. For the third passenger in the taxi, this morning was the first time.

Jimmy Wade sat quietly in the front passenger seat of the taxi, fiddling with the small haversack that contained his lunch.

It had been four o'clock that morning, just as the early dawn light was pushing back the dark of night and nobody was about, that he'd been picked up by the taxi at the bottom of Peafield Lane, just a short walk from his home.

The two other passengers were already in the taxi, having been picked up at the other end of Mansfield Woodhouse. He didn't know either of the two men, but assumed they worked on a different shift at the mine. They were laughing and joking in the back of the taxi, but Jimmy knew instinctively that the humour and levity were masking anxiety and fear.

Jimmy remained quiet throughout the journey. There was no reason for him to speak to anybody. From the moment he got into the taxi, he had spent his time looking out of the window.

Everywhere he looked, the streets were so still and quiet.

The taxi driver had deliberately taken a route that avoided the town centre of Warsop. Jimmy stared straight ahead at the cats' eyes glistening in the centre of the road, illuminated by the taxi's headlights.

It was almost hypnotic as they hurtled along the country lanes. After ten minutes of fast driving, the driver suddenly pulled into a layby at the side of the lane. Waiting in the layby were the two unmarked Ford Transit vans.

They were dark blue in colour and had been modified with

large metal grilles fitted to all the side windows, as well as the front windscreen. The side windows of the vans were made from a strong Perspex-like material, not glass. This Perspex was slightly tinted, but Jimmy could still make out that the vans were full of uniformed police officers.

Without pausing in the layby, all three vehicles quickly pulled away and continued down the country lanes to the quarry. The taxi in the centre, with a van front and rear of the small convoy.

At the metal gates that formed the entrance to Danvers & Son Stone Quarry, the vehicles stopped just long enough for two officers to jump out of the first van.

They unlocked the large padlock and swung the gates open. Once the convoy had driven through the gates, the two officers closed them immediately. They remained there while the vehicles were driven along the road towards the disused office buildings at the centre of the quarry itself.

The convoy finally came to a halt in the large car park near to the falling-down offices, well away from any prying eyes.

Jimmy hadn't been aware that this place even existed.

He and the two other passengers got out of the taxi and walked over to the buildings. Immediately, the driver of the taxi gunned the engine and sped off back towards the gates.

The two other miners who had been in the taxi walked off a short distance and stood together in the doorway of one of the buildings, leaving Jimmy standing on his own.

That suited him; he thought the two men were morons anyway. Jimmy waited quietly, sitting on the windowsill of one of the other disused buildings.

He watched, fascinated, as the policemen got out of the two vans and started donning their individual riot gear. They started to resemble medieval knights clad in ancient armour. This armour, however, was made from a hard plastic-based material and was being put on over flame-retardant overalls.

They had plates for their chests, their knees and lower legs, and also their arms and shoulders.

Finally, they put on navy blue helmets with a hard plastic visor. These were similar in appearance to a motorcycle crash helmet. Jimmy sat watching closely; he wasn't feeling nervous, just fascinated.

He had known it would be like this. There had been plenty of coverage on the news every day from other pits where miners had made the decision to return to work. They were forced to run a gauntlet of hate every morning just to get into work to feed their families. Watching those news reports had made him feel angry, not afraid.

Jimmy saw that one of the police officers had broken away from the group and was now walking towards him, carrying his blue crash helmet by its strap.

'Good morning, son, you feeling alright?' he asked in a broad cockney accent.

'I'm all good, ta,' said Jimmy.

'I'm Sergeant Mick Reynolds. I'm in charge of the two vans that are going to escort you in to the colliery. Do you want a smoke?'

Jimmy had only really registered the last part of the sentence, and right now, he could really do with a cigarette.

'A fag would be great, thanks. I'm sorry, I didn't catch your name.'

The sergeant offered the open packet of John Player Specials to Jimmy, who took one. He then struck a match and lit Jimmy's cigarette before lighting his own with the same match.

Taking a large pull on the cigarette, then exhaling a cloud of blue smoke, the policeman said, 'I'm Sergeant Reynolds. Call me Mick. You must be Jimmy Wade, the third man in our intrepid group.'

'Sergeant, I've never considered myself part of any group. Thanks for the fag, by the way.'

'You're welcome, Jimmy, and drop the sergeant bit; my name's Mick. I've always felt like that, too. It's weird, innit? I mean, I work for a massive organisation, yet I've never really felt part of the group as a whole. Does that make sense?'

'You can be part of an organisation but still retain your own personality and have your own mind. Yeah, that makes massive sense to me, Mick.'

'I can see we're gonna get on okay. I hope you're ready for what's coming, Jimmy. It's a bloody nightmare from start to finish getting into the pit. Once we're through the gates, it's fine. It's just getting through the fucking gates.'

'How do we get in? Are we all going in your vans?'

'No, Jimmy old son, this is where the lies, lies and damned lies come into it. If we all went into the pit travelling in two small vans, it'd appear as if no one's back at work. Mrs Thatcher and the government want people to think the strike's collapsing, so we travel in the vans, but you and Pinky and Perky over there will be travelling into the pit between our vans in a great big fuck-off coach.' He laughed.

'If your vans are all geared up for what's coming, how's a fucking coach going to be safe?'

But then Jimmy cast his mind back to the images on the TV, and he remembered what sort of coach it would be. He'd seen these coaches driving at speed into other pits. They were kitted out with mesh all over the windows and metal skirts protecting the tyres.

He took a last long drag from the cigarette and exhaled the smoke, saying, 'I know, we're going in on one of them so-called battle busses, aren't we!'

Mick laughed out loud. 'You've got it, Jimmy, the battle bus! Ours will be along in about ten minutes. Make sure you don't get crushed in the crowd trying to get on board. Just between you and me, we're expecting this to be the norm for the next month or so. We may get one or two more who drift back to work, but that's all. I think you'd better get used to this routine for the foreseeable future, old son.'

'Thanks, Mick, I'll be fine. Been good talking to you, and thanks for the cigarette.'

Jimmy took a last quick pull of the exhausted cigarette before throwing it on the ground and grinding it out with the heel of his boot.

Mick Reynolds was deep in thought as he walked slowly back to his men waiting by the vans. This new guy had got something about him. Mick hoped he'd keep coming into work after he saw for himself what it was like trying to get in the pit.

As Jimmy watched the sergeant walk back to his men, he felt intrigued. He had studied the man as he was speaking. There was something about Sergeant Mick Reynolds that he was fascinated by. He had a feeling they were similar in a lot of ways.

Then it came to him; he knew in that instant what was intriguing him. He knew that they were the same in one particular, special way. Jimmy always trusted his intuition; it had never been wrong before. Already he was looking forward to talking to the man again tomorrow. He couldn't wait to find out more about Police Sergeant Mick Reynolds.

He found himself smiling. He would have to be careful, the man was a police sergeant, after all, but he was excited about exploring this further. His thoughts were interrupted by the rumble of a diesel engine. Looking up, he saw a battered, cream-and-brown-coloured coach being driven up the lane towards the quarry buildings. The old coach was in such a dilapidated state Jimmy wondered how it was even allowed to be on a road.

He heard Sergeant Reynolds shouting, 'Come on, lads, look lively, the battle bus is here. The sooner we get these blokes into the pit, the quicker we get our breakfast.'

Jimmy watched, fascinated, as instantly all the cops threw

away half-drunk coffees and stood on half-smoked cigarettes before obediently jumping into their vans.

The coach came to a stop outside the buildings. Jimmy could now clearly see that it had been modified a lot and was worthy of its nickname: 'Battle Bus.'

All the windows on the coach had been replaced with the same hard Perspex material that was on the police vans, and the front windscreen was covered in a steel grille, while the side Perspex windows were covered with chicken wire. There was a metal plate covering the radiator grille, and metal skirts covered the wheel arches to protect the tyres.

The driver of the coach opened the door from the inside; there was no outer handle. He was a man in his late fifties, wearing a dirty, check flat cap and a scruffy donkey jacket over a pair of greasy, oily overalls. He had a half-smoked roll-up cigarette hanging from his mouth. 'In you get. Hurry up, we haven't got all day.'

The remnants of the roll-up fag moved as he spoke.

Jimmy and the other two men climbed into the battle bus, and the driver secured the door behind them. There was a large metal bar attached to the door that would prevent it from being yanked open.

The other two remained at the front of the bus next to each other just behind the driver. It was like they were Siamese twins, joined at the hip, thought Jimmy.

He made his way down the bus until he got about halfway along. He sat on the near side of the coach, next to the window. As the coach started moving, he saw the other men pulling scarves around their faces to hide their identities.

'Fuck that for a game of soldiers!' he said aloud.

Jimmy was wearing a black coat and a black woollen hat, which he immediately took off, revealing his blonde hair. He was fucked if he was going to hide from anybody.

The small convoy paused outside the quarry gates until the padlock had been replaced and the two cops had jumped back into their vans. They flew down the country lanes until finally Jimmy started to recognise the streets that led to Warsop Main Colliery on the outskirts of the town.

Suddenly, the bus was brought to a shuddering stop as the driver braked hard to avoid hitting the Ford Transit van directly in front of him.

Jimmy shouted, 'What the fuck's happening?'

The driver turned and said, 'The cop van has just hit a bloody dog!'

Jimmy looked out of the window and could see badly the injured dog lying on the grass verge immediately below his window. It was trying to move but was dragging its back legs, as though its spine had been injured.

The driver of the police van and another young cop had run back to the dog. Jimmy heard the younger of the two men say, 'We'd better get a vet out! The poor fucker's injured bad.'

From his vantage point, Jimmy saw Sergeant Mick Reynolds arrive from the van behind the bus.

He ordered the two cops back to their van, shouting, 'I'll deal with this. We've got to get this bus into the pit. Get going!'

As soon as the two men ran back to their van, the police sergeant had a quick look around before taking out his heavy wooden truncheon.

He glanced up and grinned at Jimmy before smashing three heavy blows down onto the dog's head, killing it.

He wiped the blood from the truncheon on the grass verge and slipped it back inside his pocket.

A look of recognition passed between Wade and Reynolds before he sprinted back to the Ford Transit van.

The diesel engine of the battle bus revved loudly, and it lurched forward as the convoy resumed its journey.

As the three vehicles approached the gates to Warsop Main Colliery, Jimmy could hear shouting and angry raised voices above the rumble of the diesel engine.

Suddenly, everything slowed down as the first police van battled its way through a sea of bodies on the road. There were well over a hundred pickets and a similar number of policemen all in the road leading to the pit entrance.

Jimmy looked out of the window and saw that many of the policemen were using large wooden batons to force the pickets back. The coach was being hit with a barrage of various objects; large rocks hammered into the Perspex. A piece of metal girder was hurled at the window near to where Jimmy sat. There was a huge bang as the piece of metal struck the Perspex and bounced off. Jimmy didn't flinch. The coach inched its way inexorably forward as the cops on the ground outside battled to clear the way for the convoy.

A loud banging noise came from the back of the coach. Jimmy quickly spun around in his seat and could see three miners were hanging off the back of the coach, trying to force open the emergency exit. Almost instantly, the three men were battered to the ground by the police and dragged away. Progress began to get a little easier, but still the missiles rained down heavily onto the coach and the two police vans that were crawling along, one at the front and one at the rear.

Then, as it became clear to the gathered pickets that the convoy was going to get through the picket line, a chant from the mob started and grew steadily to a deafening crescendo.

'Scab! Scab! Scab!'

That single word was repeated over and over again with increasing levels of venom and hatred.

Jimmy could now see the faces and the features of the striking miners, his former work colleagues. Their faces were contorted with rage and anger as they shouted that single word at the coach and its occupants. Several miners Jimmy knew personally pointed an accusing finger at him as they screamed the word, 'SCAB!' in his direction. He could almost see the veins in their heads throbbing as their faces turned red with an incandescent anger.

Jimmy started to roar with laughter at the sight of their mind-numbing stupidity. In his eyes, they were sheep: very loud and very angry sheep.

Jimmy didn't stop laughing until they were through the gates and being driven at speed to the pit head buildings away from all the mayhem. The driver stopped the battle bus. After removing the steel bar, he stretched and opened the door.

'There you are, gents, safe and sound. I'll see you this afternoon for the return journey. It's alright, don't feel you need to have a whip-round for the driver,' he cackled.

The roll-up cigarette was still dancing on his bottom lip as he spoke.

As he got off the coach, Jimmy saw Mick Reynolds standing outside his police van.

The policeman strolled over nonchalantly and said, 'How was that, then? Has it put you off coming back for more tomorrow?'

'No way. They're just morons who think they can bully people into thinking the same way as them. I'm a wolf, not a sheep. I'll be in again tomorrow; you can count on that. I'm looking forward to chatting to you some more in the morning, Mick.'

Jimmy looked directly into the eyes of the policeman, who smiled and said, 'Alright, Jimmy, see you tomorrow. Have a good shift.'

Neither of them mentioned the killing of the dog.

30

Mansfield, Notts – July 16, 1984

The days were long and hot now. Summer had arrived with a vengeance. It was already the middle of July and there was still no sign of the strike coming to an end.

The dispute between the National Union of Mineworkers and British Coal had turned into an acrimonious and bitter impasse. Neither Mrs Thatcher and the government nor Arthur Scargill and the union seemed prepared to start any kind of dialogue that could lead to an end of the strike.

As the days had turned into weeks and then months, the two sides had become more and more entrenched in their views.

There looked to be no end in sight.

With the staffing levels at work being so sparse, Danny and his small team of detectives were regularly working twelve hours or more every day, with only one day off a week.

Danny knew that Rob hadn't taken a day off for three

weeks. The tough sergeant had willingly taken on the responsibility of leading the small CID team while Danny was preoccupied with the sudden and devastating illness of his father.

Danny really appreciated the effort Rob had made on his behalf, but when he mentioned his gratitude to him over a pint, Rob had replied matter-of-factly, 'Boss, it's nothing. I know for a fact if the situation was the other way around, you'd definitely be there for me.'

Danny had made a mental note of the friendship, loyalty and hard work shown by his colleague.

Three weeks had flown by since he had gone with Sue Rhodes to have a look at the specialist nursing home at Pleasley. They had visited the home together to see if it would be suitable for his father after his stroke. The nursing home turned out to be everything Sue had promised it would be.

The building itself was old but extremely well maintained. It had once been the very grand Pleasley Manor House and was set in an acre of beautiful gardens that were all easily accessible to wheelchair users. There were several beautiful, secluded corners of the grounds where seats and benches had been placed for both patients and visitors to enjoy.

The interior of the home was beautifully appointed; each patient had a private suite of rooms and their own personal nurse, who also acted as their individual carer. The furniture was modern and the rooms spacious.

Danny had agreed straight away that if his father had to be cared for in a residential home, then this would be the one, whatever the financial cost. The only person he had to convince of the merits of the home now was his father.

Sue had been an amazing help. She had sat with Danny and his father when he had broken the news to him that he would be moving to the home at Pleasley so he could be cared for properly. It had nearly broken Danny in two when he saw the tears roll from his father's eyes and slide slowly down his cheeks. Tenderly, Danny wiped his father's tears away with a tissue and held him close for a full minute.

Patiently, and with the gentle help of Sue at his side, he carefully explained that he would only be going to the home temporarily to help him achieve a good enough recovery for him to come home.

The day had now arrived when his father was well enough to travel to the home and take up residence permanently. Sue had again taken time off work to help Danny through what was going to be a difficult day. He acknowledged to himself that he probably would have been unable to do it without her. It wasn't lost on either of them how close they were becoming. They had arrived together to collect Frank from the hospital and then driven the short journey to the nursing home at Pleasley.

As they drove through the large ornamental wrought-iron gates into the beautiful grounds, which looked resplendent in the July sun, Danny saw the beginnings of a lopsided grin forming on his father's face.

With his good hand, the old man squeezed his son's hand and mumbled the word, 'Beautiful.'

It was now Danny's turn to feel emotional, and he quickly turned away so his father didn't see the tears starting to well up in his eyes.

Danny and Sue had spent hours painstakingly deciding which of his father's personal effects he would want and need in his new rooms. Danny wanted it to be a home from home for his father, and he'd tried hard to make the move as small a wrench as possible.

Witnessing his father's positive mood after seeing the grounds for the first time, Danny was hopeful that he would readily accept the nursing home – for, in truth, he knew there was no realistic hope of his father ever being well enough to again enjoy an independent life at his old house.

Danny knew that this was undoubtedly going to be one of

the hardest things his father would ever have to accept and come to terms with.

Frank Flint had lived in the house at Mansfield all his married life, and Danny could only guess at the number of treasured memories the house held for his father. All those years with his wife, raising his family, decorating the house and making it a home.

The memories held by his father would be boundless.

As Danny stopped the car outside the front doors of the home, the owner of the home was waiting outside. As the car came to a stop, she opened the car door and immediately spoke to Danny's father.

'A very warm welcome, Mr Flint! I hope your stay here will be very comfortable.'

A wheelchair was already waiting, and two nurses assisted Frank to get out of Danny's car and into the wheelchair. He was then wheeled into the building by one of the nurses, led by the owner and followed by Danny and Sue.

Frank's eyes widened as he was pushed through the spacious comfortable lounge areas and along the well-appointed bright corridors until they arrived at his own suite of rooms.

Opening the door to his rooms, the nurse pushing his wheelchair said, 'Here you are, Mr Flint. These are your own private rooms.'

Again, Danny saw the smile appear on his father's face as he surveyed the room and saw for the first time the old photographs and personal items from the house in Mansfield, already in place.

'Very nice, son,' he mumbled.

The nurse, assisted by the owner, helped Frank get out of the wheelchair. They then made him comfortable on one of the armchairs in his room. The chair faced out of the large window overlooking the beautiful gardens that looked amazing in the afternoon sun.

To the left of the armchair where Frank now sat was a coffee table. On the table were two cherished photographs of his late wife. With his good hand, Frank reached over and picked up the first of the silver-framed photographs, kissing the picture of his wife tenderly before replacing it on the table.

The owner of the home knelt down beside him at the side of the chair and said, 'Mr Flint, this young lady is Rosie.' She indicated the nurse who had pushed the wheelchair from the front of the building.

'Rosie will be your personal nurse and carer. If there's anything you need, Mr Flint, you just let her know.'

'Frank,' he mumbled. 'Please call me Frank.'

Rosie smiled and said, 'Very well, Frank it is. I'll leave you with your son and Dr Rhodes to settle in, and I'll pop back later to discuss your preferred option for dinner this evening.'

The owner of the home and Rosie then left the room, leaving Danny and Sue alone with Frank.

Sue squeezed Danny's arm and said, 'Danny, have some time with your dad. I'll go and get a coffee. Take as long as you need.'

She smiled that beautiful enigmatic smile that always took Danny's breath away.

Returning her warm smile, he said, 'Thanks, Sue.'

As she closed the door behind her, Danny knelt in front of his father and held his hand. 'Is it okay, Dad?'

He looked directly into his father's eyes before continuing, 'If you don't like it, we can leave right now.'

Frank's face twisted into the lopsided smile once again, and he mumbled three words: 'Lovely, very happy.'

'That's great, Dad. I'll go and bring Sue back; we can all sit and have a coffee together. Dad, you know I love you, don't you?'

'Love you too, big softie,' Frank mumbled.

Danny and Sue spent a couple of hours with Frank, getting him settled and used to his new surroundings.

Rosie returned later to discuss the choices for the evening meal and to go over how things were generally run. Once again, Danny was impressed with the easy patience and understanding displayed by the nurse, Rosie. Saying their goodbyes, Danny and Sue left, with Danny promising to visit in the morning.

As they walked to the car park, Danny turned to Sue with the faintest of tears in his eyes and said, 'I can't ever thank you enough, Sue. I could never have done this without your kindness and support. I think you know how I feel about you, and I'd very much like to continue seeing you. Now I won't be seeing you most days at the hospital, that is.'

He knew his little speech had been faltering and clumsy; he could feel his face reddening.

'Detective Inspector Flint, are you asking me out on a date?' she asked playfully, again hitting him with that laser-beam smile.

'Well, I was hoping for several, actually,' he quipped back.

She stepped forward and placed both her arms over Danny's shoulders, interlocking her fingers behind his neck.

Looking up into his eyes, she said, 'The more the merrier as far as I'm concerned, Danny.'

She then tilted her head slightly so she was looking up into Danny's eyes. Taking her cue, he kissed her gently on the mouth. She returned his kiss, and they remained like that for what seemed a long time. Finally, they broke off, and she said, 'Shall we find a nice country pub for a drink and a bite to eat?'

'That definitely sounds like a plan.'

They made the short walk across the car park to his BMW. They held hands as they walked. It seemed like the natural thing to do.

31

Warsop, Nottinghamshire – August 3, 1984

For Jimmy Wade and the other miners going into work at Warsop Main Colliery, every morning was the same routine. Their day began with the taxi ride to the layby, where they were met by two Ford Transit vans full of police officers. From the layby it was a high-speed drive to the disused quarry, where they would wait thirty or so minutes for the increasingly battered battle bus. Then came the drive into the colliery itself and the daily run through the gauntlet of hate from the striking miners.

Since joining the ranks of the working miners, Jimmy Wade had been well and truly ostracised by his own community. People he'd considered as workmates before now either abused him verbally or just totally ignored him.

Jimmy had never really made close friends and hadn't been in his current house long enough to have made any lasting impression on his neighbours. He was just amazed at how fast word had travelled around the small town that Jimmy Wade was now back at work. In his own community's eyes, he was now the lowest of the low, nothing more than a scab. He would hear old men and women muttering the word under their breath as he passed them in the street. The younger members of the community were far more vociferous in their displeasure. Wherever he went, the cry of "Scab!" would follow him.

It had bothered him at first, but now he let it wash over him. The idiots would tire of saying it before he tired of listening to it, he told himself. He was unconcerned for his own safety. He was well aware that not many people would ever threaten him with violence or be prepared to have a go at him physically. It was common knowledge among the other pitmen how physically strong Jimmy Wade was.

He was worried about damage being caused to his house when he wasn't there, but so far nothing had happened. At least now the bills were getting paid, and he was no longer in danger of losing his home. Jimmy knew that as more miners returned to work, his part in breaking the strike would eventually be forgotten. He had also been carefully making plans for his future, and he knew that the venomous shouts of "SCAB!" would soon become a long-forgotten memory.

The only change in the daily routine for the miners working at Warsop Main Colliery was that there were now two cabs required. Two more men were now making the journey into the pit every day, making five in total.

It was obvious these numbers would steadily grow.

The strike was slowly crumbling. Arthur Scargill and his idiot henchmen refused to accept this was the case, and continued, at every opportunity, to rant about this famous victory over Thatcherism.

The one beacon of light in this depressing scenario had been the association he had struck up with the police sergeant from London. He would never have described it as a friendship – Jimmy Wade didn't do friendship. Every morning he and the sergeant had around half an hour of stimulating conversation before the battle bus arrived. At first, they had spoken about general everyday subjects – sport, politics and the like – but for weeks now, their talks had become more personal. Mick opened up to Jimmy about the bitch he was married to. During these deep conversations, the sergeant had said on more than one occasion that he wished his wife were dead.

When during one such conversation, Jimmy suggested to him that he should stop wishing it and just do it, he hadn't been surprised when Mick replied, 'I might just do that, Jimmy.'

That conversation had been over two weeks ago. Every day since, Mick had steered their little talks back to the subject of murder. Jimmy had let him ramble on about the various ways he intended to kill his wife, Rita. Today was no different. As soon as they arrived at the quarry, he and Mick moved away from the other miners and police officers and stood out of earshot.

Once again, it was Mick who started the conversation. 'I've thought long and hard about this, Jimmy. I'm going to do it. I can't stand being with her any longer; she's driving me insane. It's totally unfair for her to get half of everything I've worked my bollocks off for. As far as I'm concerned, I've got no option. I've made my mind up.'

'I reckon you need to think about this, Mick. If you're caught, because you're a copper, they'd lock you up forever. Anyway, I reckon it's all talk with you. I don't reckon you've got the balls to kill her. You're all wind and piss. It's one thing to smash a dog's head in, but something else to kill a person.'

He then fixed the sergeant with his cold blue eyes and said evenly, 'Have you, Mick? Have you got the balls to take a life, to snuff out your nagging bitch of a wife's very existence?'

The sergeant didn't answer.

Jimmy said, 'I knew it. You haven't got the arse to kill someone. You're all talk!'

Still the burly sergeant didn't respond, but Jimmy could see his face reddening and his lips being tightened.

Jimmy sneered, 'Hopeless. You could never do it.'

Reynolds fixed Jimmy with a steely gaze and said quietly, in a voice barely more than a whisper, 'I've done it already.'

Jimmy stifled a laugh and said in a mocking tone, 'Yeah, of course you have! What the fuck are you talking about, Mick?'

The sergeant paused and looked around before leaning in towards Jimmy, whispering conspiratorially, 'I'm telling you I've already killed somebody. So yes, for your information, I've got the fucking balls.'

It was the sergeant's turn now to stare stony-faced into the eyes of the miner.

'Yeah, of course you have,' goaded Jimmy.

'Jimmy, I've never been more serious in my life.'

'Really? So who've you killed already?'

'Back home in London, some silly little tart who was in the wrong place at the wrong time. Never mind who she was. The fact is I did it; so yes, I can take a life. I'll tell you this: I fucking enjoyed it, too. The question I need answering is this Jimmy, old son. Never mind me, what about you? Could you take a life?'

Jimmy was now thoughtful. Eventually, he said, 'I think we need to continue this talk in private, over a couple of beers when we've got more time, don't you?'

Staring at the policeman, he continued, 'I think you already know the answer to that question, Mick. I've always thought that, deep down, you and I were kindred spirits.'

He grinned. 'What do you say? Do you want to go for that talk over a beer tonight?'

'Dead right I fucking do, Jimmy. I'll go for that pint; I've been wanting to talk to somebody about this ever since it happened. I can't stop thinking about it.'

Jimmy nodded and said, 'Thinking about how exhilarated it made you feel, am I right? You end up craving that feeling of power, don't you?'

'That's it exactly. I want to feel more of that amazing adrenalin rush, the buzz or whatever other way you want to describe it. I want to feel it again. If it's not that bitch Rita, then it'll have to be some other useless fucker.'

Jimmy looked directly into the sergeant's eyes.

There was a special look in those eyes that he recognised only too well. It was the same look he saw in his own eyes, reflected back from the mirror, when his own urges were strong.

'Okay, Mick, what's the crack with you boys when you're up here? Are you allowed out at night to go for a beer?'

'Yeah, we can get out, but nowhere local to the army camp. The pubs nearby are off-limits, and we're not allowed to fraternise with the locals, in case conversation turns to argument. A lot of the blokes have got tarts on the go up here, though. None of the gaffers bat an eyelid if they go out shagging.'

'This army camp you keep mentioning, is it the old disused one up near Ollerton?'

'Yeah, it's called Proteus Camp. I've been there since the start of the fucking strike. It's a bleeding shithole.'

The distant rumble of the diesel engine of the battle bus approaching interrupted their conversation.

'I'll be in the layby outside Proteus Camp at eight o'clock tonight. I'll be sitting in a dark green Ford Cortina parked up facing away from the gates. I've got a long blonde wig that I'll put on, so if anyone sees me from behind, they'll think you're being picked up by a tart.'

'Okay, Jimmy, eight o'clock tonight. I'll see you later,' he said with a malevolent grin.

Jimmy walked over to the battle bus; he had always known his intuition about the policeman from London would be proved right. He was feeling pleased with himself; he had played Reynolds just right, waiting for him to speak first and disclose his past. It had been a relief when he finally started to talk about what they both were – stone-cold killers.

Things were about to get very interesting. For the first time in weeks, Jimmy could feel familiar urges coursing through him.

He knew he had to kill again soon.

The thing that excited him most was that he knew that Mick Reynolds was feeling exactly the same. Jimmy had never hunted for a victim before; he had always been opportunistic when it came to killing. He was feeling very excited about the prospect of a new experience. In the back of his mind he still held thoughts for the beautiful DC Moore, but he needed that to be a personal experience. It wasn't something he wanted to share with anyone else.

The meeting with the sergeant tonight couldn't come fast enough for Jimmy Wade.

32

Ollerton, Nottinghamshire – August 17, 1984

July had come and gone. The year had slipped into August, and temperatures during the day and at night had been stiflingly hot. The evenings and nights were almost unbearably sticky and humid. Just turning over in bed was enough effort to ensure most people would break out into a sweat.

As he went into work each day, Jimmy had noticed that even the pickets on the approaches and gates to Warsop Main Colliery appeared to be just going through the motions. The number of pickets had diminished, and the venom and hatred shown by the strikers in the early weeks had dissipated, too. It was as though the heat and humidity were making everything just too much of an effort.

Two weeks had passed since the night he had waited for Mick Reynolds in the layby outside Proteus Camp. The decision to wear the long blonde wig had proved extremely prudent, as he noticed in his rear-view mirror that as Mick approached his car, another off-duty copper had come sauntering out of the gate.

Mick had told Jimmy that the cop was one of the younger constables on his PSU. The officer was at least seventy-five yards away, and Jimmy had driven away quickly; the last thing he wanted was for the young copper to remember the registration number of his car.

That first night sitting in a quiet booth in the Squinting Cat pub at Clipstone Village had been a revelation for both men. Mick had gone into a lot of detail about the killing of the young woman in London, explaining to Jimmy that in his mind, he had imagined he was killing his wife, Rita. He clearly relished the chance to confide in Jimmy and told him in great detail what had happened. He bragged to Jimmy that the reason he could get away with murder was because, as a police officer, he knew the quickest way to stifle a murder enquiry was to make it impossible to identify the victim. He described in great detail how this could quite easily be achieved. He also bragged to Jimmy about his awareness of forensic science and other methods the police used to obtain vital clues.

In graphic detail, he explained to Jimmy that depriving a murder investigation of forensic evidence is like sucking the oxygen away from a fire; it will quickly die.

His final nugget of information on how to kill and avoid detection was very simplistic. The victim selected must have absolutely no connection to the murderer.

Mick explained to Jimmy that most murders were committed by people the unfortunate victim knew.

He assured Jimmy that if these three rules were followed implicitly, any police investigation would struggle and soon flounder.

Jimmy listened patiently, letting Mick incriminate himself further and further. He pretended to be in awe of the burly Londoner. The truth was, he had no desire or inclination to go into any of the details of his own two killings or the reasons for them. He still didn't trust anyone with his secrets, especially a police officer, even if that particular police officer had just admitted to a murder. Everything Reynolds had said so far could all be bullshit as far as Jimmy was concerned. When Mick spoke about the importance of identifying a victim, Jimmy questioned him on what techniques the police used to identify victims.

Mick confided in him that the two most common methods used to identify people were fingerprints and dental records. If you could deprive the investigation team of these ways of identification, things wouldn't be straightforward.

Jimmy only joined in the information-sharing once. He offered an opinion to Mick that he thought one of the most important ways to avoid detection was to divert the police into looking elsewhere. Mick readily agreed, telling Jimmy the police loved having enquiries to follow, and that if a large enough trail of breadcrumbs was left, the police would always follow it, getting further away from the truth all the time. Mick also explained to Jimmy the tremendous pressure detectives were under, not only to solve a murder, but to solve it quickly.

Jimmy lapped it up. He'd never heard anyone speak about murder and killing in the way the sergeant had. At the moment it was all just talk; the ultimate test for Reynolds would come soon enough.

Only the outcome of that test would decide how long Jimmy remained in the company of the dangerous and calculating police sergeant.

Earlier in the day at the quarry, the two men had made arrangements to meet again that evening in the layby near to Proteus Camp. Jimmy now found himself in his car, waiting for Mick Reynolds to arrive.

It was now nearly nine o'clock, and the daylight had virtually disappeared, but Jimmy still wore the blonde wig while he waited patiently.

Glancing in the car's rear-view mirror, he could now see Mick finally approaching the vehicle. He was carrying a black holdall.

Mick opened the boot of the Cortina and placed the holdall inside. He closed the boot, opened the passenger door and got in the car.

'What's in the bag, Mick?'

'With a bit of luck, I'll be able to show you later.' Mick grinned, and Jimmy noticed he had that special look in his eyes.

'I see. Have you got something in mind for tonight?'

Mick seemed agitated as he said, 'Our PSU's being stood down for a week from tomorrow. This will be my last night here for a week. I've decided I can't face the prospect of going home to that bitch Rita, so I'm going up north to Newcastle, to stay with my sister for the week. It's just that I want – no, I need – to do something special tonight. I'm sick of just talking about it, Jimmy. I need some action tonight.'

'I feel the same way. I've got something to show you later as well. I think you're going to like it. Let's just play it by ear and see what the night brings, shall we?'

Mick nodded, and a smiling Jimmy drove the car away from the layby. The two men sat in silence as Jimmy drove the Cortina steadily along Peafield Lane before turning left along the main A60 road towards Mansfield. He then took a left turn at the crossroads onto Old Mill Lane and drove into a small mining village called Forest Town.

Jimmy drove into the car park of the Prince Charles pub. As he parked the car, he said, 'I never drink in this pub, so I don't think I'll know anyone in here. It's a bit rough and ready and has a reputation as a pickup joint. The women here aren't exactly tarts, but they like their cock and by all accounts aren't too fussy about whose cock it is.'

Mick just nodded. He appeared sullen, brooding, almost trance-like. There was a real sense of anger, almost rage, bubbling below the surface, and not far below at that.

Before getting out of the car, Jimmy paused, looking at Mick. 'Are you alright? Are you sure you want to do this?'

He almost growled a reply: 'Oh yeah, I'm sure. That bitch is really going to get what she deserves tonight.'

'Listen to me, you need to lighten up, Mick. We're just two blokes having a pint in a pub. At the moment, you look like a total nutter. Nobody's going to come within a hundred yards of us while you're like that, mate.'

'Yeah, you're right, sorry, Jimmy. Let's go and get a beer, shall we?'

Jimmy was shocked at just how quickly the other man's mood changed. It was as if he changed into a different person completely.

As they got out of the car, Mick was now laughing and smiling. 'What you having, mate?' he said in a loud jovial voice.

'I'll have a bitter shandy, mate. Let's go in the public bar. Keep that accent down a bit; I've no idea what the clientele's like in here. It could be full of striking miners for all I know.'

Both men walked into the public bar of the pub. Mick quietly ordered the beers while Jimmy quickly glanced around at the other customers. In total, there were no more than twenty other punters in the bar. He could hear raucous voices from the lounge bar next door.

Jimmy leaned forward and said to the barmaid, 'Is there a do on next door, luv?'

'Yeah, it's an engagement party. A lot of the regulars are next door. You'd never guess there's a strike on, the way they're spending. It's packed in there.'

She handed over the two beers.

Both men took a long drink from their pints before walking away from the bar to sit in a booth. There was a jukebox on the wall, which was belting out the latest Wham song. Instinctively, Jimmy started to tap his fingers in rhythm to the music as he looked around the room. A group of older men were playing dominoes at a table in the corner. The only other people in the bar were couples out having a quiet drink. It was as if the pub had been turned around. The people drinking in this bar would, on any other night, be drinking in the lounge. It was obvious there was very little chance of any action in this pub. Jimmy ordered two more pints. The time was fast approaching closing time.

'This is fucking hopeless,' growled Mick as his mood changed once more.

'You're right. Let's drink this and fuck off.'

Just as they were about to drink up and leave, the door that led from the lounge bar swung open. A woman who was obviously quite drunk tottered in on ridiculously high wedges.

She staggered up to the bar and smiled at the barmaid.

'Hello, duck, it's last orders next door, but I can't get near the bar for all those drunken twats. I'll have a large Bacardi and Coke, please, duck.'

She plonked her black leather handbag loudly on the bar and fished inside for her purse. The barmaid placed the drink on the bar in front of the tipsy woman.

'You alright, Mandy? Looks like you've had a good night next door?'

The woman took a sip of her drink. 'It's been lovely. I told the silly cow not to go through with it. I've been so much better off since I've been on my own. Men are only good for one thing, and I can get that whenever I want. Variety's the spice of life, duck.' She giggled.

'You're terrible, Mandy,' replied the barmaid, chuckling.

'No one in there take your fancy tonight, then?'

'Nah luv, they're all twats in there. I'm just going to get this down me, then have a steady walk home.'

'You be careful getting home. You've had a few.'

'I'll be alright, duck. I've only got to walk down Pump Hollow Lane; it's not far.'

Both men had been watching intently and listening to the exchange between the drunken woman and the barmaid. Mick's mood was once again becoming more intense and agitated.

'This bitch will do, Jimmy,' he said, in a guttural voice that was no more than a low growl.

'I reckon you're right.'

Jimmy now looked closer at the woman.

She was probably coming up to her fiftieth birthday, but had good legs that she showed off by wearing the shortest white mini skirt he'd seen for a while. Her top was a black sheer blouse with white buttons at the front. It was unbuttoned quite low, and her ample cleavage was being held in check by a lacy black bra that was visible beneath the see-through blouse. Her hair was platinum blonde, straight out of the bottle, and the roots were starting to show dark again.

The make-up she wore was garish, trying to hold back the ravages of time and a hard life with lipstick and powder.

All in all, she looked a mess.

Jimmy truly believed that deep down she would welcome what was about to happen to her. It would be a joyous release from her shit life.

In a couple of hours, he'd know this for certain, when he looked directly into her eyes at the moment of her release.

Turning to Mick, he said quietly, 'Come on, Mick, she's nearly finished her drink. We need to get going and be waiting on Pump Hollow Lane.'

Both men quickly swallowed their drinks and walked outside. They were just getting into the car when they heard the bar door open.

'G'night, duck!' a now very drunk Mandy shouted to the barmaid as she tottered out.

There was still ten minutes to go before closing time, and

nobody else was leaving the pub; they were all inside clamouring for last orders.

Jimmy drove the car slowly out of the car park, passing the drunken woman. Three minutes later, they were parked up in the dark on Pump Hollow Lane. The street lighting here was poor, and the road was very dark.

As they waited for the woman to appear at the end of the road, Jimmy reached into the glove compartment. He pulled out a plastic document pocket.

'Look at this, Mick. Remember that deflection theory I was telling you about?'

Mick quickly scanned the short, typed document that was in the plastic wallet.

He chuckled malevolently. 'That's fucking brilliant.'

'Don't worry, I typed it with gloves on, and we'll be taking the plastic wallet with us, so there'll be no danger of any prints being left.'

'Sounds like you listened to me well, old son,' said Mick, grinning.

They could now see the woman tottering down the hill towards them. She was making slow progress, obviously feeling the effects of the alcohol.

Jimmy reached onto the back seat of the car and picked up the blonde wig and put it on.

'Be nice to her, Mick. Say I'm your wife and that I've come to pick you up. Tell her she shouldn't be walking home alone and that we'll drop her off.'

Mick nodded and wound the window down.

'Hello, luv,' he said, in his best impression of a local accent. 'My wife here says you shouldn't be walking home on your own, luv. Can we give you a lift home, duck?'

She bent over, swaying slightly as she looked into the car.

It was obvious that drink was affecting her focus as she squinted inside the car. Mick seized the initiative. Jumping out of the car, he opened the back door.

'Come on, luv, let's get you home.'

'Aw, thanks duck, but I'm alright. I don't need a lift.'

Suddenly, Mick lunged forward, grabbing the woman around the waist. He began dragging her towards the open door.

The woman began to lash out and struggle against Mick's grip. As she flailed her arms wildly, her black leather handbag flew from her grasp towards the hedgerow at the side of the road.

Finally, Mick shoved her bodily inside the car. She landed on her back on the back seat.

She shouted, 'Oi! What the fuck's going on!

Mick punched her hard in the face, rendering her unconscious, and once again the car was silent.

'No blood in the car,' said a calm Jimmy.

Taking off the blonde wig, he then drove the car away steadily.

'I know somewhere better to do this,' he said.

A fifteen-minute drive later and Jimmy steered the car into a quiet layby just outside Annesley Village.

It was a lonely desolate place that, unless you knew the area, would be difficult to find. The entrance into the layby was almost concealed and was hard to spot, especially at night.

There were no street lights here. The road was very quiet, and the layby was set back behind a row of bushes.

Mick got out of the car, taking care to only walk on the hard Tarmac. He opened the boot of the car and retrieved the grip bag.

He walked back to the open passenger door and said, 'We'll need these before we go any further.'

He opened the grip bag and pulled out a pair of light blue forensic suits, gloves and overshoes. He handed one set to Jimmy. 'Get them on before we touch anything else.'

After a couple of minutes, both men were standing at the

side of the car, totally covered in their suits. With gloved hands, Mick reached into the bag and pulled out a roll of sticky brown gaffer tape. He quickly wrapped the tape around the woman's head so it covered her mouth. She was starting to stir, slowly regaining consciousness. Mick grabbed two black cable ties from the bag and used them to bind her wrists tightly. She was now fully awake and tried to scream, but the gaffer tape stifled the scream; the noise was more like a guttural growl.

Both men smiled. Jimmy said, 'I'll bring her. Follow me.'

Unseen by Mick, Jimmy tied a length of thin cord loosely around his middle. He grabbed the now-terrified woman from the back seat, and although she tried to struggle, he easily overpowered her. Throwing her over his shoulder, he walked quickly into the woods at the side of the layby.

With the woman over one shoulder, he carried the small plastic document holder and its contents in one hand while he gripped the legs of the woman with the other.

She was only a small woman, and it felt good to him as she wriggled on his shoulder, trying to break his grip. After walking for three minutes, he found a small clearing in the trees.

Jimmy threw the woman roughly down onto the ground.

He placed the document holder on the ground, alongside the woman, who was now lying face up.

Mick stood behind him, holding the grip bag.

The woman was staring up at him, and in the bright moonlight Jimmy could see that her eyes were wide. The fear behind those eyes was evident, and Jimmy smirked. He sat astride the woman, pinning her bound arms beneath her back. She tried in vain to buck him off, but he was far too strong for her to move.

Eventually, she gave up and lay still beneath him.

Jimmy put his head six inches away from her face and stared into her eyes.

He slipped the thin cord from around his middle and wrapped it once quickly around her neck. Slowly, he started to exert pressure by pulling on each end of the thin rope until the cord was biting into her neck, cutting the oxygen off. Her eyes grew wider still, and she tried to shake her head, imploring him to stop. The last thing she would see were those intense blue eyes staring into her own. He kept pulling on the ends of the cord until he saw her eyes change from sparkling, bright, terrified eyes into dull, matte, lifeless eyes that were focussing on nothing.

Slipping the thin cord from around the woman's neck, he stood up and turned to face a scowling Mick.

'Have you killed the bitch already?' he growled, with some anger in his voice.

'No, Mick, she's just unconscious. This one's all yours. I want to see if you've actually got the bottle to do what you've been bragging about. I love these suits, by the way; are these what the coppers will be wearing later when they find her?'

'Yes, they fucking are. Now get out of the way and let me show you who's got the bottle for this.'

He stomped forward and aimed a vicious kick at the face of the already-dead woman. He then bent forward and removed the brown gaffer tape from around her head before growling, 'Shut your mouth, Rita, you fucking gobby cow!'

Jimmy stood watching as Mick's heavy boots covered by the overshoes landed kick after kick into the woman's face.

He was a man possessed; every kick was accompanied by a grunted word.

Kick: 'you!'
Kick: 'fucking!'
Kick: 'bitch!'
Kick: 'Rita!'

The woman's face was now barely recognisable.

After several minutes, Mick stopped the frenzied assault and stepped back over to the grip bag. He never even acknowledged Jimmy; he was totally oblivious to the other man's presence. He reached into the bag and took out a heavy ball-peen hammer. He then picked up the grip bag in his other hand and walked trancelike back to where the woman was lying on the grass.

Mick placed the grip bag down at the feet of the dead woman and, using the hammer, began to rain blow after blow down into the mouth of the woman until the whole jaw, both upper and lower mandibles, was smashed. Jimmy could see teeth flying as the hammer landed.

Finally, he stopped the vicious attack and, breathing heavily from his exertions, replaced the hammer in the bag.

He then took out a resealable plastic bag and a set of small garden shears.

He rolled the dead woman over onto her front, exposing her bound hands. Using the shears, he severed each of the fingers and the thumbs.

The thumbs seemed to be a lot harder to cut through, and Jimmy could hear Mick grunting with the exertion.

Finally, he cut the two black cable ties that had bound her wrists. Meticulously he picked up all the severed fingers and thumbs and put them into the ziplock bag before resealing it. He then placed the bag, the cable ties and the shears back into the grip bag before finally taking out a Stanley knife.

Using the Stanley knife blade, he repeatedly slashed at the open palms of the woman's hands until they were both a flayed, bloody mess. Having returned the Stanley knife, he then took out a black bin liner from the holdall.

He turned to Jimmy and finally spoke. 'Give me a hand to get her stripped off.'

'What the hell for? I don't want to touch her like that.'

Mick hissed, 'I'm not going to interfere with her; I'm not a bloody pervert. We need to take her clothes. There could be fibres from your car on her clothes. Better safe than sorry .'

Quickly the two men stripped the woman, placing her clothes in a bin liner from the grip bag.

The bloodied and battered body was now an image of contrast in the bright moonlight. Her skin was stark white and the blood that covered her jet black.

Mick stepped back, his breathing hard and laboured.

It was now Jimmy's turn to approach the dead woman.

'Now it's time to play some games with the coppers.' He grinned.

The first thing he did was straighten the body. The head was a mess, barely recognisable in shape or form; her face had been virtually obliterated.

Jimmy turned the woman so she was lying on her back, then straightened the arms out away from her sides until her body was shaped like a crucifix. He then opened her legs wide. He picked up the plastic document holder he'd placed on the ground earlier, and from inside, he removed a thin black plastic tube.

He thoroughly wiped the tube on the wet grass before removing the typewritten note from the plastic document holder. Rolling the note like a scroll, he placed it inside the tube. He put the document holder into the black bin liner containing the woman's bloody clothes that was sitting on top of the holdall.

He then turned towards Mick and grinned.

Mick also let out a chuckle as he realised where the tube was going. Jimmy carefully inserted the plastic tube into the dead woman's vagina.

'Just by putting that in there, we're now both sexual deviants, Mick. How long will the detectives spend trawling through list after list of sex offenders?' He laughed softly.

Mick nodded knowingly.

Jimmy reached into the holdall and removed the Stanley knife again.

He knelt at the side of the dead woman and, using the

sharp blade, he cut two words into her chest and stomach. The first word was carved just above her breasts, the second word below them.

Mick nodded approvingly. 'That will definitely get the detectives in a state of flux. I like it, Jimmy.'

Both men then stood back from the mutilated body and surveyed their grisly work. Without saying another word to each other, they slowly walked off and left the battered and defiled remains of Mandy on the cold grass, her smashed, unrecognisable face looking directly up at the bright moon.

Just before they got back to the car, Mick reached into the grip bag and removed the black bin liner that already contained the used gaffer tape and cable ties, the dead woman's clothes and the digits from her mutilated hands. Once they were standing on the tarmac at the edge of the layby, they removed the forensic suits, the overshoes and finally the gloves, placing everything into the same bin liner. They both quickly checked the area around the car to make sure they hadn't dropped anything. Jimmy opened the boot, and Mick placed the grip bag and the bin liner inside.

It was now approaching one o'clock in the morning. Jimmy slowly drove the car back towards Ollerton and the army camp.

Neither man said a word throughout the journey.

Stopping the car in the layby outside the camp, Jimmy finally broke the silence.

'What are you going to do with the bin liner?'

'It's going straight into the boiler room furnace, old son. That'll get rid of everything, no bother.'

'When will you be back from Newcastle?'

'I'm back on duty here on the twenty-fourth. I've only got a week off.'

'I'll see you at the quarry when you get back.'

'You will, mate, you will. We make a good team, you and me.'

Carrying the grip bag in one hand and the bin liner in the other, Mick walked off, disappearing into the darkness and leaving Jimmy alone in the car.

As he watched Mick walking away, Jimmy reflected on what had been a very interesting night.

Previously, he had only killed when he knew he could stage the death to look like an accident.

Tonight had been a major change for him.

The two of them had selected the woman totally at random and then killed her in such a brutal and horrific way that her death couldn't be seen as anything other than a cold and calculated murder.

He also realised now how similar, yet how very different, he was to Mick Reynolds.

Jimmy realised that the only thing they had in common was that they both enjoyed killing. The mental processes for each of them that led to the act of killing were, however, polar opposites.

Something else was now abundantly clear to Jimmy: Killing in this way meant the possibilities were endless.

He no longer had to be so patient.

Jimmy had watched Mick closely as he meticulously managed the scene of the murder so that no clue was left behind. He knew that this newfound knowledge, coupled with his cold, methodical and calculating mind, meant he could now kill whenever he wanted to and – more importantly, get away with it.

As he drove away, his thoughts turned to how killing as a pair had been so very different. He wasn't sure it was for him. He preferred to work alone.

For the foreseeable future, though, it was going to be a welcome distraction from the boredom of this fucking strike.

33

Fiskerton, Nottinghamshire – August 17, 1984

Danny Flint and Sue Rhodes were sitting outside a country pub near the picturesque village of Fiskerton on the banks of the River Trent.

It was now a beautiful balmy evening after what had been another very hot day. Only as the sun neared the horizon had the temperature finally started to become bearable.

The Bradley Arms pub was beautiful.

It was a sandstone building, draped with wisteria and other wall flowers. The walls were also adorned with several colourful hanging baskets. Wooden benches and tables had been placed at the rear of the pub, overlooking the gently flowing river.

Although it was a popular venue during the summer for a nice cool drink and a stroll along the riverbank, tonight was unusually quiet.

Swallows made the most of the last hours of daylight by

swooping low over the river, catching the myriads of insects just above the surface of the water.

Only one other couple were sitting on the benches outside the pub.

Like Danny and Sue, they too were holding hands across the table and staring out across the beautiful river to the countryside beyond.

A month had raced by since Danny had taken his father into the nursing home at Pleasley for the first time.

He had seen Sue almost every day since.

It felt easy and comfortable, like they had known each other for years.

They shared the same interests, and although she was slightly younger, their ages were close enough for it to make no difference.

Danny finished his drink and gently squeezed her hand.

'Do you fancy another drink, Sue, or shall we have a stroll along the river?'

'Let's go for that walk, shall we? It's a lovely evening and the river looks beautiful.'

The talk was relaxed as they strolled slowly along the path at the water's edge, his arm draped protectively around her shoulders, her arm around his waist.

Danny could not remember when he had last felt this happy.

'What a beautiful spot,' she purred.

The sun was sinking slowly down on the horizon, and the colour of the wide river had changed to a deep orange hue mirroring the light of the setting sun.

The water flowing nearest the bank danced over the stones in the shallows and became sparks of flame, reflecting the orange and red rays of the now quickly setting sun.

'It's stunning,' he said.

They stopped walking and turned to face each other, embracing each other and kissing slowly.

'I don't want this day to end, Danny; come back and stay with me tonight.'

Danny was keen to take their growing relationship further, but didn't want to say or do anything that would jeopardise that.

He smiled and said, 'That sounds wonderful, if you're sure.'

'I'm sure.'

They turned and walked back along the river towards the pub car park, their pace a little quicker as they both anticipated the night ahead.

34

Mansfield – August 18, 1984

The low buzzing was incessant. Gradually, the dull noise wormed its way into the consciousness of the sleeping Danny Flint. Finally, the constant low-pitched droning was enough to wake him. He slowly stirred in the large double bed and reached over to the bedside cabinet where he had left his pager the night before.

Danny turned off the alarm and squinted at the number displayed on the small screen of the pager. He became aware of Sue waking next to him, and smiled as he felt the warmth of her naked body snuggling into his back.

The night before had been one of the best nights of his life. They had arrived back at the house from their evening out at Fiskerton, and no sooner were they through the front door than they were all over each other. They'd stumbled up the stairs, removing items of clothing as they went, before falling onto the top of the large double bed.

The lovemaking had been intense and frenetic the first time, but then slower and more sensual the subsequent times.

It had been almost two o'clock in the morning when they finally fell asleep in each other's arms, exhausted.

Bleary-eyed, Danny now looked at his watch. It was only seven fifteen in the morning. The message on the pager was requesting him to contact the control room at Mansfield Police Station.

Today was Danny's scheduled day off, so he knew immediately that something must be seriously wrong if Rob Buxton couldn't handle it. He knew Rob would have arrived at work that morning around six o'clock.

'What is it, sweetheart?' said a very sleepy Sue as she slowly caressed his back with her index finger.

'My pager's gone off; I've got to phone the control room at Mansfield. Where's your phone?'

'It's in the hallway at the bottom of the stairs.'

He quickly sat up and got out of the warm bed. He retrieved his boxer shorts from the floor next to the bed, where he'd dropped them the night before.

He found his trousers in the hall at the top of the stairs, and his shirt and tie halfway down the stairs. Danny smiled as he noticed items of Sue's clothing scattered everywhere too.

Standing in just his boxer shorts, he picked up the phone and dialled the number for the control room.

'Hello, it's Detective Inspector Flint. I've received a pager message to contact you.'

The control room inspector was very matter of fact as he informed Danny the reason for the pager call.

'Yes, sir, we've had a radio message from DS Buxton. He's asking that you join him urgently at the layby on the A611, just outside Annesley Village. I'm afraid the body of a woman was found there this morning by a man out jogging. DS Buxton has already requested that Scenes of Crime officers and a Home Office pathologist attend. I've already sent messages to the other detectives on your team, asking them to come in to work early.'

Danny absorbed the message quickly.

'Okay, I'm on my way,' he said.

He added, 'Contact DS Buxton for me and inform him that I'll be there as soon as I can.'

With that, he put the phone down. He turned and saw a naked Sue standing at the top of the stairs.

'You're not coming back to bed, are you?' she said, disappointment in her voice.

He was frantically getting dressed, locating the other items of his missing clothing.

'I've got to go in to work. I'm really sorry.'

She turned and went back into the bedroom, emerging a few seconds later wearing a cream silk robe. Quickly, she made her way down the stairs until she was standing next to Danny.

'Is everything okay?' There was genuine concern in her voice now.

'I don't think it is. A woman's body has been found over at Annesley, and it sounds like she's been murdered.'

'Oh my God, Danny, that's awful.'

He grabbed his jacket from the bannister rail.

'I've got to go right now. I'm so sorry, Sue.'

'No, I understand. You hurry.'

She grabbed him by the lapels of his jacket, pulling him close, and kissed him hard on the mouth. She felt amazing beneath the silk robe.

'You were amazing last night,' she purred.

'So were you. I'm shattered.'

Sue relaxed her arms, and he slipped out of her embrace.

'Call me when you can, Danny. I love you.'

The three small words almost stopped him in his tracks.

'I love you too, sweetheart. I'll call you as soon as I can.'

35

Woods near Annesley Village – August 18, 1984

As Danny approached the layby on the A611 Annesley Bypass, he could already see the blue lights of the police vehicles parked by the side of the road.

He stopped his own car a little further back from the last marked police vehicle.

A single panda car was parked actually in the layby on the other side of the crime scene tape that cordoned off the entrance.

Rob Buxton had obviously already been busy protecting the scene. As Danny walked quickly towards the layby, he saw Rob standing in a full forensic suit, complete with overshoes and gloves, talking to a young police constable at the side of the panda car. Even from that distance, Danny could tell that the young constable had been sick. He was deathly white and was doubled over.

Waiting behind the tape, Danny shouted to Rob, 'Where's it okay to walk?'

'You're okay to walk down to us, boss. There's nothing on the road.'

Danny walked down to his sergeant. 'What have we got? The control room said a woman's body has been found?'

'It's a bad one, Danny.'

The uniformed officer doubled over and dry heaved again. Danny put his hand on the officer's back and said quietly, 'Get up onto the road and get some water, son. We'll talk to you in a little while.'

He watched as the young constable gingerly walked out of the layby and onto the road, where he was helped by his uniform colleagues.

'If he's been right down to the scene, I want his boots and his uniform at some stage,' said Danny.

'No problem, Danny, that's what I was just telling him. PC Symonds assures me he never went close to the body. He was the first officer here after it was called in. He's only got six months' service in, and I'm afraid it's been a bit much for him. It's definitely a murder, as you'll see in a minute. Scenes of Crime are here already; Rachel's down at the scene with them and has started the log. She arrived here about ten minutes after me. I've just finished talking to the jogger who found the dead woman; I've got all his details. Andy's still travelling, but he's got the furthest to come. As soon as he arrives, I'll set him on getting the statements from Mr Rose, our jogger, and also PC Symonds. I'll ensure Andy seizes all the clothing and footwear from PC Symonds and Mr Rose. I think it'd be a good idea if Andy takes the statement from PC Symonds rather than allowing him to write it himself. Andy won't miss anything.'

'Have we got a pathologist here yet?'

'The on-call Home Office pathologist has been called and is on his way. It's Seamus Carter.'

'Well, that's some good news at least. Seamus is the best.'

Danny had worked alongside Seamus Carter previously on a number of suspicious deaths. The two men were of a similar age and got on really well. They socialised off duty, mainly because of their shared passion for football. Seamus Carter was a massive Nottingham Forest supporter.

'Thanks for getting everything organised so quickly, Rob.'

'No problem, Danny.'

'Where's the body?'

'Follow the tape; it's a few minutes' walk into the woods. Keep to the left of the tape and you'll eventually come to an area where the trees thin out a bit. The woman's body is in a natural clearing in the trees.'

'Is there another forensic suit in your car? I've come here straight from home.'

'There's a couple of spares in the boot of the CID car. It's just up on the road. Give me a minute. I'll get you one.'

As Rob walked off to get the forensic suit, thoughts began racing through Danny's head.

There was no way he could investigate a murder with this small team and still be expected to provide CID cover for the division.

Something would definitely have to give now. A serious major enquiry such as this had always been his biggest fear.

Rob returned quickly with the suit, which Danny put on along with gloves and overshoes.

'This way. Stick to the left of the tape; we've kept off the main footpath. Scenes of crime are interested in some foot marks along there. I've instructed one of the PCs up at the road to look out for Seamus Carter and to radio me when he arrives so I can bring him down to the scene.'

The two detectives made their way through the wood, being extremely careful and observant as to where they placed their feet. They also deliberately avoided brushing against branches and shrubs along the route. The last thing they wanted to do was destroy any potential evidence by being careless. When Danny saw the body of the murdered woman, he understood completely why young PC Symonds had been so affected.

The scene was one of utter carnage and depravity.

Danny could see the body of the woman lying naked on her back, her arms outstretched in the crucifix position, her legs wide open, exposing her genitalia.

Her face no longer existed; it had been smashed to a pulp and was now just a black mess of dried blood, matted blonde hair and disfigured flesh and bone.

He saw that both the hands had been mutilated – all the fingers and both thumbs had been severed and were nowhere to be seen. Carefully, he made his way nearer to the body. On closer inspection he could see ligature marks around the wrists. She had been bound at some stage.

Perhaps the single most disturbing thing about this horrific sight was two words carved into the flesh of the woman's chest and stomach. The wounds had been caused by a very sharp blade and had started to pare back. The lettering was now distorted, but still legible.

The first word just above her breasts said 'SCAB'.

The second word on her stomach below the breasts said 'LOVER'.

'Jesus Christ!' muttered Danny

He turned to see Tim Donnelly, the man in charge of the Scenes of Crime team, standing at the tree line, holding an evidence bag.

'Morning, Tim, have you found anything we can use?'

'It's early days, sir, but so far nothing. Everything's been taken away.'

'What do you mean, taken away?'

'Well, things we'd usually expect to find at murder scenes, we just aren't finding here. Obviously, she's naked, but her clothes have been taken away. She was killed here – the blood spatter on the plants shows us that all this damage was caused here – but her clothes have been stripped from her afterwards. You can see marks in the blood on her body where it stopped at her clothing. Which means the clothing was removed after the injuries were caused. You've spotted the ligature marks on her wrists; well, whatever she was bound with has also been removed. Weapons have been used, and some sort of cutting implement was used to damage her hands, but there's no sign of any of them. The fingers and both thumbs are all missing. My preliminary observations of the body reveal no obvious fibres from clothing, but like I say, it's still early days.'

'Thanks, Tim.'

A message came over Rob Buxton's radio, informing him that Seamus Carter had arrived. He immediately began to retrace his steps to meet the pathologist and guide him back into the scene. Danny then turned to a very pale-looking Rachel; she was standing in her forensic suit at the edge of the clearing, clutching a clipboard that contained the log of the scene.

Rachel was staring transfixed at the body of the murdered woman.

Danny asked, 'Are you okay, Rachel?'

'I don't understand. How could anyone do this to another human being?'

'I've no answer to that question, Rachel. All I know is that we've got to do everything we can to find the monster capable of doing this. We need to find them and lock them up so they never have the chance to do it again. Have you logged me into the scene?'

'Yes. Boss, I logged you and the sarge in, and I've logged him back out again.' There was now more than a hint of steel in her voice.

Danny squatted down near to the left side of the body.

He slowly rubbed his chin with his left hand. He was perplexed by what his Scenes of Crime officer had said.

There should be things here.

His thoughts were interrupted by the sound of approaching voices. He recognised the booming voice and raw Irish brogue of Seamus Carter, the pathologist.

Seamus was a bear of a man. He was over six feet five and weighed around eighteen stone, with a mop of red hair and a large bushy red beard. He had a big personality to match. As he entered the clearing and saw the body, he slowly exhaled in a low whistle.

'Sweet Jesus! What kind of maniac have we got in our midst? Morning, Danny, what can you tell me? Any ideas who she is yet?'

'Nothing yet, Seamus. I'm hoping you can maybe help me out with who she is.'

'Working on first impressions and from what I can see so far, I think I'm going to struggle. Obviously, dental records won't help because of the huge damage to the face, and her hands have been mutilated to stop us obtaining prints. I'll see if I can help you out with a time of death, though.'

He set to work with his examination. Twenty minutes later, he again stood up.

'Well, she was definitely killed here at this location. Sometime last night, around midnight, is my best estimate. Are the undertakers on their way?'

'They're travelling, sir,' said Rob.

'Good, I want to get the body out of here and crack on with the post-mortem as soon as possible. Danny, have you noticed there's an object of some kind protruding slightly from the vagina?'

Danny shook his head slowly. Bending down to look closer, he could just about see it.

'I've no idea what it is yet; that's why I want to get this poor woman out of here as soon as possible.' He looked directly at Rob.

Rob said to Danny, 'Undertakers and transport will be here in five minutes, boss.'

'Tim, have you got all the photographs you need of the body in situ?' asked Danny.

'Yes, boss, we've got everything we need. Once the body's been removed, we'll scan this area with a fine-tooth comb. If there's anything here, we'll find it.'

'Thanks, Tim. Seamus, are you okay? Is there anything else you need to do while the body's still in situ, or can we move her?'

'I'm fine, thank you. Let's get her over to the mortuary at Mansfield.'

The big Irishman glanced at his watch. 'It's just coming up to eight thirty. Shall we say nine thirty at the mortuary?'

'Okay, I've got to finish up here at the scene first. Then I'll join you there as quick as I can.'

Danny tried to remain optimistic for his team, but he was extremely worried. He could already see that whoever was responsible for this brutal killing was showing signs of being extremely forensically aware. The mutilation of the face and hands was obviously an attempt at trying to delay or prevent identification of the woman.

Then, on top of all that, there was the macabre message carved into the torso of the woman.

Unanswered questions were racing through Danny's mind.

Was it at all possible that this murder could be politically motivated?

Could a murder as horrific and savage as this one possibly have any connection to the ongoing bitter industrial dispute?

Danny's thoughts then turned to the object that had been inserted into the dead woman's vagina.

It was gearing up to be every detective's worst nightmare. There was the frenzied attack, plus evidence of a calculating and organised killer, and the possibility of a sexual or political motive, or both.

Finally, to top it all off, Danny knew he had nowhere near enough staff to investigate it properly.

The undertakers arrived and began the grisly task of removing the body under the close supervision of the pathologist and the Scenes of Crime team.

Danny looked on, wondering how it could possibly be that less than twelve hours ago he'd been the happiest he'd been in years. Now he felt like a three-ton weight was slowly grinding him into the floor.

36

Mansfield Mortuary – August 18, 1984

'Come in, gentlemen,' said Seamus Carter.

The pathologist stood on the far side of the stainless-steel examination table. Standing next to him was a young woman.

As the two detectives walked into the examination room at Mansfield Mortuary, Danny's thoughts turned to the last time he and Rob were in this room a couple of months ago. On that occasion they'd attended the post-mortem examination of Albie Jones, the miner who'd been found dead at Warsop Main Colliery.

Carter said, 'Detectives, this young lady is my student. Stephanie Bridges. She is here to assist me with the post-mortem examination and will be taking photographs throughout.'

Danny nodded towards the young woman before staring down at the examination table.

Laid out in front of them was the body of the woman

recovered from Annesley Woods.

Now in this sterilised, clinical setting, under the glaring white lights, the enormous damage caused to the woman's face and head could be clearly seen. The lower jawbone had been exposed and was jutting out grotesquely from the side of the woman's head. The gaping hole that had once been her mouth was now totally devoid of any teeth.

Both eyes had been obliterated, as had the sockets that once housed them. The creamy-coloured bone of the skull could be seen on her forehead, where a large flap of skin had been pared back, the huge fractures on the forehead visible.

'Danny, I don't need to tell you that you're dealing with a monster here, right enough,' said the big Irishman quietly.

He pointed to the smashed skull. 'The level of violence used to cause all these devastating injuries is way more than was necessary to cause her death. Even if, as I suspect, it has been done to avoid or hinder the identification process, it's way over the top. Whoever did this firstly really hates women, and secondly really enjoys the violence.'

Danny tried to remain focused and not be overwhelmed by the grisly injuries.

'Any idea what was used to cause the injuries?' he asked.

'Now that I've had the chance to have a close look under these powerful lights, I can see what appears to be scuff marks around the sides of the head and the remnants of the ears. I would normally associate that type of marking with kicking. I think the murderer started the assault by kicking her around the head and face. Most of the subsequent and more significant damage has been caused by a heavy blunt instrument. My best guess would be some kind of hammer. At the centre of one of the fractures on the forehead is a round indentation, but the width considerable. Therefore, a large hammer.'

'What about the injuries to her hands?' asked Rob.

'I think something like small garden shears or bolt croppers to remove the fingers and thumbs. The damage to the palms of her hands, however, has been caused by a very sharp blade, possibly a craft knife or a Stanley knife. Whatever was used to slash the hands, it was also the same instrument used to carve out the two words on her torso.'

He paused, turning to his assistant Stephanie Bridges, who was standing ready with the camera.

'Steph, have you got all the pictures needed of the injuries to the head and face?'

The young assistant nodded.

Seamus returned his attention to the detectives.

'Okay then, gents, shall we see what's been inserted in her vagina? Steph, I want photos of every stage as we remove this item, okay?'

'I'm on it,' the assistant said eagerly.

She positioned herself at the foot of the examination table and quickly changed the film in the camera.

It was possible for police Scenes of Crime officers to obtain these photographs, but Seamus Carter always preferred to have his own assistant in the examination room. He believed it served as a valuable learning aid for his students to assist him at post-mortem examinations.

Using a pair of thin forceps, very slowly the pathologist gently eased the foreign object out of the vagina. The camera constantly clicked throughout this process, with Stephanie eager to record every detail. Finally, the object was fully extracted and was revealed to be a black plastic tube approximately one inch in diameter and six inches in length.

Seamus picked the object up with the forceps and placed it carefully on a plastic tray. He then carried it over to a bench at the side of the examination room. On this bench was a large magnifying glass that was surrounded by a fluorescent light.

Both Danny and Rob watched closely as the pathologist examined the object under the magnifying glass.

'This is getting ever more bizarre, Danny. There's something inside the tube.'

Using a small set of tweezers, Seamus eased a rolled-up piece of paper out of the tube. Once again, Stephanie's camera was clicking and whirring constantly. Eventually, using great care, Seamus delicately unfurled the paper, then assisted by Stephanie, he placed the sheet of paper on a separate tray.

Danny leaned forward to look at the paper. 'There may be fingerprints on the paper, Seamus. I'll need to get it nin tested as soon as possible.

'Stephanie, can you get plenty of photographs of the paper, please?'

'Will do, sir.'

The assistant understood the instruction. She knew that the ninhydrin, or nin, test was a process used to obtain fingerprints from paper. It was extremely effective but could seriously discolour the original paper.

Both detectives examined the paper closely. They could see that on the paper was a typewritten note.

Seamus said, 'Alright, Detectives, don't keep me in suspense. What's the message from our murderer?'

Rob read the note aloud:

This scab loving bitch is just the first.
While EVIL Thatcher and her storm trooper coppers are killing the coalfields
I will continue to kill more scab loving whores
The Coal Killer

THE NOTE HAD BEEN PREPARED USING a typewriter. The lower case letter *c* was slightly raised above the line of writing.

'Danny, have you noticed the typewriter key for the letter *c* is damaged?' said Rob.

'Well spotted! That'll make the typewriter identifiable, at

least. The press will have a field day with this. "The Coal Killer," for Christ's sake.'

Seamus returned to the body of the young woman and began the full post-mortem examination. As he worked, he dictated his findings into a Dictaphone; a comprehensive written report would be prepared later. His work was steady and very methodical. As he worked, he handed Rob various items for recording as exhibits. The detectives listened intently, knowing not to interrupt and to save any questions until after he had completely finished his examination.

Finally, the post-mortem was complete.

Seamus took off his gloves and turned to Danny.

'Okay, I'll give you a quick summary and go into more detail in my written report, if that's okay?'

'Of course, Seamus, fire away.'

'Despite all of the horrific injuries to her head and face, the actual cause of death was asphyxia. She was strangled to death by a very thin cord, probably of a nylon make. Very thin but very strong. There are profound ligature marks on the skin of the neck, and because the cord was so thin, there is considerable damage to the windpipe. I'm pretty certain that the rest of this woman's horrendous injuries were all caused after her death. Reasonably quickly after her death, but definitely post-mortem.'

He continued, 'There's absolutely no evidence of any sexual activity, which is surprising to me, only because of the way the body was staged at deposition. That and the fact that a foreign object had been placed in the vagina. There's no evidence of penetration or semen anywhere. I would estimate that our victim was a woman in her late forties, early fifties. Quite a heavy drinker and a smoker. There are no tattoos or operation scars that might help you with the identification. I hope somebody's going to miss this poor woman, or you're going to struggle to find out who she was. Sorry, Danny.'

'Do you have any thoughts on the excessive violence used

to cause all these massive injuries?'

'I'm sorry, that's a psychologist's territory. I can give an opinion, but that's all it would be, just an educated guess. Please don't hold me to it.'

'I appreciate that, Seamus, but I'd still very much like to hear your opinion.'

'Well, bizarrely, it's like looking at the work of a number of different types of killers. We've all heard the theories about ordered and organised killers in comparison to the disorganised, frenzied killers. Just looking at the injuries inflicted on this woman, it looks like she's been unfortunate enough to meet all the different types of killer rolled into one. It's either that, or everything we see before us today is just an elaborate game of smoke and mirrors. Sorry, I'm not helping much, am I?'

'No, that's fine. How soon can I have your report and copies of the photographs?'

'Barring any other call-outs today, will tomorrow morning be okay?'

'That would be great, Seamus, thanks.'

Danny then turned to Rob. 'Have you finished bagging and labelling all the exhibits?'

'Yes, boss.'

'Right then, we need to get back to the nick. I'm going to need more staff; there's no way Jackson can refuse now. Let's get back and regroup. Rachel will have finished up at the scene now, and Andy should have finished getting the statements of Mr Rose and PC Symonds. We need to sort out where we're going with this and quickly. You saw the note; there's a very real prospect of this maniac doing this again. '

As they walked towards the door of the mortuary, Seamus Carter bellowed after them in his booming voice, 'Good hunting, Detectives!'

Danny and Rob nodded grimly and continued out the door without looking back.

37

Mansfield Police Station – August 18, 1984

It was now almost two o'clock in the afternoon. The small CID team were gathered in their office; they had been joined by Tim Donnelly from the Scenes of Crime Department.

Danny raised a hand and addressed the small gathering.

'Right, let's get cracking; I've got a meeting with Superintendent Jackson in an hour to get more staff. I'm not taking no for an answer this time. Right, Rachel and Tim, what have we got at the scene?'

It was Tim who spoke. 'I'm afraid there's very little at the scene. We've found footprints leading down to the scene and back up to the layby that we know definitely haven't been made by the police officers who subsequently attended. The significance of this being that the marks found appear to be of shoes or boots that are covered. We see the same type of footprints left by police officers when they're wearing overshoes. We've found absolutely no fibres of any kind on the ground or the surrounding vegetation. Again, as a general rule, it's something we'd expect to find at a scene such as this one. It's already very evident that your killer's extremely forensically aware and has taken every precaution to prevent leaving any trace evidence. I'm convinced this is also the reason why the clothes of the deceased were removed from the scene by the killer. It's been done purely and simply to prevent us finding fibres that may have been transferred onto her clothes from either the killer or whatever was used to transport her to that location.'

'Thanks, Tim. Have we got anything at all, exhibit-wise, from the scene?'

'We've found a number of broken teeth around the scene, which we've bagged up. I don't think they're going to be any use to you for identification purposes.'

'Any observations of the scene from you, Rachel?'

'No, boss, other than, as Tim says, I've never been to such a sterile crime scene. The only other thing worth mentioning is how out-of-the-way the deposition site is. Unless you know that area well, you'd never know that layby existed. It's hardly visible from the road.'

'That's a good point, Rachel. I'd like you, as of right now, to start going through all our missing persons reports. Let the control room know that you're to be notified immediately if anyone reports a female, between forty and fifty-five years of age, missing. We know she was blonde, quite slim and about five feet two inches tall. She liked a drink and was either a smoker or has recently stopped. I know it's not much to go on, but it's all we have. Hopefully, somewhere out there, somebody will be missing a wife, a mum, a sister or a daughter. We need a break, and we need it fast.'

'Okay, boss, no problem. I'll let the control room know straight away.'

'Thanks, Rachel. Andy, tell me about our witnesses, please?'

'Our jogger, Mr Nathan Rose, is a twenty-year-old student currently studying at Nottingham Trent University out at Brackenhurst near Southwell. He's originally from Stone in Staffordshire. He's currently living at Chapel Terrace in Newstead Village, in a rented house he shares with two other students. The other two students have already gone home for the summer, one to Newcastle and one to London. Those two have been back home for the past four weeks and aren't expected back in Newstead for at least another fortnight. Nathan has the loan of a horse at Blidworth, so he's had to stay here to take care of it. He's studying equine dentistry at Brackenhurst, so his passion is horses. I've checked him on the PNC, and he's got no record of any convictions. I've checked his housemates, and they're both clean, too. This afternoon I made a discreet enquiry at Brackenhurst College. They're closed for the summer holidays, but the secretaries are there this week. The secretary I spoke to knows Nathan quite well; apparently he's a model student who's well into keep-fit and athletics as well as everything horsy. Unlike most students, he's not interested in drinking. When I spoke to Nathan, he told me that he regularly runs between Newstead and Hucknall to keep fit. He uses several different routes that either go through the woodland or around the farmers' fields. There was no particular reason for choosing the route he took today. I've also seized his running gear and his trainers for comparison with foot marks found at the scene. They are Nike Fireblades.'

Tim Donnelly interrupted. 'We've taken impressions of a training shoe print, but it was in an area well away from the body.'

Andy continued. 'Yeah, that would tie in with what he's saying, Tim. He told me that he realised it was a body straight away. He made a mental note of his location and then ran to the nearest phone box, which was back in Newstead Village. Having made the three nines call to the police, telling them what he'd found, he then ran back to the layby and waited for the cops to arrive. He was waiting in the layby when the panda car arrived. He then took PC Symonds into the woods and showed him the location of the body. Nathan told me that he then helped the officer back to the police car as he was being sick. I've checked, and the call was made from the telephone box he described. Although embarrassed a little about throwing up, Symonds corroborates everything Nathan Rose has said. I think Rose is a stand-up guy, boss, but just to be on the safe side, I've fired a check into the local police in Stone, Staffordshire, to make sure there aren't any dark secrets lurking at home. Rose has promised to stick around and to be available if we need anything else.'

'Does he have a girlfriend, Andy?' asked Danny.

'Nobody special at the moment, boss. He's seeing a girl from the college, but it's low key. Nathan says they just date if there's a movie they both want to see, that sort of thing.'

'Can PC Symonds add anything else?'

'Not really, but just for the record, I've seized the uniform and footwear he was wearing today, in case any fibres are found at a later date.'

'Thanks, Andy, good work. Have they both made written statements?'

'Yes, boss, I've taken them.'

'Thanks, Andy. Rob, is there anything else you can add?'

'When I left the scene earlier, I took several different routes to and from the layby. There isn't a CCTV camera in sight anywhere, so we're getting no help in that area. There are no other houses or buildings of any kind within a mile of the deposition site, so there's no house-to-house to be done yet. If we get any further information on who our victim is or where she was abducted from, then we might need a team of officers for house-to-house enquiries. I'm happy that there's no chance we've missed anything at the scene. The uniform lads, along with Tim's team, have done a very thorough fingertip search. Sorry, no pun intended, boss. They found nothing apart from the few broken teeth we spoke about earlier. I've had the photos of the typed note left by the killer blown up for later use, should we ever manage to find the typewriter used. We can maybe get an exact match from the damaged key.'

Once Rob had finished, Tim Donnelly spoke up. 'I've had the Ninhydrin test on the killer's note fast-tracked, and the result's back already. Unfortunately, it's a big fat zero. There were no marks of any kind found on the note.'

Danny took a brief moment to absorb all the information he'd just received.

'Right, folks, I'm going to see Superintendent Jackson now about staffing levels. I'll also be having a conversation with him about what details we are prepared to release to the press at this stage. I have made arrangements to do a full press release for the TV later today. My personal view is that, for the time being, we at least keep the contents of the note and the fact that words have been carved into the body to ourselves. I can't see any merits in releasing that information to the press right now. Andy, did you impress on Nathan Rose that he wasn't to discuss the details of what he saw this morning with anybody?'

'I did, and he assures me that he's no intention of talking to anybody about it.'

Danny turned to his small team.

'I want all our efforts for the time being to be focussed on the identification of the dead woman. The fact is, we've got no worthwhile witnesses and no forensic evidence to follow up, so until we can identify our victim, we're struggling. Unless anybody has anything to add, or any questions, let's get cracking.'

Nothing was said, and the team immediately began getting on with their individual tasks.

38

Mansfield Police Station – August 18, 1984

'This is bad, Danny, really bad.'

Superintendent Ken Jackson was shaking his head as he tried to take in what Danny had just told him.

'As soon as you've done your press appeal later, there'll be every shade of shit hitting the fan. I totally agree with you: We keep both the message carved on the body and the typewritten note to ourselves. I'll go over to the chief constable's office this afternoon to brief him. Will you be available to attend that briefing this afternoon?'

'Yes, sir, of course I can attend the briefing, but what I really need is more staff!'

'From what I've heard so far, Danny, until you discover the identity of this dead woman, there aren't any manpower-intensive enquiries to do, or have I misunderstood that?'

'No, sir, you haven't misunderstood me. But I'm confident

that with more staff on the ground, we'll be able to identify this woman a lot quicker. Believe me, when you've seen the handiwork of this maniac close up, time really is of the essence here. The last thing we can afford to do is drag our feet and allow another woman to be murdered.'

'Danny, don't try to play emotional blackmail with me. As soon as the woman's been identified, I promise you I'll re-evaluate the levels of manpower you need for each enquiry and provide more staff accordingly. The best I can do, in the meantime, is to get two of your detectives recalled from strike duty to run the CID office while your team remains focussed on this murder enquiry.'

'Look, sir, with respect, you're missing the point: The more manpower I have, the easier it'll be to swamp the area and try to ascertain who this woman is.'

'No, you're the one who's missing the point! What I've just offered you is the best I can do at the moment. This strike isn't going away any time soon, and our resources are already stretched to the limit. I cannot justify taking any more men from the PSUs.'

Danny was starting to get annoyed and frustrated.

'And how will you justify the death of another innocent woman if this maniac means what he said in the note, and this woman is just the first?'

'That note contains nothing more than the ramblings of a lunatic. I don't put any credibility into that claim, and I'm sure the chief constable will agree with me this afternoon. I'm warning you, Detective Inspector Flint, you'd better moderate your tone this afternoon, is that clear?'

'Oh yes, crystal clear, sir.'

'Be back here at three thirty sharp, ready to travel over to headquarters.'

'Yes, sir. In the meantime, I'll make arrangements for the press appeal to be done after that at headquarters. Will you be joining me on the press appeal, sir?'

'No. I'm sure you can handle that.'

Danny came out of the office feeling exhausted, and walked slowly back to his office. He couldn't believe what he'd just heard: 'the ramblings of a lunatic,' the superintendent had said.

They were exactly that, but he'd missed off one word. He should have described the note as the ramblings of a *homicidal* lunatic.

He slumped down in a chair in the CID office.

'Everything okay, Danny? You look shattered,' said Rob.

Danny started to explain to Rob about the two extra staff and the rest of the conversation he'd just had with Ken Jackson.

Suddenly, Rachel came hurtling into the office.

'I think we've just had a huge slice of luck. The barmaid at the Prince Charles pub in Forest Town has just phoned the nick to complain about a bloke coming into the pub demanding to know where his girlfriend is. He'd threatened to smash the pub up if the barmaid didn't tell him the name of the bloke his girlfriend had gone off with when she left the pub last night. The uniform lads have got the guy at the pub now. He's still kicking off and has been arrested.'

'Exactly how is that lucky for us?' asked Rob.

'Because the barmaid says the woman in question is always going off with different blokes. Her name's Mandy Stokes, she's forty-seven years old, a blonde, and apparently has legs to die for. The sergeant in the control room thought she sounded similar to the missing person reports.'

'Right, you two, get straight over to the Prince Charles pub. Let the cops arrest the guy kicking off for a breach of the peace; he can be left in the cells here for us to talk to later. First of all, I want this barmaid talking to properly; fetch her back here. I want chapter and verse on this Mandy Stokes. I'm going with Jackson to see the chief constable at headquarters later to discuss staffing levels, and I've still got to make the arrangements for a full press appeal. Rob, I want a full update from you the minute I get back.'

'Yes, boss!' Rob shouted as he and Rachel legged it out the door.

39

Mansfield Police Station – August 18, 1984

'I'm not one to moan, Detective. I just don't know why I had to come down here, that's all I'm saying.'

The complaining voice belonged to Trisha Miller, the barmaid from the Prince Charles pub, who had called the police about the disturbance earlier.

She continued angrily, 'I could've told you everything I know at the pub. I bloody hate cop shops.'

Rachel tried to soothe the angry barmaid.

'Look, Trisha, I've got a lot to ask you, and it's not going to take five minutes. The pub was heaving, and this is important; surely you realise that. I can't talk to you in between you pulling pints for the punters, now can I?'

'Okay, I get it, but how long's this going to take?'

'I'll try to get through everything as quick as I can. The landlord's fine with it; he's told me to take as long as I need. He's assured me he won't be stopping your money. I'll be as quick as I can, I promise you, but I have to be thorough as well. I can't afford to miss anything out.'

Trisha sat open-mouthed for a few seconds before smiling and saying, 'Bloody hell, I can't believe you've got that tight bastard at the pub to pay my wages while I'm stuck down here. How did you manage that, sweetheart?'

'I can be very persuasive when I have to be, Trisha, so don't worry about losing any money. I need you to concentrate fully on what we're going to be talking about.'

Trisha Miller shrugged in resignation.

She was still an attractive woman, with a pretty face and bright blue eyes. Her blonde hair was cut in an elfin style. Even after having her three children, she still managed to keep her figure. She considered her full breasts to be her best asset and always wore low-cut blouses.

Today was no different, and she'd already noticed more than one appreciative glance from the boys in blue at the police station.

Leaning back in the chair, Trisha took a sip of the coffee she'd been given. 'Okay, what do you want to know?'

Rachel leaned forward, placing her elbows on the table. 'When did you last see Mandy Stokes?'

'Mandy was in the pub yesterday evening; she'd been at the engagement party in the lounge bar most of the night. I didn't see much of her in there, because I was serving in the public bar last night. Mandy only came into that bar to get a drink at last orders, because she couldn't get served in the lounge bar.'

'How did she seem?'

'She was well on her way to being drunk. Let's say she'd certainly had a few, that's for sure.'

'Was she with anybody?'

'When she came into the public bar, she was on her own. I don't know if she'd been with anybody next door.'

'What did she order?'

'That's easy. Mandy always has the same drink, Bacardi and Coke.'

'How many did she have?'

'In the public bar, just one; it was last orders.'

'Did you have a chat with her or just serve her a drink?'

'We chatted, but only briefly.'

'What about?'

'Basically, I asked her if she'd copped off. Mandy said she hadn't and that they were all twats next door. She told me she'd be walking home alone as soon as she'd finished her drink.'

'Did she say which way she was going home?'

'Yeah, she did, as it happens. She said she only had to walk down Pump Hollow Lane. I remember it because I'd told her to be careful walking home on her own.'

'Can you remember what Mandy was wearing last night?'

'She'd got a short skirt on, as usual. You can't blame the girl; she's got great legs for her age. I think the skirt was white, and she'd got a black see-through blouse on.'

'How well do you know Mandy?'

'Everyone in the village knows Mandy, as she's a bugger for the men. That knobhead who came in the pub shouting the odds today thinks he's her boyfriend. Mandy's got lots of blokes on the go, if you know what I mean, Detective?'

'Is she very promiscuous?'

'If that means does she shag about, then yes, she does!'

'And you're certain Mandy left the pub alone and was going to go straight home?'

'That's what she said, and I didn't see anybody leave with her or after her.'

Rachel paused thoughtfully.

'All these men she sees, have you ever heard any of them make any kind of threat to her face, or threaten her behind her back?'

'No, I've never heard anything like that. All the blokes

involved with Mandy know exactly what she's like. I think they just enjoy copping off with her. She must be hot stuff, eh?'

Trisha winked at the detective.

'What about the guy we arrested at the pub today?'

'You mean Mr Knobhead? I don't really know him; he's a lorry driver from out of town. I think he stays with Mandy when he's up this way.'

'Was he in the pub last night?'

'I didn't see him, and Mandy did tell me she was going home on her own.'

Rachel had nearly finished.

'Trisha, have you ever been to Mandy's house?'

'No, never. I like her, but we're not friends, if you know what I mean. I know where her house is, but I've never been inside.'

'Does Mandy have any kids or other next of kin that live nearby?'

'I think she's got a grown-up daughter, but I haven't a clue where she lives. I know her husband left the area when they split up; he went back to Ireland, I think. Mandy's lived on her own ever since. As long as I've known her, Mandy's always been footloose and fancy-free.'

Not anymore, thought Rachel, *if Mandy does turn out to be the murdered woman.*

'Okay, Trisha, thanks. You've been a great help. I need to take a written statement from you, so I can get down on paper what you've just told me about last night. I promise you it won't take long.'

Trisha sighed loudly. 'Alright, Detective, but before you start, is there any chance I can have another coffee, please?'

'Of course you can. I'll go and grab us some coffee. I'll have one with you while I'm writing your statement.'

At the same time as Rachel was talking to Trisha Miller,

just along the corridor in the cell block area, Rob was going into an interview room with Ted Grozier.

He was the lorry driver from out of town who had been arrested to prevent a breach of the peace at the Prince Charles pub.

Grozier had been technically released without charge, now that there was no likelihood of the breach of the peace, which he had instigated, reoccurring.

He was now assisting Rob voluntarily with his enquiries.

Ted Grozier was forty-three years old and was quite short and stocky, with receding brown hair. He was wearing a pair of bottle-green overalls with the name 'Kleenwipes' embroidered in yellow thread on the left breast pocket.

He had a ruddy complexion and the biggest hands the detective had ever seen.

Rob sat quietly and stared directly across the interview desk at Grozier.

'Ted, my name's Detective Sergeant Rob Buxton. I've a few questions for you before you leave the police station. Are you happy to stay and assist me with my enquiries?'

Grozier simply nodded.

'Ted, we're concerned that Mandy Stokes appears to have gone missing. I need to find out if there's anything you know that might assist us in finding her.'

'Okay, Sergeant, if there's any way I can help you, I will.'

Even though, technically, Grozier had been released from custody, Rob had no intention of letting him leave the police station. If Grozier made any attempt to leave, Rob had already made up his mind to arrest him on suspicion of murder. But for now, he wanted to try to keep Grozier happy and helping voluntarily.

Rob had noted a strong Welsh accent from Grozier's first reply.

'That's not a local accent, Ted. Where are you from?'

'I'm from Rhyl in Wales. I drive an HGV, delivering toilet rolls all over the UK.'

'Which firm do you drive for?'

'It's a firm called Kleenwipes.'

He pointed to the embroidered name badge on his overalls and continued, 'They're a big company. They provide toilet rolls and tissues to hotels all over the country.'

'Do you drive all over the UK, then?'

'Yes, everywhere. It depends on where the orders are. I can be in Scotland one day, then back down to the Midlands the next.'

'So you don't do a regular delivery, then?'

'No. I'm all over everywhere, me, Detective.'

'How long you've known Mandy Stokes?'

'I've known my Mandy for just over a year now. We first met when she was on holiday in Rhyl, my home town, see. We had a few drinks together and got on really well. We're both single and, well, you know, one thing led to another, and we ended up sleeping together. She gave me her address up here, and said if ever I was delivering up this way, I should call in.'

'Do you see her up here very often?'

He thought for a moment, and made eye contact with the detective. 'I only deliver up here once in a blue moon. Since we first met in Rhyl, I think I've only seen Mandy about five times. When I found out yesterday that I was coming up to Nottingham today, I called Mandy and arranged to see her. I did my drop at the Grosvenor Hotel in Nottingham at about half past four this morning, and then drove straight to Mandy's house. I won't lie to you, Detective; I was bloody angry when she wasn't at home. I knew she was going to that party last night, and I just assumed she'd copped off with another bloke. That's why I was angry, see.'

'I can see why that would get you annoyed, Ted. So what time did you arrive at Mandy's house this morning?'

'I got to Mandy's place at around five fifteen. There was no answer when I knocked on the door. I thought that was odd, because normally Mandy's up and waiting for me when she knows I'm coming over. It's always the same routine: She does me some nice bacon and eggs, standing there in her little nightie, teasing me with her great legs and arse. I eat my breakfast while she has a cup of coffee and a fag, and then we go back to bed. You know what I'm saying, Detective, you're a man of the world. I don't have to spell it out to you, do I?'

'No, I get the picture. Did you go into Mandy's house this morning?'

'Yeah, that's how I knew she hadn't been home. Mandy always leaves a spare front door key under a brick in the front garden. The key was there, so I went in. It was obvious she hadn't been home.'

'Where's this front door key now, Ted?'

'It's here.' Grozier fumbled in his trouser pocket and removed a Yale door key, which he handed over to Rob.

'Ted, why did you assume that Mandy had gone off with another bloke last night?'

'Come off it, Detective, I'm not stupid. I know what my Mandy's like; she's the kind of woman who needs a man in her bed. I'm not daft enough to think I'm the only one.'

'Why get so angry about it at the pub, then?'

'I don't know, really. The anger, it just came over me, I suppose. I think it was just because we'd made a set arrangement, and she knew I was coming over. I just thought with her knowing I was coming, she would've been at home. I was looking forward to my bacon and eggs, not to mention the afters.'

He grinned at Rob.

'Do you know if Mandy has any family local?' asked Rob, ignoring the grin.

'All Mandy told me was that her husband had fucked off back to Ireland years ago, and that she had one daughter, who's now grown up and that she doesn't see. I think her daughter lives on the east coast somewhere, at one of the holiday places. Yeah, that's right, I think it's Skegness or maybe Mablethorpe. That's why she was having a holiday in Rhyl, so she didn't bump into her daughter.'

'Okay, Ted, thanks for being so open and honest with me. I'll need to know the name of your transport manager at Kleenwipes so I can verify your deliveries and times for today's run, and I'll also need the name of the person you spoke to at the Grosvenor Hotel in Nottingham, so I can verify what time you left there. I'll then need to take a written statement from you about everything you've told me about Mandy Stokes. Are you alright for time?'

'No problem, Detective. I'm not picking my next load up until first thing tomorrow morning. I'd planned to be spending the whole day with Mandy.'

He then looked thoughtful. 'Can I ask you a question, Detective? Why are you lot so interested in my Mandy?'

'We're just a little concerned about her being missing, that's all. Now what's the name of your transport manager?'

'His name's Brian Davies. I won't be getting into trouble with the firm when you call him, will I?'

'Don't worry about that, Ted. I'll make the call myself and tell him you witnessed a road accident or something.'

'Thanks, Detective. The other guy you wanted who works at the hotel, he's an Asian bloke. I know his first name's Manjeet, but I'm not sure of his last name. He deals with all their deliveries and unloading.'

'Thanks. Do you want a drink before I start on your written statement?'

'A cup of tea would be great, mind. Thanks.'

Rob left the room, leaving a uniformed constable outside the door. He made the two phone calls to Kleenwipes and the Grosvenor Hotel. Both calls confirmed exactly what Grozier had said about the timings of his pickup and deliveries.

He was telling the truth.

Rob returned to the interview room with two cups of tea. 'Right, Ted, let's get cracking on this statement, shall we?'

The lorry driver picked up the mug in his giant hands, sipped his tea, and nodded.

40

Pump Hollow Lane, Mansfield – August 18, 1984

Rob parked the CID car outside the row of semi-detached houses on Martyn Avenue, a quiet street just off Pump Hollow Lane at Forest Town. In the car with him were Danny and Ted Grozier.

Danny had rushed back from headquarters after doing the press appeal in front of the television cameras, standing outside the main headquarters building. He had kept the information given to the media deliberately vague, just informing them of the discovery of a woman's body off the A611 in Annesley. He had said enquiries were ongoing to establish the identity of the victim, and that he would welcome anyone who had been in the area the night before to contact him directly at Mansfield Police Station.

On his return, he had quickly been briefed by Rob, and had decided to travel with his sergeant and the lorry driver to the house on Martyn Avenue.

Grozier pointed to a large HGV that was parked up a little

further down Martyn Avenue. 'That's my wagon over there, see. I can never park the bloody thing right outside Mandy's house; it's just too long for the bend. That's her house over there, number 34.'

Rob looked over his shoulder into the rear of the car and said, 'Okay, Mr Grozier, we may need to speak to you again at some point, but for now, thanks for your help, and try to keep that temper of yours in check.'

'I will, Detective. I was only gobbing off, see. I would never hurt anyone. You'll let me know when you find Mandy, won't you? I really do like her; she's a great girl.'

'We will, Ted. Try not to worry.'

Grozier then got out of the car and walked up the road towards his HGV. The two detectives also got out of the car and made their way to the front door of 34 Martyn Avenue.

Rob knocked once; then using the key he had been given by Grozier, Rob opened the front door.

It was a typical three-bedroom, semi-detached house.

There was a lounge that went right through into a small dining room, a kitchen, hall stairs and landing, and three bedrooms and a bathroom.

The house was neat, tidy and very clean.

There were no pots and pans in the sink, the kitchen was spotless. There was plenty of food in the refrigerator. Rob took out a pack of bacon and noted that it had a long sell-by date. There was also a tray of fresh eggs.

The three bedrooms were all clean and tidy, although the third bedroom was being used more as a large store cupboard than a bedroom.

The main bedroom was a very feminine room. It had been decorated in a dusky pink theme. A large double bed covered with a thick, fresh white duvet dominated the room, and there was a large white sheepskin rug on the floor.

The bathroom was a neutral cream colour and was full of women's toiletries, bath salts, hair conditioners and the like.

There wasn't a razor blade or any aftershave. It was obvious no man lived at the house.

The detectives did a thorough search, but there was nothing to suggest that Mandy Stokes had decided to take a sudden holiday. Rob found an in-date passport for Mandy Stokes in one of the bedside table drawers in the main bedroom.

In the box room upstairs, Danny found a photo album. The album was full of pictures of a pretty, petite woman with blonde hair and long legs. In nearly every photo, the woman was wearing either a miniskirt or very short shorts.

Danny held up one of the photos. 'This must be Mandy.'

'We can soon get it verified with the barmaid at the Prince Charles, boss.'

'Yeah, let's do that. What do you reckon, Rob? Do you think Mandy Stokes is our dead woman?'

'I'd put my mortgage on it, Danny. Mandy left the pub at around eleven o'clock last night, intending to walk home alone. I think the reason she never made it home is because she was intercepted by our killer. She'd made an arrangement to see somebody today that she hasn't kept, she fits the description perfectly, and the time of death fits, as well.'

'I agree. We can't get a visual identification, but let's start doing enquiries with her local GP and get blood group, medical history, etc. I recall seeing the dead woman's blood group is AB negative, which is extremely rare. I'll talk to Seamus Carter again; I need to ascertain if the dead woman had ever been pregnant. I don't recall reading about a pregnancy in his report. I might've just missed him referring to it.'

As they left the house, Danny locked the front door and said, 'I've made my mind up. I've got to regard Mandy Stokes as our dead woman until proved otherwise. First thing in the morning, as soon as it gets light, I want a full search of this area. Start on Pump Hollow Lane from its junction with

Martyn Avenue, and work back up the hill towards the Prince Charles pub.'

'Okay, boss, I'll get that sorted.'

'I also want all the houses on Martyn Avenue, Pump Hollow Lane and the other two roads on the estate to have a full house-to-house enquiry. I want a full team on it; I want every house visited as a matter of urgency. I'll go and see Jackson and see if he's as good as his word. We definitely need the extra manpower now. You'd better have a word with Rachel and Andy; there'll be no days off for the foreseeable future. Obviously, that goes for me and you as well.'

'No problem, boss. Good luck with the extra staff. I know how stubborn Superintendent Jackson can be.'

'Stubborn or not, we've got to be given more manpower; this is a murder enquiry, for Christ's sake. One other thing, Rob, arrange for Andy to be down here at first light with the search teams so he can brief them properly. I want the Special Operations Unit out to do the search. I don't care what strike duties they've got tomorrow; this takes precedence. Andy can brief them and then the house-to-house teams. I want the house-to-house enquiries to start no later than eight o'clock in the morning.'

'Okay, Danny, I'll get it organised.'

'I know I sound like a broken record, and I know I'm fast becoming a pain in the arse!'

'I can't say I've noticed any change!'

'Very funny! I just know that we need to get cracking on this. I'm convinced that we haven't heard the last of this lunatic.'

'I know what you mean, boss, and for what it's worth, I think you're dead right. I'll get everything organised.'

41

Pump Hollow Lane, Mansfield – August 19, 1984

It was four thirty in the morning.
The early morning sky was changing from the black of night to the purple hues that appear just before the sun creeps slowly over the horizon.

The air was refreshingly cool. A group of police officers were standing outside two plain white police vans that were parked at the junction of Martyn Avenue and Pump Hollow Lane. The men spoke in hushed whispers out of deference to the early hour and the close proximity to residential properties.

Two full sections of the Special Operations Unit were being briefed by Detective Constable Andy Wills. The briefing only lasted five minutes; it was to the point. Andy quickly explained that it was suspected that a woman had been abducted from somewhere along this stretch of the road.

He made it clear to the gathered officers that he was interested in anything, however small, that looked out of place or that looked like it had recently been dropped there. He was also very interested in any signs of a struggle.

Pump Hollow Lane had been closed in both directions for the duration of the search. The entire stretch of road, between the junction of Martyn Avenue and the crossroads where the Prince Charles pub was located, was almost six hundred yards long. The road varied in width along the way, being narrower at the Martyn Avenue end.

It wasn't a busy road, especially so at this time of day, and Andy hoped his decision to close the road wouldn't cause too many issues.

Ever since the start of the strike, motorists in the area had become used to having their travel plans disrupted. All too often, the residents of this and other towns across Nottinghamshire had seen main roads closed without notice to prevent large numbers of pickets getting through to the coal mines.

At an instruction from one of the two sergeants present, the two sections of Special Ops officers spread themselves out in a line that spanned from one side of Pump Hollow Lane to the other.

From hedgerow to hedgerow, the officers were on their knees, moving slowly. Intermittently, an officer would raise his hand, and the whole line would stop. One of the section sergeants would take possession of whatever had been found and then place the object into an evidence bag before completing the relevant exhibit label.

Andy walked slowly with the two Special Ops sergeants, staying behind the line of kneeling officers, as they slowly and methodically searched every inch of the road.

After fifteen minutes of agonisingly slow progress, the man to the extreme far right of the search line stopped and raised his right arm. Once again, the entire line stopped, and as before, the section sergeant approached the man.

The sergeant turned and shouted, 'Detective, I think you'll want to see this.'

Andy walked briskly over to the far right of the line. 'What have you got, Sarge?'

'Just there, right in the bottom of the hedge.'

The sergeant indicated a handbag lying in the hedge bottom. Andy saw immediately that the handbag was clean and looked relatively dry. It was obvious it hadn't been in the hedgerow very long. The handbag was made from black leather and had a gold chain as a strap.

'Do you still have the Polaroid Instamatic cameras on the vans?' Andy asked.

'We certainly do. I'll get a couple of photographs of it in situ before we recover it.'

'Thanks, Sarge.'

The second of the two sergeants indicated for the rest of the men to resume the search while his colleague walked off to retrieve the camera from the van.

Andy looked around him. Pump Hollow Lane narrowed slightly here; the pavements were quite narrow, and he could see that there was only one old street light for this whole area. With just the one street light, this particular stretch of the road would be very dark at night.

The sergeant returned and took a couple of Polaroid photographs of the bag still lying in the hedge bottom before removing it carefully and placing it in a brown evidence bag. He completed the exhibit label and then passed everything to Andy.

Andy carried the brown bag back to his car.

He opened the boot of his car and placed a paper sheet on the floor of the boot before putting on a pair of latex gloves and removing the handbag from the evidence bag.

Andy then carefully opened the handbag and placed the individual items on the paper sheet.

There were only three items in the handbag.

A small black leather purse, a bright red lipstick and a Benson & Hedges packet that contained eleven cigarettes and a slim plastic lighter.

He opened the black purse.

The first thing he saw was a membership card for Blockbuster Video that had the name M. Stokes on the back.

'Bingo!' he said aloud, and began to replace everything. He then placed the handbag back into the evidence bag.

He left a message with the control room, instructing either DI Flint or DS Buxton to contact him at the search site as soon as they came on duty at six o'clock that morning.

42

Mansfield Police Station – August 21, 1984

It was now the morning of the third day.
Three days had come and gone since the discovery of Mandy Stokes's battered remains in Annesley Woods.

Danny had gathered his small team together in the CID office to assess how far the enquiries into her murder had progressed. He looked around the room at his team; they were all exhausted. Every one of them had remained at work since the discovery of the body, taking naps in between enquiries at work. Phone calls had been made regularly to their loved ones explaining why they were staying at work and not coming home.

The handbag found on Pump Hollow Lane during the fingertip search carried out by the Special Operations Unit had been positively identified by Trisha Miller, the barmaid at the Prince Charles pub.

She was certain that it was the bag Mandy Stokes had with

her in the pub on the night she disappeared. Trisha could remember in detail the way a drunken Mandy had noisily placed the bag on the bar as she ordered her drink.

Specifically, she recalled the gold chain-link strap that had rattled so noisily on the hard wooden bar of the pub.

Danny now addressed the team.

'I'm certain now that Mandy Stokes is our victim. The enquiries that have been made with her GP over her medical history and the fact that her blood group matches our victim have convinced me. I don't think we'll ever get a cast-iron identification, but all the evidence we have suggests that Mandy was abducted from Pump Hollow Lane and taken to Annesley Woods, where she was murdered. It occurs to me that not realising she'd dropped her handbag was the first mistake our killer has made. He's been so careful, so forensically aware, that if he'd seen her drop the bag, there's no way he would've left it behind.'

Andy then spoke up. 'Nothing else of any relevance was found on the search. I've been back there at night, and where the bag was found is the darkest part of the road. The level of street lighting is really bad.'

'There's nothing from the house-to-house as yet, either,' said Rachel.

Rob spoke next: 'I've tracked down all of Mandy's casual lovers that we know about. They can all account for their movements that night, and all their alibis check out. I've also confirmed that Ted Grozier was picking a load up in Cardiff at 12.30 a.m. on the morning Mandy was killed, which rules him out completely.'

Danny paused, taking in the information he had been given.

'Thanks, everyone. Your efforts have been amazing; I know the hours you've all put in. The good news is we're now officially dedicated to this murder enquiry full time. The superintendent has finally agreed to take one more DC and a DS off the PSUs to help take care of the everyday work generated by the CID office. This will stay the same for the duration of the strike or until we solve this murder. So, from today, all your efforts will be focussed on catching this killer. I know we don't have much to go on, but there are some enquiries still outstanding.'

Andy said, 'I'm still trying to identify the paper the note was typed on. I've sent it to the lab for analysis. I'll keep chasing it so I can then get a list of suppliers. I'm also trying to identify the make of the typewriter used from the impressions made by the keys.'

'Good work, Andy, make sure you keep at them,' said Danny.

Rachel said, 'I'm still working my way through the guest list for the engagement party at the Prince Charles pub. So far everyone remembers Mandy being there, but nobody remembers her being with anybody else.'

'How many have you still got to talk to?'

She quickly looked down at the list of names and addresses in front of her. 'I've spoken to twenty-seven of them, but there's at least another forty-six still to get through.'

'Rob, can you give Rachel a dig out on that enquiry; let's get these people seen as a matter of urgency, please. While we're at it, let's talk to Trisha Miller again and see if she can remember anything about the punters in the public bar. Up to now, we've only concentrated on the engagement party in the lounge. Let's make it a priority to identify as many punters as possible from the public bar and talk to them as well. Any one of them may have seen Mandy leaving with someone.'

'Okay, boss, we're on it,' said Rob.

'I've got to go over to headquarters again this morning to talk to the chief constable about the new television appeal that's scheduled to be broadcast this evening on the local news at half past six. I don't think he's going to want any of the items that relate to the strike forming part of the release, but we'll see. It's twenty past eight now. I want everyone back here at six o'clock this evening, before the press appeal is shown on the TV. You never know, the phones might start ringing with new information. It's going to be another long day, folks.'

43

Warsop, Nottinghamshire – August 31, 1984

As the month of August drew to a close, the number of miners regularly going into work at Warsop Main Colliery had grown to fifteen.

It was still the same routine every morning, getting the men in and out of work. The only difference was that the taxis being used to pick up the men in the morning had now been replaced by two hired Ford Transit vans.

Sergeant Mick Reynolds was still in charge of the Metropolitan Police PSU that escorted the miners into work every day.

As soon as the small convoy reached the standby point at the quarry, all the miners and the police officers would get out of the vans to stretch their legs before the 'battle bus' arrived.

The police officers would also use the time to start getting their protective clothing on. All the men, miners and police officers alike, took the opportunity to have a quick hot drink and a cigarette. And every morning, without fail, Mick Reynolds would seek out Jimmy Wade. The two men would disappear to a quiet corner of the yard to talk and smoke a cigarette over a cup of tea while they waited to make the journey into the colliery.

The other police officers in the PSU had thought it all a bit strange. They knew their sergeant kept his cards very close to his chest, so they found it slightly weird that he could find so much to laugh and joke about with the striking miner.

On one occasion, one of the young constables made a comment in the van about 'the odd couple'. Unfortunately, his careless remark was overheard by the sergeant. The young cop received an almighty dressing-down by a clearly livid Reynolds. After that incident, nobody else had dared to comment out loud again. The men all came to the decision that if he wanted to be friends with the scab miner, let him get on with it. Today was no different: the two men stood well away from the rest of the gathering. They were both smoking cigarettes and sipping hot tea.

'It's September tomorrow, for Christ's sake. I say we find another one, Jimmy.'

'The dust hasn't settled from the last one yet, Mick; we'd be crazy to go again already. You've seen the TV coverage as well as I have. That big cop is always on the telly lately. What's his name, Flint or something?'

'That's just where you're wrong, old son; it's the perfect time. That cop you're on about, Detective Inspector Flint, he knows they've got nothing. I've seen the appeals they've put out on the TV; it was pathetic. They're shit scared. They never once mentioned the connections to the strike that we left evidence for. You saw it, Jimmy. Flint never said a word about the note, nothing about the state of the body, and no mention of "the Coal Killer". Trust me, the chief constable will be more bothered about all that getting out into the public domain.'

'I don't know, Mick. I reckon just to be on the safe side, we let the dust settle for another week; then we go again.'

Mick sighed and shrugged his shoulders, finally accepting that he wasn't going to be able to change the other man's mind.

'Okay, if you insist. My deployment here finishes next week on 7 September. I'll be going home for a week the following day; I won't be back up here until the fifteenth. I'm happy to do as you say and wait another week, as long as we go again before I've got to go back. How about the night before on Thursday, 6 September?'

'Alright, you're on. I'll check out a couple of different venues this time. Last time was all a bit hit and miss. I want to make sure we go to a busy venue next time, where we can just blend in, and where there's plenty of targets to choose from.'

He smiled and fixed Mick with those cold blue eyes. 'It's my turn to actually do the killing this time, though. You hogged all the fun last time.'

Mick let out a small chuckle. 'Whatever you say, Jimmy, whatever you say.'

44

Ollerton, Nottinghamshire – September 6, 1984

Mick threw the black holdall into the boot before opening the front passenger door and getting in next to the blonde with the long hair.

'Hello, Jimmy, my old son. I swear with that wig on and with those sparkling blue eyes, you get more gorgeous every time I see you.'

He laughed raucously.

'Not funny, Mick, not funny at all.'

As soon as he had driven the car away from the layby outside Proteus Camp, Jimmy took off the wig and threw it onto the back seat of the car.

'So, Jimmy, what delightful establishment have you got lined up for us tonight?'

'We're going to a pub called the Archer. It's at a small pit village called Rainworth, about seven or eight miles from here. It's nine o'clock now, so we should be in the pub for around nine thirty.'

'Why the Archer?'

'I went one night earlier this week, and there's a Northern Soul disco on tonight. Apparently, for these music nights, the place gets rammed with birds. The pub itself is sort of out in the sticks, but it's within walking distance of both Rainworth and the next village, Blidworth. I reckon come closing time we'll be able to intercept some silly tart walking home on her own. Then it's down to us to do what we do best.'

'I can see you've been busy, old son. It all sounds very promising, very promising indeed.'

Both men laughed.

'Let's go for a pint in a different boozer first, Jimmy. I'm dying of thirst.'

'Yeah, why not?'

'Is there somewhere on the way to Rainworth?'

'Not really, but we could get a quick pint at the Robin Hood pub in Rainworth itself. You'll have to keep your gob well and truly shut in there; there'll be lads who are definitely out on strike.'

'No problem. I'll keep quiet and let you get the beers in.'

'We'll have a swift one in there; then we can park the car just up the road from the Archer and wait to see what little darling comes our way.'

'It's a marvellous plan. I'll have a cold pint of lager when we get there, cheers!'

45

Blidworth, Notts – September 6, 1984

June Hayes had been looking forward to going out all week. The other women at the Pretty Polly hosiery factory had spent all week talking the very shy June into having a night out with the girls. All the women caught the minibus, which took them from Rainworth over to the factory at Sutton in Ashfield, every day. The other women who caught the minibus all lived in Rainworth. June was the only one that lived in Blidworth. Every morning, she walked from her house in Blidworth to the Joseph Whitaker School in Rainworth to catch the bus.

The driver of the minibus always made a point of going through Blidworth first on the way home, though, so he could drop June off outside her house. The girls on the minibus had been quick to point out to June that the Archer pub was only a twenty-minute walk from her house in Blidworth and was only five minutes further down the road than the Joseph Whitaker School.

Reluctantly, she had finally agreed to go on the night out, arranging to walk to the pub and meet the other girls in there at seven thirty.

FOR THE REST of the week, the conversation on the bus was all about the Northern Soul disco at the Archer.

The girls discussed at length what they would be wearing, and the single women – and some of the married ones – had spent the week speculating on what men from the two villages would be there. Much to her own surprise, June found herself really looking forward to finally having a night out, where she could let her hair down and have some fun.

Her husband, Dave, was all for it and had readily volunteered to look after their two children for the night, a boy of eight and a girl of six.

Dave was a self-employed plumber, so although he was not directly involved in the strike, his work had suffered badly, as people in the community put off having jobs done. As the strike went on and on, there was less and less money around in the village and surrounding areas. Without the emergency work that was, more often than not, paid for by insurance companies, his little plumbing business would have gone bust a long time ago.

Dave did appreciate the extra hours June worked at the factory, trying to make ends meet. He encouraged her to go out, telling her she thoroughly deserved to have some fun with the girls.

He watched her closely as she got ready to go out.

June was thirty-two years old on her next birthday, and was still a very sexy woman. He hardly ever saw her fully made-up these days, and now, as he watched her get ready, he was still wowed by her appearance.

She had let her stunning long red hair down for the night; it was usually tied up ready for the factory. Her eyes were the brightest, most beautiful, exquisite green colour he'd ever seen. There were fine lines at the corners of her eyes that only appeared when she smiled, and that made her eyes even more beguiling.

Her figure was fuller now, after motherhood, but was still very attractive. June oozed sex appeal, which was heightened even more by the fact that she had absolutely no idea how sexy she actually was, or of the effect she had on most men.

As her husband watched her get ready to leave the house, he thought to himself just how lucky he was. He absolutely adored his stunning wife.

'Have a lovely night, sweetheart,' he said as he tried to kiss her.

She turned her head right at the last moment.

'Don't smudge my lippy.' She laughed.

He kissed her gently on the cheek.

'Are you sure you don't want picking up from the pub later? I think I should, June; it'll be late.'

'No, Dave, I'll be fine. You can't leave the kids on their own in the house just to come and fetch me.'

'They'd be fine for ten minutes.'

'Definitely not, Dave. I won't hear of it. It's way too risky. If anything happened to them, I'd never forgive myself.'

'Well, get a cab, then. I just don't think you should walk home that late at night.'

'Don't be daft, Dave; we can't afford a taxi! It's only a fifteen-minute walk, twenty tops. I'll be fine. I walk it every day to catch the bus to work. Now stop fussing or you're going to make me late.'

As she walked up the path, he shouted after her, 'I love you, sweetheart.'

'I love you too,' she said.

As he watched her walk away from the house, he thought

how amazing she looked in her figure-hugging, navy blue jumpsuit.

JUNE only ever felt comfortable in trousers and never wore skirts or dresses. This was because both her legs, from the knees down, were terribly scarred.

The scarring was the result of an unfortunate accident when she was a very young toddler. Her mother had stood her straight into a bath that had been run by her father. By a tragic oversight, she failed to check the temperature of the bathwater first.

The burns caused by the scalding hot water were terrible, and meant that as she got older, June had to endure numerous operations to apply skin grafts to the badly burned and disfigured areas of her legs.

Now as she walked from her house towards the Archer pub, thoughts of her childhood and the terrible burns were a long way from her mind.

As she strolled along, she was happily singing her favourite northern soul songs. 'Skiing in the Snow' was her favourite track of all time, and she found herself belting out the lyrics at the top of her voice as she walked. This was followed by her loud rendition of the Smokey Robinson classic 'Tears of a Clown'. By the time she reached the pub, June was virtually skipping along. She couldn't wait to meet her friends inside and start dancing.

She could already hear the beat of the northern soul music booming out from the pub.

June knew she was really going to enjoy tonight.

46

Blidworth, Notts – September 6, 1984

June Hayes couldn't remember the last time she had enjoyed herself so much. The music in the pub had been fantastic; all the girls had been dancing around their handbags on the small dance floor. Her workmates from the factory had been brilliant fun, and they'd all danced for most of the night.

June had smiled to herself when she saw a couple of the younger single girls kissing men as they enjoyed the last slow dance of the night. It had taken her back to when she first met Dave, back to that special giddy feeling of a new romance.

She felt warm and happy. The warmth might have had something to do with the three glasses of Mateus Rose wine she'd drunk throughout the evening.

When the bar staff finally called last orders, the girls from the factory all booed loudly. Feeling under pressure to carry on, the DJ didn't switch the decks off until twenty past eleven.

June and her friends were now standing outside the pub, laughing, chatting and saying their goodbyes.

'Are you sure you'll be alright walking home on your own, June?' asked one of her friends.

'Of course I will. It's not far, and there's plenty of street lights along the way.'

She spread her arms wide, giggled, and said, 'Who'd want to come after an old bird like me anyway?'

'Just be careful, June. You must've seen on the telly what happened to that poor woman they found over at Annesley. They still haven't caught anybody for that yet.'

'I'll be fine, Glo. Annesley's miles from here. If anyone comes after me, they'll get one of these shoes up the side of their head. They don't call 'em killer heels for nothing!'

June waved one of her high-heel shoes above her head and laughed. 'Don't worry, I'll see you lot bright and breezy on the bus in the morning. Can't say I'm looking forward to the noise of the factory tomorrow morning though.'

The women all agreed with that as they started walking off their separate ways.

June slowly started on the twenty-minute walk from the Archer to her house. Only five minutes had gone by when she noticed how different it felt walking home in the dark, to how it had been walking down to the pub.

She had been happy, singing on the way down the hill, the sun had been shining, and the countryside either side of the lane looked beautiful.

It was totally different now. For a start, she was walking up the hill, and after a night of dancing, her feet were killing her.

Her progress was slow.

She looked up and saw a really bright moon; the light from the moon made her feel a little better, as the street lights were dismal and were spaced around a hundred yards apart.

Because of the long distance between street lights, there

were areas of the path where it was really dark. She quickened her pace slightly through these darker areas.

June shivered involuntarily, as for the first time she felt the night chill. The warmth from the wine was quickly wearing off. A single cloud obscured the moon, and suddenly it was very dark.

Looking along the straight road, she grimaced and let out an audible sigh, realising how far she still had to walk.

Another five minutes passed, and she was now well away from the last of the houses at the Rainworth end of the road. Joseph Whitaker School was also way behind her. She was now on the stretch of road where it narrowed and became little more than a country lane.

Here, there was nothing but fields either side of the road.

For the moment June wasn't concerned; she had walked along this road a thousand times or more. She could think of many occasions when she had walked along the road in the dark during the cold winter months. The bright moon was now frequently covered by passing clouds, everywhere becoming instantly darker as the moon disappeared. Once again, she shuddered involuntarily.

It wasn't fear; she wasn't scared. It was more a feeling of apprehension that she experienced every time a cloud flitted across the moon.

Ahead of her, in the distance, she could now see the slight bend in the road. She knew that just after that bend, the houses of Blidworth village would start to come into view.

Using the street lights dotted ahead to judge the distance, June calculated that after another three or four minutes of walking, she would reach the bend.

The sound of a sharp crack that sounded like a twig snapping broke the deathly quiet.

The noise had come from directly behind her.

Instantly, all of June's senses became alert. She tried to

quicken her pace a little, but her high heels wouldn't allow her to go much faster.

She listened intently, desperately trying to hear another noise. Suddenly, there it was: Above the silence, she heard the unmistakeable sound of footsteps approaching her from behind. Real fear began to seep through her body now; quickly she glanced over her shoulder.

There was nothing there.

Inwardly she scolded herself, saying under her breath, 'Calm down, June. Stop being so bloody stupid. Nobody's there.'

Her breathing was shallow, and her heart was racing.

She walked on, quicker now.

Tears were starting to sting her eyes, and she felt clammy all over. Another couple of minutes passed by. She was nearly at the bend.

Suddenly, she heard the sound again, definitely footsteps.

June didn't want to, but she had to look back.

Forcing herself to look, she turned her head quickly. Just as she did so, the moon slid from behind a cloud, bathing everywhere in bright moonlight.

To her horror, she clearly saw a man.

He was about eighty yards behind her and was crouched over, very close to the hedgerow.

She watched in horror as the man moved away from the hedgerow across the grass verge and onto the pavement. He was now walking quite quickly. Because he was crouched over, he resembled a large ape.

Immediately, June turned back the way she was going and began trying to walk even faster.

She could hear the man's footsteps clearly on the path behind her now. It was obvious he knew she'd seen him, and he was now intent on catching her up.

The footsteps sounded close, and a terrified June again

glanced over her shoulder. To her horror, she saw that the man was now no more than fifty yards away.

She felt tears start to well in her eyes, and a panicked sob escaped her lips. Quickly, she kicked off her high-heeled shoes and picked them up before walking on barefoot. The hard, cold pavement made her feet hurt like hell, but at least she could walk faster now.

The first house was no more than a couple of hundred yards away. She was terrified and thought about breaking into a run just to reach the bend and the sanctuary of that first house.

The footsteps behind her were getting louder; the man was getting closer. June didn't dare to look back again and was just about to break into a desperate run when she heard a car approaching from behind her.

Now she did risk a glance over her shoulder. To her relief, she saw that the man had stopped and was waiting for the car to pass him.

She knew this was her chance.

As the car approached, she stepped to the side of the road and waved her arms, frantically signalling for the driver to stop.

June prayed the driver of the car would see her and stop.

She could still see the stalker some thirty yards behind her. He was now standing stock-still, like a statue. The approaching car's headlights illuminated the man from behind. She could see he was staring at her.

The man watched impassively as the car sped past him.

June desperately tried to stop it, waving her arms and shouting.

To her horror, the car did not stop. Her heart sank. Her eyes initially followed the car as it sped by; then, quickly, she turned to look back down the road.

June saw that the man had begun to walk slowly towards her again. She turned and began to run for her life.

As she turned to run, she saw that the car was now about forty yards ahead of her, but its brake lights were coming on. The car was stopping.

Sprinting now, she ignored the pain in her feet and desperately ran towards the stationary car that was now only about fifteen yards in front of her.

The driver of the car reached over and opened the front passenger door. As the door swung open, the interior light of the car came on, and June got a glimpse of the driver.

Thank God, long blonde hair, the driver was a woman.

June reached the car and desperately yanked the passenger door open wider.

She blurted out loudly, 'Help me, please. There's a man after me!'

Too late, and to her horror, June realised that the driver of the car was also a man.

'I know that, darling!' the driver snarled. 'He's with me.'

As she turned away from the car door to run, she was terrified to see the man who had been following her was now right behind her.

June was trapped between the open car door and the man. She screamed and swung one of her high heels at the man's face. The shoe narrowly missed its mark, and the stalker pushed her roughly backwards against the car. She hit the side of the car with such force that it knocked all the breath from her body, and she felt her knees buckle and strong hands pushing her into the back of the car. She was pushed down onto the back seat and managed one more piercing scream before she saw a bunched fist heading straight for her.

Suddenly, everything went black.

'Close the door, for Christ's sake, and keep her quiet. Let's get out of here.'

'Just a second; she's dropped her shoes.'

Having retrieved the shoes with the killer heels, Mick got into the car, climbing onto the back seat after the woman.

Jimmy could hear whimpering noises coming from the back seat as the woman began to recover from the punch that had landed flush on her mouth. He then heard the taut screech of gaffer tape being removed from the roll. The gag was applied, and everything went quiet again.

'All sorted, Jimmy,' growled Mick.

'Thank Christ for that,' muttered Jimmy as he slowly drove the green Cortina away.

About a hundred yards away, on a small hill in the fields, looking down over the road, stood Stan Briggs.

Briggs had heard the piercing scream made by the woman and turned in the direction of the noise. He saw the car and heard the door close, then heard one more scream from inside the car before it was driven off at speed towards Blidworth.

'Another bloody domestic,' he muttered to himself.

He picked up the dead rabbits on the string and his high-powered, silenced .22 air rifle. He shouldered the rifle and tied the rabbits to his waist. Lastly, he picked up the large portable lamp that he'd used to transfix the rabbits, making them remain still as he shot them.

Stan Briggs was nearing fifty-six years of age. He had thought his lamping days were behind him, but for a striking miner, times were now very hard. He'd been forced to revert to his youth, back to the old poaching method to supplement food for his family.

He was on private land, and he knew that poaching was illegal, but he had to provide meat for his wife, kids and grandkids. Stan decided the three rabbits he'd already shot would have to be enough for one night. The cold night air was starting to seep through his camouflage overalls. He felt cold and damp and was ready for a hot cup of tea.

As he slowly trudged across the muddy fields back towards his home in Rainworth, the woman's screams were already forgotten.

47

Woods near Blidworth Village – September 7, 1984

It had just turned midnight.
June Hayes was conscious again. She was shivering with the cold and could feel the damp grass on the bare skin of her back. The realisation that she was now totally naked shocked her, and she whimpered.

Her mouth felt bruised. She tried to lick her swollen lips beneath the tape that covered her mouth, but winced at the pain it caused. She ran her tongue along the bottom edges of her front teeth and could tell by the rough texture that a couple of them were broken.

Her head was throbbing, the pain travelling in waves from the back of her head to the area immediately behind her eyes. Slowly, as more of her senses returned, she looked around urgently, terrified at what she might see.

June could see she was surrounded by tall trees. The moon kept dancing from behind the clouds, intermittently shining through the leaves of the trees above her. The moonlight also afforded glimpses of the small clearing in the trees where she lay.

Her hands were tightly bound behind her back, and she could feel whatever was used to bind her wrists starting to dig deep into her skin. She tried to raise her head off the ground, but went dizzy as a rush of pain swept over her.

Ignoring the pain and dizziness, June looked down along her body. She had been stripped naked and was bound around her ankles as well as her wrists.

The gag across her mouth felt sticky and had a strong smell of glue. Now fully aware of her situation, panic rushed through her, questions bursting into her head.

Where were the men who had brought her here? Would they be coming back to rape her?

Her friends' warning, as she left the pub, about the murder of the woman at Annesley then came crashing into her consciousness. June felt tears sting her eyes and trickle down her cheeks, and she started to shiver violently as the cold of the damp grass seeped in.

Suddenly, an overwhelming sense of anger gripped her. With a renewed strength and determination, she struggled against her bindings and forced herself to sit up.

As she finally managed to do so, she was confronted by an image that terrified her to the bone.

June felt the warmth between her legs as her bladder loosened at the terrifying sight in front of her.

Illuminated clearly, as a cloud slipped past the bright moon, were two figures silently watching her.

They stood ten yards away and were dressed from head to foot in light blue nylon suits with hoods. They had covers on their shoes, and their hands were a ghostly white. She realised they were wearing gloves.

They looked like surgeons preparing to operate.

The stark white light of the moon gave the figures an ethereal glow.

A strangled scream erupted from her throat, but was stifled by the gaffer tape. Thoughts of her husband and two children came into her mind. In that instant, June knew for certain that she'd never see any of them again.

One of the figures bent down, and she watched in horror as he silently reached into a black bag at his feet.

Fleetingly, the moon disappeared, and the figures evaporated in the darkness. Then, just as suddenly, they were both standing there again, bathed in white light as the moon emerged from behind the clouds once more.

Her eyes widened in fear when she saw that the figure who had bent down to the bag was now holding a set of small gardening shears.

Without making a sound, the figure slowly walked towards her, watched intently by the other one. The fact that everything was done in deathly silence only heightened the feeling of utter dread she now felt.

Suddenly, she felt gloved hands on her naked shoulders as the man pushed her back down onto her back. He then turned her over roughly, so she was now lying on her side. She struggled gamely, but felt a heavy blow to her kidneys.

The fight and anger were quickly replaced with a feeling of total helplessness, and June lay unmoving on the damp grass, quietly sobbing.

Her hands were now exposed, and she felt the coldness of the metal shears against her thumb. A lightning bolt of pain shot up her arm as she felt the blades of the shears slice off her thumb. She felt two more fingers being severed before the pain caused her, mercifully, to black out.

The figure watching tutted loudly. 'Now look what you've done, Mick. I told you the pain would be too much for her to stand.'

'She'll be back with us soon enough, you'll see. It's so much more satisfying when they're awake to feel it.'

'Sort the fingers and her hands out now, while she's out of it. We'll be here all night at this rate.'

'Who put you in charge?'

'Just do it, or I'll finish her off now and the fun will be over, got it?'

Grumbling to himself, Mick severed each digit from the hands of the unconscious woman before picking them up and placing them in a ziplock bag.

He then walked back to the grip bag and took out the Stanley knife. Returning to the woman, he made long, deep lacerations across the palms of both her hands until the skin resembled a latticework.

Now bleeding substantially from the wounds to her hands, the unconscious woman was then rolled over onto her back again. Carefully, he turned her head to one side so she didn't swallow her tongue. The two men then stood together watching her in silence as they waited patiently for her to come around.

Fifteen minutes passed before she stirred again; another five before she was fully awake. Her hands felt strange, and when the realisation of what had happened became apparent, June felt herself gag; the acid of the wine consumed earlier burned her throat as she almost vomited. Forcing herself, she swallowed the burning bile.

It was either that or choke.

With a feeling of dread, she saw that the other, slightly taller figure was now moving towards her.

He knelt beside her and moved close enough for her to see his face clearly. He smiled at her benignly, saying, 'Don't worry, this will all be over soon. I know that all you want is to leave this place. Do you, sweetheart? Do you want to leave this place?' he asked softly.

June nodded vigorously, ignoring the pain in her head.

She thought he'd meant leaving these woods, leaving these monsters, returning home to her loving family.

It was not what Jimmy Wade had meant at all.

He slowly showed her the thin nylon cord that he gripped in both hands and smiled again.

The reality of his intentions now rushed into her head, and she shook her head, pleading with her eyes.

She looked directly into those cold, unfeeling, unblinking blue eyes, imploring him not to hurt her any more.

Very slowly, he wound the thin cord once around her neck. Her eyes widened with terror as she felt the cord tighten around her throat as he exerted slow gradual pressure. Jimmy Wade continued to squeeze the life from her, watching her beautiful green eyes intently as he did so.

After five minutes it was over, and he stood up quickly, removing the cord from around her neck.

June Hayes was dead.

'At last. What a performance! Do you mind if I have a play now?' a voice growled from the shadows.

Jimmy took a step back from the woman, turned and walked away, allowing Mick Reynolds to approach the dead woman. He knew what was coming next and was totally disinterested in it, almost bored by it.

Standing just ten yards away from the dead woman, he looked up at the moon as he heard the orgy of violence begin.

Jimmy could see no point to it. He knew there was absolutely no chance this woman wouldn't be missed; she was obviously married and would quickly be reported missing from home.

Deep down, Jimmy knew that Mick Reynolds was completely mad. The only reason he tolerated him was so he could fulfil his own needs and achieve that special feeling that only came as he actually extinguished a life.

Having achieved that already, he was now feeling extremely bored.

'Hurry up, Mick. We need to get out of here. We haven't got all night. I need to get you back to Ollerton.'

There was just a grunt of acknowledgement.

'Nearly done. Have you got the letter and the Stanley knife, so we can leave another message for the cops?'

Jimmy nodded and walked back towards the shattered remains of June Hayes to play out the final part of their macabre ritual.

48

Mansfield Police Station – September 7, 1984

'Good morning, sir; it's Sergeant Clark at the front counter. I've got a Mr David Hayes here. He's insisting on speaking to someone from the CID urgently. Apparently, his wife, June, didn't come home from a night out at the Archer pub in Rainworth last night.'

'Okay, I'll be up there shortly with DS Buxton.'

It was the phone call Danny had been dreading ever since the body of Mandy Stokes was discovered at Annesley.

The investigation into her horrific murder was going nowhere fast. No new leads or lines of enquiry were coming through, and time was passing quickly by.

The appeal for information that he had made personally across all the television networks had yielded nothing of any note.

It was now four weeks since Mandy Stokes had been brutally murdered. A feeling of dread washed over him as he walked quickly towards the front desk of the police station.

Rob walked in silence at his side. Neither man said anything, but both were already thinking the worst.

Another murder. Another dead woman.

AT THE FRONT COUNTER, Danny saw a man sitting alone. He looked dishevelled, his skin colour was grey, and looking at his eyes, it was obvious he hadn't slept.

'Mr Hayes, I'm Detective Inspector Flint, and this is Detective Sergeant Buxton. The sergeant tells me you want to speak to the CID.'

The man stood up and nodded. 'It's about my wife, June; she never came home last night.'

Danny showed David Hayes into an interview room where they could talk in private.

Once everyone was seated, Danny said, 'You're saying your wife didn't come home last night. Is that unusual for her?'

'My wife's never stayed out, Inspector. That's just not like her.'

'The desk sergeant has told me your wife was at the Archer pub last night. What was the occasion?'

'There was no occasion. It was just a night out with the girls from work.'

'Does she go out with the girls from work regularly?'

'No, it's the first time she's had a night out in months. We've got two young kids.'

'Where does your wife work, Mr Hayes?' asked Rob.

'June works at the Pretty Polly factory over at Sutton in Ashfield. It was just a night out with the other girls who catch the laid on transport every morning from Rainworth to the factory.'

'What were the arrangements for your wife to get home last night?'

David Hayes put his head in his hands and looked down at

the floor. In a faltering voice cracking with emotion, he said, 'She said she'd walk home. I knew I should've picked her up. This is all my fault.'

Trying to placate the man's obvious fears, Rob said, 'We don't know anything's wrong yet, Mr Hayes. Is it possible your wife just didn't fancy the walk home and stayed with one of her friends for the night?'

'I thought that myself, Sergeant, but I've phoned the factory this morning at half past eight. All the girls who were out last night are at work except June. She wasn't on the minibus this morning. That's when I knew something was seriously wrong. I've taken the kids to school and then came straight here to report her missing.'

Danny glanced at his watch. It was now just after nine o'clock. 'How far is it from the Archer pub to your house?'

'Probably half a mile, three-quarters at the most. We live at the end of Blidworth that's nearest to Rainworth.'

'How long should it have taken your wife to walk home?'

'It should only take twenty or so minutes.'

'Do you know what time your wife left the Archer?'

'I've spoken to Glo – sorry, Gloria – her best friend at Pretty Polly, and she told me that June left the pub at about half past eleven, and she saw her start to walk home. June should've been home way before midnight. Earlier this morning, while the kids were still asleep in bed, I walked all the way along the route she would've taken last night. I can't find anything. There's no trace of her, Inspector. Something awful's happened; I know it has. People don't just disappear into thin air.'

David Hayes then fixed Danny with a glassy-eyed stare before saying, 'Inspector, have you caught that nutter who killed the woman in Annesley Woods yet?'

Danny said softly, 'Let's not jump to any conclusions, Mr Hayes. There could be any number of reasons why your wife didn't come home last night. I'll get DS Buxton to run you home so he can obtain all the details we'll need about your wife. I'll organise a proper search along her route home and start making some enquiries at the pub. Have you contacted any of the local hospitals yet?'

'No, I haven't. Do you think she might be there?'

'It's possible; she may have had an accident. I'll call them all now and let Rob know the outcome, so he can tell you straight away.'

Danny stood up. 'I know it's difficult, Mr Hayes, but try not to worry. We're going to do everything we can to find your wife.'

Again, the distraught husband seemed to visibly crumple in front of Danny.

'Thanks. Inspector.'

Danny left the room, leaving Rob to take David Hayes back to his home.

The main reason Danny had arranged for Rob to take Hayes home was so he could search the family home thoroughly.

Danny had to keep an open mind. June Hayes could have made it home safe and well and then fallen foul of domestic violence as her husband flew into a jealous rage about his wife having a night out with the girls.

Having spoken to the obviously worried husband, Danny doubted this was the likely scenario in this instance.

He needed to organise manpower for a search. There was a body out there somewhere. Every instinct in his body was screaming to Danny that June Hayes was already dead.

After leaving the interview room, Danny went straight to Superintendent Jackson's office. He needed the senior officer to authorise the manpower needed for a search.

Just an hour later, arrangements had been made via strike control to release three PSUs from their duties on the dispute. They would assist in the search of the surrounding farmland

and woods adjacent to the route June Hayes would have taken on her way home last night.

Three PSUs meant a total of thirty-three men. Danny was satisfied that a large area of the surrounding countryside could be searched properly by that number of officers. He would have liked more, but was thankful he'd managed to get that many.

Danny returned to the CID office, where he briefed Andy and Rachel about the disappearance of June Hayes.

'Rachel, I want you to go straight to the Pretty Polly factory over in Sutton and speak to all the women June Hayes was out with last night. Start with her best friend, this Glo. From what the husband says, it appears that Glo may've been the last person to see her. I definitely want a full and detailed statement taken from her, but play it by ear for the other women; statement them if necessary. If there's anything startling that comes to light, like a secret lover, et cetera, let me know straight away.'

'No problem, boss, I'll get over there right now unless there's something else you want me to look at as well?'

'No, that's more than enough to be getting on with, Rachel. I don't know how many of the factory girls were out last night, but I suspect it'll be quite a few. I also want you to talk to the minibus driver who takes the women to the factory every day. He could be a gold mine of information. I bet he listens to all the juicy gossip.'

'Right you are, boss.'

'Keep me posted if there are any developments, okay?'

Grabbing her coat, a set of car keys and a bundle of statement paper, Rachel hurriedly left the office.

Danny turned to Andy: 'I want you to stay here and do all the background checks on the husband and the Hayes family in general. I want to know everything about them. Have either of them ever had an extramarital affair? Have there been any domestics? Do they have money troubles?'

'No problem.'

'Sorry, Andy, I'm not trying to teach you to suck eggs. You know what I want.'

'I know, boss. I'll shout Rob up for a chat once he's got over to the Hayes house, and get all the details from him.'

'I'm going over to Blidworth now to help organise the search with the inspector from the Special Operations Unit. Superintendent Jackson has arranged for him to come over and co-ordinate the searches being carried out by the foreign-force PSUs. Once I've spoken to him, I'll join Rob up at the Hayes family home. We'll then make a start on the enquiries at the Archer pub. Andy, I want you to make sure we all keep in touch by radio. My gut feeling's telling me that we've another murder on our hands. Obviously, I hope I'm wrong. It could just be that June Hayes was hit by a car last night and is lying unconscious in a ditch somewhere. Either way, time is of the essence.'

Danny walked out into the car park and took two or three deep breaths before climbing into the CID car.

He sat quietly for a moment. It felt like the world was closing in around him. As he drove out of the police station, he was already rehearsing in his mind how he was going to break the worst news imaginable to David Hayes.

49

Warsop Main Colliery – September 7, 1984

The Metropolitan Police PSU had just finished escorting the working miners through the picket lines at Warsop Main Colliery. The usual cries of 'SCAB!' were still ringing in their ears. The men had just begun removing the protective clothing they wore every morning and beginning to think about yet another fried breakfast when the radio in the Transit van crackled into life.

'Mike Alpha One Zero. Over.'

Three times the call sign was repeated before a disgruntled Sergeant Reynolds answered the radio.

'Go ahead, Control. Mike Alpha One Zero over.'

He answered the radio begrudgingly, because he was desperately hoping his PSU wouldn't be given another task to carry out. Today was the last day of their deployment; they would be heading back to London first thing tomorrow morning for a well-earned week of rest days.

The answer he was dreading came soon enough as the

control room operator's voice said, 'Mike Alpha One Zero, resume immediately from Warsop Main Colliery and travel to Blidworth Police Station. Upon arrival at that location, liaise with Inspector Richardson of the Special Operations Unit.'

Mick let out a low groan before saying, 'Will do, Control. What's the commitment? We're standing down for a week this evening, and obviously we've got a lot of kit to get stowed. Mike Alpha One Zero over.'

'Mike Alpha One Zero, we're aware it's your last day. You're required to assist in the search of countryside around the Rainworth and Blidworth area for a missing woman. Over.'

'No problem, Control, we're just finishing off at Warsop Main. Show us travelling to Blidworth Police Station.'

There was a loud chorus of moans and groans from the men in the back of the Transit.

'All right, you lot, shut it! Is everybody here?'

'We're three missing, Sarge. They went to get a brew.'

That's all I need, thought Mick.

Of course, he knew exactly where the missing woman was. He and Jimmy had left her in a small clearing just off a bridle path in the woods. He hoped that he didn't get that area to search with his PSU. He didn't want any connection to the woman.

He quickly located his missing men. 'Come on, you three, look lively! We've got a search commitment to get done before we can pack up and go home.'

The moans came thick and fast from the three men, who had anticipated an early finish, ready for home.

Mick rounded on them sharply. 'Stop whining and get your gear on board. The sooner we're there and get it done, the sooner we can get packed up, ready for home.'

The three men reluctantly binned their coffees and climbed into the back of the Transit van.

As the Transit was driven towards the rendezvous point,

Mick subconsciously reached into his trouser pocket and began to feel the two small gold rings inside.

Making sure the van driver was watching the road, Mick surreptitiously removed the rings from his pocket to look at them. One was a small gold wedding band, the other a gold ring with a single solitaire diamond.

When he came to dispose of the items from the site of last night's killing, he'd seen the two rings still on one of the fingers he had severed.

He'd removed the rings before throwing the severed digits into the furnace.

As he looked down at the tiny rings sitting in the palm of his hand, Mick smiled. The memories they instantly stirred felt delicious; he felt an overwhelming surge of excitement. He played with the rings, slipping them on and off his own little finger, before quickly replacing them back into his pocket. For the time being, at least, his secret double life was safe.

As the police van was driven nearer to Blidworth Police Station, he was praying his PSU wouldn't be tasked to search the area between Blidworth Lane and the main A60 road that ran between Mansfield and Nottingham.

50

Blidworth Police Station – September 9, 1984

For two days, the police search had concentrated on the area of open countryside between the villages of Rainworth and Blidworth. The police had meticulously searched vast areas of the open gorse land that lies between the two townships.

On the first day of the search, the Metropolitan Police PSU led by Sergeant Mick Reynolds searched the area immediately behind the Archer public house until finally being stood down at last light.

Reynolds had known the search in that area was a pointless exercise, but he still bullied and cajoled his men to carry out as thorough a search as was possible.

All the Metropolitan Police PSUs in that particular serial had now gone home for a week of rest days. They would not be back in the Nottinghamshire coalfield again until September 15.

The search for the missing woman had been carried on by

PSUs from Hampshire Constabulary. Once again, the search areas were concentrated towards the village of Rainworth.

All the searches so far had drawn a blank.

IT WAS NOW ENTERING the third day that June Hayes had been missing, and everybody in the community was starting to fear the worst.

Danny had travelled to Blidworth Police Station at half past six that morning to meet with Jim Richardson, the Special Operations Unit inspector, so they could discuss the areas to be searched that day. The search was going to be extended, moving further out from the Archer public house, the location June Hayes had last been seen alive.

While ever June was only missing, there was still hope.

Both men sipped a steaming hot cup of coffee as they examined the Ordnance Survey maps of the area.

Inspector Richardson pointed at the map, saying, 'Right, Danny, I propose we extend the search into this area of woodland today. If we get the search teams to gradually spread out from Blidworth over towards the A60, we might have some joy. It seems a natural direction of travel away from the point of abduction.'

The two men had long ago dismissed any other scenario than an abduction. The SOU inspector continued, 'We haven't got many PSUs at our disposal today, but some of the villagers will no doubt turn out to help. It's another huge area, and some of the terrain's quite difficult. There's a large area of pine forest here that I think we should start with. I'll deploy the PSUs there first thing this morning; then we'll extend the search out into the general woodland later this afternoon.'

Danny nodded his agreement.

The discussion was taking place in a mobile control and command centre that had been set up in the car park of Blidworth Police Station.

This mobile control centre also served as the incident room for the enquiry. If a body was discovered, the incident room would be transferred to the police station at Mansfield, but for the time being the mobile control centre would suffice for a missing person enquiry.

Danny had made another press release on the evening of the first day, asking for anyone with information to contact the mobile control centre. It had been constantly manned around the clock.

There had been five bogus sightings of June Hayes so far. All of these sightings had to be investigated thoroughly before they could be discounted. It was yet another drain on an already limited resource, that of manpower.

Danny again carefully studied the search areas identified on the map. 'That looks good to me, Jim. I'll leave you to co-ordinate the search teams this morning, and I'll liaise back here with you at two o'clock this afternoon.'

'Yes, of course; no problem. I know you're running a skeleton crew doing the enquiries. So, any way I can help, I will.'

'Thanks, Jim, I really appreciate that. What time are the PSUs arriving for the briefing?'

'Any time now. I told them to be here no later than seven. I want them out on the ground as soon as it's properly light at about seven thirty.'

'How many have you got today?'

'Only three again. Thirty-three men in total.'

'Okay, I'll see you at two this afternoon. Contact me on the radio if you find anything in the meantime.'

'Will do, Danny.'

Danny made his way out to the car park and sat in his car.

Again, he allowed himself the luxury of a few minutes to gather his thoughts before beginning the fifteen-minute drive back to Mansfield. He had another briefing with his own staff scheduled for seven thirty before updating Superintendent Jackson at nine o'clock.

As he drove his car along the country lanes, he made a mental note to call Sue; he needed to have a proper conversation with her, not just a two-minute chat.

It seemed as though his whole life had been taken over at the moment by the pressure of work.

Danny had only seen his father, in the new care home, a couple of times in the last three weeks.

He had a fledgling relationship with Sue, who, again, he hadn't seen properly for over two weeks.

It was a blessing that Sue was kind enough to be a regular visitor to the care home. Her daily visits had helped his father enormously to settle into his new surroundings.

Her thoughtful attitude had allowed Danny the time to concentrate solely on trying to find the killer in their midst.

51

Ricket Lane, Blidworth – September 9, 1984

The two teenagers had been up since six o'clock that morning. They quickly ate their breakfast and made their way straight to the stables.

Lizzie and Polly Thornley, like a lot of teenage girls, loved horses more than anything else in the world. Both girls were nearly fifteen and had been riding the horses kept at their father's livery stables since they were eight years of age.

The twins were not identical to look at, but they were definitely identical when it came to their interests.

The girls loved riding and especially show jumping.

This morning they were both up early to muck out the stables. They would then have the opportunity to exercise two of the horses liveried at the stables.

The women who owned the horses couldn't always get in to ride them, due to work and family commitments. Whenever this was the case, it was left to Lizzie and Polly to exercise the horses.

The exercise for the horses would be a steady hack through the local woods, along one of the many bridle paths situated around the village of Blidworth.

The horses they were going to ride this morning were two of their favourites. Both horses were mares and a beautiful chestnut colour; they stood almost seventeen hands. Both animals had lovely temperaments.

They had been trained as dressage horses and were very sensitive to each little command given by the teenagers.

Both girls were excited about taking the horses out and were really looking forward to their hack through the woodland between Blidworth and Papplewick Village.

Their father's business, Thornley Livery Stables, was located just outside Blidworth on a stretch of land that lay between the village and the small upmarket town of Ravenshead, not far from the main A60 road.

There was a secluded bridle path that ran virtually the whole way from Blidworth to Papplewick. It was very seldom used by anyone, and for that reason, was the Thornley girls' favourite.

It was a beautiful clear morning, and the sun was just creeping over the horizon when the girls set off from the stables. They wore identical gear of black riding helmets, blue quilted anoraks over chest protectors, beige-coloured jodhpurs and black boots.

The horses they were riding may have good temperaments, but it was never worth riding without the proper protective clothing on.

A horse could be spooked at any time, for any reason.

Their father had always instilled in them that it was better to be safe than sorry.

After saddling the two horses, the young girls mounted their rides and set off at a walk out of the livery yard.

The two girls were chatting happily as they rode the horses out of the yard and along the secluded bridle path.

. . .

AFTER TEN MINUTES, the girls had reached the stretch of the bridle path that passed directly below Ricket Lane. The path here was bordered on both sides by a tall hawthorn hedgerow. The horses were so big, however, that both Lizzie and Polly could see over the top of the hedgerow and into the woodland beyond.

Suddenly, Lizzie gasped and said, 'Whoa!' as she pulled on the reins.

Polly, who was riding just behind Lizzie, immediately stopped her horse as well.

'What's the matter?'

'Polly, come here and look over the hedge into the clearing.'

Polly could tell by her sister's voice that she was afraid.

She guided her horse next to Lizzie and looked over the hedge.

Immediately, she saw what had made her sister gasp. Lying face up on a small area of grass in the woodland, she could see the naked body of a woman.

'Oh my God! Come on, we need to get back and tell Dad what's up here.'

The two girls immediately turned the horses around and trotted them back to the stables.

Polly was shouting as they entered the stable yard: 'Dad! Dad!'

Having heard the girls shouting, their mother came out into the yard from the house. The girl's father emerged from one of the stables with a face like thunder.

'Whatever do you think you're doing, shouting like that? You know better than that! The horse could spook and throw you off. Be quiet, right now.'

Once the girls had halted their horses, Polly handed the reins of her horse to Lizzie. Dismounting quickly, she ran the short distance towards her father. Jack Thornley could see instantly that something was wrong. He saw how pale Polly looked, and could tell she'd been crying.

'Whatever's the matter, girl?' he said.

'Dad, there's a dead woman in the woods up near Ricket Lane!'

'What are you talking about, a dead woman in the woods? Talk sense, girl,' said their mother.

'I'm not messing about, Mum! There's a dead woman in the woods. She's got no clothes on, and her face is horrible.'

The girl was now crying loudly.

Lizzie also dismounted and walked the two horses towards her father.

'It's true, Dad. I saw the woman as well. It's horrible.'

'Right, girls, get them horses seen to and stabled. I'm calling the police. Will you be able to show them where this woman is?'

It was Polly who answered her father.

'Can you go, Dad? I'm too scared. I don't want to go back up there. It's horrible. I don't want to see it again.'

'Me neither,' sobbed an equally upset Lizzie.

'Alright, calm down, girls. Exactly where is this woman?'

'Go along Ricket Lane as far as the Lightning Oak. Once you reach the oak tree, go down the bank and onto the bridle path where the hawthorn hedges are tall. The woman's in the woods on the other side of the bridle path.'

'Okay, girls, I know where you mean. Now get these horses unsaddled and stabled before you do anything else. I'll call the police and take them up to the Lightning Oak.'

Both girls were still sobbing as they led the horses into the stables, followed by their concerned mother.

Jack Thornley ran inside the house to call the police.

52

Ricket Lane, Blidworth – September 9, 1984

The telephone call from Jack Thornley had come into Mansfield Police Station just after eight o'clock as Danny was finishing briefing his staff.

It was the call Danny had always known would come, but it still felt like a hammer blow when the control room passed the call down to the CID office.

It had been Rob who answered the phone.

'Danny, a woman's body's been found,' he said quietly.

'By the search teams?' asked Danny.

'No, by a couple of young lasses horse riding over near Blidworth.'

'Who called it in?'

'It was the girls' father, a bloke by the name of Jack Thornley. He owns the livery stables just outside Blidworth.'

Without saying another word, all four detectives dropped what they were doing and ran out of the station.

Taking two cars, the four of them travelled at speed to

Thornley Livery Stables, where they were met by a very worried-looking Jack Thornley.

WITHIN MINUTES of arriving at the stables and speaking to Mr Thornley, Danny and his team were following him as he drove his Land Rover up onto Ricket Lane.

Still on Ricket Lane, but about two hundred yards from the main A60 road, he stopped the Land Rover in a layby.

At one end was a very old, gnarled oak tree that still bore the black scorch marks of a lightning strike.

The two CID cars pulled in behind the Land Rover.

'My girls said the dead woman's in the woods down here. I'm afraid you'll have to go on foot from here.'

Danny turned to his team. 'Andy, wait here and start a log. If the information's right and it's a body, we can use this layby as the rendezvous point. Rob, get some tape from the car and mark the route we're taking in, please.'

Rob was back quickly with the tape. Tying it to a tree, he started to mark their descent from Ricket Lane down onto the bridle path where the girls had been.

'The woman might be difficult for us to see,' said Jack Thornley.

'Why's that?' asked Rob.

'My girls were on horses that are seventeen hands high, so they were able to see over these hawthorn hedges. They told me the woman was in some sort of clearing in the trees beyond the far hedge.'

Danny, Rob and Rachel all bent at the waist, trying to look under the hedgerow as they moved slowly from left to right along the bridle path.

Suddenly, Rachel stopped and held her hand to her mouth.

'Over here, boss! She's over here!'

Rachel turned and took two paces away from what she'd seen and dry heaved, retching loudly.

Danny and Rob ran over. 'Are you okay?' asked Danny.

She said nothing and just pointed behind her.

Danny and Rob bent over so they could see below the hedgerow. Instantly, they saw the mutilated remains of the naked woman.

'Christ Almighty!' muttered Rob.

'Right, Rob, take Rachel with you and get back up to the cars. Take Mr Thornley with you as well, please. Rachel, are you okay?'

Rachel looked as white as a sheet. 'I'm okay, boss. It was just a shock, that's all. I'm sorry.'

'Don't apologise; you've done nothing wrong. I want you to go back with Mr Thornley and speak to his girls. I want statements from both of them, whenever they're able. Just take your time with them; they've had a massive shock too. Rob, when you get back up to the cars, get Scenes of Crime travelling. I want Tim Donnelly in charge of the team, and the Home Office pathologist travelling as well. If at all possible, I want Seamus Carter on this. No, scratch that: I *insist* on Seamus Carter coming out to this scene. The whole thing looks exactly the same as Annesley to me. Last thing, Rob, get on the radio to Inspector Richardson and tell him to meet me here. We're going to have to redeploy our search teams. Tell him, from me, that I want all his search teams on standby at Blidworth Police Station.'

'Okay, Danny.'

Rob turned to Rachel. 'Come on, Rachel, let's get you back up onto the road.'

Danny shouted to Rob as he made his way back up the banking: 'Once you've got the circus travelling, bring a couple of suits and overshoes back down with you. We'll try to find the easiest way through the hedgerow to get to where she is.'

. . .

TEN MINUTES LATER, Danny and Rob were walking slowly along the hedge line, trying to find a suitable gap to get through.

Both were now wearing forensic suits, gloves and overshoes. Rob continued to mark the route. About twenty yards along the bridle path from where they'd first seen the body, Danny saw an opening in the hedge.

The opening was about five yards across. Carefully, both men scanned the area for any sign that the offender had used the same gap.

At the nearest point, they could see some indentations in the mud, and the grass had been flattened a little.

Rob taped off that area, and the two detectives carefully skirted around and entered the grassy area from the far side.

Tying the tape to a small tree, Rob then allowed the tape to trail behind them as he and Danny made their way into the area where they had seen the body. There were small saplings everywhere, and larger trees further in.

Suddenly, the ground rose a little, and there in the middle of a grassy clearing was the dead woman.

'Oh, for fuck's sake,' whispered Rob.

'I know; it's fucking identical. I can see that from here.'

Moving carefully, the two detectives got as close as they could to the body.

There were marks and indentations in the grass immediately around the body, where obviously the killer had been walking.

From where he stood, a distance of about eight feet away, Danny could see the woman was lying face up. She was in the same crucifix position, with her arms stretched out wide and her legs slightly open.

The hands had been mutilated in the same way as Mandy Stokes. The head injuries were horrendous and appeared worse after being out in the open, exposed to vermin and the elements for three days.

The same two words had been carved into the woman's torso, but the wounds had started to pare back with decomposition and were barely legible.

'What's the betting the bastard has left us another note, boss?'

'It wouldn't surprise me. There's no sign of any clothing anywhere.'

'I can't see any, but this is definitely June Hayes.'

'Why are you so sure?'

'Look at the legs below the knees.'

'You're right; I can see the scarring that was mentioned in the statement you took from her husband.'

'Yeah, she was scalded as a kid. The scarring's on both legs from the knee down.'

'Right, stay here; I'm going back up to meet and brief the Scenes of Crime team and Seamus Carter as soon as they get here. I'll talk to Inspector Richardson on the radio and get the search teams organised and ready to move in as soon as Scenes of Crime have finished. I'd like you to manage the scene again. You know, chapter and verse, what was at the Annesley scene.'

'Makes sense, Danny, no problem.'

'As soon as I've briefed Tim and spoken to Seamus, I'll go straight over to Blidworth and see David Hayes. I want to inform him personally that we've found a body. I don't want him hearing anything through the grapevine.'

'I don't envy you that job.'

'I'll make sure there's a policewoman available to meet me at Blidworth Police Station. She can help to look after the two children while I talk to their dad.'

Carefully, Danny retraced his steps and made his way back up on to Ricket Lane to await the arrival of Scenes of Crime and Seamus Carter. He quickly spoke to Inspector Richardson on the radio and appraised him of the situation and that a search team would be required at this location shortly. Having finished the radio call, Danny leaned on the bonnet of his car and took several deep breaths.

This was fast becoming a nightmare.

Two women killed brutally in an identical way. God knows what the note left by the killer, if there was one, would say this time.

No new leads or lines of enquiry of any consequence from the first killing. He prayed the killer had been more careless this time and left something of some evidential value behind at the scene.

Danny exhaled and then said aloud, 'I won't hold my fucking breath!'

53

Mansfield Police Station – September 9, 1984

It had already been a very long day.
In half an hour's time, at seven thirty, Danny and Rob would be making the short walk from the police station to the mortuary. Danny had arranged to meet Seamus Carter, the Home Office pathologist, there. He and Rob could then observe the post-mortem examination of June Hayes and take any relevant exhibits.

The murder scene at Ricket Lane had proved to be just as frustratingly sterile as the one at Annesley Woods.

Nothing at all of any evidential value had been found.

Indeed, had it not been for the scarring on the legs of the dead woman, they would have, once again, been struggling for a formal identification.

The scarring from both the original injury and the subsequent skin grafting all matched perfectly to the medical records of June Hayes.

There were signs at the Ricket Lane scene, identified by

Seamus Carter to Rob, that once again an object had been inserted in the dead woman's vagina.

Seamus could only estimate that the time of death had been somewhere between midnight and four o'clock on 7 September. He was unable to be any more specific, due to the amount of time that had lapsed and the level of decomposition.

Rachel had patiently interviewed both Polly and Lizzie Thornley at length, one after the other. She had taken detailed statements from them individually in the presence of their mother and father.

It had been a long drawn-out process, as both girls had been traumatised by what they'd seen and frequently broke down in floods of tears.

Rachel could empathise with their feelings and had struggled not to shed a few tears herself alongside the youngsters. Eventually, after several hours, two very detailed and informative witness statements had been obtained.

Rob had managed the crime scene at Ricket Lane until the body had been removed and Scenes of Crime had finished their forensic examination. He had then, together with Inspector Richardson, co-ordinated a fingertip search of the area.

Nothing had been recovered.

Danny had spent most of the day with David Hayes.

Initially, he'd broken the terrible news to him, then, very patiently and gently, he coaxed every last piece of information he could glean from him about his wife's medical history.

This process had also taken a long time. Danny was only too aware of how upsetting and traumatic a time this was for the entire Hayes family.

Danny and the policewoman who had gone with him only left when David's brother and sister-in-law arrived from Matlock to stay with him and the children.

Now back in the CID office, Danny addressed his team,

'Okay, I know this is exactly what we've all been dreading. Another murder of an innocent woman, obviously carried out by the same sick individual. Once again, there's absolutely nothing for us at the scene. Andy and Rachel, get a quick bite to eat, and then get yourselves up to the Archer pub at Blidworth. I want you to talk to as many of the regulars as you can. I know it's been a few days since the Northern Soul night, but I guarantee there'll be people in there this evening who were in that night. I need you to find me something, anything. I don't care if it's rumour, speculation or Fantasy fucking Island; we need a break to kickstart this enquiry. Our killer isn't going to stop any time soon. If we don't catch him, this is going to keep happening. More women will die. I'm going with Rob to the mortuary shortly. Once we've finished there, Rob will join Rachel and Andy up at the pub while I'm thrashing out the detail of tonight's press release. I think it's important we get something out to the public tonight. I know you're knackered, but I want you all to make phone calls home and let your other halves know what's happening. Okay, let's go.'

At exactly seven thirty, Danny and Rob walked into the mortuary. Waiting for them was Seamus Carter.

In the centre of the room, lying on a stainless-steel bench, was the putrefying remains of June Hayes. Once again, under the stark white lights, the detectives saw exactly how defiled and mutilated her body was.

In silence, Danny and Rob donned the protective overalls, and this time, they slipped masks over their faces and dabbed Vicks vapour rub just below their nostrils on their top lips. The smell of decaying flesh in the room was already overpowering, and both men knew the stench would only get worse once Seamus Carter commenced his examination.

'First things first, then, gents. Let's see what little insight into his depraved tiny mind the killer's left for us this time?'

Danny nodded wearily and watched closely as Seamus removed the object from the vagina.

Using exactly the same method as he had with Mandy Stokes, the pathologist removed the rolled-up paper from the black plastic tube.

'Everything looks identical. Obviously you'll need to get it tested, but the tubing looks as though it's been cut from the same material, and the paper also looks the same.'

Slowly, he unfurled the paper.

Typed on the paper was a chilling message, which Seamus read aloud:

I WARNED you the first one wouldn't be the last
Thatcher and her police boot boys haven't stopped
They continue to kill the coalfields
So I will continue to kill scab loving whores
Until the next time, Detectives
'The Coal Killer'

'LOOKS like he's making this personal now, Danny,' said Seamus.

Danny said nothing.

Finally, after a minute's silence, Danny said softly, 'Okay, Seamus, let's get this done, shall we?'

At the end of the full autopsy, Seamus took a deep breath.

'In my opinion, Danny, this horrendous act has definitely been committed by the same individual who killed Mandy Stokes. The wounds to the hands are identical; the same instruments have been used. The level of violence is escalating, though.'

'How can it have escalated? The wounds are the same.'

'When Mandy Stokes was killed, all the wounds to the hands had been made post-mortem. This poor woman was alive when they severed her fingers and mutilated the hands. The injuries to the face and head, however, have all once again been caused post-mortem.'

'Jesus Christ,' whispered Rob.

Pointing to the dead woman's neck area, Seamus continued, 'The cause of death is exactly the same. Strangulation with the same type of thin cord. Once again, there's no evidence of any sexual activity apart from the insertion of the tube containing the note into the vagina. The note has the same dropped letter c, so undoubtedly the same typewriter was used.'

'Thanks, Seamus.'

'I'll get my report over to you as soon as possible.'

Danny nodded wearily. 'Thanks.'

'I know I said it last time, but this bastard will keep doing this until you catch him and make him stop.'

'Tell me something I don't know,' said an exhausted Danny.

54

Mansfield – September 10, 1984

Jimmy Wade hadn't forgotten about the beautiful, enigmatic detective who had visited him at his home, asking questions about the death of Albie Jones.

He had watched her slim elegant fingers caress the mug when she drank the coffee he'd made her. He remembered how she had looked longingly into his eyes.

He'd seen her full red lips pout as she blew the hot coffee. He had tasted the lipstick ring she left on that mug.

Jimmy enjoyed fantasising, again and again, how her young voluptuous body must look beneath the business suit she'd been wearing. He imagined the lacy black underwear, the stockings on those long slim legs.

Jimmy wanted her in every way.

She aroused him sexually.

Just thinking about her, he was once again starting to feel the same familiar lustful stirrings.

He also wanted her in that most exquisite, special way.

He had looked into her beautiful eyes, and he knew that she yearned for that beautiful release from her humdrum, boring little life.

Once he finished playing games with that ignoramus Mick Reynolds, he would return to the planning, capture and subsequent demise of the beautiful detective. Jimmy was weary of the Neanderthal policeman. It had been fun, a distraction, but it was never destined to be a long-term thing.

The plans he'd set in motion were slowly coming to fruition. Very soon, it would be time to call a halt to his current life and start afresh.

The time to move on had arrived. He needed to concentrate on Detective Rachel Moore.

Her time to shine was approaching fast.

55

Wembley, London – September 14, 1984

It was the day before Mick Reynolds was due to travel back to the Nottinghamshire coalfields to resume his duties policing the miners' strike.

His mood was dark.

He cut a brooding, menacing figure as he paced up and down the lounge of his three-bedroom semi in Wembley.

His foul mood had been caused by two things: the prospect of another month of boredom in Nottinghamshire and a week spent in the company of his nagging bitch of a wife, Rita.

She'd spent the entire week moaning at him to take her out for a drive in the car. The weather had been glorious; the country was in the grip of an Indian summer, the sun was shining, and the days were pleasantly warm. She'd constantly nagged to be taken out here, there and everywhere. He was never going to agree to that; he was fully aware the police were searching for his Ford Sierra.

He knew he had to get rid of the car sooner rather than later. It had been impossible to arrange the disposal of the car while ever he kept having to go north for strike duty.

Again, the strident voice of his wife, Rita, screeched from upstairs, 'What's the point of having the frigging car if we never go out in the bleeding thing?'

'It needs repairing. How many more times have I got to tell you the same thing, ya daft cow!'

He could hear her stomping down the stairs.

Here it comes, he thought as she stormed into the lounge.

'What's wrong with the bloody car?' she demanded.

Trying desperately hard to control the rage building inside him, he shouted back, 'The big end's gone. I've told you a dozen times already!'

She sneered, 'Oh! The big end, is it? Well, I bet that's the first time anyone's ever said that to you, eh, darling?' She chuckled spitefully.

'Fuck off, ya evil bitch!'

'I'm a bitch, am I? Is that what you call your tarts when you're fucking them?'

'What ya talking about? What tarts?'

Their voices were getting louder and louder as each tried to shout down the other: 'Do you think I'm fucking stupid, Mick? I know you go and see tarts. They're the only silly bitches that would accept your poor excuse for a cock!'

'Shut it. Rita, I'm warning ya!'

'They're the only women you don't have to satisfy, aren't they? You just pay them, don't you, Mick. You fucking sad act!'

Mick Reynolds then did something he had never even dreamed of doing before.

He punched Rita full in the mouth as hard as he could. The force of the blow knocked her to the floor.

He stood over her and bellowed, 'Shut ya poisonous mouth, bitch!'

Rita was as shocked as she was hurt.

'Bastard!' she yelled through gritted teeth as she sat stunned on the floor.

She could already begin to taste the blood in her mouth as she slowly got to her feet. She pointed an accusing finger and was just about to tell Mick what she thought of him, when he stepped across the room towards her, raising a clenched fist. She quickly changed her mind about saying anything and cowered away.

'Rita, get the fuck out of my house,' he said quietly, but with real menace.

She went to respond, but he held up his hand and said, 'If you open your fucking poisonous mouth again, I'll kill you right here, right now.'

The last sentence was said in barely a whisper, and for the first time in their relationship, Rita was afraid, really afraid.

She had never seen her husband act this way. There was a dark and dangerous look in his eyes that she'd never seen before. It was as though something inside him had finally snapped.

Grabbing her door keys, coat and a handbag, Rita fled out of the house and ran down the street.

Mick slammed the front door behind her and went back into the lounge. He sat on the settee, breathing heavily. He could feel beads of sweat trickling down his face.

Slowly, he felt himself calming down.

He smiled to himself. He felt great.

Mick knew Rita would be back as soon as he left the house to travel back to Nottinghamshire, but right then he didn't care; he had drawn the line. If she ever crossed that line again, he knew he'd kill her on the spot. There'd be no second chances. He knew he'd only been a fraction of a second away from killing her today.

Mick walked out of the lounge, went upstairs and started to pack his kit, ready for deployment.

56

Wembley, London – September 14, 1984

After fleeing the house to escape from her enraged husband, Rita had run to the phone box at the end of the street. Breathless and in a state of panic, she had phoned her best friend, Sue Jessop.

Rita had arranged to meet Sue in the Green Dragon pub on Wembley High Street in ten minutes.

Both women now sat in the scruffy public bar of the pub, slowly sipping their drinks. The pub was a proper shithole; the old wooden floor was sticky underfoot, and the whole place reeked of stale, spilt beer and cigarette smoke.

It was a hard drinker's pub, the sort of place you went to if all you were interested in was getting drunk.

The only other customers in the bar were two old geezers sitting at the bar, drinking pints of Double Diamond with Bell's whisky chasers.

An indignant Sue Jessop sipped her pint of lager and lime and said, 'Rita, you're coming over to my flat in Peckham, and you're staying with me until that animal's gone back up bloody north. I'm not having any arguments.'

Sue Jessop was forty-three years old, a divorcee with one grown-up son.

The boy had left home on the day of his sixteenth birthday to join the Army. Truth be told, the boy would probably have joined the French Foreign Legion if it meant he could get away from his mother.

Sue Jessop was a mess. She dressed like a twenty-year-old, had peroxide blonde hair with jet-black roots and chain-smoked John Player Special fags.

She was very short and about two stones overweight.

By far the biggest problem with Sue was that she thought men found her irresistible. The procession of different men, who only ever wanted sex, into her bed every weekend had been the main reason her son wanted to leave home so badly.

She was now right up on her soapbox as she poured out advice and sympathy to her equally slutty best friend, Rita.

'You don't have to put up with any of that shit, Rita love. That man's lucky to have you. Look at you, darlin', you're bloody gorgeous. How dare he lay a finger on you! You should go to his bosses and get him sacked.'

'What good would that do, you stupid cow? It's his job that keeps me in money.'

'You can't accept it, Rita. Trust me, girl, if a man hits you once, he'll sure as hell do it again.'

'I must admit, he scared the shit out of me today. I've never seen him like that before; he wasn't like my Mick at all. He's usually such a soft twat. When he said he'd kill me, I knew he meant it.'

'What are you gonna do?'

'I've got to stay with him, Sue. I've got no choice; it's my home, and he gives me everything I want. Just do me a favour, if ever you don't hear from me for more than a few days, please go to the police station and tell them everything. Will you do that for me?'

'Fuckin 'ell, Rita, are you that scared?'

'I don't know, maybe I'm being a bit overdramatic, but there was definitely something in his eyes today. When I go home, I'll call you twice a day for a chat; it's what we do now anyway. If for some reason I don't call you and you can't contact me, then you'll know something's happened. Just go to the cops and tell them something's wrong.'

'Of course I will, darling, us girls have got to look out for each other. Shall we have another before we go back to mine?'

'Pint of Carling with a splash of blackcurrant, thanks.'

'Coming right up, darling!'

Rainworth, Nottinghamshire – September 14, 1984

Rob Buxton was standing at the bar in the lounge of the Jolly Friar pub on the outskirts of Rainworth village.

He glanced at his watch and took another sip of the half-pint of lager he was nursing while he waited for Jamie Towle to arrive. Jamie had phoned the incident room the day before, saying he'd got information on the recent murders.

He was a striking miner and had point-blank refused to walk into Mansfield Police Station as a matter of principle.

Instead, he'd agreed to meet early doors at the Jolly Friar pub. The small pub was on the very edge of the village and was usually a quiet place. Jamie knew there was less chance of him being seen talking to the police if he arranged to meet them there.

Rob was given the task of meeting Jamie and had arrived at the pub ten minutes before the agreed time.

The pub was empty. That wasn't unusual; ever since the strike started to bite, the local pubs had suffered.

Any drinking by striking miners was being done at the Welfare as the men mulled over the progress, or lack of it, of the strike.

Rob was glad the place was empty; it would make it easier for Jamie Towle to speak to him openly. He took his lager and sat in one of the small booths that formed part of the lounge bar.

He sat well away from the bar and faced the door so he could see Jamie Towle when he walked in.

Another five minutes ticked slowly by; then Rob saw the door to the lounge bar open quietly. A skinny youth who looked too young to drink in pubs looked inside.

Seeing the pub was empty except for Rob, he walked in.

The youth was dressed in scruffy jeans and a donkey jacket that looked two sizes too big for him. His hair was long and greasy, and he had a face full of acne.

After having one more quick furtive glance around him, he walked straight over to Rob, ignoring the bar and the barman, who glared markedly at him.

In an overly aggressive manner, he said, 'You the cop?'

'I'm DS Buxton; are you Jamie Towle?'

'Yeah, that's me. Let's get this done quick. I don't want anyone seeing me talking to you lot.'

'Okay, Jamie, let's get things straight. You asked me to come here; here I am. Sit down and let's talk properly. Exactly what information have you got for me?'

Jamie sat down, leaned forward and, in a conspiratorial whisper, said, 'It's this bloke at the Welfare. All he does is talk about the two women who've been murdered. He's just a bit weird, that's all.'

'What do you mean? In what way is this man weird?'

'He's weird coz he's a total fucking nutjob; you know what I mean! He said the other day if he couldn't kill Maggie

Thatcher, some other tart would have to do. I'm not the only one who thinks he's strange. Half the miners at the Welfare keep their distance from him. He gets really nasty and violent when he's had a few beers.'

'Have you seen him get violent yourself?'

'Yeah, I've seen it. When he's had a drink, he just goes mental. He'll fight anybody.'

'Does he work down the pit?'

'Yeah, he works at Rainworth. He's the same when he's at work down the pit. People avoid him.'

'Is he on strike?'

'Yeah, and he fucking hates scabs. I mean, we all hate scabs, but he *really* hates them. He's always saying how we should start taking them out. That's what I mean. I'm telling you, he's fucking nuts.'

Jamie paused, looking around him again before continuing, his voice now even more of a whisper. 'Then, the other morning, he comes into the Welfare wearing overalls that are like camouflage. Well, there's blood all over the front of them. One of the other blokes in the Welfare asked him what he'd been up to, and he just told him to fuck off and mind his own business. He's getting on a bit now, he must be fifty odd, but a lot of people in the village are still shit scared of him. The rumour is that he's got weapons as well.'

'Weapons?'

'Yeah, some of the blokes in the Welfare reckon that he's got guns and a load of knives.'

'Okay, Jamie, what's this man's name, and where does he live?'

'Me talking to you like this, it's not going to come back on me, is it? If people around here find out I've been talking to the cops, I'll get battered.'

'No, it won't come back on you; I won't be telling anybody we've had this little chat. So if you don't say anything to anyone, you'll be fine.'

'I won't be making any statements, and I definitely ain't going to court.'

'That's fine, too. Just give me the name.'

'Stan Briggs. His name's Stan Briggs.'

'Where can I find Stan?'

'He lives on Hardcastle Road in Rainworth, but he spends most of the day at the Welfare.'

'Thanks, Jamie. Who else lives with him at Hardcastle Road?'

'It's just his old lady who lives with him now. He's got two daughters who live in Blidworth with their husbands. I know the husbands; they're on strike, too. They don't like Stan either; they think he's mental. I think both his daughters have got kids as well.'

'Thanks for telling me all this. Can I give you some money for a drink or something?'

'I don't want your money, copper. I ain't a grass, but it ain't right what's happened to them women, either. I'm out of here.'

Jamie then stood up and took off out of the pub like a scalded cat.

Rob waited for two minutes; then he also left the pub, leaving the now flat, half-drunk glass of lager on the table.

He walked back to his car and drove out of the car park and set off back towards Mansfield.

As he drove the car down Python Hill, away from the pub, he passed Jamie walking along the street. Neither man acknowledged the other.

Rob made a left turn onto Little John Avenue and then took another left onto Hardcastle Road.

He noted that the houses with odd numbers on Hardcastle Road all backed onto fields. The fields at the back of these houses all led directly towards the rear of the Archer pub.

Rob slowly drove his car to number 15 Hardcastle Road.

It was a large semi-detached house, identical in design to every other pit house in the village.

The house was very scruffy and run-down.

Hardcastle Road was a cul-de-sac, and number 15 was the last house on the street. The other half of the semi-detached was almost derelict with an overgrown garden and a couple of smashed windows. It appeared as though number 13 had been unoccupied for a long time.

There was a rusting wreck of a car on the front garden of number 15. The grass where the car had been abandoned was as high as the wheel arches of the car.

The paint on the front door and window frames of the house was flaking off. There were filthy dirty net curtains hanging in all the windows.

Rob turned the car around in the cul-de-sac and again drove slowly passed the house. This time, he looked down the side of the house. He could see a large coal bunker, which was empty.

Looking beyond the coal bunker, Rob noted there was a falling-down fence at the back of the property. He could also see there was clear access onto the fields behind the house.

'Okay, Stan Briggs, let's see what we know about you already, shall we?' he said quietly to himself as he drove his car out of Hardcastle Road.

58

Mansfield Police Station – September 15, 1984

It was six o'clock in the morning, and a full section of the Special Operations Unit were being briefed by Danny and Rob at Blidworth Police Station.

Rob cleared his throat, and the men stopped talking and listened as he began the briefing. 'Right, gents, our target today is a man named Stan Briggs. There's an up-to-date photograph of Briggs in your briefing pack. We've received information that he may be connected in some way to our recent murders. The address on the warrant is 15 Hardcastle Road at Rainworth. Briggs was a nasty bastard in his youth; he's got two previous convictions for Sec 18 wounding. He's also got numerous convictions for minor assaults, and three of these have been for attacks on women. There are numerous calls logged to his home address following domestic disputes. Basically, Stan Briggs is violent and is no fan of women. Our information is that he hates scabs with a passion and has recently tried to incite violence against working miners. He's also been heard recently making threats against women, connecting the threat to the strike. He was heard to say, "If I can't kill Maggie Thatcher, some other tart will have to do."

'We're particularly interested in locating and seizing a set of overalls with a camouflage pattern, that may or may not be bloodstained, any weapons, any typewriters, or any other article you think may be connected to our two recent murders. I want to be on the road by ten past six and at the address no later than six fifteen. Any questions?' asked Rob.

A voice from the back of the gathering spoke up. 'Are there any firearms registered to the address?'

'The source suggested that Briggs does have access to firearms. Our records indicate that he doesn't legally own any firearms or shotguns, but as we all know, that doesn't prevent the possibility of him having an illegal weapon. This is one of the reasons I want a very rapid entry to the house. Hopefully, Briggs will still be in bed asleep, and you'll be able to contain him before he stirs. Any other questions?'

There were no other questions.

Five minutes later, the two vans containing the Special Operations Unit drove out of the police station, followed by a car containing the two detectives.

'How good's the information, Rob?' asked Danny.

'It was good enough to get a warrant from the magistrates, but it's not the best. It's uncorroborated and the word of an untested informant, but we've got to act on it. Let's face it, there's not much else coming in. You never know, it might just be spot on.'

'We'll soon find out, won't we?'

The house at 15 Hardcastle Road was in darkness when the small convoy of police vehicles pulled up quietly outside.

Quickly, the men from the SOU surrounded the house.

As soon as he was satisfied that all exits to the house were covered, the sergeant in charge indicated to the man with the sledgehammer to knock the front door in.

With one almighty blow directly onto the mortise lock, the front door flew open. Immediately, officers sprinted through the door and ran straight up the stairs.

Danny and Rob remained outside on the road and saw lights coming on in various rooms and heard shouts emanating from the first floor of the house. Less than a minute later, the sergeant in charge of the raid emerged from the front of the house.

'The house is secure, Inspector; your man's getting dressed upstairs. He's secured, but he hasn't been arrested yet.'

Danny turned to Rob. 'Do the honours, Rob, arrest him on suspicion of murder. It might just focus his mind away from the strike.'

The SOU sergeant spoke up. 'That might be a very good call, sir. When we grabbed him, the first thing he started spouting on about was Thatcher's boot boys.'

Rob looked knowingly at Danny before walking into the house and up the stairs to the main bedroom.

Stan Briggs was a very angry man. He was now fully dressed and had been handcuffed behind his back, and he was threatening anybody who could be bothered to listen.

Rob looked closely at him. Yes, he was obnoxious, and yes, he was violent, but was he a murderer?

Right now, he looked pathetic, his puffy, bloated face red from shouting.

He was a very scruffy, short, stocky man. He'd not shaved for days, and his hair was long and lank. His clothes were unwashed, and they smelled.

Basically, the man was a shambolic mess.

The house was even more of a shithole inside than it was on the outside. It smelled of damp and mould, stale fried food and cigarette smoke. There was rubbish and old unwashed clothes piled everywhere.

Rob looked at Briggs, took hold of his right arm, and said

evenly, 'Stan Briggs, you're under arrest on suspicion of the murders of Mandy Stokes and June Hayes.'

Rob then cautioned Briggs.

There was a long silence before Briggs spluttered a response. 'Did you say murder? This has got to be a fucking joke. I've never killed anybody.'

Briggs was suddenly very subdued and stopped shouting.

Rob took him downstairs and through the kitchen.

Briggs's wife, wearing a shabby old dressing gown, had rolled herself a cigarette and was now smoking it in the kitchen. Rob heard her talking to the officers who were starting the search of the property.

'What exactly is it you're looking for? He's not one of the great train robbers, you know,' she said wearily.

Rob escorted Briggs out of the house and walked him towards Danny and the waiting car.

'Are you his boss?' asked Briggs quietly.

'I'm Detective Inspector Flint, why?'

'You've got it all wrong, chief. I'm not a murderer; this is a huge mistake.'

'Let's get you over to the police station at Mansfield; then you can tell us everything you know about the murder of Mandy Stokes and June Hayes.'

There was now a level of panic in Briggs's voice.

'I don't know anything; I've never heard of either of those women.'

The return journey to the police station was made in silence. The only noise in the car was from Briggs sitting in the back of the car, constantly muttering the word 'no' to himself.

AT MANSFIELD POLICE STATION, Briggs was immediately taken to the cells, where he complained to the sergeant in charge of the cell block.

'This is all wrong, Sarge!' he whined.

Briggs was put in a cell, and Danny and Rob made their way to the CID office. They had a quick cup of tea while they waited for the Special Ops team to arrive with the result of the house search at 15 Hardcastle Road.

'What do you think, Danny?'

'I honestly don't know. Like you, I heard the comment he made to the Special Ops lads, the one that's also on the note, but looking at him?' He shook his head.

'I hope the search of the house yields something, boss. This killer's so careful and meticulous at the scenes, with everything being planned in minute detail, it's hard to imagine him being so different in the way he lives his everyday life.'

'I know; that's exactly what's bothering me the most: Our killer's an extremely organised individual, and Briggs, on face value, looks like the most disorganised man I've ever seen. Let's just wait and see what the SOU lads bring back from the search. You never know your luck in a raffle.'

The two men then set about planning the interview they were about to have with Briggs. Initially, they had to plan as though nothing was found at the house.

When the SOU team arrived at Mansfield, having completed the search, they had good news.

The sergeant walked into the CID office with the search log in his hand.

'I'll give you the highlights of what's been seized, then you can have the search logs. We've recovered the camouflage overalls, and there's what looks like a lot of blood on the front and both sleeves of them. We've got two very sharp filleting knives, a .22 silenced air rifle, a headlamp attached to a car battery and, most surprisingly of all, an Olivetti typewriter. The last item being found in one of the unused bedrooms in amongst a load of other junk.'

'Did the wife say anything to you about any of the items recovered at the house?' asked Danny.

'I asked her specifically about the typewriter, and she told me it belonged to one of her daughters and that Briggs had borrowed it at the start of the strike. I didn't ask her about the other things we've recovered. They all look pretty straightforward to me; that's a full poaching kit we've recovered. My guess is that the staining on the overalls will turn out to be rabbit's blood.'

'Okay, Sarge, thanks. It was another very professional job this morning. Will you thank your men for me?'

'Will do, boss. All the recovered items have been booked into the property store, everything's labelled up, and the statements from the officers who found the items will be on your desk by the end of the day.'

'Thanks, Sarge.'

As soon as the sergeant left the room, Rob grabbed a plain piece of paper and was on his feet, racing out the door, quickly followed by Danny.

At the property store, Rob got out the Olivetti typewriter recovered from Hardcastle Road, quickly inserted the sheet of paper, and typed out a random sentence.

'Bollocks!' he exclaimed before continuing, 'It types perfectly, Danny. Look at the letter *c*. It's aligned correctly.'

'I can see it is,' said a very disappointed Danny.

An hour later, Danny and Rob were sitting opposite a very quiet and subdued Stan Briggs in an interview room.

A uniformed constable was also standing at the back of the room, having brought Briggs from the cells to the interview room.

Danny started the interview.

'Okay, Mr Briggs, first things first. Tell me your movements on the night of Thursday, 6 September?'

'I was at home with my old lady most of the night.'

'What does "most of the night" mean?'

'I was at home until about ten o'clock at night; then I went out.'

'Where'd you go?'

'Just out. I went for a walk.'

'Exactly where did you go for a walk?'

'I walked around the streets, nowhere in particular.'

Danny looked at the desk and shook his head slowly, finally looking up and staring directly into Briggs's eyes.

'Why are you lying?'

'I'm not lying.'

'Don't waste my fucking time, Briggs. We both know you weren't walking the streets of Rainworth; now, where did you go?'

Briggs let out a long sigh. 'I might as well tell you; you've got all my gear anyway. I was out in the fields at the back of my house.'

'Doing what exactly?'

'I was fucking poaching. I was out lamping for rabbits. I've got to get food for my daughters and their little ones. They've got no money coming in now, thanks to that cow Thatcher.'

'Exactly where were you poaching?' asked Rob.

'I was only out for about two hours. I remember it was freezing that night, and I started to get cold.'

'Where were you, Briggs!' said Rob, raising his voice.

'Alright, alright. I was on the private farmland behind the Archer pub.'

Danny looked directly at Briggs.

'Let me get this straight: You were on the fields behind the Archer pub between eleven and eleven forty-five on Thursday, 6 September?'

'Was that the night all the music was on at the pub?'

'YES!'

'Were you still there after the music finished?'

'Yeah, I was. I got three small rabbits early doors about ten thirty, then I didn't see anything else for an hour or so. I gave up just after I heard the couple arguing.'

'What couple?'

'Well, I think it was a couple. They must've had a row or something, because I heard the woman scream.'

'Exactly where were this couple?'

'Down on the road that runs from the pub towards Blidworth.'

'Whereabouts on the road?'

'Up towards the Blidworth end; I was up there at that time.'

'What did you see?'

'After I heard the scream, I turned around and looked in the direction it came from. I saw the car, and I heard the door being slammed shut. I heard another, quieter scream from inside the car; then the car was driven off quickly towards Blidworth. Like I said, they must've had a row. She was probably talking when she should have been listening. You know what women are like.'

'I want you to think very carefully: How far away from all this commotion were you?'

'A good seventy-five yards easy, but I was looking down from the top of the hill, so I had a good view. The car was sort of in between the street lights, so it was quite dark where it was.'

'Did you get a better look at the car as it was driven off, passing the street lights?'

'I suppose I did, slightly.'

'Can you remember what type of car it was?'

'It looked like an old one. It definitely wasn't a modern car; the shape looked old. I remember it was a dark colour, but it's hard to tell the colour in them orange street lights.'

'Did you see the woman who screamed?'

'No, I never saw her. I just heard the scream.'

'Did you see the man in the car?'

'No.'

'Have you ever seen that car before?'

'No.'

'When you were being arrested this morning, you used the phrase "Thatcher's boot boys". Is that something you say often?'

'Any striking miner you talk to refers to the cops like that, not just me.'

'You also said that you had never heard of Mandy Stokes or June Hayes. Is that true?'

'I've heard their names. They've both been all over the news, and people are talking about what happened to them. I was panicking when you arrested me for murder. I haven't hurt those women, Detective. I've never seen either of them in my life.'

Danny nodded to the uniform PC who was standing in the interview room, indicating for him to keep an eye on Briggs.

He and Rob then walked out of the interview room.

Once outside the room, Danny said, 'Briggs isn't our killer, but I think he may have seen our killer abducting June Hayes!'

Rob nodded.

Danny said, 'Rob, arrange for the blood to be tested, though I'm pretty certain it'll turn out to be rabbit's blood like the SOU sergeant suggested. Get a statement from Briggs, and spend as much time as you can on the car he saw. Take him around garages if you have to. I want to know what type of car he saw. Make, model and colour. If we can find that car, we may just find our killer.'

59

Mansfield Police Station – September 29, 1984

All the optimism Danny felt about finding a witness to the abduction of June Hayes had now evaporated.

Two weeks had flown by since the arrest of Stan Briggs and the subsequent discovery that the poacher had witnessed the moment June Hayes had been abducted and bundled into a car on her way home from a night out at the Archer pub in Rainworth.

After making a witness statement, Briggs had been released. Disappointingly, he was unable to specifically identify the type of car used by the killer, despite the best efforts of Rob Buxton to jog his memory.

The only thing Briggs had been able to say with any degree of certainty was that it was an older car, possibly a Ford Cortina, and dark in colour.

Danny was now sitting in the CID office with his team, discussing the sparse evidence they had, and more importantly, if there was anything else they could do to progress the enquiry.

It was Rob who spoke up first. 'I've been on the phone to the lab this morning. They've finally completed all the tests on the camouflage overalls we recovered. As we suspected from the outset, the blood isn't human; it's from an animal, most likely a rabbit. The typewriter's also been fully examined, and there are no recent repairs to any of the keys.'

'Thanks, Rob, I think it's fair to say that we can now discount Briggs from this enquiry other than as a witness, albeit a reluctant, misogynistic one,' said a weary Danny.

He paused before continuing, 'Are we missing something here, people? Is there something blatantly obvious staring us in the face?'

The team were silent for a minute or two before Andy spoke up. 'There's one thing that's nagged at me about both of these murders, and that's the total lack of forensic evidence at either scene. We've all moaned about it, but have we asked the question, why? Who'd have the knowledge to commit crimes like these and leave absolutely no trace of forensic evidence? Who'd even know what we look for at scenes and the processes we use to obtain it?'

Rachel now carried Andy's theme on. 'Add to that the deliberate acts taken under the guise of a frenzied assault, to obliterate the identity of the victims.'

'What do you mean "under the guise of a frenzied assault"?' asked Danny.

'Well, the cause of death in each case has been strangulation; the rest is all window dressing, in a sense. Albeit very careful and calculated window dressing, I'll grant you. The identification of the victims could have been made difficult without going to such lengths. I think it's all staged. He wants us to think he's out of control and that his motive for killing is hatred, but personally, I think that's the opposite of the truth.'

She continued, 'And what about the messages left on the

body and the typed notes? Am I the only person in this room who doesn't believe there's any political motive to these murders? I think all that's a massive red herring left deliberately to throw us off the scent.'

Andy spoke again: 'Who's got the forensic awareness?'

Danny had listened carefully to his two junior officers, then said, 'I'm going to say out loud what I believe you're all thinking anyway. Should we be looking for a police officer?'

Rob replied, 'It's a good question, Danny. Scenes of Crime have already said they've found marks from overshoes at both murder scenes where they can be sure no police officers or Scenes of Crime personnel had been.'

'Do you think our killer was wearing a forensic suit when he killed these women?' asked Danny.

'It would certainly explain a lot.'

A thought suddenly came into Danny's head. 'Rob, how many police officers from foreign forces are currently working in Nottinghamshire?'

'Thousands, and they're chopping and changing every week. They're arriving from virtually every police force in the land on mutual aid. I think there's over five hundred officers deployed from the Metropolitan Police alone. Obviously, they're not all here at the same time.'

'How many remain in Nottinghamshire for the duration of their deployment?' asked Danny.

It was Andy who answered the question. 'All of them who are based too far away to be deployed from their home force on a daily basis. That's most of them.'

Danny stroked his chin and thought for a long time before saying, 'Right, Andy and Rachel, I want you to start contacting the personnel departments of all forces that are currently providing mutual aid in the shape of Police Support Units to this force. I want you to start obtaining comprehensive lists of police officers that have been seconded to Nottinghamshire from all these foreign forces. It's going to be a hell of an undertaking, and I'll need you to be very discreet in your enquiries. I don't want it known outside of these four walls what we suspect. If the public got wind of this enquiry, it would be a public relations disaster. The level of bad feeling between the community and the police is already the worst I've ever known. I want accurate lists drawn up. I want you to include officers that have only been deployed in Nottinghamshire for a few days. I want the dates each individual has been in the county. Once we've got all that information, we can then cross-check it with the dates of our murders. That will narrow down the suspect list massively.'

'That's a mammoth task, Danny,' said Rob.

'I don't see any other option. I think you're all on the right track. I think we could be looking for a serving, or recently retired, police officer with a good knowledge of the investigation of murder and a good understanding of forensic evidence and how we obtain it. I believe it will also be an individual who still has ready access to forensic suits. I think it's time to move this investigation forward. We've no significant leads or lines of enquiry outstanding at this time, so I want to get started on this enquiry today. I think our killer's name will be somewhere on one of those lists.'

60

Warsop Main Colliery – October 8, 1984

The strike was crumbling. The number of miners returning to work across the country was growing steadily. The number going in to Warsop Main Colliery had now reached twenty-four.

The levels of picketing at the gates to the mine had also declined. The usual number of pickets each day was now down to around fifty. The strike was losing all impetus and was dying a slow death.

Once in a while, pickets from the Yorkshire coalfields would get through the intercept points and boost the numbers picketing the mine. As the numbers of pickets had reduced, the policing of them had intensified. Pickets were getting arrested and put before the courts for the least little thing. Once before the court, stringent bail conditions were imposed that meant if an arrested picket returned to the mine entrance again, he would risk being sent to prison.

The miners' strike was being slowly and mercilessly crushed to death by the judiciary.

AT THE DISUSED QUARRY, the groups of miners and police officers milled about as usual while they waited the twenty or so minutes before the two battle buses arrived.

While waiting for the buses, Mick Reynolds immediately sought out the company of Jimmy Wade.

Once he found him, Mick steered Jimmy furtively out of earshot of the rest of the gathering.

'Are you deliberately trying to avoid me?' said a disgruntled Mick softly, through gritted teeth.

'Of course not! What makes you say that?'

'We haven't had one of our little chats for a while, that's all.'

For the last couple of days, Jimmy had stood in amongst the groups of other miners to deliberately avoid having a conversation with the irritating cockney sergeant.

Jimmy had grown tired of Mick's constant moaning about Rita, and boasting about how he'd dealt with her the last time he was home, and saying that if she stepped out of line again, he was going to finish her once and for all.

'I think it's time we went out on the prowl again, Jimmy. We need to let them know we're still here.'

'Haven't you seen the paper? The cops are looking for an old Ford Cortina that's a dark colour. I'm sorry, but at the moment it's not an option to go anywhere. We have to lie low for the time being. I can't risk driving my car around now. I've got it safely locked up in my garage.'

'Don't be so soft, old son. We'd be fine. I'm telling you, I need to go again!'

Jimmy could see that the sergeant was getting angry, so he tried to placate him.

'It's not that I don't want to, Mick, but there's so many of your lot everywhere, we'd be bound to get a pull, and then it really would be game over.'

'Are you too scared?'

Growing angry at the pathetic goading, Jimmy snarled, 'Grow up, Mick. I don't want to spend the rest of my life behind bars just to please you! Now fuck off!'

Jimmy started to walk away.

Mick shouted after him, 'I don't need you, Jimmy. I'll go myself!'

Angrily, Jimmy spun around to face him. 'Don't be a fucking idiot. All we've got to do is just bide our time.'

'We'll see, shall we? I'm not waiting any longer. I need to do one more up here, so the next time I'm home in London, I can do Rita as well. That bitch has had it coming long enough.'

'What about your rules? I thought one of them was "Never kill anyone you know"?'

'This is different. I've been planning it for ages. I've found a place to dump her where she'll never be found.'

'And why do you have to do one up here to kill Rita? It's madness.'

'I need to do one more here so I'm ready for her. You don't understand.'

'Bloody right, I don't understand! You're talking like a crazy man. You need to get a grip of yourself; we need to wait. I'm going to swap my car soon; then we can go out again.'

'When?'

'When you get back after your next rest days, I'll have swapped the car. I promise you we'll go out again then.'

'I go back to London on rest days from the twentieth of this month. I'm back up here on the twenty-seventh. Are you saying we can definitely go out on the twenty-eighth?'

'It's a deal. We just need to be careful and take our time. One more thing, Mick, no more talk about killing your old lady when you're back home. That would be madness at this moment in time.'

'Can't promise that, old son.'

THE BATTLE BUSES were now powering up the lane to where the men had gathered. Once the transport had come to a stop, Jimmy took the front seat on the first bus.

He watched through the front window of the bus as Sergeant Reynolds mustered his men into their police vans.

Jimmy was deep in thought now. He was glad he had made the preparations. It was nearly time to move them forward. The time was coming for him to deal with the police sergeant, who was quickly becoming a dangerous liability.

Jimmy didn't trust Reynolds; he knew he was crazy enough to go out on his own and risk getting caught. He also knew that eventually Mick would kill his wife, and then it would seriously come on top. Jimmy had made his mind up: The problem of Mick Reynolds had to be sorted out once and for all. They'd be going out again on the night of the twenty-eighth, alright, and there would definitely be a killing.

Jimmy grinned at the prospect.

Sitting in the front seat of his police van, Mick Reynolds was also thinking.

Who the fuck does Jimmy Wade think he is?

Mick considered himself to be the brains and the driving force behind their little ventures. He made the decision when it was okay to go, not Jimmy.

'Fuck Jimmy Wade!' he mumbled to himself.

His mumbled words were lost in the noise of the Ford Transit van's engine as it was driven at speed along the country lane.

By the time they reached the entrance to the mine, Mick had made his mind up. With or without Jimmy Wade, he was going to have one more bitch before he went back to London.

61

Edwinstowe – October 19, 1984

Mick Reynolds checked his watch again. It had just turned nine thirty at night as he slipped silently out of his bed. He had to be careful; he was in the Nissen hut he shared with the rest of his PSU. He looked around at the men. They were all still sleeping. They had a four o'clock start the next morning, and there was nothing else to do anyway. He was carrying a small grip bag as he carefully closed the door of the Nissen hut and made his way stealthily across the disused army base.

Mick was wearing a black jacket, black jeans and gloves, and in his pocket was a black ski mask. He also had his warrant card in his jeans pocket, just in case he was stopped by some overzealous local copper.

Having made his way carefully out of the camp without being spotted, he walked down the long driveway to the main road. It was a really dark night; the night sky was full of cloud, and there was no moonlight whatsoever. It felt like a storm was coming. There was definitely the feeling of rain in the air.

Once on the main road, he knew it would take just over three-quarters of an hour to walk from the entrance of the army camp to the small village of Edwinstowe.

There were no street lights along the road until he reached the outskirts of the village. As he walked along the dark road, dressed from head to toe in black, he felt totally invisible. He'd made a couple of visits to Edwinstowe over the last week or so to check out the geography of the village and to pick out likely places where he might find a young woman walking alone at night.

He had a loose plan in his mind, and as he neared the village, he could feel a tingling excitement racing through his body. His intention was to grab a woman off the street and drag her into the woodland that surrounded the village.

Once in a quiet location, he could then take his time and make sure he got rid of any evidence.

As he walked towards the village, he cursed Jimmy Wade quietly under his breath.

'Fuckin' yellow bastard,' he muttered.

Just under an hour later, he had reached Edwinstowe without any major dramas. There was only one incident, when he'd had to dart back into the hedgerow to allow a car to pass by.

Having reached the village, he made his way, unseen, to the Forest Tavern pub, right on the outskirts of the village. He squatted down behind a privet hedge so he could observe the front door of the pub opposite.

For just over half an hour he remained in the same position, watching the front door of the pub. Mick had chosen the white-walled pub because of its proximity to the surrounding woodland. It was the last building at this end of the village; the road went out into dense woodland immediately after the pub. There was a large beer garden at the side of the pub that overlooked the woods.

As he patiently waited, he thought to himself what a beautiful spot it must be in the summer.

He checked his watch. It was now almost eleven o'clock; last orders would have been called. Mick slipped further back into the shadows cast by the large privet hedge across the road from the pub.

He could hear voices laughing and joking now, and he saw groups of people starting to leave the pub.

Mick cursed silently as he saw that the people leaving the pub were all couples. After the last pair left, he saw the front door of the pub close and heard the bolts slide across.

He cursed his luck and was just about to leave his hiding place and head back to Proteus Camp, when he heard the bolts on the front door slide back again. Moving back into the shadows, he watched as a young girl stepped out of the door.

'Good night, Tony,' she said.

He heard a male voice reply, 'Good night, Sarah, see you tomorrow evening.'

Bar staff, thought Mick.

Perfect.

He now watched intently, his eyes glistening in the dark, as the young girl stood near to the gate of the beer garden and lit a cigarette. She was standing with her back to the woods. This was going to be easier than he'd thought. As he watched the girl, he licked his lips in anticipation. She was young, probably around nineteen.

She was very petite, just over five feet tall, with long blonde hair tied back in a ponytail.

As she stood beneath the single white street light, he could see that she was an extremely pretty girl.

'I bet you're popular with the punters,' Mick said softly to himself.

The young girl was wearing tight blue denim jeans and a

cream-coloured blouse underneath a thin dark blue cardigan, and black flat shoes.

As she took a long drag on the cigarette, she glanced down at her wristwatch.

'Shit!' he whispered to himself.

He suddenly realised that the girl was waiting for somebody or something. Maybe she'd called a taxi to take her home. He knew he had to move fast.

Silently, he slipped out from behind the cover of the privet hedge and manoeuvred around until he was directly behind her. He could now approach her from the direction of the woods.

He slipped the black ski mask over his face and crept stealthily through the beer garden towards her, carrying the small black grip bag in his left hand.

He got to within five yards of her and caught a faint smell of her perfume as it was carried towards him on the slight breeze. The perfume smell was then replaced by the smell of tobacco as she exhaled smoke from her cigarette.

He could hear the young girl humming a song, which he recognised from the charts.

Mick was now only a couple of strides away from the girl.

He felt empowered as he realised she still had no idea of his deadly presence. He paused momentarily; then as the girl took another long pull on the cigarette, he pounced.

Placing the grip bag on the ground, he stepped forward and punched the girl once, hard, on the back of her head. The force of the punch sent the cigarette flying out of her mouth. The cigarette travelled in a high arc before landing in the gutter.

The girl's legs buckled beneath her, and she crumpled in a heap, knocked out cold from the force of the blow.

He immediately reached down and started to drag the unconscious girl back across the beer garden to the woods.

Mick was about to bodily pick the girl up so he could

carry her off when he heard footsteps running towards him as he struggled to lift the girl.

He looked up and saw a young man hurtling up the street towards him. The youth was quite slight and skinny and looked to be of a similar age to the girl.

He was approaching very fast though, and Mick could now hear the youth shouting, 'Get the fuck off her!'

Mick let the girl drop, then, as the youth was almost upon him, he stepped forward and met him with a hard punch to the face, knocking him backwards onto the ground.

The shouting and commotion from outside had raised people in the pub. The lights inside were again being turned on.

As the boy gamely started to get to his feet, Mick stepped forward and kicked him hard in the face. The force of the kick spun him over onto his back and knocked him unconscious.

Mick could now hear the bolts on the pub door being drawn back once more.

'Bollocks!' he muttered under his breath before picking up his bag and sprinting away in the direction of the woods beyond the beer garden. As soon as he reached the cover of the woods, Mick stopped briefly and watched as the landlord emerged from the pub.

The landlord saw the two unconscious teenagers and immediately shouted to his wife to call the police and an ambulance.

Mick turned away from the pub and briskly walked off into the woods.

He knew he could get back onto the road that led back to the army base a little further on.

It was time to get back to Proteus Camp.

As he walked away, he replayed the events of the night in his mind, and he cursed the outcome. Another couple of minutes and he would have been able to carry the girl into the woods, where he wouldn't have been disturbed.

Now he was well away from the pub, he took off the ski mask and dropped it into his grip bag. He made his way from the woods back out onto the road that led from Edwinstowe to Ollerton.

As Mick walked slowly along the road, staying close to the hedgerows in case any cars came along, he again cursed Jimmy Wade for being too scared to join in tonight's activity.

Mick fantasised about what he would be doing right now if he and Jimmy had both been there.

Suddenly, his attention was snapped back to the present as he saw blue lights approaching fast from the direction of Ollerton. Quickly, he dropped down into the ditch that ran alongside the road. From his concealed position, he watched as the police panda car raced by.

He waited a minute, then got to his feet and began to jog slowly back towards Ollerton. Ten minutes passed before Mick silently slipped into the army camp. Once inside the camp, it was easy to make his way unseen back to his own Nissen hut. He quietly opened the door and slipped inside the hut.

Everyone inside was still fast asleep.

He glanced at his watch before undressing.

It was now almost one o'clock in the morning; three more hours and he would be getting up. He knew he wouldn't be able to sleep. He could still feel the adrenalin pumping through him.

As soon as he closed his eyes, his mind was full of images of him raging over the smashed and battered body of the dead young barmaid.

He opened his eyes again and placed his hands behind his head as he stared at the ceiling of the hut.

'Who needs fucking sleep anyway,' he growled softly.

62

Edwinstowe – October 20, 1984

The two detectives stood outside the Forest Tavern at Edwinstowe. It was still early morning, and everywhere was covered in a heavy dew; the sky was grey and brooding. The clouds above looked full of rain. There was definitely a storm coming.

'It's a vicious attack; do you think it's our killer?' asked Rob.

'I really don't know. Compared to the other two attacks, this seems a bit disorganised. It's way too risky, too haphazard.'

'It's certainly a weird one.'

'What about our victims? What are they saying?'

'The barmaid, Sarah Featherstone, can't give us any description whatsoever. All she remembers is standing outside the pub, having a cigarette, waiting for her boyfriend, then wham! The next thing she remembers is coming to in the ambulance. She never saw or heard a thing.'

'What about the boyfriend? Can he help us out?'

'I've just spoken to him at the hospital before driving over here; his name's Steve Pepper. The hospital kept him in overnight because he took such a nasty whack to the head. The doctor I spoke to at the hospital thinks the young lad was kicked in the head near to the temple. He wouldn't let me speak to him until first thing this morning. All Steve Pepper can tell us is that he saw a figure dressed in black from head to foot standing over his girlfriend. He thought the man had knocked her down and was trying to pick her up. He can recall being scared for his girlfriend and shouting at the man before running at him. He remembers getting punched in the face and falling backwards to the ground. He says he tried to get up again, but as he was on his hands and knees, he was hit again and knocked out. He didn't come around until they were at the hospital.'

'Can he give any sort of description of the attacker?'

'Not really. He says the guy was bigger than him, not taller but stockier, and that he was wearing one of them black woollen ski masks.'

'He sounds a brave young lad.'

'Yeah, he is. He was more concerned about his girlfriend's welfare. When he came to, the first thing he asked was how she was. He works for the Forestry Commission at the moment, but he was telling me that he's recently applied to join the police. The poor kid's only just turned eighteen.'

'Okay, is there anything else?'

'Oh yeah, sorry, Danny, there's one other thing. Steve also thinks he saw a black bag near the feet of his attacker.'

Danny paused, deep in thought. 'That changes things, Rob. I was ready to treat this as a random attack that's not connected to the two murders. Now I'm not so sure. Maybe the bag is significant. Perhaps that's where he keeps the forensic suit and tools he uses until he's somewhere quieter, where he won't be disturbed. It's possible the attacker was trying to pick the girl up and take her into the woods, where God knows what would have happened to her. I think maybe we've had a lucky escape here, thanks to the bravery of Steve Pepper. Remind me to write him a commendation letter; you never know, it might help him get on the force at a later date.'

'Will do, Danny. Neither of the witnesses made any mention of a car being involved though.'

'That could've been parked up anywhere, for him to go back to later. The car's something else that's been bothering me. If our theory's right, where would a deployed officer from another force get hold of an old car?'

'It's a good question, Danny. Perhaps they've already got links in this area. Maybe it's not a cop who's on deployment. Maybe it's one of our own.'

Danny shuddered involuntarily.

'Can you organise a press release to go out later this morning. The usual stuff: women to be vigilant, etc. I don't want to link it to the other attacks at the moment, so don't mention the bag, or some bright journalist might link them anyway.'

'Will do. I've left Andy and Rachel back at the station. They're hard at it, talking to the foreign forces personnel departments.'

'Thanks, Rob. I know I keep dumping work on you, but I really do have to go and see my father at the nursing home today. I haven't been over to see him for weeks. Thank God Sue's been over to see him every day.'

'She's a very nice lady, Danny. How's that all going, by the way?'

'Apart from the fact that since all this started, we've hardly had five minutes together, it's going very well, thanks for asking.' He laughed.

As they walked back to their cars, Rob said, 'Danny, there's something I do need to talk to you about. I'm starting to get a little concerned about Andy. He doesn't seem himself lately, and I've noticed he's coming to work unshaven, and a couple of times he's been wearing the same shirt for a few days. I know that's not the end of the world, but it's just not Andy. We both know he's normally very sharp and smart with his appearance.'

'Do you think he's having problems at home?'

'I don't know, Danny, possibly. At work he's as focused as ever, but something's definitely changed. Would you take him to one side and have a word with him when you get back from seeing your father?'

'I'll talk to him over a beer at the Railway this evening after work.'

'Thanks, Danny. He's a hard worker and a bloody good lad, but something's not right.'

'I'm sure I'll get to the bottom of what's bothering him over a beer or two.'

When he'd reached his car, and Rob had sped off, Danny took a moment and sat quietly behind the wheel. He chastised himself for not spotting that Andy was maybe having problems. He should be the one to look after the welfare of his staff. It shouldn't be down to Rob to inform him that something was amiss.

He started his car and drove off.

63

Mansfield – October 20, 1984

The lounge bar in the Railway pub was almost empty. An old man sat in the corner next to the roaring open fire, eating a bag of pork scratchings. He was eating them at the rate of one scratching every five minutes.

He was washing them down equally as slowly with his pint of Mansfield Mild.

Danny and Andy walked into the pub and closed the door hurriedly. The cold autumnal nights were really setting in, and the warmth of the fire was definitely welcome.

Both men walked straight to the bar.

'Evening, gents, what can I get you?' asked the landlord.

'My shout, Andy. What you having?'

'Guinness for me, boss, thanks.'

'Make that two pints of Guinness, then, please, Billy.'

'Coming right up, Mr Flint.'

The Railway pub was frequented by detectives, as the police station was less than a hundred yards away. The landlord of the pub, Billy Steele, knew most of the detectives by name.

As he waited for the Guinness to settle, Billy said, 'I heard you nicked someone for the murders of those poor women, is that right?'

'That's right, Billy; we did make an arrest, but unfortunately he wasn't our man. We're still looking.'

Billy placed the two black beers on the bar.

'Good luck, gents. I hope you get the bastard locked up soon. Could you do me a favour, Mr Flint, when you go over to your seats, just check and make sure old Fred's still breathing. I haven't seen him move for twenty minutes now!'

'Will do, Billy.'

Danny and Andy both chuckled as they took their beers and moved away from the bar.

'Let's sit over here, Andy.'

'Okay, boss.'

'We're off duty; just call me Danny.'

'Okay. Is everything alright?'

'That's what I wanted to ask you, Andy. You don't seem yourself lately.'

'Is there a problem with my work?' Andy asked defensively.

'Not at all, your work and your effort is the same as it always is, exemplary. No, I mean in yourself. You don't seem like your old self.'

Andy now slowly turned his glass on the beer mat before lifting the glass and taking a long drink of the black beer. He carefully placed his glass back on the beer mat before looking directly at Danny. 'My wife, Sally, and I have separated.'

Danny was shocked. 'What do you mean, separated? A temporary thing or permanent?'

'She says it's only temporary, but I don't know. It's the hours we're all working, Danny. I'm never at home. Because I live over at Retford, most days I leave the house just before seven o'clock, and if I get home at all, it isn't until after nine o'clock at night. The straw that broke the camel's back, so to speak, was a few weeks ago when I completely forgot our wedding anniversary. I didn't get in from work until gone nine o'clock that night. Then the next day, June Hayes was reported missing. I've hardly been home since.'

He took another long drink of the Guinness. 'One night I got home, late as usual, and found a note from Sally saying she'd gone back to her parents' house in Gainsborough. The note said she was going to stay there until I knew what I wanted, a marriage or a career in the police force.'

'Bloody hell, Andy! Why haven't you said anything to me before?'

'What can I say? I'm not working any harder or putting in any more hours than the rest of us. This is my job; it's what I do. I thought Sally would understand, that's all.'

'Andy, you need to get this situation sorted out right now. I want you to go home tonight, get tidied up, get a shave and drive over to her parents' house at Gainsborough. You need to do everything you can to save your marriage, mate.'

'It's not that simple.'

'It is that simple. Trust me, I know. I had exactly the same situation, and I chose not to fight for my marriage and just let it go. I've regretted that decision every day since. If you love Sally, which I know you do, you'll go home and sort this out now. This isn't a request, Andy. I know I've just said we're off duty, but this is an order. I want you to go home and speak to Sally, take two weeks off work, and get your marriage back on track.'

'It's going to be difficult to talk to her at her parents' house. Her father's never really liked me anyway.'

'Then take her away on holiday somewhere. Get away from this fucking strike and these fucking murders. Andy, you're a valued member of the team, and I'll miss your hard work and endeavour, but this is way more important. Sort this out, and it'll make you and Sally stronger.'

'Danny, I'm not taking two weeks off and leaving you all in the shit. I know how much work there is for me and Rachel still to do. There's a shitload of stuff with the foreign force enquiries alone.'

'You won't be leaving us in the shit. I've got two more detectives starting on the team tomorrow. Superintendent Jackson's finally relented and agreed that we need more staff. I'd planned to feed them into you and Rachel in the morning to help with the foreign force enquiry.'

Andy suddenly looked alive. He sat up straight. 'That's great news! Are you sure it's okay for me to take two weeks off, though?'

'I'm sure, Andy. Now finish your pint and get going.'

'I've had enough of the beer, thanks. If it's all the same to you, I'm going to get off home.'

He stood up and made for the door, pausing just before he went out.

'See you in two weeks' time. Thanks, boss.'

Smiling broadly, Andy left the pub, leaving Danny to finish his pint alone.

Danny wondered how Rachel would take the news that she was now on her own doing the foreign force enquiry.

There were no more detectives starting tomorrow.

He hoped Rachel would understand.

64

Bristol University – October 23, 1984

Seamus Carter hated seminars with a passion. As he walked into the Brunel Lecture Hall at Bristol University, he immediately knew it was going to be a torturous day for him.

Carter was a huge bear of a man, and he sighed audibly as he saw the small size of the hard plastic chairs all lined up in rows, facing the stage, where a small lectern stood to the left of a large white screen. He could see a cable running from the lectern across the stage and then down through the middle of the twenty or so chairs to a portable overhead projector.

'Oh, great, death by overhead!' he groaned.

'I don't think it'll be quite that bad,' said a woman's voice, with a chuckle.

Seamus turned around, startled.

He hadn't been aware anybody else was in the room.

Walking towards him was a very attractive blonde woman, in her early thirties, with a broad smile on her face.

'You must be Seamus Carter,' she said.

He grinned and said, 'Was it my bad mood that gave it away?'

'Oh, that and the fact that I can't think of any other pathologists who are six feet five inches tall with a shock of red hair and a beard that would put Grizzly Adams to shame.'

They both laughed before Seamus said, 'I'm sorry, I don't want to appear rude, but I don't think we've met.'

'No, I'm sorry, I should've introduced myself. I'm Emily Cook. I graduated from this university a couple of years ago. Professor Mason, giving the lecture on facial mapping today, was my professor.'

'Oh, now I understand why you said it wouldn't be too bad. Is he an interesting chap, this Professor Mason?'

'He's more than interesting; Professor Mason is a brilliant man. He recently helped me out with the identification of a woman who'd been murdered in Peckham. I cover most of the South London area when I'm on call.'

'Now I know who you are, so I do. You took over from Jock McArdle in London when he retired, didn't you?'

'That's right, I did, and I've enjoyed every minute so far.'

'I've heard good things about you, Mrs Cook.'

'It's Ms Cook, but call me Emily, please.'

'I'll gladly do that, Emily, and you must call me Seamus. Do we have a deal?'

'We certainly do, Seamus.'

'I'm very interested in hearing a bit more about your Peckham case. I'm fascinated by facial mapping, but I've never had the opportunity to employ the technique.'

'I know the Peckham case will be forming part of the professor's lecture today, so I won't steal his thunder. Why don't we listen to the lecture and then go for a bite to eat and a drink? There's a very nice Italian restaurant just up the road. We can have a proper civilised conversation over a plate of delicious food and a nice glass of red.'

'That sounds a terrific idea,' gushed the big Irishman.

All of a sudden, Seamus Carter decided he was a massive fan of seminars.

The lecture itself from Professor Mason was very informative, and mercifully for Seamus's back, it wasn't too long. He had found himself listening intently to the description of the injuries suffered by the victim in the Peckham murder. The mutilation of the hands, the severing of the digits. The massive injuries to the face and jaw.

The injuries were almost identical to the two murder victims he'd recently performed post-mortems on in Nottinghamshire. The conversation with Emily that evening was going to be even more interesting than he'd first thought.

An hour after the seminar had finished, Seamus opened the door for Emily to enter Giovanni's, the small Italian restaurant a short walk from the university.

Having been shown to a table for two by the waiter, they sat down and perused the menus. After enquiring whether Emily preferred red or white wine, Seamus ordered a bottle of Valpolicella Reserve red wine.

Emily ordered the spinach and ricotta cannelloni, while Seamus ordered the pollo a la creme chicken dish. While they waited for their food to be prepared, they sipped the velvety red wine and talked quietly about the lecture.

'Emily, I'm fascinated by your Peckham murder case. Is it still unsolved?'

'Yes, I believe so. I can check when I get back to London. Why do you ask?'

'I've recently carried out two post-mortem examinations on murdered women in Nottinghamshire, where I've seen almost identical injuries to the hands and fingers, as well as massive trauma to the heads – especially the jaw. What was the actual cause of death of your Peckham victim?'

'The cause of death was a massive brain haemorrhage caused by repeated blunt force trauma to the skull.'

'You see, from what you've told me so far and what I heard in the lecture, that there's the only difference. The two women I examined had both been strangled prior to the injuries being caused. Tell me, is it just the one victim you've seen with these injuries?'

'Yes, only one, she was a young prostitute. There was something very strange about the case, though.'

'Strange?' echoed Seamus.

'Yes, strange; it was like looking at the handiwork of two textbook murder scenarios in one go.'

'I'm sorry if I'm being a little dense, but I don't understand.'

'Well, there were definite elements of rage involved, but there was also a strong element of cold calculation. I also know that the detective in charge was bemoaning the total lack of evidence found at the scene.'

'What do you mean?'

'There was absolutely no forensic evidence left, either at the murder scene or the deposition site. It really was quite an unusual case.'

Seamus stroked his bushy beard thoughtfully. 'Emily, I really think that the Peckham murder and the two murders in Nottinghamshire could be linked; there are so many similarities. I think it would be a good idea if you pass onto me the details of the detective in charge of the Peckham case so I can put him in touch with Detective Inspector Flint, who's investigating the murders in Nottinghamshire.'

'No problem at all. If you think there could be a connection, I'll get that information to your office first thing in the morning.'

'Anyway, I think that's more than enough talk about work for one night, so it is. Now, would you like another glass of this lovely red wine before you tell me all about yourself and your new life in London?'

Emily smiled and said, 'That would be lovely, Seamus, thank you.'

Seamus looked across the candlelit table and hoped this would be the first of many meals with the beautiful Emily Cook.

65

Peckham Police Station, London – October 26, 1984

On the third ring, Glyn Johnson answered the telephone in his office: 'Hello, Detective Inspector Johnson, can I help you?'

'Good morning, my name's Detective Inspector Danny Flint, Nottinghamshire CID. I'd like to talk to you about the unsolved murder of a young girl in Peckham. The victim's name is Jenny Taylor.'

Glyn answered the request brusquely.

'Give me your contact number, Detective Inspector Flint, and I'll call you straight back. I'm not being funny here, but I ain't about to start discussing a murder case over the phone with somebody I've never even heard of before. No offence.'

Equally brief and to the point, Danny answered, 'None taken; I'd be exactly the same. As I said, my name's Detective Inspector Danny Flint. I'm stationed at Mansfield Police Station in Nottinghamshire. My direct line will be in the Police Almanac on your desk. Talk to you shortly.'

Glyn hung up the phone and muttered, 'Cheeky bugger!'

He opened his desk drawer and rummaged through the contents until he found the beige-coloured book that listed the telephone numbers of every police station in the UK.

Quickly thumbing through it, he found the pages for Nottinghamshire Constabulary. He scanned the pages and found the number for the direct line into the CID office at Mansfield Police Station. He picked up the phone and dialled the number. It was answered on the first ring.

'Detective Inspector Flint.'

'Danny, it's Glyn Johnson from Peckham. What do you want to know about Jenny Taylor?'

'Thanks for getting straight back to me. I had an interesting telephone call from a pathologist last night by the name of Seamus Carter. He told me that very recently he attended a seminar at Bristol University, where he bumped into Emily Cook, the Home Office pathologist who, I believe, covers your area. The seminar he attended was a lecture about facial mapping by Professor Mason, and the case of Jenny Taylor formed part of that lecture. From what Seamus told me last night, it would appear that the injuries suffered by Jenny Taylor are almost identical to the injuries found on two murder victims up here in Nottinghamshire.'

'That's interesting. Have you got a suspect in mind for your cases?'

'No, both our cases are still unsolved.'

'These injuries you mentioned on the victims in your cases, what were they specifically, and how are they similar to those inflicted on Jenny Taylor?'

'Both of our victims suffered mutilations to their hands and massive injuries to the head and face. According to Seamus, these injuries are identical in every way to those found on Jenny Taylor. The only thing that differs is the actual cause of death. Our women were strangled using a thin nylon cord. Jenny Taylor, I believe, died as a result of a massive brain injury caused by blunt force trauma to the skull.'

'That does sound remarkably similar. Tell me something, Danny, have you got much to go on evidentially with your cases?'

'Forensically, we've got absolutely nothing.'

'The scenes were totally sterile, right?'

'Totally.'

'Have your Scenes of Crime people found any foot marks?'

'Yes, at both scenes.'

'Don't tell me, they were footmarks covered by overshoes. Am I right?'

'Spot on, Glyn. This goes no further, but between you and me, I've started looking at the possibility that a serving police officer is responsible for our two murders.'

'That's exactly what we've started to look at down here on the Jenny Taylor case as well. I'm looking at serving or recently retired police officers. Unfortunately, my investigation has ground to a halt down here. My guv'nors are slowly pulling the plug on the Jenny Taylor enquiry, and unless something drastic comes to light, this murder will stay unsolved. Danny, would you mind if I travelled up with my skipper, Craig Fraser, to see you and your team? That way, we can compare notes and see exactly what common ground we have.'

'I think that would be a good idea. When can you get up here?'

'I'll have to clear it with my guv'nor down here first and tidy a few things up, but I should be able to get up to you on the twenty-ninth. If I give you a call later with the time we'll be arriving, could you arrange for somebody to pick us up from the railway station in Nottingham?'

'No problem; I can arrange that. I look forward to seeing you on the twenty-ninth.'

Glyn hung up the telephone and sat back in his chair.

'Interesting,' he said aloud.

66

Wembley, London – October 27, 1984

'What time are you going back to Nottingham?' a very timid Rita asked Mick. She'd stayed away from the house all week, only popping in and out when she absolutely needed to. Something about her husband had definitely changed.

He stalked around the house in his dirty vest and pants, just lying on the sofa, watching TV. He hadn't been out all week, refusing to tidy up after himself. He'd not had a wash or shave all the time he'd been home.

Only once had she dared to make a comment about the state of the house. He had simply glared at her before walking over and raising his hand as if to slap her.

Rita had cowered away and quickly slipped out of the house without saying another word. She'd stayed with her best friend, Sue Jessop, at her flat in Peckham every night.

Lying on the settee, Mick angrily responded to Rita's

question. 'What the fuck's it got to do with you when I'm going back?'

'I'm sorry, love, I was just going to iron your shirts, that's all.'

He sneered at her. 'Iron my shirts; you've changed your fucking tune, haven't you? I don't know, Rita darlin', I reckon I should've given you a slap years ago.'

Rita was fighting the urge to make a comment back. She knew he was goading her, but she was terrified of him in this menacing mood.

'There's no need for that, love; you know I care about you,' she said.

'All you care about, you dirty slag, is your next shag pressed up the wall of some dark alley behind some dingy pub in the East End!'

She could bite her lip no longer. Before she thought about the consequences, she snapped back at him, 'Yeah, well, at least I don't fuck tarts!'

'You're a fucking tart, Rita. Don't think for one minute that I don't know you've been dossing down at Sue Jessop's flat. She's another fat slag. I bet you've both had a different bloke every night!'

Rita desperately tried to bite her tongue, but it was too much for her. She railed back, 'Who could blame me! All I've ever wanted was a proper man, not some ugly retard with a cock the size of an acorn, and that's when it's fucking hard!' she screamed.

Mick jumped up from the settee, and with one powerful hand, he grabbed Rita by the throat, pushing her backwards until she slammed hard against the lounge wall.

The force with which she hit the wall caused ornaments to fall from the mantelpiece above the fireplace.

'Apologise, you bitch,' he snarled. 'If you don't say sorry in the next ten seconds, I'll kill you right now!' he said through gritted teeth.

Desperately, Rita tried to say the word, but his powerful hand was gradually crushing her windpipe.

A noise escaped her mouth, but it was just an inaudible rasp.

'Sorry, what did you say, love?' He laughed and then squeezed harder.

'I can't fucking hear you!' he mocked.

He put his other hand around Rita's throat and now squeezed in earnest, slowly lifting her off the floor. He watched as her eyes bulged and her tongue started to protrude from her mouth. Her face was getting darker and darker. He could feel her feet kicking his legs and her hands pounding his head and shoulders.

Still he squeezed.

Eventually, her feet and hands became still, and his hands and arms grew tired. After ten minutes Mick slowly relaxed his grip. Rita had been dead for the last four.

He let go of her completely, and she dropped lifeless to the floor.

'Finally, some peace and fucking quiet!' he roared.

He stepped over her body and walked from the lounge into the hallway. He opened the door that led from the hallway into the attached garage.

The dark blue Ford Sierra was there.

He grabbed the car keys from the hook above the work bench at the back of the garage and unlocked the boot. Lifting the boot lid, he removed a few items, clearing the entire boot space.

He then walked out of the garage and back into the lounge. He contemptuously rolled Rita's body out of the way with his foot and carefully replaced the ornaments that had fallen onto the floor from the mantelpiece.

Trance-like, he walked from the lounge into the kitchen and got a glass of cold water from the tap. He drank the water quickly before picking up the kettle and filling it.

Mick then took a mug from the cupboard and threw a tea bag in.

While the kettle was boiling, he walked back into the lounge. Grunting loudly, he lifted his wife's body off the floor and over his shoulder. Rita was quite heavy, and he struggled at first with her dead weight. He carried her into the garage and threw her down roughly into the boot of the car. He grabbed an old dust sheet from the back of the garage and threw it on top of her body.

He slammed the boot shut.

'Good riddance, bitch!' he said under his breath.

Mick then locked the boot of the car and hung the car keys back on the hook before leaving the garage.

Closing the interior door, he walked into the kitchen and finished making his mug of tea. Gradually calming down, he sat at the kitchen table and took a sip of the hot drink.

Ten minutes ticked by as he slowly finished his tea. He placed the mug on the table and looked at his watch. Three hours to wait before he would be travelling back up the M1 motorway, back up to Nottinghamshire.

Mick couldn't wait to see Jimmy Wade and tell him the news about Rita. He'd tell him before they went out for some proper action tomorrow night.

He would deal with Rita's body when he came back on rest days next time. He knew exactly where he intended to dispose of her body.

Mick sat at the table, closed his eyes and began to plan it all out in his head.

First, he'd buy an old van for a couple of hundred quid; then he'd chuck Rita's body in the van and drive down to the old tin mine in Cornwall. He was confident that her weighted body would never be discovered down the flooded mineshaft. Once he'd dumped her body, he would scrap the van down there in Truro, then catch the train from Cornwall back to London.

He would then scrap his own Ford Sierra to avoid any implication in the prostitute's death. The last thing he'd have to do would be to buy a brand-new motor with the proceeds of all the overtime he'd worked during the strike.

It was a perfect plan.

Rita would just have to stay in the boot of the car for now.

After all, it wasn't like she was going anywhere.

That thought made him chuckle.

At last, he was free.

67

Ollerton, Nottinghamshire – October 28, 1984

Mick was in a buoyant mood. He quickly climbed into the front seat of the dark green Ford Cortina that was parked in the layby outside Proteus Camp.

'Hello, Jimmy, it was good to see you again at the quarry today, old son. Have you missed me?'

He frowned before continuing, 'You didn't say much today. Was that because you were shocked when I told you about Rita?'

'This was you, wasn't it?' said a disgruntled Jimmy without looking up.

'What was me?'

Jimmy thrust a copy of the local *Observer* newspaper towards Mick. The newspaper headline read 'Woman attacked in Edwinstowe'.

'Yeah, it was me, so what?'

'I thought we agreed to wait until tonight.'

'No, you agreed. Anyway, I thought you said you were going to change the motor?'

'No need to. The cops are looking for a silver-coloured Nissan Bluebird now.'

'How come?'

'Because the smart one in this team made an anonymous phone call saying he'd seen a silver Nissan Bluebird speeding away from the lane where we dumped the second woman, that's how come.'

'Sweet, good thinking, Jimmy.'

It was a lie.

There had been no phone call to the police. Jimmy was prepared to risk using the Cortina for one more night.

'Talking of Rita, what were you babbling on about at the quarry earlier? Have you really done her in?'

Mick replied triumphantly, 'Oh yes! I couldn't stand another minute listening to her nagging, grating voice.'

'I thought we'd agreed that you would hold off at this moment in time.'

'I never agreed to that. I told you I couldn't promise anything. She just wound me up once too often.'

'What've you done with her?'

'If you must know, I throttled the bitch. Look, it's fine, nobody's going to miss her, and nobody's going to find her. Just relax, will you? Everything's fine and dandy.'

'I don't like it.'

Mick glared at him. 'You don't have to like it, old son. It's done. Get over it!'

But Mick didn't want to risk Jimmy getting so annoyed that he cancelled tonight, so he said in an acquiescent manner, 'Alright, Jimmy, I'm sorry. I know I shouldn't have snapped with Rita, but I just couldn't help it, okay?'

'You've got to stay in control. I know what it's like when the urges are strong, but you've got to remember the most important thing is not getting caught.'

'You're right, and I'm sorry. Trust me, though, I've taken care of everything down there. Rita won't ever be found. Now, where are we going tonight?'

'Oh, I've got a proper treat for you tonight, Mick. We're going over to a small village called Newstead. I've been watching a woman who walks a little terrier dog on her own through the grounds of Newstead Abbey at night.'

'Silly bitch!' grunted Mick.

'You're going to love this one, mate. She's really fit.'

'Nice one, Jimmy. This is more like it, the two of us back in the groove.'

The journey over to Newstead village was made in silence. Jimmy was constantly on the lookout for police cars or a roadblock.

Luckily, they saw neither.

After half an hour, Jimmy drove the car into Newstead village. He drove straight through the village and turned into the grounds of Newstead Abbey. After two minutes, he pulled off the main lane and turned onto a very narrow, very bumpy dirt track.

Finally, he stopped the car.

'Bloody hell, this bird must have a death wish, walking down here on her own.'

'No, she walks along the lane up the top, but I don't want her to see the car. The plan is, we wait up there by the side of the lane, grab her, kill the dog and then bring her down here to have some fun. What do you think?'

'It sounds perfect to me. Tell me about the woman; is she a blonde?'

'Yeah, she's a blonde.'

'Great stuff. I'll get the bag out of the boot.'

'There's no need. We can leave the bag in the car. We're bringing the woman back down here, away from the lane, remember?'

'What about the dog? We'll need something to deal with the dog.'

'Don't you worry about the dog; I've got some stuff here to deal with that.'

Jimmy held up a small brown bottle and a rag. 'One whiff of this stuff and the little rat will be history. You concentrate on grabbing the woman. Let me worry about the dog.'

'How long before she gets here?'

'She'll be along soon enough. We need to get up to the lane.'

Both men got out of the car. It was very cold, and frost was starting to form on the ground.

'Fucking hell, it's brass monkeys out here, Jimmy!'

'For Christ's sake, keep the noise down! She'll hear us.'

'Sorry, guv'nor!' Mick said, in an exaggerated sarcastic whisper.

They crept stealthily through the woods until they were ten yards from the main lane.

'Wait here, and I'll see if she's coming. I won't be long.'

'Okay.'

Jimmy disappeared into the dark woods.

Mick hadn't felt this excited about any of the others. He felt aroused and had already decided that before he killed this woman, he was going to have some fun with her. The more he thought about all the deviant acts he was going to do to the silly cow, the more aroused he became. It was her own fault; fancy walking down here at night on her own. She was asking for it.

His mind had wandered so much that he never heard Jimmy stealthily approaching him from behind.

Suddenly, a chloroform-soaked rag was clamped firmly over Mick's mouth and nose. He struggled briefly, but Jimmy was strong and held the rag firmly in place.

Within a few seconds, Mick had slumped into unconsciousness and fell to the ground in a heap.

'Now for the hard part,' Jimmy said aloud.

Mick was quite short, but he was a stocky man. Getting a good grip on his clothes, Jimmy hoisted him over his shoulder into a fireman's lift.

He retraced his steps through the woods before dropping Mick down onto the ground, twenty yards in front of the car. Once again, he clamped the chloroform-soaked rag over Mick's mouth and nose before walking over to the car and flicking the headlights on. The beams of the headlights picked out a rope with a hangman's noose swinging from an oak tree.

The rope had been tied off onto a lower branch, and the noose was hanging about four feet off the ground.

After a hard struggle, Jimmy managed to manoeuvre Mick's head through the noose. Mick was still totally unconscious; he was now hanging from the noose with his arms dangling by his sides.

His knees were still resting on the ground, taking most, but not all of his weight.

Jimmy could hear a gurgling sound coming from Mick as the rope of the noose began to dig into his windpipe. He quickly walked over to where he had tied the end of the rope off. He untied the rope and took up the strain of the weight of Mick's body.

Using all his strength, Jimmy hauled on the rope until Mick was completely suspended from the rope, his feet no longer touching the ground.

Jimmy pulled again, hoisting the dead weight further up, until the sergeant's feet were about two feet above the ground.

Maintaining the tension on the rope, Jimmy tied it off again on the lower branch of the tree. Once the rope was fastened securely, he stepped back and watched, grinning, as Mick began to thrash around.

He had obviously started to come around as the effects of the chloroform began to wear off. He was now kicking his legs, and his hands went up to the rope that was now biting hard into his neck. Desperately, he tried to claw his fingers behind the rope to allow some air in.

His thrashing limbs, illuminated by the headlights, caused shadows to dance against the surrounding trees.

Jimmy chuckled as he watched the sergeant dancing at the end of the rope like some crazed puppet. Finally, the thrashing stopped, replaced by a few twitching movements. Eventually, even those stopped, and everything became still, the arms limp at the sides of the hanging body.

Mick Reynolds slowly swung at the end of the rope. Jimmy walked over to take a closer look.

It was grotesque.

Mick's head was nearly black and looked swollen. His eyes were bulging almost out of their sockets, and his bloated swollen tongue was already protruding slightly from his mouth.

'You just wouldn't listen, would you?' said Jimmy to the dead man.

He put gloves on before he reached into his pocket and took out a black plastic tube, placing it in Mick's inside coat pocket. He had typed out the final message from the 'Coal Killer' earlier that day.

There was one other thing left to do. Reaching up, he found what he was looking for under the dead man's jumper. Quickly he removed the object, stashing it in his own coat pocket.

Jimmy walked back to the car and grabbed Mick's grip bag from the boot. He quickly checked the contents to ensure there was nothing in there that would incriminate him. He was unconcerned that there were two forensic suits in the bag. Anybody finding the bag later would just assume that the sergeant had carried a spare. He placed the bag next to the carefully staged overturned wooden crate.

It looked perfect. It looked like the sergeant had taken his own life.

Jimmy had only used the bare minimum of chloroform to incapacitate Mick; he wrongly assumed that any traces of the stupefying drug would have worn off by the time the body was discovered.

Having left the grip bag by the side of the hanging man, Jimmy returned to the car and threw the chloroform bottle and rag inside the already open boot.

From inside the boot, he retrieved a full petrol can.

Returning to the hanging man, he splashed a little petrol on the sleeves of the dead man's coat.

Jimmy then walked back to the car, his precious Cortina, and began splashing petrol in the boot, in the footwells and finally all over the engine.

He quickly removed the registration plates from the front and the back of the car. He couldn't risk removing the registration plates until now. He'd already removed the chassis plate, engine number and the vehicle identification number plate earlier that day. He knew exactly where he was going to dump the registration plates later.

Having filled the car with petrol, Jimmy took a step back before lighting a rag he'd taken from his pocket. He then threw the lit rag into the car. There was a loud whooshing noise as the car erupted into a ball of flame.

Once again Jimmy chuckled as the hanging body of Sergeant Mick Reynolds, illuminated this time by the car fire, caused eerie shadows to dance in the surrounding woodland.

He walked over and pushed the legs of the hanging man to make the dance even more animated.

Finally, Jimmy picked up the two number plates he'd removed from the car and walked off through the woods.

He'd played here as a child and knew these woods like the back of his hand. After ten minutes' walking, he came to the edge of the wood.

In front of him was an open field.

The field was rock hard with the frost, so Jimmy was

unconcerned about leaving footprints. He walked straight over the field towards the small copse in the middle.

At the centre of this tiny copse was a small, deep pond.

The pond held a special childhood memory for Jimmy Wade, and he smiled as he looked at the black water that was reflecting the bright full moon like a mirror.

Jimmy hurled the two number plates into the middle of the pond.

He stared in wonder as ripples disrupted the solid disc of the reflected bright moon into a myriad of exploding white stars.

Silently, he watched until the water settled down again and the moon became a whole entity once more.

He then left the small copse and walked back out across the frosty field, this time heading in the opposite direction, back towards Newstead village.

Jimmy planned to walk as far as the first phone box in nearby Annesley and then call a taxi to take him back to Mansfield Woodhouse.

As he walked, he felt free, totally unburdened. No more Police Sergeant Mick Reynolds to worry about.

His thoughts immediately turned to Detective Rachel Moore; he knew it would be her time very soon.

The careful planning for the future was starting to come together now, and he couldn't help smiling as he walked briskly towards Annesley.

68

Peckham Police Station – October 29, 1984

The West Indian cleaner paused at the door, her hand shooting towards her mouth. She gasped, 'Bloody hell, Glyn, you gave me such a fright, man!'

It was seven o'clock in the morning. Glyn and Craig were already at their desks in the Peckham CID office; both were busy clearing paperwork.

Glyn looked up at the startled cleaner. 'Don't worry about it, Florence sweetheart. I won't be making a habit of it. You can leave this room today.'

'Thank you for that anyway, kind sir.' She smiled before moving on along the corridor.

Glyn took another sip of his black coffee and then reached for the telephone. He dialled the number for the Mansfield CID office on the off chance that Danny Flint had also started his day early.

The phone was answered on the second ring.

'Good morning, Danny, it's Glyn Johnson here. Sorry it's a bit early.'

'No problem, Glyn, it's good to hear from you. Are you still okay to travel up here today?'

'Yeah, well, that's the reason for my call, Danny. Myself and DS Fraser have come on duty early to get the decks cleared. We intend catching the midday train from St Pancras. It's due to arrive at Nottingham Midland Station at approximately two thirty this afternoon. Will you be able to arrange for someone to meet us there?'

'No problem. It will probably be DC Rachel Moore. Shall I get her to wear a pink carnation?'

Glyn laughed. 'That's not a bad idea, but I'm sure we'll spot each other. Just tell her to look out for one devastatingly handsome black dude and one ugly Scottish dwarf!'

'Charming,' muttered Craig.

'Nice one. We'll see you later and have a chat over a few beers,' said Danny.

'Sounds like a plan, Danny. See you later this afternoon.'

No sooner had Glyn put the phone down than it started to ring again.

'Bloody hell, don't people realise it's only seven in the morning!'

Sweeping up the phone, he answered the call tersely: 'DI Johnson!'

'I know it's early, guv'nor, but I saw you come in. It's Sergeant Collins at the front desk.'

'Bloody hell, Sarge, I've come on early for a reason. What's so important that it can't wait?'

'Sorry, guv, I've got a woman by the name of Sue Jessop in reception. She says her best friend's missing, and she reckons she's been done in. I wouldn't normally bother you straight away, but the missing woman's married to a cop over at Wembley nick.'

'Can't we send her over there, then, and let Wembley deal with it?'

'That's the problem. This Sue Jessop's saying it's the husband who's done her in, and she's too scared to go into Wembley nick coz that's where he works.'

'Bloody hell, this just keeps getting better. What's the missing person's name, and who's the cop?'

'Her name's Rita Reynolds, and his name's Sergeant Mick Reynolds.'

'Okay, Sarge, I'm on my way down.'

'Thanks, guv'nor.'

Glyn turned to Craig and said, 'Come on, we'd better go downstairs and listen to this load of old shit before we book the train tickets.'

Craig said nothing. The two men grabbed their jackets and made their way out the door.

'See what happens when you come in early, Craig?'

'I know, guv, that's why I always try my hardest to be late.'

'Yeah, ain't that the truth.'

Five minutes later and Craig was showing Sue Jessop into the interview room where Glyn was waiting.

'Good morning, Mrs Jessop, is it? I'm Detective Inspector Johnson, and this is Detective Sergeant Fraser. I understand you've got some concerns over a friend of yours?'

'That's right, I have. It's my best friend Rita Reynolds; she's married to one of your lot. He's an arsehole, and he punched her in the face the last time he was home.'

'What do you mean the last time he was home?'

'He's always away on this bloody miners' strike thing.'

'So how do you know your friend was punched by her husband?' said Craig.

'I saw her straight after she'd run out of the house. Her face was a right mess.'

'Why didn't she report it?'

'Look, I'll be straight with you. Rita's no angel, and she gives Mick a hard time sometimes, but that's still no excuse to belt her one, is it?'

'No, it certainly isn't, Mrs Jessop. Why are you so concerned about Rita's well-being this morning?' asked Glyn.

'Well, he came home last week, and he's been a proper swine to her all week. Anyway, after he smashed her face in the last time, he was home, Rita made me promise that I'd phone her every evening and every morning to make sure she was okay.'

'That's a bit drastic, isn't it?'

'Rita's terrified of him. He threatened to kill her last time, and she thinks he meant it.'

'When did you last speak to Rita?'

'Well, she'd been staying at mine for that week he was home, but she went back over to her house on the morning of the twenty-sixth.'

'That was three days ago, Sue. Why haven't you been in before?'

'I don't know, coz he's a copper, I suppose. I was too scared to go into Wembley nick. I went over there twice but bottled it; I just daren't go in. That's why I've come here today and not Wembley. I don't want to be talking to his mates, do I?'

'Why did he hit Rita last time he was home?' asked Craig.

'Rita says it was nothing. Apparently it was all to do with the fact that he wouldn't take her out for a trip in the car. They've got a lovely dark blue car, and he refuses to use it. Anyway, he wouldn't take her out for a ride, they ended up arguing, and Rita gave him some grief about seeing prostitutes.'

Glyn now leaned forward and placed his elbows on the desk. 'Hang on a minute, Mrs Jessop. Did you say this police sergeant sees prostitutes?'

'Yeah, the dirty sod. Apparently – well, according to Rita

– he's down the red-light areas all the time. He likes to get off with the tarts. Rita reckons the younger the better, filthy perv!'

'Do you know what sort of car they've got?'

'Nah, I'm useless with cars. I've only seen it once. It's quite big, almost brand new, and it's dark blue. That's all I know about the car.'

Glyn was thoughtful for a moment.

'Okay, Mrs Jessop, where does your friend Rita live?'

'It's on Miller Street over at Wembley – number 29, I think. It's a nice semi, with a garage 'n' everything.'

'Is there anything else you can tell us, Sue?' asked Craig.

'Yeah, I've got a key for their front door. Rita gave it to me two weeks ago in case anything was wrong.'

She took the Yale key out of her coat pocket and offered it to Glyn.

'Blimey! She must've been worried to give you a key,' said Glyn.

'She isn't worried; Rita's *terrified*. Mick's a proper nasty bastard! Sorry, I know he's one of your lot, but he is. I hope she's alright.'

Glyn took the key. 'Well, thanks for coming in, Mrs Jessop. We'll have a drive over to Miller Street and make sure everything's okay.'

'Will you let me know that Rita's okay, please?'

'Of course we will. Give Detective Sergeant Fraser a phone number where we can reach you.'

'Thanks. I'm so worried about her.'

Craig stood up and escorted Sue Jessop out of the police station.

When he returned to the interview room, Glyn was still sitting there. He was rubbing his chin and looked deep in thought.

'Penny for 'em, guv'nor?' asked the tough Scot.

'I'm probably clutching at straws here, but a big blue car, prostitutes, a copper who's violent towards women ... I think me and you need to get over to Wembley and check this out.'

'Okay, guv, I'll make a quick call and find out what shift Sergeant Reynolds is working today.'

Fifteen minutes later, Craig walked back into the office.

'Right, I've done some ringing around. Sergeant Mick Reynolds returned to Nottinghamshire on the night of the twenty-seventh. He's doing four weeks on and one week off. The call sign of his PSU is Mike Alpha One Zero. They're currently being billeted at a place called Proteus Camp near a town called Ollerton. It's actually a disused army camp that the local Army cadets use. It's a bit of a shithole, by all accounts.'

'Right, let's get over to Wembley and check out Reynolds's house.'

'Do you want me to contact Wembley nick and let them know what we're doing?'

'Nah, not yet; Sue Jessop might be giving us a load of old pony. We've got a front door key; let's check it out ourselves first. It'll only take five minutes. Straight in, make sure the wife's okay, straight out.'

'Right you are, guv'nor. I'll grab some car keys. I reckon I know where Miller Street is. If I remember rightly, it's in quite a nice area, not far from Wembley Stadium.'

It took forty-five minutes to drive over to Wembley; the rush-hour traffic was just starting to build up.

Finally, Craig parked the car directly outside 29 Miller Street.

'Looks a nice place, guv'nor.'

Mimicking Sue Jessop's description of the house, Glyn replied, 'Yeah, it's got a garage 'n' everything.'

The two detectives got out of the car and walked up the path to the front door. Glyn banged loudly on the door with his fist. When there was no answer, he tried the key. He turned the key and, with a gentle push, opened the front door.

As they walked in, Glyn shouted, 'Anybody home!'

It was a typical semi-detached house.

The front door opened directly into the hallway, the lounge door was off to the right, the stairs went straight up from the hallway, and just past the stairs was the kitchen door. Glyn walked into the lounge, and Craig went straight upstairs.

He shouted down from upstairs, 'Guv, you'd better come up here and have a look at this!'

Glyn climbed the stairs three at a time and found Craig in the small third bedroom. 'What is it?'

'Over here, have a look in the bottom of this wardrobe.'

Glyn stepped forward and saw a stack of four or five blue forensic suits still in their plastic packets. Lying at the side of them, in a clear plastic packet that had been torn open, were black tie wraps.

On the other side of the suits were two rolls of brown gaffer tape.

'Get Scenes of Crime out here to photograph this lot. I'm going back downstairs to check out the garage. It looks like there's an internal door that leads into the garage from the hallway.'

Glyn went downstairs and through the internal door into the garage.

Immediately, the stench hit him.

Doing his best to ignore the foul smell, Glyn saw a dark blue Ford Sierra.

'Craig, you'd better get down here, mate! I think I've found Rita!'

Craig came downstairs and walked into the garage, 'Bloody hell, guv'nor, I see what you mean. That smell's only going to be one thing, a body. Have you seen any keys for the car?'

Both men quickly looked around the garage, and Glyn saw the keys on the hook above the workbench.

'Before we do anything, Craig, nip out to the car and grab us a pair of gloves each.'

'Okay, guv.'

Craig was glad to get out of the garage, even if it was only for a minute; the smell was already unbearable. The heating was on full in the house, and there was a small radiator near the back of the car in the garage.

While he waited for Craig to return with the gloves, Glyn looked closely at the registration plates that were on the Ford Sierra.

He could see that the plates had been tampered with using black tape.

The actual number beneath the tape was B 623 FJH.

The black tape had been cleverly used to change the number 3 to an 8 and the letter *F* to an *E*, changing the registration number to B 628 EJH.

Glyn got out his notebook and compared the tampered registration plate to the number Lee Skipton had scribbled down the night Jenny Taylor had been abducted and killed.

They were identical. This was the car Skipton had seen Jenny Taylor getting into on the night she was abducted and murdered.

Craig returned with the gloves.

'Craig, look at the plates. This is the car that was used to abduct Jenny Taylor.'

'Bloody hell, guv'nor, we've cracked it!'

Having put on the gloves, Glyn grabbed the car keys from the hook and opened the boot.

Both detectives involuntarily took a step back, as the action of the boot opening wafted the stench directly up towards them.

'Jesus Christ!' said Craig.

The light in the garage was dim, and it was hard to see into the boot properly.

Glyn held his gloved hand over his mouth and nose.

'Craig, there's a light switch over there near the door; flick it on, mate.'

Craig flicked on the switch, and a light bulb directly over the workbench came on. With the light now on, Glyn could see there was a bundle in the boot covered by an old dust sheet. He could see that parts of the dust sheet were moving.

Glyn reached into the boot and pulled away the dust sheet. The sight that greeted him was horrific.

Although it had only been a few days since Rita had been dumped in the boot of the car, the central heating, which came on automatically in the house, was so high that her body had started to decompose very quickly.

Her face was black and grotesquely bloated, distorting her features. Her tongue had swollen so much that it resembled an arm trying to escape from her mouth. Glyn could see maggots moving around her face, crawling in and out of any orifice they could find. It was the maggots crawling around the head and face that had caused the dust sheet to appear to be moving slightly.

The stench of putrefying flesh was overpowering.

Having opened the boot to confirm their suspicions, both Glyn and Craig quickly moved out of the garage and then out of the house.

ONCE OUTSIDE THE HOUSE, both men took deep breaths, filling their lungs with the cold morning air to try to remove the cloying stench from their nostrils.

'Fuck me, guv'nor, what a mess!'

'I've seen some bad sights in my time, Craig, but bloody hell, that's right up there with the worst.'

'I know what you mean. I think I'll be smelling that stench for the rest of the week.'

Glyn took a minute to take a few more deep breaths of fresh air.

'Get back on the radio. I want a full Scenes of Crime team turning out, and I want a Home Office pathologist travelling immediately. If at all possible, I'd like it to be Emily Cook.'

'I'm on it.'

'Also, I'm going to need you to manage the scene here for a little while. I've got to get back to the nick and make a phone call up to Nottinghamshire. They've got to be told what we've found down here.'

'No problem, guv, I can sort it out here. Can you send me a couple more blokes to help with the bagging and labelling?'

'Will do. As soon as I've made the call up to Mansfield CID, I'll be back here myself. I need a chat with Danny Flint first; we need to get things moving up in Nottinghamshire.'

69

Mansfield Police Station – October 29, 1984

The telephone in the CID office at Mansfield Police Station was ringing off the hook. Rob ran back into the office and picked up the phone. 'Hello, DS Buxton. Can I help you?'

'It's Detective Inspector Johnson from the Met. Is your guv'nor around?'

'He is, sir, just a second.'

Rob placed the receiver on the desk and ran down to the canteen, where Danny was just taking the first bite of a sausage sandwich.

'Boss, there's a phone call for you in the office. It's that DI from the Met.'

Danny grabbed the sandwich and raced back to the office. Picking up the phone, he said, 'Hello again, Glyn, what's up?'

'Danny, we've had a major breakthrough down here. We've just found the body of a dead woman in a house in Wembley. It would appear on first look that she's been murdered, and we've found forensic suits, black cable ties and gaffer tape all at the scene.'

'Forensic suits still at the scene? We've never found any at the scenes. Was your suspect disturbed?'

'Sorry, I'm not being very clear. I've just left the scene, and I'm still a bit hyped up.'

'Don't worry, Glyn; take your time.'

'The house where we found the body is the deceased's home address. She'd been stuffed into the boot of the family car. I think her name's Rita Reynolds. The man she's married to is a serving police officer, Sergeant Mick Reynolds. The forensic suits were all still in their packets. There were five of them.'

'Go on.'

Danny was now trying hard to restrain his own growing excitement at what he was hearing.

'Danny, this Sergeant Reynolds has been in charge of a Metropolitan Police PSU in Nottinghamshire for the entire duration of the miners' strike. The PSU call sign is Mike Alpha One Zero. Reynolds and his PSU have been billeted at Proteus Army Camp near Ollerton in Nottinghamshire. They're still there now.'

'Bloody hell! This has got to be our man.'

'It certainly looks promising. I've already contacted the strike control room, and they've informed me that call sign Mike Alpha One Zero is currently escorting working miners into Warsop Main Colliery. They're due to stand down at around nine thirty this morning.'

Danny's brain was going into overdrive.

'Glyn, do me a favour. Get back onto the control room and tell them to instruct Mike Alpha One Zero to return to Proteus Camp as soon as they stand down from Warsop Main for a special commitment. We'll start travelling out to Proteus Camp immediately.'

'Will do. Obviously, we won't be travelling up to

Nottingham today as planned. We've got a major crime scene to sort out here. Keep me informed, and let me know as soon as Reynolds is nicked. Cheers.'

'Will do. I'll arrest him on suspicion of the murder of Jenny Taylor for starters; we can always arrest him for the murder of his wife later if your body down there is subsequently identified as being Rita Reynolds. In respect of our outstanding murders, I'll wait until I know exactly what we've got to connect him to the killings up here. First things first, let's get him in.'

'Okay, that sounds like a plan. I'm going back over to Wembley now to meet the Detective Inspector from that nick to sort out a plan to deal with this latest murder. Technically, it's not in my area, but I think it's so obviously linked to the murder of Jenny Taylor that I'll be taking charge.'

'Okay, Glyn, talk to you later.'

Danny put the phone down.

Both Rob and Rachel were staring intently at him, having heard one side of the conversation.

'What's happening, boss?' said Rachel.

'I think we might've just identified our killer.'

'Come on, spill the beans,' said an excited Rob.

'Rachel, have you started your enquiries with the Metropolitan Police personnel department yet?'

'Yes, sir, I finished the Met yesterday. I'm starting on North Yorkshire today.'

'I want you to forget about North Yorkshire now and go back to the records of the Met and dig out everything we know about the deployment of Police Sergeant Mick Reynolds from Wembley Police Station. He's been on duty up here, off and on, since the start of the strike. I want to know exactly when he was up here and when he was back down in London. His PSU call sign is Mike Alpha One Zero. I want to know from the strike control room exactly when that call sign was actively on duty and when they were stood down. Can you manage all that?'

'Yes, sir. Is this Sergeant Reynolds our killer?'

'I don't know yet, but it's looking good. I'll give you a full update when we get back.'

He grabbed his jacket and coat from the back of the chair.

'Come on, Rob, we need to get to Proteus Camp at Ollerton. I'll brief you on the way.'

Rob grabbed his coat and a set of car keys.

Five minutes later the CID car was being driven at speed through Forest Town as it headed towards Ollerton.

'Ease off the pedal a bit, Rob. Let's get there in one piece.'

'Sorry, boss.' Rob eased back on the accelerator. 'I heard some of your conversation with the Met DI, but not all of it. What's happening?'

Danny took a deep breath. 'It would appear that Sergeant Reynolds has killed his wife and dumped her in the boot of the family car in the garage at their home. The Met detectives have found forensic suits still in the packets, cable ties and rolls of gaffer tape all at the house. They strongly believe Reynolds is responsible for killing his wife, as well as a prostitute in London.'

'Jenny Taylor, the murder in London that Seamus told us about? The one that had the similar MO to the murders of Mandy Stokes and June Hayes.'

'That's right, Jenny Taylor. If the dates and times of Reynolds's deployment tie in with the dates and times of our two murders, then maybe we can link him to the deaths of Mandy Stokes and June Hayes. All that painstaking work by Rachel and Andy could prove vital.'

'Bloody hell, boss, a serving cop. The shit's really going to hit the fan when this gets out to the media.'

'I don't give a toss about the media; I just want this nutter off the street. If it turns out he's a nutter who's also a cop, so be it.'

'Dead right. What's the plan once we've got hold of him?'

'We'll arrest him on suspicion of the murder of Jenny Taylor to get him in and hold him at the police station. Once he's locked up, then the hard work, trying to link him to both the murders here and the murder of Rita Reynolds and Jenny Taylor in London, can begin.'

They were now on the main road between Clipstone and Ollerton, and the road was clear. Once again, Rob gunned the engine, and the car accelerated away. Within ten minutes they were driving along the lane that led to Proteus Camp.

A police sergeant from Hampshire Constabulary was standing at the gate.

Danny showed the sergeant his warrant card and asked him for directions to the Metropolitan Police PSU billets. In particular, the billet for Mike Alpha One Zero.

The sergeant checked a list on a clipboard and directed them towards the far end of the camp and hut 23.

Rob parked the car on the hard standing nearest to a Nissen hut that had the number 23 painted in white on the side wall.

Danny was surprised to see a uniform chief inspector waiting outside the door of the hut. As soon as their car came to a stop, the chief inspector walked purposefully over. Danny wound the car window down as the senior officer approached.

'Good morning, gentlemen, my name's Chief Inspector Delaney. I'm the liaison officer in charge of the Metropolitan Police Mutual Aid. I've been informed by strike control in London that there's a situation I need to be informed about.'

Fucking jungle drums have been beating already, thought Danny.

'It's a little bit more than a "situation", sir. My name's Detective Inspector Flint. I'm here at the request of Detective Inspector Johnson from Peckham Police Station in the Met, to locate and arrest Sergeant Mick Reynolds on suspicion of the murder of Jenny Taylor.'

The chief inspector looked shocked to hear that an officer was to be detained for murder. He rubbed his chin thoughtfully before saying shakily, 'Very good, Inspector, kindly let me know when Sergeant Reynolds is under arrest, please.'

He started to hurry away.

Danny shouted after him, 'Before you go, sir, would you arrange for this hut to be padlocked for the time being? I'll also need an empty hut we can use to temporarily house the rest of the PSU in. We're obviously going to need to search this hut without it being disturbed.'

'Hut 24 next door to this one is empty at the moment. You can use that. The PSU normally using it left yesterday, to begin a week of rest days. I'll arrange for a padlock for this hut to be brought over to you immediately.'

Chief Inspector Delaney then quickly strode away. He couldn't get away from the detectives and the situation quick enough.

Danny wound the car window up.

'That was all a bit bizarre,' said Rob.

'I think that's the closest Chief Inspector Delaney has been to police work for a few years. I reckon the words "arrest" and "murder" used in the same sentence seemed to surprise him a little, don't you think?'

'Yeah, I think you're right. I reckon he's rushed straight back to the canteen to finish his bacon and eggs and forget about the two detectives causing him a problem.'

Both men chuckled and then settled down to await the arrival of Police Support Unit call sign Mike Alpha One Zero and Sergeant Mick Reynolds.

70

Proteus Army Camp – October 29, 1984

Thirty minutes had ticked slowly by since Chief Inspector Delaney had hurriedly left the two detectives.

Five minutes after he beat a hasty retreat, a very young constable turned up with a gleaming new padlock and a bar to go across the door of the hut. The bar was quickly put in place and the padlock fitted. The constable handed Danny the two keys for the lock and scooted off.

Almost immediately after the padlock was fitted, it began to rain heavily. Danny and Rob were thankful they had grabbed their overcoats as they ran out of Mansfield nick.

Rob was sitting in the driver's seat, constantly flicking his handcuffs closed before opening them again, clicking the metal teeth along the ratchet of the locking mechanism.

The rain was beating loudly on the metal roof of the car, and the car windows were starting to steam up because of the warmth being generated inside the vehicle.

Using his sleeve to wipe the condensation from the windscreen, Danny saw two dark blue Ford Transit vans approaching.

Both the vans had metallic grilles attached to the windscreens.

Danny could see the windscreen wipers of the leading van swiping rapidly from side to side beneath the metal grilles. The two vans came to a stop and parked on the same hard standing as the CID car.

Danny stared intently at the front passenger seat of the lead van, waiting for Sergeant Reynolds to get out of the vehicle.

The side doors of both vans opened, and six officers clambered out, heading straight for hut 23. There were howls of protest as the men realised they couldn't get into the hut and out of the rain. Quickly getting drenched by the downpour, the men returned to the vans to get out of the rain.

The driver of the first van then got out and started to head towards the door of the hut. Danny and Rob got out of the car and approached the constable.

Danny showed the officer his warrant card.

'I'm Detective Inspector Flint; this is Detective Sergeant Buxton. We need to talk to Sergeant Reynolds.'

'He's not here, guv'nor,' said the driver.

'What do you mean he's not here?'

'Just that, guv. I'm not being awkward. He went out last night with that blonde tart of his and didn't come back. I've been covering for the daft sod all day. She must be good, that's all I can say, coz he's gonna be right in the shit when he gets back.'

'What's your name, Constable?' asked Rob.

'Oh, don't say I'm in the shit for covering for him; he'll be back later. It's the first time he's missed a shift.'

'Your name?'

'PC Ken Drury. Look, I don't need to be in the shit over

this. I need the money this strike's bringing. You ain't gonna send me back to Wembley, are you?'

Danny held his hands up to placate PC Drury, saying, 'Ken, calm down. Nobody's sending you back to Wembley. You and the rest of the lads will have to use the hut next door temporarily. We've had to seal off this hut. Is there a room I can talk to you and the rest of the PSU? I want to know everything you can tell me about this blonde woman your sergeant's been seeing.'

A relieved look came over the face of Ken Drury.

'There's a small room at the end of each of the huts that's got a table and chairs in. You can use that if you like. What shall I say to the lads about the hut being temporarily out of bounds?'

'Tell them we're from the Complaints Department and that if we don't get full co-operation, we'll make sure this entire PSU is sent back to Wembley. We've already spoken to Chief Inspector Delaney and told him we're here about Sergeant Reynolds and his activities with this woman.'

PC Drury then walked back over to the vans and spoke to the men sitting inside.

Drury was followed by the two detectives.

Danny introduced himself and Rob to the men and reiterated what PC Drury had told them already, that they were investigating Sergeant Reynolds for a clandestine affair he was having with a married woman.

Rob told the men to use hut 24 for the time being.

Once they had made their way into that hut, Rob unlocked the padlock securing hut 23 and walked in, followed by Glyn and PC Drury.

Rob looked around the room. 'Okay, Ken, which is Sergeant Reynolds's bed space?' he asked.

The officer stepped forward and pointed. 'The skipper uses this bed.'

The bed he indicated was the nearest to the small room they would be using to talk to the officers.

Danny took PC Drury into the small room. 'Take a seat, Ken. I'll be with you in a minute.'

Danny left the room and closed the door.

'Rob, I want a Scenes of Crime team out here to photograph the sergeant's bed space; then I want every bit of the bedding and all his kit bagged and tagged.'

Danny took Rob further away from the door to the small room before adding, 'We need to locate Reynolds urgently. Make contact with Rachel back at the station and tell her to get him circulated as wanted on the Police National Computer as soon as possible.'

'Okay, Danny.'

Danny then walked into the small room where he'd left Ken Drury.

'Sit down, PC Drury. You're obviously quite tight with your sergeant, or you wouldn't have covered for him today. How long have you known him?'

Drury sighed and said, 'Mick Reynolds has been my skipper at Wembley nick for the last six years. We were PCs together for three years before that.'

'Are you surprised he's been seeing this woman?'

'Not really, guv'nor. I know things haven't been great between him and his old lady for some time now. Between you and me, she leads him a dog's life.'

'How long's he been seeing this other woman?'

'I honestly don't know the answer to that question. He's a bit of a closed book, is Mick; he plays his cards very close to his chest. He's never told me about her or anything. I only know about her coz one of the lads saw him getting in her motor at the end of the lane here.'

'Who's the constable who saw him getting in her car?'

'Tony Jones, one of the younger lads. I told him to keep

quiet and not to go blabbing it around. I didn't want it to become common knowledge among the lads. I was trying to prevent the skipper getting into strife over it.'

'How do you know PC Jones saw this?'

'Tony told me what he'd seen. It was quite a few weeks ago. Tony had been going to the shops in Ollerton for a walk. It gets bloody boring in here all the time. So anyway, he sees the skipper walking up the lane about sixty or seventy yards in front of him. He told me that at first he was gonna run to catch him up, but then he couldn't be arsed.'

'Go on.'

'Well, when Tony gets to the end of the lane, he looks along the layby and sees the skipper getting into the passenger side of this motor.'

'Who was driving, did he say?'

'You'll have to ask him that; all he said to me was that it was a bird with long blonde hair.'

'Okay, Ken, that's all for now. Send in PC Jones to see me next. I know I don't need to tell you this, but don't say anything to the other lads about our conversation. The less they know, the better. I don't want to drop your mate Mick Reynolds any deeper in the shit than he already is.'

'Right you are, guv'nor; no problem. I'll send in Tony.'

'One last thing, PC Drury: Where do you think Mick Reynolds is now?'

'Knowing that randy bastard, he's probably in bed somewhere shagging that blonde. He's always talking about skirt. What he wouldn't want to do to this tart or that tart. You know what I mean, guv. When we're driving around, there isn't a single bird he doesn't clock; he's woman mad.'

Danny knew everything would be out soon enough, but he didn't want the rumour mill to go into overdrive until after they'd located and detained Sergeant Reynolds.

Rob popped his head around the door. 'Scenes of Crime are here.'

'Alright, get them into the hut. I want the entire bed space photographed. Anything suspicious they find I want photographed in situ before it's recovered. Then I want everything removed from Reynolds's bed space. Blankets, sheets, pillowcases ... I mean everything. I want the entire contents of his locker emptied and bagged up properly. Make a full inventory while they're bagging everything, so we can go through it all back at Mansfield. You crack on with that while I talk to PC Tony Jones.'

A couple of minutes passed before there was a knock on the door.

A young, fresh-faced cop stuck his face around the door.

'Sir, PC Tony Jones, you wanted to talk to me?'

The young officer, who looked fresh out of training school, came in and sat down.

'How much service have you got, Tony?'

'I was only two weeks out of my probation when all this lot started. This is my first PSU duty. I've only been training once. I've got to tell you, sir, it's boring the tits off me.'

'Tony, I'm going to ask you some questions about your sergeant. I know you're young in service, but don't try to avoid answering any of my questions thinking you're doing him a favour. Do you understand?'

'I understand, sir. I'll answer if I can.'

'Good lad. I want to ask you about this woman you saw your sergeant with a few weeks back.'

'The blonde?'

'Have there been others?'

'No, sir, I don't know, sir. I mean, I only saw him with a blonde.'

'Tony, you're not in any trouble, okay? Just listen to the questions and answer them if you can. No one's trying to trip you up.'

'Okay, sir, sorry.'

'Right, tell me about this blonde woman.'

'I can't remember when it was for sure, but it's quite a few weeks ago, now. I was walking into town to get some biscuits from the shop one evening. Anyway, as I'm walking along the lane up to the road, I see the skipper in front of me. He's a bit too far ahead for me to run and catch up with him. The skipper then turns off the lane and into the layby. By the time I got up to the layby, he was already getting in the car being driven by the blonde.'

'How far away from the car were you?'

'Forty or fifty yards, I guess.'

'What time was it?'

'It was getting quite late, but it was still light.'

'Could you see the driver?'

'Honestly, all I could see was long blonde hair. She never turned around, so I never saw her face. As soon as he got in the car, they drove off quickly.'

'Are you sure there's nothing else you can tell me about her?'

'Positive, sir, sorry.'

'Okay, what about the car?'

'That's a bit easier; it was an old Ford Cortina. I'm sure of that; my dad had one when I was a kid.'

'What colour was it?'

'It was a dark green colour. That British racing green you see on older cars.'

'What else can you tell me about the car? Could you see the plates?'

'I was close enough to see them, but I honestly can't remember the number. Sorry, sir.'

'Anything else about the car that springs to mind?'

'Only that it looked in mint condition for an old motor.'

'Did you speak to Sergeant Reynolds about what you'd seen?'

'Bloody hell! No way, sir. I told Ken Drury; he's the

driver of our van. He told me to shut the fuck up and not to repeat it or I'd be shipped back to Wembley.'

'So, you haven't told anybody else on your PSU?'

'No, sir.'

'Do you have any idea where your sergeant is right now?'

'Haven't got a clue, sir; he just wasn't around this morning when we set off for Warsop Main pit.'

'Has the sergeant ever missed a shift before?'

'No, definitely not. He goes out some nights and doesn't get back until late, but he's always been back for the shift to start – except for today, that is.'

'How late?'

'I've seen him come back into the hut a few times during the early hours of the morning.'

'Thanks, Tony, that'll be all. Don't talk to your colleagues about what we've discussed. Do you understand?'

'Yes, sir.'

PC Jones then left the small room.

Danny knew it was probably going to be a pointless exercise, but nevertheless, he spoke to every one of the officers on the PSU individually. Not one of the constables had any idea where their sergeant had spent the night.

A couple of them confirmed what PC Jones had already said: that they'd noticed Sergeant Reynolds slipping out of the hut during the evenings. None of them could remember when.

By the time Danny had finished the interviews with the PSU officers, the Scenes of Crime team were just bagging up the last of Reynolds's belongings and bedding.

'Have we got everything, Rob?'

'We've left nothing; I've logged everything as we've gone along.'

'Anything of note?'

'Definitely, boss. There are four forensic suits still in the wrappers, a roll of gaffer tape and an open packet of black tie wraps. There's also a black woollen ski mask stuffed at the bottom of a bag full of dirty washing. One last thing: I found these in a small tin at the bottom of his PSU bag.'

Rob indicated a small evidence bag in his hand that contained a small gold wedding band and an engagement ring, and said, 'We've never recovered the rings worn by June Hayes.'

'Was everything photographed in situ before recovery?'

'Yes.'

'The black ski mask? Are you thinking Edwinstowe last week?'

'Who knows, boss? It could well be; there's plenty of dark clothing to go with it.'

'I'll need to get the rings over to Mr Hayes as soon as possible for identification.'

As they left the Nissen hut, Rob secured it again with the padlock.

'Rob, I want this entire PSU stood down until we find Reynolds. You never know, they could all be covering for him. I doubt it, but I don't want this lot allowed off this camp until Reynolds is found and arrested.'

'What about all their gear in hut 23?'

'If we haven't found Reynolds by morning, they can enter the hut one at a time, under supervision, to remove what they need. Hopefully, we'll have Reynolds in custody before morning.'

'I'll fire a phone call in to strike control to get that organised as soon as we get back to Mansfield nick.'

'Thanks, Rob. I need to let Glyn Johnson know that Reynolds is still on his toes. I don't think he'd make his way back to London, but you never know.'

Danny thought for a moment, then said, 'The key to all this is finding the mystery blonde. The description of the car she drives isn't a million miles away from the one Stan Briggs gave us. Find the car, the blonde, or both, and we'll get Reynolds. Let's get on with it.'

Danny and Rob, helped by the Scenes of Crime officers, then loaded the CID car with the bagged items from Reynolds's bed space.

Once the car was loaded with the exhibits, Rob started the engine and drove slowly out of Proteus Camp.

71

Mansfield Police Station – November 3, 1984

It had been five days since Danny and Rob had gone to Proteus Camp intending to arrest Mick Reynolds for the murder of the young prostitute in London.

During those five days, there had been no sightings of either Reynolds or the old-style, dark green Ford Cortina.

Danny and Glyn were in constant touch over the hunt for Reynolds; both detectives were certain they had identified the man responsible for the murders both in London and Nottinghamshire.

Glyn assured Danny that he was now in a position to charge Reynolds with the murders of both Jenny Taylor and Rita Reynolds.

Between them, they'd organised a nationwide press appeal to try to help track down the man the papers were now labelling as Britain's most wanted.

Danny had taken the two rings found in Reynolds's PSU bag to David Hayes. The distraught husband had identified them as his wife's engagement and wedding ring. Danny then had to explain to David Hayes that he was unable to release the two rings back to him until after any future trial.

In spite of this damning evidence, the police had still not publicly linked Reynolds to the Nottinghamshire murders of Mandy Stokes and June Hayes. They had, however, released to the press that Reynolds was wanted in connection with both the murder of his wife, Rita, and the young prostitute Jenny Taylor.

DANNY, Rob and Rachel were working tirelessly around the clock, trying to establish the links that would implicate Reynolds in the murder of Mandy Stokes, as well as that of June Hayes.

Through her meticulous and painstaking enquiries, Rachel had been able to establish that not only was Sergeant Reynolds in Nottinghamshire at the times of the murders, but that he had also been off duty and kicking his heels at Proteus Camp.

The same was also true of the assault on the two teenagers at Edwinstowe. Danny was hopeful that forensic testing would establish whether blood matching either of the two young victims was to be found on clothing seized from Proteus Camp.

DANNY LOOKED at the wall clock in the CID office. It was five o'clock in the evening.

'Okay, Rob, Rachel, that's enough for today. There's nothing more we can do this evening. I want you both to go home, put your feet up and have a meal with your families. Let's be back here at seven in the morning to start a fresh day. One other thing: Andy phoned me earlier today. He's back tomorrow, so the team will be back together.'

'Trust him to come back now all the work's done and we know who the killer is.' Rachel laughed.

'I know it's typical; now get off home, both of you.'

Rob instantly grabbed his jacket, saying, 'That's great, Danny. I could do with seeing the wife and kids before they go to bed. See you in the morning.'

Rob was up and out the door quickly, leaving Danny and Rachel alone in the office.

'What about you, Rachel? What's your plans for tonight?'

'The usual stuff: Get home, eat a frozen meal for one while I watch a bit of telly, and then bed.'

'Look, Rach, I've just phoned Sue; she's cooking at my house tonight. Why don't you join us for a home-cooked meal before you go home?'

'Are you sure you two wouldn't like to spend the evening together? Just the two of you?'

'Rachel, come and eat with us. Dinner's going to be ready for six o'clock. Me and Sue can still get an early night later, if you know what I mean.'

'Only if you're sure Sue won't mind, boss.'

'I'll let you into a secret, Rachel: it was Sue's idea to ask you.'

'In that case, what's for dinner?'

'Her famous beef stew and dumplings, I think.'

'Why's it famous?'

'I've absolutely no idea.'

He laughed as he held the door open for Rachel before switching off the lights in the office.

As the two cars left the police station car park, another car slipped in behind Rachel's Mini. Neither Rachel nor Danny paid any attention to the small Datsun that followed them up to Danny's house.

Jimmy Wade stopped the Datsun and watched as the two detectives walked up the pathway towards the house.

As he watched, he said aloud to himself, 'Being very

friendly towards your staff, aren't you, Detective Inspector Flint?'

As the detectives approached, the front door to the house was opened. Wade could see it was a woman who'd opened the door.

Wade relaxed a little, again speaking aloud: 'That's okay then, Inspector.'

To his surprise, Jimmy realised that he'd begun to feel angry when he thought the inspector had designs on Rachel Moore.

He was waiting in the shadows, as it was his intention to follow Rachel to her home tonight and make one last recce before he paid her the visit that would ultimately end in her death. Accepting how he had felt earlier, when he thought Rachel would be spending the night with her boss, he had come to a decision.

Jimmy had decided that he would allow himself some intimate time with Rachel when he visited her that final time. He felt he owed it to himself. He couldn't deny that he found the policewoman very attractive. He knew that with the plans he'd already put in place, it would be okay for him to pleasure himself fully before finally killing her.

It had been a long time since he last enjoyed any proper intimacy with a woman. Especially one as attractive as Rachel Moore.

He licked his lips in anticipation.

Newstead Abbey grounds – November 4, 1984

Winter had arrived with a vengeance. The ice cold wind was driving the freezing sleet into the face of Tommy Dawson. The old man pulled his check woollen scarf tighter around his neck and took his grey flat cap off before putting it back on again, this time making sure it was tighter on his head.

The black donkey jacket that covered the thick Aran jumper he was wearing helped to keep out the biting wind.

His gloved hands held on tightly to the leather dog lead.

It was just beginning to get light; the night sky was fading fast, but dawn hadn't quite broken yet.

The small wire-haired terrier was pulling hard on the lead.

He yanked the dog lead back sharply and snapped, 'Sam, stop bloody pulling, lad!'

The dog stopped pulling for a few seconds before resuming the tug of war he was having with his master.

Evil in Mind

It was six thirty in the morning, and Tommy was making his way from Newstead village to Newstead Abbey. Every day since he'd retired from Annesley Colliery a year ago, the ex-miner had taken an early morning walk into the grounds of the Newstead Abbey estate. It mattered not to Tommy what the weather was like.

His constant companion on these daily walks was his little dog, Sam.

Tommy pulled hard on the lead again, trying to control the little dog, before saying, 'I know, Sam, it's time for you to have your run.'

Bending down, he unclipped the lead from the collar, letting the little dog off the leash. Tommy grinned as Sam immediately darted off into the woods.

He shouted after the small dog, 'You'll do well to find any squirrels to chase today, lad!'

Tommy whistled a melodic tune as he continued his slow stroll along the tree-lined lane that ran through the centre of the abbey grounds.

He never tired of the beauty of this place.

For a man who had spent his entire working life underground at Annesley Colliery, it was now a simple pleasure to spend a small part of every single day walking through this beautiful estate.

Each of the seasons brought its own beauty.

The spring held the promise of new life. Everywhere new leaves would be beginning to show, and the light pastel green colours were always beautiful to see. The bluebells would cover the floor of the woodland with their deep blue and purple hues.

Summer was full of birdsong and colour as the forest burst into life. Rabbits and squirrels were abundant, and Sam had hours of fun desperately trying to catch them.

Tommy's favourite season was the autumn as the leaves changed colour. Every morning, he would be treated to a dazzling display of deep reds and golden yellows. A cold crisp morning in September or October, with the sun shining down onto the colourful leaves, was hard to beat.

Today was a proper winter's day and was extremely cold.

The bitterly cold wind made the sleet feel like shards of freezing ice biting into his skin. Slowly the sun crept over the horizon, and Tommy watched as the sky gradually changed colour above the leafless branches of the trees.

Suddenly, Tommy could hear his small dog a long way off in the woods.

The dog was barking fiercely.

'Where are you, lad!' he shouted.

He continued to walk along the lane, grateful that the sleet was easing and had nearly stopped.

The dog continued to bark.

The light was getting better now as the sun cleared the horizon. Tommy could see a small track that ran from the lane off into the woods. The noise of Sam's barking was coming from the end of the track.

'Come on, Sam, stop playing silly beggars. We need to head for home now. I'm ready for my tea and toast.'

The dog carried on barking incessantly. Losing patience, Tommy shouted, 'Come on, Sam, get here now!'

He took off his gloves and put his fingers to his mouth, using them to make a shrill whistle.

Still the dog carried on barking.

Tommy realised the dog wasn't going to come back on his own. He put the gloves back on his freezing cold hands and set off down the track towards the sound of the barking.

The sleet had now stopped altogether, and as Tommy made his way into the woods and out of the chill wind, he immediately felt warmer.

The long grass underfoot was sodden, though, and Tommy could feel his boots and the lower part of his trousers quickly becoming saturated.

The wet trees were dripping icy water, and whenever Tommy brushed against a branch, he was showered with freezing cold rainwater.

He shouted after his dog again: 'Come on, Sam, stop messing about now, old lad. Your Tommy's getting soaked here!'

The dog just continued to bark.

Tommy knew instinctively that something was wrong. Sam was not usually a yapping dog. He continued to walk along the track further into the woods. The sound of the barking was closer now.

He was about to shout the dog's name again, but the sight that now confronted him took his breath away.

After the shock passed, Tommy said out loud, 'Good God Almighty!'

About ten feet away, directly in front of him, was a rotting corpse hanging from the branch of an oak tree.

The neck of the dead man had stretched, and looked to be almost a foot long. The head was tilted at a grotesque angle to the neck and looked ready to separate from the body at any time. The feet of the corpse were now just brushing the ground.

In between barks, the little dog was growling and tugging at the trouser leg of the rotting corpse.

'Get away from there, Sam! Get here now, boy!'

Slowly the dog cowered towards him, unsure of the tone in his master's voice.

Tommy grabbed the dog by the scruff of its neck and clipped the lead back onto the collar. With the dog finally under control, Tommy had a closer look around the macabre scene. He could see a sodden leather bag and an upturned crate near the feet of the hanging man.

He yelled at his dog, which was again barking, 'Shut up, Sam!'

Finally, the dog stopped barking and sat quietly at his

master's feet.

'What else have we got here, then, Sam?' said Tommy as he walked around.

Looking beyond the corpse, Tommy could see the charred remains of a burned-out car. He walked around the hanging man towards the torched car. Carefully, he walked slowly around the car, finally stopping again behind the hanging man.

A gust of wind suddenly blew into the small clearing and was enough to cause the corpse to begin gently swinging on the creaking branch.

Feeling uneasy, Tommy said aloud, 'Come on, Sam lad, let's get out of here. We need to fetch the police, I reckon.'

Tommy knew there was an old gate lodge that was occupied about half a mile along the lane. He walked quickly through the woods along the track and back up onto the lane. After a brisk ten-minute walk along the lane, Tommy stood outside the front door of the small stone lodge.

He began to hammer urgently on the wooden door.

The resident of the lodge, Frank Bennett, was a labourer who worked on the nearby Harris Farm.

After the old man repeatedly banged on the front door for five minutes, it was finally opened.

'Bloody hell! It's you, Tommy. Don't you know what time it is? What's all the commotion about?' said a shocked and bewildered Frank Bennett.

'Have you got a phone here?'

'Yeah, I've got a phone; what's the problem?'

'Frank, call the police straight away and tell them to drive up to the lane about half a mile back towards Newstead. I'll wait for them there.'

'What's up?'

'I've found a body in the woods. There's a bloke who's hanged himself, and there's a burned-out car down there as well.'

Tommy started to walk off, heading back along the lane.

Frank shouted after the old man, 'Tommy, you're not making this shit up, are you?'

Tommy turned around and shouted angrily back, 'Don't be so fucking stupid, Frank. Of course I'm not bloody well making it up! Get the bloody cops out here now, as quick as you can!'

Tommy turned and continued to walk back along the lane.

The sun was creeping up into the sky, and the weak light was getting stronger.

Tommy had just reached the entrance to the track again when he heard the sound of a car being driven along the lane from the direction of the abbey. He turned around and began to wave his arm, indicating to the driver of the police car to stop.

As the car came to a stop alongside him, Tommy could see there were two officers in the car. He knew the policeman who was driving the car. PC Steve Jarvis regularly patrolled Newstead Abbey and Newstead village.

PC Jarvis got out of the car and said, 'Hello, Tommy, what's all this about a dead body?'

The policeman bent down and made a fuss of Sam as he waited for Tommy to reply.

'Hello, Mr Jarvis; it's just down this track here. There's a bloke who's hanged himself and a burned-out car as well.'

Sam immediately started barking again.

'Sam, bloody well be quiet now!' said Tommy, firmly pulling on the lead.

The dog fell silent, and Tommy continued, 'It was the dog that found the body, when he went for his run.'

PC Jarvis turned to the younger officer and said, 'Wait in the car, Nick, and monitor the radio. I'll go down and have a look.'

PC Jarvis turned back to the old man. 'Come on then, Tommy owd lad, show me where this body is.'

Tommy walked back into the woods down the track with

the police officer following. After five minutes, they had reached the hanging man.

'Bloody hell, Tommy! It looks like he's been here a while.'

Tommy nodded; he was starting to feel cold now in his wet clothes. All he wanted was to get home for his cup of tea and a slice of hot buttered toast.

A shivering Tommy pointed out the torched car to the officer. 'Looks like an old Ford Cortina to me. What do you reckon?'

'I think you're right. Come on, let's get back up to the car.'

They walked out of the woods, along the track back to the lane.

PC Jarvis spoke to the other officer. 'There's a body down there alright. The burned-out car looks like an old Ford Cortina.'

The younger officer said, 'We're supposed to be on the lookout for a Ford Cortina. Do you remember the briefing the other morning? That Met copper they want for the murders in London, he's supposed to be driving a dark green Ford Cortina.'

'Bloody hell, you're right. Get on the radio and tell the control room what's down here, and tell them to get the CID out of their beds.'

Tommy sniffed loudly.

PC Jarvis looked at the old man and saw that he was shivering. 'You alright, Tommy? You look frozen to the bone, pal.'

'Sam and me, we're both ready for our tea and toast.'

'I'll bet you are, owd lad, it's bloody freezing this morning. Hop in, I'll nip you home. Byron Terrace, isn't it, Tommy?'

Tommy climbed into the back of the police car, clutching Sam tightly on his lap.

'It's number sixteen, that's grand. Thanks ever so much, Mr Jarvis.'

'It's no bother, Tommy. We've got time before the CID get out here. We'll drop you off for your tea and toast and then get back up here. The CID might want to talk to you later, though.'

Tommy laughed. 'I'll be in all day; they can come over any time. I'll have the kettle on; they can have a brew with me.'

The police car sped off down the lane to take Tommy and Sam home.

Left alone in the woods, the hanging man continued to drift slowly from side to side in the breeze.

Soon the only sounds in the woods were the dripping rainwater and the creaking of the oak branch straining under the weight of the dead Sergeant Reynolds.

Mansfield Police Station – November 4, 1984

It was six thirty in the morning, and the shift was just about to start. Danny was sitting alone in the CID office, sipping a coffee. The office door opened, and in walked a suntanned and smiling Andy Wills.

'Hello, Andy, how was the break?'

'Just what Sally and I needed, thanks.'

'Did you manage to have a good talk and sort things out?'

'We certainly did. We've had ten glorious days in Cyprus at Sally's parents' villa in Paphos. You were right, Danny; all we needed was to spend a bit of quality time together to talk things through and get back on track.'

'I take it that Sally's behind you and supporting your career again, then, Andy?'

'The news is better than that. It turns out the reason she was having a crisis about the two of us was because it'll soon be the three of us.'

'Do you mean …?'

'Yes, Danny, I'm going to be a dad. Sally was all over the place emotionally when she found out she was pregnant. All it needed was reassurance from me that we'd be a proper family and that I'd commit to being a proper father. I assured her that I'd like nothing better than being a dad. I've always wanted children; she knew that anyway. I even talked to her about Rob, how he works long hours and still manages to be a fantastic father.'

Just at that second, the door to the office opened and Rob walked in.

'Did I hear my name?'

'You did, Sarge. I was just telling the boss my news. I'm going to be a dad.'

Rob stepped forward and warmly shook Andy's hand.

'That's fantastic news, Andy! Congratulations.'

Danny stood up and also shook Andy's hand, saying, 'Yes, congratulations, Andy. I'm glad you got everything sorted out.'

'I think I'm the one who should be thanking you, boss. I've heard on the grapevine the extra staff you told me about never actually existed and that you've been running the enquiry with just you, Rob and Rachel. I'm really grateful for what you did, Danny. I'm going to buy Rachel the biggest bunch of flowers as a big thank-you for taking on all my work as well as her own without complaining. I really do appreciate it. Thanks.'

Danny shrugged. 'It's all sorted now, Andy; that's the main thing. Anyway, have you heard the developments here?'

'Of course I have. It's all over the news. As soon as I got off the plane from Cyprus, I saw it. I thought, "That's bloody typical. Trust me to miss it." Have you arrested Reynolds yet?'

'Unfortunately not, he's still on his toes. It's only a matter of time, though.'

Andy walked over and grabbed the kettle. 'I'll fill this up and make us all a brew.'

Rachel walked into the office just as Andy was leaving with the kettle in his hand.

'Ah, perfect timing, I've missed my tea, bastard!' She laughed.

'That's charming, and just when I was singing your praises as well.' Andy laughed.

Ten minutes later, they were all sat in the office with a cup of tea, discussing the joyous news of Andy's impending fatherhood. There was a knock on the office door, and a young police cadet stepped nervously into the CID office.

'Excuse me, sir,' he said timidly.

'Come in, son, what's the problem?' asked Danny.

'The sergeant in the control room asked me to nip down and tell you there's been a suicide at Newstead Abbey. A man's been found hanged in the woods not far from the Abbey.'

Andy put his mug of tea down, saying, 'I'll go, boss.'

The young cadet continued, 'The sergeant told me to make sure I tell you that there's a burned-out Ford Cortina near to the dead body, as well.'

Danny was already grabbing his coat. 'We'll all go. Exactly where is it, son?' he asked the cadet.

'The local panda car is already at the scene. They're parked on the lane between the abbey and Newstead village, sir.'

Within seconds, all four detectives had abandoned their drinks and run out of the office, leaving a very bewildered police cadet standing in the CID office.

Rob Buxton was the last to leave. He winked and said, 'You're in charge, son!'

74

Newstead Abbey, Nottinghamshire – November 4, 1984

The two CID cars raced to Newstead Abbey. Entering the grounds through the gated entrance off the main A60 road, they sped past the beautiful lake and the abbey building itself.

Heading along the lane towards Newstead village, they quickly saw the panda car parked at the side of the lane.

The two uniformed officers who had been sitting in the panda car now got out of the vehicle. The CID cars skidded to a halt behind the police car, and Danny and his team quickly got out.

Danny walked over to the two officers. 'Where's the scene?' he asked.

'It's down here, sir,' said PC Jarvis.

The uniformed officer walked down the track in front of Danny and Rob. Andy and Rachel remained on the lane, talking to the other officer.

'The body's just through here.'

PC Jarvis stood to one side and allowed the two detectives to pass by him into the small clearing where the body was hanging from the tree.

Danny turned to PC Jarvis. 'Have you asked for Scenes of Crime to attend yet?'

'Yes, sir, just after I informed the control room what was here. I've not cut him down yet, for obvious reasons.'

'No, you did right. How long do you think he's been here?'

'I've seen a few suicides in these woods. Going on the state of him, I'd say he's been here about a week.'

'Right, as soon as Scenes of Crime have got their photographs, we'll get him down. Get back on the radio and put a call in to control. I want the on-call undertakers attending to remove the body. I also want the vehicle examiners here to check over the vehicle.'

'Will do, sir.'

Just as PC Jarvis was about to walk back to his car, Rob asked, 'Who found the body?'

PC Jarvis replied, 'Tommy Dawson, he's an old retired miner from the village who walks his dog down here every day. Apparently, it was the dog that found it.'

'Why isn't Mr Dawson still here?'

'I took him home, Sarge. He's an old man, and he was freezing. I took him home so he could get a hot drink inside him. Is that a problem?'

Danny intervened, 'No, it isn't a problem. Where does he live?'

'He lives at 16 Byron Terrace in Newstead, sir.'

'Okay, thanks; make the calls to the control room, requesting the undertakers and the vehicle examiners, please. Would you also, on my behalf, tell DC Moore and DC Wills that I want them to go straight to 16 Byron Terrace and interview Tommy Dawson at his home? Thanks.'

'Will do, sir.'

PC Jarvis exchanged glares with Rob before walking off up the track.

As the constable disappeared back up to the lane, Rob shook his head. 'He knows better than that; he should've kept the witness here so we could question him.'

'No, for once, my good friend, you're dead wrong. PC Jarvis did exactly the right thing taking the old man home to get warm. For one thing, we don't want a witness with hypothermia, and for another he'll now think the police are the best thing since sliced bread and will bend over backwards to help.'

Rob held his hands up. 'If you say so.'

'I do. Now let's have a proper look at what we've got here. What do you think? First impressions?'

'Looks like suicide to me. You can see the box he's used to stand on, and his feet are only touching the ground now because over the week, his neck has stretched.'

'Have a look at the knot that fastens the rope to the lower branch.'

'I don't see anything unusual.'

'I agree; I can't see anything odd about the knot, but look at how deep the foot marks are below the knot. Why d'you reckon they're so deep?'

'I don't know; the ground does look really wet there.'

'Or could it be where someone else has used a lot of effort to hoist the body up?'

Danny then turned his attention to the upturned crate and the bag.

'Let's have a look at what's in the bag at his feet.'

Rob walked over to the wet bag, put on a pair of gloves, and carefully opened up the bag.

'The bag's absolutely sodden; we won't be getting any prints off it, that's for sure. Everything inside's wet through, as well.'

Opening the bag, he carefully picked out two forensic suits still in the plastic packets.

'These are dripping wet, too. There's also several loose black cable ties, a roll of gaffer tape, a hammer, garden secateurs and a Stanley knife in here. The suits, ties and tape look the same as the ones we recovered from Reynolds's bed space.'

'Looks like we've finally found the elusive Sergeant Mick Reynolds, then,' said Danny.

PC Jarvis then returned to the clearing, followed by Tim Donnelly. 'Scenes of Crime are here, sir, and your detectives have gone off to see old Tommy. Do you still need me and Nick to remain up on the lane?'

'Yes, please, until the undertakers and the vehicle examiners arrive. That will free us up to examine the scene properly.'

'Of course, sir. No problem.'

'Once they've both arrived, you can both resume. I'll need your statements before you go off duty today as well, please,' said Danny.

PC Jarvis nodded and once again made his way up the track.

'Hello, Tim,' Danny said. 'Can you get busy with your camera so we can get the body cut down? I'm also interested in some deep foot marks around the area below the knot used to tie the rope to the lower branch. They look deeper than maybe they should be just to tie a knot off.'

'Of course, Danny.'

Immediately the Scenes of Crime officer began to take photographs of the areas pointed out by Danny. The first pictures he took showed the entire scene; then, gradually, he made his way towards the body. Finally, he took close-up shots of the knots in the rope, the upturned crate and the corpse.

Standing right next to the corpse, Tim pointed at the dead man's jacket. 'Have you seen this?'

'Seen what?'

'There's a black tube sticking out of his jacket pocket. I'm not a betting man, but it looks the same as the tubing we found inside the murdered women.'

Danny walked over and looked at the tubing that was just protruding out the top of the dead man's jacket pocket.

'Have you photographed it?'

'Yes, I've got a few shots of it in situ.'

Danny slipped on gloves and removed the tube from the jacket. 'The tubing's soaked, but I can see there's a note inside.'

'I'd strongly advise against taking the note out of the tube here. You should do it somewhere dry; the last thing you want is for the note itself to get wet. If the paper's still dry inside the tube, we might be able to nin test it. I'll dry the tube and bag it up properly, with a view to saving the paper.'

'Thanks, Tim, I'll leave you to it. Have you got all the photos you need?'

'Yes, thanks, boss.'

'Right then, let's get the body cut down.'

Tim Donnelly was the tallest, so it was he who reached up with the knife and sliced through the rope. Danny and Rob had the unpleasant task of supporting the soaking wet corpse while he did. He made the cut well away from the knot that formed the makeshift noose.

Finally, the soaking wet rope gave way, and Danny and Rob lowered the rotting body to the ground.

The remainder of the rope was then removed from the tree and placed into a sack and labelled. The contents of the bag, the bag itself and the crate that had all been beneath the corpse were also placed in exhibit bags and labelled.

All the exhibits would need to be dried out slowly and

carefully in the specialist drying cabinets back at the police station.

PC Jarvis returned to the clearing, this time followed by the undertakers and two men in blue overalls.

'The undertakers and vehicle examiners are here now, sir.'

'Thanks, PC Jarvis, you've done a cracking job today. You can resume your patrol now.'

'Thanks, sir.'

'Don't forget I'll need your statements today.'

'No problem, sir.'

The undertakers quickly placed the sodden, decomposing body into a black plastic body bag and carried it back up the track to their waiting hearse.

'Mansfield Mortuary, please, gents,' said Rob.

He had already arranged for the coroner's officer to be waiting for the arrival of the body at the mortuary.

The two vehicle examiners walked over to Danny.

'Hello, Danny, long time no see.' The voice belonged to Peter Cameron.

'Pete, how are you?' replied Danny.

'I'm good, thanks. It's been a good many years since I tutored you as a young cop fresh out of training school, and you're a detective inspector now? Well done, you.'

'Thanks, Pete. How's working part time with the Vehicle Examiners Department suiting you?'

'It's great; the money supplements my sergeant's pension perfectly. You know me; I've always loved motors. Anyway, enough of all this chit-chat. What do you want us to look at, Danny?'

'You're right; we'd better get on. It's good to see you looking so well, though. The motor I want you to have a look at is over there.' Danny pointed over to the burned-out wreck.

Quickly, Pete and his colleague were all over the vehicle.

'Well, it's definitely a Ford Cortina Mk 1. There's a little bit of paint over the rear wheel arch that hasn't been touched by the fire. It's dark green, possibly similar to British racing green.'

'Can you identify the car?'

'I'm struggling to do that; obviously there's no registration plates on the vehicle, and it would appear that the VIN plate, chassis number and engine number have all either been removed or ground off. Without any of them, there's no way we can identify who the owner of the car is. Sorry, Danny.'

'It's not your fault, Pete. Can you arrange for a full lift to get the car removed and taken to force headquarters?'

'Yeah, I reckon we'll be able to get the tow truck down this track, so it shouldn't be a problem.'

'Was the car torched deliberately?'

'Definitely. Petrol's been used to burn this; you can still smell it.'

'Thanks, Pete. Give me a call when the car's arrived at the forensic bay at headquarters, please. Oh, and will you pass on my regards to Maggie?'

'Will do, Danny. It's good to see you again.'

Danny then turned to Tim. 'Have you finished? Have you got all the photos of the car you need?'

'Yes, we're all done.'

'Right, let's get back to Mansfield and see if there's anything else we can glean from the body.'

Mansfield Mortuary – November 4, 1984

Stewart Henson, the coroner's officer, was waiting for Danny and Rob when they walked into the mortuary.

'Good morning, gents. I've stripped the body and laid all the clothes out separately in the drying room next door. We can look at them after you've viewed the body if you like.'

'That sounds like a plan. First things first, though: Have you found any identification on the body?'

'Oh yes, it's your man, alright. I found his Metropolitan Police warrant card in his left trouser pocket and also one of his shirt epaulettes showing his police number.'

'Only one?' asked Rob.

'Yes, there's only one epaulette. He might've lost one or got changed in a hurry; who knows? He was still wearing a police uniform shirt, but non-uniform jeans and a jumper. Anyway, the body's ready if you want to view it.'

Danny and Rob followed Stewart into the same examination room where they'd watched the post-mortem examinations of Mandy Stokes and June Hayes.

Laid out on the stainless-steel table was the naked body of Police Sergeant Mick Reynolds.

'There are no marks of violence on the body at all.' Stewart turned the body so that the detectives could view the back as well as the front. This was no easy task due to the level of decomposition that had already taken place.

'The neck's abnormally elongated due to the length of time the body's been suspended. A few more days and the head may have become detached completely. It's been really windy of late, and I think the body's taken quite a buffeting from the elements.'

'Lovely,' said Rob.

Stewart continued, 'There are some marks around the bottom of the legs and around the face and neck. These are consistent with the attention of vermin such as rats and birds, probably carrion crows.'

'What time's the post-mortem?' asked Danny.

'It will probably be later this afternoon.'

'Have you spotted any signs of possible foul play, Stewart?'

'Nothing at all. I've seen countless hangings, and this looks like suicide plain and simple to me.'

'Can you let me have the pathologist's report as soon as possible for the inquest?'

'Of course, Danny. Do you want to see the clothing now?'

Danny and Rob followed the man dubbed 'Dr Death' into the adjacent drying room. The dead man's clothes were all stretched out on benches. The heating was high in this room compared to the cold of the examination room. They could smell the familiar odour of death emanating from the clothes that until recently had been covering a rotting corpse.

On the benches were a pair of black lace-up Dr Martens shoes, black woollen socks, a pair of white Y-fronts, a white vest, a police uniform shirt with one epaulette attached, a navy blue woollen jumper, a pair of dark blue denim jeans and a black reefer-style coat.

Also drying on the bench was the short length of rope that Stewart had cut from around the neck of Reynolds. The knot was still intact. The pathologist would want to examine the rope and the knot later to compare it against any surface or underlying injuries he found during the post-mortem examination.

'Anything startling on the clothing apart from the warrant card and the epaulette?' asked Rob.

'No, not really. There were some sodden paper tissues in one of the trouser pockets. The only other thing worthy of note is that on both sleeves of the coat, there's a faint smell of petrol.'

'Really? How on earth can you smell petrol above the other stench?' asked Rob.

Stewart grinned. 'I suppose it's all a matter of what you get used to, Sergeant.'

'I'll ask Tim to come down and swab the sleeves. He can test it later to see if it's petrol. The car was torched before he killed himself, so it's not unreasonable to believe he may have splashed some on his jacket,' said Danny.

'I hear you might have a suicide note, Danny?'

'That's the next stop. Tim's drying it out slowly for us. It'll be interesting to see what's on it.'

The two detectives left the mortuary and made the short walk back to the police station. They walked straight through the station and into another specialist drying room. This time, it was at the exhibits store, where Tim was already busy working on the exhibits recovered from Newstead Abbey.

'There's nothing else in the bag other than what you've already seen. The make of the forensic suits is identical to those found at Proteus Camp. The cable ties match the ones found in the opened bag at the camp, too,' he said.

'Thanks. What about the note?' asked Danny.

'I'm almost ready to take it out of the tube now. The tubing material looks identical to the two found on the women. I'll be checking it forensically to make sure. I want to photograph the note once it's out of the tube, then send it straight for nin testing to check for any possible fingerprints.'

'Okay, let's have a look,' said Danny.

Tim slowly removed the paper from the tube and unfurled it very carefully. Once again, there was a typewritten note on the paper, and once again the letter *c* was slightly below the line of type.

Placing the notepaper on a tray, Tim stood back to allow Danny and Rob to read the note.

I CANNOT CONTINUE on this path of destruction
  I killed Rita and I know I'll be caught
  I killed the others because Rita drove me to it
  The girl in London and the two women here
  The Coal Killer was a fantasy I made up
  I cannot go to jail
  Death is the only way out for me

'IT LOOKS like it's been typed on the same typewriter,' said Rob.

Danny scowled. 'Send it for testing, Tim, but don't expect to find any prints. Come on, Rob.'

Five minutes later, the two detectives were sitting in the CID office.

'Thank Christ that's over. What a sick fuck,' said Rob.

'I'm not buying it, Rob.'

'What do you mean?'

'It's been bothering me ever since I saw those deep foot marks below the branch the rope was tied to. The examination of the vehicle heightened my suspicions, and now the note has just confirmed it.'

'What are you talking about? Confirmed what?'

Danny picked the phone up and dialled a number from memory. There was a long pause before he said, 'Hello, Seamus, it's Danny here. Can you do me a huge favour? We've recovered the body of the police sergeant suspected of committing our murders. He's apparently hanged himself. There are no obvious signs of foul play, but I'm not convinced. Would you be able to carry out the post-mortem at Mansfield later today?'

There was a long pause.

'Thanks, Seamus, I owe you one.'

Danny hung up, then dialled again. 'Hello, Stewart, I've arranged for Seamus Carter to do the post-mortem on Reynolds later this afternoon. Are you able to be there to observe?'

Again, a pause, this time shorter.

'Thanks, you're a star.'

Rob was puzzled. 'What's going on?'

'Doesn't it seem at all strange to you that someone who's intent on killing himself would go to all the trouble of obliterating every identifying feature of the car?'

Rob stroked his chin thoughtfully, then said, 'He may have done it to protect this blonde woman, whoever she is.'

Danny continued, 'And if you're going to kill yourself, why take the bag with the forensic suits and all the rest?'

'Maybe they were already in the car, and he got them out before he torched it.'

Danny shook his head. 'Why would he do that? You mentioned the blonde; do you think she knows more about our two murders than we think? I guarantee you, Rob, there'll be no marks on the typed note. So why take the trouble to ensure there are no fingerprints on the note if you're intending to kill yourself?'

'So what you're saying is that you think Reynolds's death isn't a suicide?'

'I don't know yet, but I want Seamus to have a bloody good look and make sure. I'm not prepared to write this investigation up as closed just yet.'

Danny then picked up the telephone and dialled again. 'Hello, Glyn, it's Danny. We've found Mick Reynolds. Unfortunately, he's now in our mortuary. It looks like he hanged himself in the woods, at a place called Newstead Abbey.'

There was a brief pause.

'There's a note we found with the body in which Reynolds confesses to killing Rita and a girl in London. I'll send you a full report and photographs of the note. I think that's going to be case closed for you. I've still got a couple of questions I need answering about the two murders up here. Sorry we couldn't find him alive, Glyn.'

Another pause, this time longer.

'Yeah, I know what you're saying; definitely the coward's way out. I'll need to liaise with you further anyway. I need to see all your paperwork regarding the enquiry into the deaths of Rita Reynolds and Jenny Taylor, ready for the coroner's inquest into Sergeant Reynolds's death. Take care, Glyn; I'll talk to you again soon.'

76

Peckham, London – November 4, 1984

In the CID office at Peckham Police Station, Craig watched as Glyn slowly replaced the telephone back on its cradle.

'You look shocked, guv'nor. Is everything all right?'

'That was Danny Flint on the phone from Nottingham. They've finally found Mick Reynolds; he's bloody well topped himself. The cowardly bastard has hanged himself in the woods up in Nottingham.'

'Bloody hell!'

'That's not all. Danny says they've recovered a suicide note from Reynolds's body and that he's admitted killing both his wife, Rita, and a young girl in London.'

'Well, the young girl's got to be Jenny Taylor, hasn't it?'

'God, I'm pissed off. That evil bastard has taken the easy way out and won't ever have to answer for his crimes.'

'I know where you're coming from, guv, but at least

nobody else's gonna get hurt by him, the cases here are solved, and we can start to close the enquiries down.'

'That's all very true, but we'd got more than enough evidence to secure convictions against him for both the murders here. Danny's asked me to prepare a report summarising our enquiries into the murders of Jenny Taylor and Rita Reynolds, ready for the coroner's inquest that'll be held up in Nottingham.'

'I can crack on with that, guv. I've got everything I need on my desk, anyway.'

'Thanks, Craig. It sounds to me like Danny's not happy about something up in Nottinghamshire, though. He's just said to me he still needs a couple of questions answered.'

'Wonder what that's all about?'

'I don't know. I'll call him in a few days' time and find out. I'm curious is all.'

'Anyway, I know you're a little bit pissed off at the way that bastard Reynolds has dodged his final reckoning, but there's something else that we do need to pay attention to as a matter of urgency.'

'Pub?' said Glyn.

'Pub!' said Craig.

Mansfield – November 11, 1984

It had been a week since the body of Sergeant Mick Reynolds had been found hanging from a gnarled oak tree in Newstead Abbey.

Danny had finally received most of the outstanding forensic test results. The only matters still outstanding were the toxicology results from the samples taken at the post-mortem examination. As he'd expected, there were no marks of any evidential value found on the typewritten note left on the sergeant's body.

The burned-out car had been forensically examined at headquarters, and no identifying features were found that could help trace the owner.

Sitting in the lounge at Sue's house, Danny leaned forward on her sofa and grimaced. He shook his head in disbelief as he watched the press release being delivered on the evening news by Superintendent Ken Jackson.

Jackson was smiling, telling the television audience that

women in the area could once again feel safe and that the hunt for the killer of Mandy Stokes and June Hayes was over. He praised the efforts of the police and thanked the public for their assistance and support.

Danny remained perched on the edge of the sofa; he was not impressed.

'What the hell's he doing?' he yelled.

Sue asked, 'What's wrong, Danny?'

'I can't believe Jackson's sitting there in front of the cameras, spouting all this rubbish. He doesn't know what he's talking about, and what's more, he hasn't even had the professional courtesy of speaking to me about the progress of the case first.'

'But surely it's good news. That monster you've been working so tirelessly to find is now dead.'

'You're right, Sue. Sergeant Mick Reynolds is dead, and yes, I'm sure he was a monster, but I don't think this is all over yet. I've got a nasty feeling we're being fed a line here somehow. There are too many things that don't make sense to me. Jackson should've spoken to me first before going public like this. I still haven't received the toxicology test results from the Reynolds post-mortem yet, and the forensic results I have got back have only confirmed my nagging doubts about this case.'

'I don't get it; do you think women are still in danger?'

'I just don't think that everything's as crystal clear as Jackson would want us to believe, and yes, I really think women may still be in danger.'

'But Sergeant Reynolds is dead. Surely that's it; it's all over.'

'I hope you're right, Sue. I really hope you're right.'

Gently, Sue pulled him back from the edge of the sofa and cuddled him.

'Well, I for one think it's good news. Now the case is closed, I might get to see a bit more of you.'

'I'm not arguing with that. There's nothing I want more than to spend more time with you, but I'll be seeing Superintendent bloody Jackson first thing in the morning. I want to keep the murder team working. I just know something about this isn't right. The case shouldn't be closed yet.'

Sue knew that Danny wasn't going to lighten his mood, so she just snuggled into him, trying her best to calm him down and take his mind off his anxieties.

78

Mansfield Police Station – November 12, 1984

Danny had waited patiently for Superintendent Ken Jackson to arrive at the police station that morning. When he finally arrived, Danny had followed him straight into his office and closed the door.

'Sir, we really need to talk. That press release shouldn't have been made without you at least having the professional courtesy to speak to me about the progress of the case first.'

As he hung his jacket on the coat hook on the back of the office door, Ken Jackson made eye contact with Danny and glared angrily. 'I really don't see what your problem is, Danny.'

'My problem is you should've spoken to me first. I'm not happy about closing down the enquiry into the murders of either Mandy Stokes or June Hayes at this time, sir!'

'Exactly what aren't you happy about? You've got a dead suspect who's left a suicide note with a full confession, for Christ's sake. The Met have closed their enquiries. They're quite happy that Reynolds was the man responsible for the death of his wife, Rita, and Jenny Taylor.'

'With respect, sir! I don't really give a flying fuck what the Met have done. The murders in London, although linked in some ways, are totally different to what we've got here!'

Ken Jackson, having retreated behind his desk, had remained standing. He scratched his head and slowly walked over to the office window, gazing out, deep in thought.

'Exactly what are these issues that you're not happy with? Explain them to me so I can understand what the hell it is you're talking about.'

Danny took a deep breath and began. 'I think the person responsible for murdering Mandy Stokes and June Hayes is still out there.'

Jackson spun around now, his anger mounting. 'You're losing the plot here, Inspector! What on earth gives you that idea?'

'Sir, I'm of the opinion that Reynolds didn't kill the women by himself. I believe he's always worked alongside somebody else; I'm convinced it's this second person who's actually carrying out the murders.'

'I've never heard anything so ridiculous! What possible evidence have you got to support this ludicrous theory of yours? I've gone on TV telling the public that they're safe and that the killer's been found, and now you're standing here telling me this rubbish!'

'That's why, with respect, you should've spoken to me before last night's TV broadcast!'

'Look, Danny, the chief constable himself ordered that TV bulletin to be broadcast last night. In case you hadn't noticed, the Nottinghamshire Police force has been getting some severe criticism lately; embarrassing questions have been asked. Why hadn't we found Reynolds until he was dead? Why hadn't we solved the murders here before he killed his wife? The whole thing's been a public relations disaster. The media are having a feeding frenzy at our expense. I'm not prepared to go to the chief constable this morning and say, "Did you see the press release on TV last night, sir? Oh, and by the way, sir, really sorry, sir, but actually the real killer's still on the loose, sir." Not a chance, Inspector!'

'Even if it turns out to be true?'

Superintendent Jackson walked back around his desk and sat down, trying to calm himself down. He looked squarely at Danny and said, 'Okay, sit down and tell me exactly what evidence you've got to back up this fantastic theory.'

Danny sat down opposite the superintendent and began to speak quietly. 'There are a number of things that have bothered me throughout this investigation, sir. The first was the massive injuries to both victims, the rage displayed causing those injuries was enormous, but conflictingly, the cause of death in both cases was strangulation. It was as though the rage was either being staged to throw us off the scent, or there were two individuals involved in the murders. One of them motivated by rage, which would have been Reynolds. The other motivated by something else completely – a cold, calculating killer. Two individuals, with different motivations, working together to carry out horrific murders.'

Danny continued, 'As the investigation progressed and Reynolds was identified, other things came to light that supported this theory.'

'Such as?'

'Such as the blonde woman described by the young PC at Proteus Camp. Who is this woman? The young cop only saw long blonde hair from behind, so how do we even know for sure this person's a woman? This blonde, male or female, is still outstanding and has yet to be traced.'

Danny took a breath and pressed on. 'Then there's the car. There was a green Ford Cortina seen by the PC at Proteus Camp, and also by Stan Briggs on the night of the Hayes murder. A green Cortina was subsequently found burned out at the side of Reynolds's body. Who actually owned that car? Why would someone about to take their own life be bothered about obliterating every identifying mark on that vehicle? It doesn't make any sense.'

'Is that it, or do you have more of this nonsense?'

Danny threw his hands up in despair, anger creeping into his voice. 'Yes, there's more, if you can be bothered to hear it, sir!'

'Carry on, Detective Inspector Flint. I'm all ears!'

'We've done an awful lot of background checks into Mick Reynolds. Before his deployment on the strike, he'd never been to Nottinghamshire. Think for a second about the remote locations used by the killer as deposition sites for Mandy Stokes and June Hayes. Then think about the location where Reynolds's body was discovered. How would Reynolds possibly know about these locations? Surely this fact alone suggests the involvement of somebody else. Somebody who has good local knowledge.'

Danny paused to allow that point to sink in before continuing. 'Then there's the fact that the suicide note found on Reynolds's body was typed, using the same typewriter as the notes left on the murder victims. We've still not recovered that typewriter. I've checked with the Met, and there isn't a typewriter at the Reynolds home, and Detective Inspector Johnson has had every typewriter at Wembley Police Station checked. I've even checked every typewriter I can find at police stations throughout this county that his PSU have visited, as well as every typewriter at Proteus Camp. There are no typewriters with a dropped letter *c* anywhere. My question to you is a simple one. Is Reynolds the author of the notes? Or could it be that the typewriter used for the notes is still in possession of this second individual?'

Ken Jackson shook his head slowly.

Danny ignored the negativity emanating from his senior officer and continued, 'Finally, the suicide note itself found on the body of Reynolds has been nin tested. There's absolutely nothing on the paper, not a mark of value anywhere. Would a person typing their own suicide note be bothered about leaving fingerprints on the paper used, when he's about to kill himself?'

Danny leaned forward, resting his elbows on his knees, and took a deep breath, having finished outlining his theory.

After a long pause, Jackson steepled his fingers beneath his chin and said, 'That's all very interesting, Inspector – but that's all it is, an interesting theory. Supposition at best on your part. I've read the pathologist's report, and there's nothing to suggest Reynolds's death was anything other than suicide.'

'Sir, in his report, Seamus Carter said he could find nothing that would indicate anything other than suicide, but he also said it wouldn't have been impossible for somebody else to hang Reynolds. Don't forget the very deep foot marks that were found below where the rope was tied to the lower branch. They could've easily been made by somebody using a lot of effort to raise a dead weight. And another thing, I still haven't received the toxicology results from the post-mortem yet.'

'That's only your opinion about the foot marks, Danny, more supposition that you're using to help promote your theory of a second killer. Did Seamus Carter say it wouldn't have been impossible for somebody else to hang the sergeant in answer to a specific question put by you, Inspector?'

'Yes, he did, but–'

Jackson cut him off. 'Then it means nothing. The bottom line is this: Carter thinks Reynolds's death was suicide. I'm sorry, but I can't agree with you, Inspector. The reality of this situation is we're fortunate that this man took his own life rather than continue his killing spree because, let's face it, you and your team were no nearer catching him, were you?'

Jackson had subtly gone on the attack.

Danny countered by saying, 'Sir, let me remind you of the enquiry I'd instigated, tracking the movements of visiting officers. I'm confident that enquiry would've eventually led us to Reynolds. Are you prepared to discount the toxicology reports before we've even had them?'

With a self-satisfied smile, Jackson said, 'Yes, I am. I'm confident that those tests will show absolutely nothing suspicious. You have actually just made my point for me. You said "would" have led us to Sergeant Reynolds. Not to some phantom, blonde-haired maniac who's still out there, waiting to strike!'

Danny sat back in his chair; he already knew what was coming next.

'Inspector Flint, as of today, the murder enquiry team's disbanded. You and your staff will resume normal CID duties. I don't want you, or any of the detectives under your command, wasting any more time on these murder enquiries. As far as Nottinghamshire Police are concerned, they're solved. Case closed; move on.'

Danny stood up to leave. As he was going out the door, he paused and said angrily, 'There's none as blind as those who want to be. I hope for everyone's sake you're proved right about this, sir!'

Without even looking up from the paperwork on his desk, Jackson had the last word: 'Think about taking some leave, Inspector!'

Mansfield Police Station – November 12, 1984

Danny was fuming as he walked back into the CID office. He looked around at the detectives in the small office and said angrily, 'Rob, Rachel, Andy … as of this moment, you'll all resume normal CID duties. There'll be no further enquiries carried out into the murders of Mandy Stokes and June Hayes. I'll take care of the paperwork for the coroner's inquest into Reynolds's death, and I'll close the files on Mandy Stokes and June Hayes.'

For the first time since the strike started, Danny walked through the general office and into his own office, closing the door behind him.

After ten minutes, there was a polite knock on the door.

'Come in,' he shouted.

Rob opened the door, walked in and said quietly, 'I'm guessing Jackson didn't go for your theory, then?'

'Shut the door and sit down, Rob.'

As soon as Rob had closed the door and sat down, Danny spoke again. 'That man's a fucking idiot. He always takes the line of least resistance. I spelt it out for him chapter and verse, but he wouldn't listen – worse, he didn't *want* to listen. As far as the force is concerned, it's "case closed; move on". He actually said those words to me, Rob!'

'So that's it, then, boss, "The Coal Killer" enquiries are to be put to bed?'

'Be honest with me, Rob: Do you think this is all over? Tell me straight if you think I'm being paranoid.'

'I can see some merit in every point you raise, such as the local knowledge needed for the deposition sites, the anomalies with the suicide, the car, the blonde – all of it makes sense.'

'I sense a "but" coming, Rob.'

'You're right, there is a "but", Danny. I think we've got to accept what Seamus Carter told us, that Reynolds's death was suicide. My other problem with your theory is this: Even if there's a second individual involved in these crimes, what's his connection to Reynolds?'

'Firstly, I keep banging on about this, but we still haven't had the toxicology results. The other point you raise is valid, and I really don't know the answer. There's got to be a connection between Reynolds and the second man somewhere; it's just finding it.'

'If there's a second man, Danny.'

'Anyway, it's all hypothetical, as there are to be no more enquiries made, so it's back to work for everyone. Will you do me a favour, Rob? Ask Andy and Rachel to come in here for a minute.'

Rob nodded and left the office. Seconds later the door opened again, and Rachel and Andy walked in. Danny indicated for them both to be seated. 'Grab a chair, both of you. As from today, the official line is that the investigation into the Coal Killer murders is now closed. We're not to spend any more time on enquiries into the two murders. I just wanted to personally thank you for your tireless work. I know it hasn't been without impact on your personal lives. I'll be seeking a chief constable's commendation for both of you.'

'Thanks, boss,' said Andy.

'That's great; thanks,' Rachel agreed. 'Do we start on the old shift pattern again, then, or are we staying on the rota we started when the strike began?'

'I think we'll be reverting back to the strike hours, so generally day shifts, but with plenty of overtime.'

Rachel smiled. 'My brother's coming up to stay for a week on the fourteenth. Would it be okay to book a week's leave from that date? We plan to do some walking up in Derbyshire.'

'No problem at all. Andy, you can cover if anything drastic comes in, can't you?'

'It's the least I can do, boss. Rachel covered all my work for a fortnight.'

'That's sorted, then, Rachel. You can take leave for a week from the fourteenth. Just drop an annual leave request form on my desk, and I'll sign it through.'

'Thanks, boss, will do.'

'That's that, then, folks. Thanks again, both of you, for all your efforts.'

Rachel and Andy left the office, leaving Danny alone, thinking about what Rob had said to him.

Connection was the key.

Rob had been right when he'd asked what was the connection between Reynolds and the second killer. The thought suddenly came into Danny's mind: What if the connection was somebody Reynolds had met while on strike duty? Suddenly, feeling very enthused, he stood up and stuck his head around his office door.

'Rachel, could you get me a list of all the deployments

undertaken by Mick Reynolds's PSU, Mike Alpha One Zero? I need it for the coroner's file.'

'Of course, boss,' said Rachel.

Danny closed the door. *No more enquiries to be done, my arse. Jackson can go fuck himself,* he thought.

80

Mansfield, Nottinghamshire – November 13, 1984

Jimmy Wade had been waiting a long time for this day to arrive. The anticipation inside him was growing steadily; he felt like a volcano about to erupt.

His Datsun car was parked just around the corner from the block of flats where Rachel Moore lived with her cat. He'd spent hours watching her, stalking her, getting to know her routine.

Jimmy hadn't bothered going back into work after dealing with the idiotic police sergeant. Everything was now in place; there was absolutely no reason or any need for him to keep going down the mine. He'd purchased the Datsun secondhand. It was a runner and was cheap enough to be discarded later.

The painstaking preparations he'd made to get to this point were all now in place. Rachel Moore was the last piece of his perfect jigsaw.

Thinking about her made the anticipation he felt even

stronger. It had been a long time since he'd enjoyed a woman properly, intimately, and Jimmy fully intended to enjoy Rachel in every way before finally dispatching her to a better place than this one.

He sat patiently waiting in the car, biding his time, watching the entrance to the block of four flats.

Glancing over his shoulder, he saw the large suitcase on the back seat of the car. There was another bigger case in the boot. After tonight, if all went to plan, he would need a long break. He looked down at his watch. It was almost three o'clock in the afternoon. Still a few more hours to wait before she'd be due to arrive home.

Suddenly, the opportunity he'd been waiting patiently for seemed about to happen. An elderly woman walked slowly towards the communal entrance, carrying a couple of heavy bags full of shopping.

Instantly, Jimmy jumped out of the car. Having locked the car door, he strode purposefully over, saying, 'Here, let me help you with those heavy bags.'

'That's very kind of you, thank you. I live on the top floor, and it's a bit of a struggle getting the bags up the stairs. Would you mind carrying them up the stairs for me, darling?'

Perfect, thought Jimmy.

'No, not at all,' he said. Quickly taking both the bags of shopping from the old lady, he took a step back to allow her to open the communal door with her key. He followed the old lady slowly up the stairs to the first floor until he was standing outside her door.

The old lady's flat was directly opposite Rachel's flat.

'That's lovely: thank you so much. I can manage them from here.'

'No problem at all,' Jimmy said. 'Be seeing you.'

He turned and walked noisily back down the stairs.

Once downstairs, he opened and then slammed the communal door shut, remaining on the inside. Very quietly he stepped under the stairwell. He waited until he heard the old lady close and lock the door to her flat; then he crept back up the stairs, taking his wallet out as he did so. He removed a plastic credit card and put on a pair of the light blue latex gloves that Reynolds had introduced him to. The fact that the gloves were police issue gave him an additional thrill.

Very carefully, he slipped the thin plastic card between the door frame and the lock. After a few seconds of wriggling the card, he felt the latch slide open.

He slowly pushed open the door and stepped inside Rachel's flat, closing the door softly behind him.

He made a quick check inside the flat to make sure there were no unexpected visitors. Happy he was alone in the flat, he returned the plastic card to his wallet.

Suddenly, he was startled by something brushing against his leg.

It was Rachel's black-and-white cat. He snatched up the cat and shut it inside what appeared to be the second bedroom.

Jimmy hated cats with a passion and was tempted to throw the animal out of the first-floor window. He quickly discounted this idea; the bloody thing might hang around outside, and then Rachel would wonder how it had got out of the flat. No, the small bedroom would have to do.

Jimmy began to have a close look at all the rooms.

There was a small kitchen just off the hallway that was clean and tidy; there were no dirty dishes left in the sink. He opened the well-stocked fridge and thought about helping himself to some fresh orange juice. He decided not to and walked along the hallway through an interior door. This led into a spacious room that was used as a lounge and dining area. At the end of the room nearest the kitchen was a small teak table and four chairs. Beside the table and chairs was a large teak wall unit with a stereo at one end and a heavy cut-glass vase at the other. There were no flowers in the vase. A large record collection and a vast number of books took up the remaining space on the wall unit.

The other end of the lounge was dominated by a dark brown leather, three-seater sofa covered in beige-coloured scatter cushions. It looked extremely comfortable.

He could see that the end of the sofa nearest the colour television was obviously where Rachel spent most of her evenings. There was a noticeable indentation where she sat, and there were a couple of the scatter cushions strategically placed to aid her comfort while watching the television.

At the side of the sofa was a carefully placed small teak coffee table. It still had last night's coffee mug on a bamboo coaster. In front of the sofa was a cream-coloured sheepskin rug.

Closing his eyes briefly, he imagined himself with Rachel, writhing around on the rug in the throes of passionate lovemaking.

From the lounge, he made his way into the bathroom. Again, neutral colours made up the bath, toilet and basin. There was a chrome showerhead above the bath, with a glass screen at the side of the bath.

An image came crashing into his brain: Rachel standing in the shower with lather from her scented body gel cascading down her naked body.

Quickly he checked his imagination and walked into the main bedroom.

It was exactly how he had imagined her room would be.

The room was dominated by a large double bed covered with a very thick, ivory-coloured duvet. There were two ivory pillows at the top of the bed. Smaller chocolate brown scatter cushions made of silk were haphazardly placed on the bed. The headboard was a brass frame, with brass bed knobs on the pillars. At either side of the bed were small cream-coloured bedside cabinets with matching lamps. The lamp shades were a very subtle light beige, and the stands were intricately carved mock ivory.

There were cream-coloured fitted wardrobes down one entire wall of the bedroom, and a matching chest of drawers on the other side of the room had a stand-alone vanity mirror sitting on the top. In front of these drawers was a matching stool.

Jimmy could imagine Rachel sitting naked on the stool, applying her make-up before getting dressed every morning.

Regaining his concentration, Jimmy opened the top drawer of the chest of drawers and pulled out the contents, spreading them all over the white duvet.

All of Rachel's silky underwear was now on display for him to inspect. He lingered over the black bras and panties for twenty minutes, picking them up and allowing the silky material to slide slowly across his face.

He glanced at his watch; it was nearly four thirty.

Not long to wait now.

'Hurry home, Rachel,' he said aloud.

81

Mansfield Police Station – November 13, 1984

Danny looked at his watch and said, 'Rachel, why are you still here?'

'I've just got to finish this report before I go home, boss.'

'I thought I'd signed a leave pass for you to be off for a week from tomorrow. Isn't your brother coming up from Plymouth today? You don't want to leave him stuck outside on the doorstep, do you?'

'He isn't due to arrive until about six o'clock this evening. What's the time now?'

'It's getting on for five thirty; time you weren't here. Your brother will curse you if you're not at home to welcome him.'

Rachel laughed out loud. 'I doubt it, not our Joe. He'd just let himself in and make a brew. He's very self-sufficient, like all Royal Marines. The first thing I did when I got the flat was give him a key, that way whenever he gets some leave and fancies a base to go walking, he can come up and stay, without worrying what shift I'm on.'

'Rachel, get yourself home. Whatever that report is, it'll keep, and if it won't, I'll get Andy to sort it in the morning. Go home, enjoy a week with your brother, then come back refreshed and raring to go.'

Rachel put down the paperwork. 'Thanks, boss, you've talked me into it. It's only an intelligence report for a sighting of a suspect motor we saw yesterday. Andy will know which one it is.'

'Don't worry, I'll make sure Andy gets it sorted. Enjoy your leave. You've earned it.'

'Will do! See you next week.'

Rachel grabbed her coat and walked out to the car park.

Throwing the coat onto the seat beside her, she started her car and drove out of the car park. Her head was already full of the different walks she'd be doing with her brother in the coming week.

Edale and Kinder Scout in the Derbyshire Peak District would be the first. They always liked to start a week's walking with the long climb up Jacob's Ladder on to the moors. The view from the top of the climb was breathtakingly beautiful and helped to raise their spirits at the start of the week.

Eventually, she pulled her Mini onto the car park next to Bateman Court and made her way into the block of flats.

Wearily, she trudged up the flight of stairs until she reached her front door. Unlocking the door, she walked in, flicking the light on as she entered and calling out for her cat, 'Come on, Mr Tibbs, where are you?'

She walked straight past the kitchen and opened the door into the lounge diner, throwing her coat onto the back of the nearest dining chair.

Jimmy Wade was waiting silently in the main bedroom.

He could now hear her footsteps walking towards the bedroom.

With a growing sense of excitement, he watched as the brass door handle moved slowly down.

The door opened.

He saw her eyes widen in terror when she finally saw him standing directly in front of her. She was too startled to react to the threat, and although she saw the punch coming, she couldn't move quickly enough.

He punched her once hard on the forehead directly above the bridge of her nose. The force of the blow was enough to stun her and knock her backwards into the living room. She fell onto the sheepskin rug and lay there dazed.

Quickly he was upon her, trying to grab her wrists and to feed them into the cable ties.

Rachel regained her senses. Now fully aware of what was happening, she began to fight back in earnest.

A strong and fit young woman, she refused to curl up and submit to this maniac.

Rachel began lashing out with fists and feet, fighting hard for her life. She felt her fists connect with her attacker's face. Instinctively, she raised her right knee sharply upwards, forcing it hard into the groin of her attacker, and heard him gasp as pain racked through him.

Wade now realised he had a fight on his hands. He dropped the cable ties, concentrating solely on subduing her. After the painful blow to his groin, all thoughts of sexual activity had quickly disappeared from his mind. All he wanted now was to control the bitch so he could savour the moment of killing her.

Fighting desperately against her much bigger and much stronger assailant, Rachel knew she was losing.

She cried out at the top of her voice, 'Help me!'

Wade instantly let go of her wrist and punched her hard in the face.

The blow landed heavily, flush on Rachel's left cheekbone.

Once again, she was momentarily stunned. He used this pause to straddle her arms with his legs, pinning her to the floor. Regaining her senses again, Rachel started to buck and thrash wildly with her legs, trying to dislodge him.

Wade was too heavy and too strong; she was pinned to the floor and couldn't move. His weight was crushing her chest, and she struggled to breathe. She could feel his hands around her throat now.

Frantically, Rachel tried to twist her head from side to side, trying to prevent him getting a good grip.

It was useless; she couldn't stop him and could now feel his hands closing around her throat. Then she felt him starting to squeeze. All the fight suddenly left her; she couldn't offer anything else and just remained still.

Rachel stared up at her attacker's face and looked into his eyes. Her last thought was that she knew who he was, that she'd stared into those piercing blue eyes before.

Even as her eyes rolled back, Wade continued to strangle her. Rachel was completely still now, and he knew she was dead. Finally, he released the pressure on her throat.

Very slowly, he started to edge back along her torso until her arms were no longer beneath his legs. He was now sitting on her waist. Her arms lay limp at the sides of her body.

He calmed his breathing down, then slowly began to unbutton her sheer maroon-coloured blouse, exposing the black lacy bra beneath.

When he'd undone the last button, he opened the blouse fully, pushing the black bra up towards her neck, exposing Rachel's firm breasts.

He removed the latex gloves he was wearing, stuffing them into his jacket pocket. Slowly, he cupped his hands around her breasts, gently caressing them. He then bent forward and kissed each nipple, saying softly, 'Stupid girl, this would've been so much better if you hadn't struggled so hard.'

Suddenly, Jimmy heard the sound of a key being inserted in the door behind him.

He jumped off Rachel and stood behind the door that led from the hallway into the lounge, grabbing the heavy cut-glass vase from the wall unit.

He heard the front door slam. A man's voice said, 'Hello, Rach, I'm here. Where are you, sis?'

The door opened, and a short, powerfully built man stepped into the lounge.

Rachel's brother, Joe, saw his sister lying on the floor in front of him.

'What the fuck!' he shouted.

Jimmy stepped out behind him and crashed the heavy vase onto the back of his head. The glass vase smashed into a thousand pieces, and Joe was knocked out cold.

Knowing the commotion would have alerted the neighbours, Jimmy ran out of the flat, down the stairs, and across the street to his waiting car.

He jumped into the car and drove quickly away, leaving the disaster in the flat behind him. It would take him less than a quarter of an hour to reach the M1 motorway.

His visit to Rachel Moore hadn't gone exactly to plan. He deeply regretted not being able to have sex with her. He had thought of little else for weeks. He consoled himself with the fact that he had succeeded in killing the beautiful, enigmatic detective who had consumed his thoughts for so long. That had to be a good thing. It would now be a new beginning for him in every sense.

BACK AT BATEMAN COURT, Rachel's brother, Joe, was starting to come round from the enormous blow to the back of his head.

Slowly, he shook his head, and the fog started to clear

from his brain. He looked around and saw his sister lying motionless on the floor.

Quickly, he reached over and felt her neck for a pulse. It was very weak, but it was there. Rachel was still alive.

His head throbbing with pain, he dragged himself over to the telephone on the wall unit. He pulled the phone onto the floor and, trying hard to focus, dialled 999.

His head began to swim once again as the operator's voice came on the line.

He spoke in a soft faltering voice. 'I need an ambulance and the police right now. I'm at 4 Bateman Court, Mansfield. My sister's been attacked, and she's unconscious.'

Having made the call for help, Joe dragged himself back across the floor to where Rachel was lying. Tenderly, he pulled his sister's bra back down until it was once again covering her breasts.

Using all the reserves of his considerable strength to overcome the pain in his head, he rolled Rachel over into the recovery position. He then remained at her side, holding her hand and talking to her constantly, waiting for the ambulance to arrive.

Every so often he checked for a pulse. It was still there, very weak, but it was still there.

He repeated over and over again, 'Keep fighting, Rach. Hang in there. I'm right here with you.'

82

Mansfield, Notts – November 14, 1984

The blue lights of the gathered emergency vehicles splashed across the concrete walls of Bateman Court.

Danny and Rob parked their cars across the road and quickly walked towards the block of flats. An ambulance cranked up the two-tones as it sped away from the flats, back down the hill, heading towards Mansfield.

A uniform policewoman was standing at the communal door to the flats, notebook in hand.

'Oh, shit,' muttered Danny.

Rob got out his warrant card and showed it to the young policewoman.

'DS Buxton and DI Flint,' he said.

'It's the flat upstairs, on the left.'

Danny muttered under his breath, 'I know which bloody flat it is.'

At the top of the stairs, waiting outside Rachel's flat, was a very worried-looking Andy Wills. He'd been returning to the police station from an enquiry at Rainworth when he heard the call on the radio. He'd driven directly to Bateman Court and arrived first on the scene, seconds before the first panda car.

'What's the news, Andy?' asked Danny.

'She's still alive, boss, just.'

'Thank God for that. Who called it in?'

'Her brother, Joe; he walked in and found her unconscious, stepped forward to help her and was whacked from behind. By the time he came around, the attacker was long gone.'

'Where's Joe now?'

'He's gone in the same ambulance as Rachel. He wouldn't leave her. He's talking to her constantly, telling her to hang in there and keep fighting. He needs checking over as well, boss. He's had a really nasty blow to the back of his head.'

'Did the ambulance crew say anything?' asked Rob.

'Nothing at all, Sarge. They were too busy working on her. She's in a really bad way; it's touch and go, I'm afraid. They've just this second left for King's Mill Hospital.'

Danny took a deep breath. 'Rob, get things started here. I want Scenes of Crime out here sharpish. I want officers talking to the neighbours in the flats and also up and down the street. I'm going to the hospital to see how Rachel's doing, and find out what the prognosis is. I'll also talk to Joe down there once he's been seen by the doctors.'

'Okay, Danny, I'm on it,' said Rob as he walked back to the car.

'This has all the hallmarks of a sex attack, boss,' said Andy.

'What do you mean?'

'Well, when I first got here, I had a quick look through the flat, and nothing appears to be missing. There's a lot of valuable stuff that would've been nicked in a burglary. Her knicker drawer's been tipped out onto the bed, and her underwear's strewn all over the place. Rachel's blouse was totally unbuttoned as well. So it looks more like a sex attack than a burglary to me.'

'You could well be right, Andy, and that's a line of enquiry we can definitely look at later. Right now, I want you to crack on with the enquiries I've asked you to do. Concentrate on the neighbours first.'

'Okay, boss.'

Danny walked back to Rob. 'Are Scenes of Crime on their way yet?'

'I've just fired another call in to them, boss; they're travelling. It's Tim Appleby who's coming out.'

'Okay, if Tim's team find anything, let me know straight away. Rachel's one of our own, and we're going to find whoever did this to her.'

Danny started down the stairs.

Rob shouted after him, 'Let us know how she's doing, Danny.'

Danny looked up and saw the look of concern on the faces of the two detectives.

Danny nodded and was then running to the car. He gunned the engine and sped off down the hill towards the hospital. Ten minutes later, he ran into the Casualty Department at King's Mill Hospital.

He took out his warrant card and was just about to ask the receptionist where Rachel and Joe had been taken when he saw Sue walking quickly towards him.

'Oh, Danny, I'm so sorry,' she said.

'Rachel's not dead, is she?'

'No, she isn't. She's alive; I don't quite know how, though. The ambulance crew had to revive her in the ambulance. Her heart stopped; she didn't have a pulse for over two minutes before they got her heart started again. It's touch and go, Danny. They've rushed her straight up to the Intensive Care Unit.'

'How's she doing now?'

'Like I said, it's touch and go, Danny; they've stabilised her, but she's in a coma.'

'Thank God she's still alive.'

'I saw her when they first brought her in. She's got a couple of really nasty injuries to her head and face, but she's been strangled almost to death. Somebody's tried to kill her and then had a bloody good go at killing her brother, Joe.'

'Where is Joe?'

'He's in the treatment room next door. The wound he received is very bad; my colleague's putting quite a few stitches into the back of his head. I'll tell you something, these Marines are tough. By rights, he should still be out for the count. It's a good job he came around pretty quickly or Rachel would be dead.'

'I need to talk to Joe as soon as I can.'

Sue took his arm, gently restraining him as he walked towards the treatment room. 'Take your time, Danny. I know you want to find who did this, but don't forget he's just taken a tremendous whack to the back of his head. Tough or not, he could get forgetful or drowsy at any time, so go easy.'

'Okay, Sue, I will. After I've spoken to Joe, will I be able to go and see Rachel on ICU?'

'I'll take you up to ICU as soon as you're ready.'

'Thanks, Sue.'

Danny stepped forward and kissed her gently on the lips before walking into the treatment room.

Joe Moore was sitting on the treatment couch. His blue denim shirt was covered in blood, and he had dried blood on his face and hands. He didn't flinch as the attending doctor put yet another stitch into his head wound.

'Joe, I'm Danny Flint. Rachel's boss.'

'How's my sister, Inspector?'

'I've just spoken to the doctor, and Rachel's stable now, in the Intensive Care Unit. But I'm sorry to have to tell you ... she's in a coma.'

Relief washed over Joe's features, and he said quietly, 'She's still fighting, then.'

'Yes, your sister's still fighting. She's a very strong and determined young woman.'

The doctor placed the final stitch in the wound, then stood up from behind Joe, saying, 'That's all done, Mr Moore, but I'd like to keep you here overnight for observation. That was one hell of a clout you took. I've put twenty-two stitches in that cut.'

'Don't worry, Doctor, I'm not leaving this hospital without my big sister.'

As the doctor walked towards the door to leave, he looked directly at Danny, saying, 'Not too many questions, Detective. Mr Moore needs to rest.'

Danny nodded.

Joe waited for the doctor to leave, then said, 'Ask as many questions as you like, Inspector. I'm fine.'

Danny looked at the young Marine.

Joe was twenty-three, around five feet seven inches tall and looked about three feet wide. He was a very stocky, very powerful man. Rachel had told Danny that Joe had been a Royal Marine for five years and had fought in the Falklands War.

'What can you tell me, Joe?'

'I arrived at the flat around six fifteen, I guess. I've got keys, so I let myself in the communal door, then into her flat. I walked into the living room and saw her lying on the floor. I thought she was dead, Inspector.'

'Call me Danny. What happened then?'

'Okay, Danny. So I remember I shouted her name and started to bend down towards her. The next thing I know, I'm on the floor as well. Someone must have been hiding behind the lounge door and gave me a right clout.'

'Do you know what it was that hit you?'

'Rachel's got a big glass vase on her wall unit. It's heavy crystal. I've got some flowers in my car to put in it. I always bring flowers for my sister. Anyway, I'm guessing whoever hit me used the vase. When I came around, I was surrounded by smashed glass. The flat door was wide open, and whoever whacked me was long gone.'

'How was Rachel when you first saw her?'

'She was out cold, totally unresponsive. Her pulse was very weak.'

'One of my detectives said when he arrived, he noticed Rachel's blouse had been unbuttoned. Did you do that, to find a pulse?'

'No, I didn't. Her blouse was unbuttoned, and her bra had been pushed up around her neck. I reckon I disturbed whoever did this just as he was copping a feel of my sister, the sick, pervy bastard.'

He went silent, then said softly, 'I promise you one thing, Danny. You'd better find whoever did this before I do. If I get to him first, I'll just bury the bastard.'

Danny nodded his head as he saw the tears well in the eyes of the tough Marine.

'Come on, Joe. Let's go and see your sister.'

He helped Joe off the treatment couch and walked slowly outside the room into the corridor.

Sue was waiting outside.

'Do you want to go to ICU now, Danny?'

'Yes, please. Joe's coming along, too. He needs to see his sister.'

'Are you sure you're okay, Joe? You really do need to rest,' said a concerned Sue.

'What I really need, Doctor, is to see my big sister.'

They took the lift up to the Intensive Care Unit, then stood in silence at the foot of the bed where Rachel now lay.

She was connected to several machines that were breathing for her, monitoring her heartbeat and other vital signs. There was total silence in the ward apart from the noise of the machines hissing and beeping as they kept Rachel Moore alive.

Sue addressed the two men quietly. 'Rachel's in a coma because her brain was starved of oxygen during the attack. We can't say how long she'll remain in this state. Unfortunately, it's not an exact science; all we can do is monitor her progress.'

Joe looked down at his sister and said, 'Rachel's a fighter, Doc. She has been all her life. I know she'll come through this.'

'I need to get back up to the flat now, Joe. I take it you're staying here?' said Danny.

'Definitely, I won't be leaving here without my sister, Danny.'

Sue put a reassuring hand on Joe's arm. 'You won't be able to stay on the ICU ward, but I can find you a room just along the corridor. I'm on duty all night, and I need to monitor your vital signs anyway, so I'll keep you updated if there's any change in your sister's condition.'

'Okay, thanks.'

Joe then turned to Danny, saying, 'You'd better find this bloke quickly. I meant what I said earlier.'

'I know you did, Joe.'

DANNY LEFT the hospital and drove back to the flat.

When he arrived, the policewoman was still guarding the communal door.

'Is DS Buxton inside?' he asked.

She nodded, saying, 'I'll sign you in again, sir.'

'Thanks.'

Danny walked up the stairs two at a time.

He paused at the door to Rachel's flat and watched as Tim Appleby went about his work. He was busy taking swabs of blood droplets that were on the sheepskin rug.

'Found anything, Tim?' he asked.

'I've found some glove marks here and there; looks like our offender was wearing them.'

Danny looked down at the remains of the heavy crystal vase. The base was still quite intact.

'Have you printed that glass yet?'

'That's my next job.'

Rob appeared from the bedroom. 'I thought I heard your voice, Danny. How's our girl doing?'

'She's stable, but in a coma, and still on the critical list.'

'Bloody hell! What about Joe?'

'He's fine. He's had quite a few stitches in his head, but he's a tough sod.'

'It's a bloody good job he turned up when he did.'

'Tell me about it. Have we got anywhere with the neighbours?'

'We might have something there. The old lady who lives opposite Rachel's flat told us a young man helped her up to her flat with some shopping earlier today. Andy's with her now, getting a statement. I've got a police sketch artist travelling to try to get a likeness from her. He might be a perfectly innocent guy who was just helping the old lady out.'

'Yeah, and he might just be the bastard who's done this!'

'One of the uniform lads doing the house-to-house around the corner has found another possible witness. This guy lives in one of the houses just down the road from Bateman Court. The witness says he saw a Datsun car parked up for a few hours earlier today. He saw a man run to the car and drive off at speed back towards Mansfield at around six thirty.'

'Any description of the man he saw?'

'It appears to be very similar to the description given by the old lady.'

'Okay, get the artist to talk to him as well. Any details on the car?'

'No, boss, just a dark-coloured Datsun; no registration plate, nothing.'

'Make sure we get a proper statement from that man as well.'

'Will do, boss. I'm really struggling to get my head around this. Why would anybody want to attack Rachel?'

'I don't know, Rob; I really don't. Let's get the artist's impressions sorted; then tomorrow morning, all of us can start trawling through the sex offenders lists to see if any are likely. We're going to have to start rattling a few trees first thing tomorrow. I'll see you, Andy, and Tim for a debriefing in our office at eight o'clock sharp. I'm going back to the hospital now to get a written statement from Joe while everything's fresh in his mind. I'll let you know if there's any change with Rachel. See you in the morning, Rob.'

'Okay, Danny, see you tomorrow.'

Mansfield, Nottinghamshire – December 20, 1985

The letter box in the front door rattled as the postman pushed through that day's delivery of letters.

Sitting in the kitchen, sipping a cup of tea, Louise Smedley said, 'That's the post, love. Are you going to get it?'

Dave Smedley had built his hopes up too many times before. He shook his head, saying, 'Nah, love. You go and get it if you want. There won't be anything out there for me.'

Ever since he'd resigned from his deputy's job at British Coal, he had struggled to find work. He had written to countless firms up and down the country, all to no avail. As a last resort, he'd written out the job application that was advertised in the press. He was a realist and didn't hold out too much hope of success.

This was the reason for his apathy.

Dave Smedley was also a haunted man.

He knew that scheming bastard Jimmy Wade had tricked

him over the death of Albie Jones at Warsop pit, and now he was struggling to come to terms with the fact that, deep down, he knew it was his conduct that had made it easy for Wade to get away with killing Albie Jones.

The hardest thing for him to accept was that he had behaved that way for purely selfish reasons.

At the time, he had based his decisions on money. Albie Jones had died because he, Dave Smedley, could only think about money.

He had also allowed Wade to get away with it because of money. He'd been so intent on safeguarding his own job and wages as a deputy that he'd gladly gone along with Wade's deception.

Trying to push those dark thoughts to the back of his mind, he buttered another slice of toast and was just dipping the knife into the marmalade jar when his wife Louise rushed back into the dining room.

'There's a letter for you, Dave, love. It's got an Australian postmark on,' she said excitedly.

Dave almost dropped the butter knife. He grabbed the letter from his wife and ripped it open. Quickly, he scanned the document. There it was, in black and white, on the page.

Louise was beside herself with excitement. 'Come on, love, don't keep me in suspense. What does it say?'

In a trembling voice, Dave read the letter aloud to his wife.

Dear Mr Smedley

We are pleased to offer you the position of mines supervisor at the Beltana Mine, Singleton, New South Wales.

This offer is subject to your attendance at Canberra

House, London, for a medical and also subject to the granting of a twelve-month work visa.

Should the medical and visa application be successful, your employment will start from March 1, 1985.

The company will not assist you to travel to Australia, and this will have to be undertaken at your own expense.

Please notify this office at your earliest convenience if you intend to take up this offer of employment.

I look forward to hearing from you in the very near future.

Yours sincerely

Royce Goudy
Head of Development
The Baluga Coal Management Company

He put the letter down and looked at his wife, who was beaming.

'Looks like we're off to Australia, sweetheart,' he said as tears welled in his eyes.

His wife was equally excited. 'That's fantastic news, love; we need to get cracking. We've got to get the house sold, make arrangements to get the medical passed, as well as getting the visa and making travel arrangements.'

The Smedleys had always been childless, so they only had themselves to worry about. This bolt-out-of-the-blue job offer was in every way a lifeline.

It was a chance for Dave Smedley to start a new life, away from the memories of Albie Jones and Jimmy Wade.

A new beginning in every sense! He could feel his mood

lifting already. He grabbed his wife, and they hugged each other tightly.

They began to dance around the breakfast table, singing together. 'We're on our way to Australia!'

After a couple of minutes, a breathless Dave Smedley said, 'Make us a fresh cuppa, love; there's a sweetheart.'

As he watched his beaming wife filling the kettle, Dave Smedley made a decision. Before he left for Australia, he needed to go to the police station and tell somebody his suspicions about Jimmy Wade.

84

Mansfield Police Station – November 15, 1984

The mood in the CID office was a sombre one.

It was still only seven thirty in the morning when Danny walked in. Already waiting in the office were Rob, Andy, and the Scenes of Crime officer Tim Appleby.

'There's a cuppa in the pot, Danny,' said Andy.

Danny poured himself a hot cup of tea before sitting down at Rachel's desk.

He took a swig of his tea, then said, 'Thanks for getting here promptly, everyone. Let's start with you, Tim. What have we got from the flat?'

'There are definitely three blood groups found at the scene. I've cross-checked with the hospital for Rachel's and Joe's blood groups. It means our offender is blood group O positive. It also means he may have sustained injuries to his face, meaning that Rachel fought back bravely. I've checked with all casualty departments across the county for any males presenting with facial injuries that are O positive.'

'Anything so far, Tim?'

'Nothing yet, but I've asked them to call this office should anyone present throughout the day matching those parameters.'

Tim continued, 'I've also lifted what looks like a partial thumbprint from the base of the vase. The print's too large to be Rachel's, and I've checked with Joe at the hospital, and he hasn't touched the vase. This partial print is currently being checked against our systems. I've also lifted a lot of glove marks throughout the flat, in particular the drawer containing her underwear. The significance of this being, at some stage, our offender took off his gloves.'

Danny interrupted, saying, 'Joe told me last night that when he first saw Rachel on the floor, her bra had been pushed up, revealing her breasts. I reckon our attacker took off his gloves and was having a proper grope before he was disturbed by Joe coming into the flat.'

Tim continued, 'That's definitely possible. I've got Rachel's clothing from the hospital to test for fibres today. I'll also test for the powder used in latex gloves, to see if there are any traces on her clothing.'

'Good work, Tim. Let me know about the powder as soon as possible, please.'

'Will do, Danny.'

Danny turned to Andy. 'Right, Andy, what about the description of the man seen by the neighbour?'

'The neighbour, Edith Balshaw, describes the man as being about six feet tall, with short blonde hair. He was dressed smartly in a black crew-neck jumper and blue jeans. Edith reckons he's about the same age as her grandson, who is mid to late twenties. The most striking thing she remembered was the man's eyes. She reckons she hasn't seen eyes that blue since Paul Newman.'

'How did she get on with the police artist?'

'Pretty good. This is the image they came up with.'

Andy passed the picture around the table.

'Did this man say anything to the neighbour?'

'Nothing of note. He asked if she needed a hand with her heavy shopping bags, that's all.'

'Did she see where he'd come from?'

'I asked that question, and all she could say was that she thought it was from behind her, from down the road a little way.'

'Is that where the other witness saw the car parked, the Datsun?'

'Yes.'

'Okay, what about that witness?'

'He describes the man he saw as being around thirty, six feet tall, slim build with short blonde hair, wearing dark clothing.'

'Any good with the artist?'

'Didn't come up with anything. He reckoned he was too far away to get any sort of look at the man's face.'

'What about the car?'

'He did his best, but all he can say is that he thinks it was definitely a Datsun and was dark coloured, possibly dark blue. He thinks it may have been a Datsun Cherry.'

'Have you got statements from both witnesses?'

'Yes, boss.'

'That's good work, Andy. What time did you get off last night?'

'I don't know; sometime around three o'clock, I reckon.'

'I want you to get that artist's impression printed and circulated out to all patrols, along with as much information about the car as we have.'

'Yes, boss.'

'Andy, don't be too late getting off today. You're no good to me exhausted. This could well turn out to be another long and protracted enquiry. That goes for everyone in this room. I've been assured by Superintendent Jackson that manpower is not an issue on this case, so don't think we've got to do everything ourselves.'

'Right, Rob, sex offenders. Have we compiled a list yet?'

'Yes, boss, I've been in touch with all the divisional intelligence officers across the divisions. They're compiling lists of all the sex offenders who live in their respective areas, and they are going to fax the completed lists over to us. There are detectives en route to us from Worksop and the City divisions. I'll team them up into pairs; then we can gradually work through all the names on the sex offender lists. I've warned the cells that it might get busy later, when we start dragging their sorry arses in for questioning.'

Danny allowed a grim smile before saying, 'It's a good start; well done, all of you. Before you go, I've an update from the hospital. Sue spoke to me just before I came into work. Rachel's condition has remained stable overnight, and there's been no change, which I'm assured at this stage is a good sign. Joe's had a restful night and is now at his sister's bedside, talking to her about fell walking. I don't need to tell you what needs doing, so let's get cracking. I want this bastard locked up.'

85

Mansfield Police Station – December 14, 1984

It was now a month since Rachel Moore had been brutally attacked and left for dead in her own home. She was still in a coma.

Her brother, Joe, had been granted special leave from the Royal Navy in order to stay at his sister's bedside. He had been living at Rachel's flat for the past three weeks.

A search made on the partial thumbprint lifted from the smashed crystal vase in Rachel's flat had yielded nothing. The attacker's prints were not in any database held by the police.

Detectives drawn from every division had spent over two and a half weeks working through the sex offender lists provided by the divisional intelligence officers from across the force.

Twenty-four men, all with previous convictions for attacking women in their own homes, had been arrested and questioned at length.

The criteria for arrest had been left extremely loose. Even

if the men only vaguely fitted the description provided by the witnesses, they were brought in for questioning.

The result of all this time-consuming, painstaking, labour-intensive work had been nothing. No positive leads or lines of enquiry were forthcoming.

Once again, Danny could feel the pressure of working a case with very little evidence to go on. Today, as he walked into the control room, he was in a very despondent mood.

'Anything for me, Sarge? I'm just nipping out to get a turkey cob from the Railway pub,' he said.

'Sorry, sir, I didn't know you were in the building. I've been looking for someone from the CID to talk to a bloke at the front counter. I've been phoning the CID office, but nobody's picking up.'

'They're all out on enquiries. What's this bloke's problem?'

'His name's Dave Smedley. He says he wants to talk to someone about a miner who died underground at Warsop Main Colliery back in March.'

'Did he say the name of the dead miner?'

The sergeant looked at his notepad and said, 'Jones, sir, Albie Jones.'

'I'll talk to him. I dealt with Albie's death.'

Danny walked out to the front office and looked at the man waiting there. 'I'm Detective Inspector Flint. I understand you wanted to talk to me about the death of Albie Jones.'

'That's right, Inspector. I do.'

'And who might you be?'

'My name's Dave Smedley. On the day Albie Jones died at the pit, I was the deputy in charge of the men working on the face.'

'I didn't think Albie was working on the face that day.'

'He wasn't, but he was in my work detail, working further

down the loader gate. I really need to talk to you about the events of that day.'

Danny was intrigued. He showed Dave Smedley into an interview room, where both men sat down. It was obvious to Danny that Dave Smedley was extremely nervous.

'Is it okay if I smoke, Inspector?'

Danny nodded, then declined Smedley's offer of a cigarette. Dave Smedley lit his cigarette and took a long drag, inhaling the smoke deep into his lungs before exhaling. His hands holding the cigarette were shaking; he looked a very worried man.

'Right, Mr Smedley, you've obviously got something you want to get off your chest. What is it you need to tell me about the death of Albie Jones?'

'Before I say anything, Inspector, I want you to know that at the time Albie died, nobody ever suggested that his death was anything other than an accident. There was never any question of a criminal enquiry.'

'Why exactly is that important?'

There was a long silence. Smedley took another long pull on his cigarette before stammering, 'Because at the time, when I was questioned by the Mines Inspectorate, I lied to them.'

'You did what?'

'I lied to them. I've left the coal industry now, so they can't take my deputy's papers off me. That's what I was scared of, you see. I'd broken the rules that day, but I couldn't say anything about it, or I would've lost my papers. I'm not proud of what I did, and now I need to tell somebody the truth.'

'What exactly did you lie about, Mr Smedley?'

'I told the Mines Inspectorate that I'd escorted an injured miner all the way to the pit bottom, and that I'd passed Albie Jones twice. I told them Jones was alive both times I saw him.

All that was a lie. I never escorted the injured miner; he walked out by himself. I never saw Jones alive at that time.'

Danny was thoughtful for a moment; then he said, 'Yes, I remember this now. There was a miner on your team who had an eye injury. He had to leave the face and go topside to get it treated.'

'That's right.'

'And you're telling me now that the miner with the injury to his eye left the pit bottom and walked out on his own unsupervised?'

'That's it exactly.'

'Why haven't you said anything before?'

'I wanted to. I was in two minds whether or not to come clean to the Inspectorate about the whole lying business. Then, when the strike started, I was shipped off down to Wales. They were short of deputies to carry out the essential safety maintenance down the mines there. I only came back here last month, and I've now resigned from my job at Warsop Main Colliery. I reckon the coal industry in Britain's finished. I've started looking for new work.'

'Why say anything at all, Mr Smedley? You could've just kept quiet about everything.'

'The reason's simple, Inspector. What I did that day has bothered me ever since. There was something strange about the miner who walked out of the pit that day. I went to see him at his house after the shift, to make sure he'd stick to the story. I swear that he already knew Albie was dead. This is the part that's bothered me ever since, because there's no way he could've known about the death. Albie wasn't found until the afters shift came down the pit later, way after he would've walked past him on the loader gate. The only way he could've known about Albie was if he was already dead when he walked past him to get to the pit bottom.'

'There is one other explanation, Mr Smedley.'

'What's that?'

'The miner who walked out of the pit that day was responsible for the death of Albie Jones.'

'Oh my God!'

Smedley put his head in his hands. He was visibly shaking.

Danny leaned forward, staring intently at Smedley. 'Remind me again, what was the name of the miner with the injured eye?'

'His name's Jimmy Wade.'

'You said you went to his house that night. Where does Jimmy Wade live?'

'He lives on Marples Avenue at Mansfield Woodhouse. I think it's number 56.'

'Thank you, Mr Smedley. You should thank your lucky stars that at the time, Mr Jones's death wasn't a criminal investigation. If it had been, I'd be locking your lying arse up for a very long time. I want a full written statement from you, right now!'

'I'm sorry, Inspector. I never meant any harm; I was just trying to protect my job and my livelihood.'

'Where do you live?'

Dave Smedley gave Danny the details of his home address before asking sheepishly, 'How long will the statement take? My wife's waiting outside.'

'It will take as long as it takes.'

'I'm sorry I lied. I truly am.'

'Yeah, me too,' said Danny as he stepped out of the interview room.

He turned to the desk sergeant and said, 'Do me a favour, Sarge, step in the interview room and sit with him until I can get a detective up here to get his statement. He's not under arrest, but I don't want him walking out of here either. Is that clear?'

'Yes, sir.'

Danny walked quickly back to the CID office, where he found Andy and Rob eating lunch.

He said, 'Sorry, Andy, can you leave that and go up to the interview room at the front desk. There's a bloke called Dave Smedley in there. He's got information relating to the death of Albie Jones, a miner who died at Warsop Main Colliery back in March. I want a full witness statement taken from him. I don't care how long it takes; I want every detail, okay?'

'No problem, boss. I remember that job. It was at the beginning of the strike, wasn't it?'

'That's the one. Apparently when Smedley was questioned by the Mines Inspectorate, he was less than forthcoming about what occurred that day.'

'I'm on it.'

Andy took a last bite of his sandwich, scooped up a large stack of statement forms, and strode out the door.

Rob was just about to have the second bite of his own cheese and ham sandwich when Danny said, 'Come on, Rob, get your jacket. We're going out. Bring that sarnie with you.'

Rob grabbed his jacket and put it on while he held the cheese and ham sandwich in his mouth. Still chewing, he mumbled, 'Where we going, Danny?'

'We're going to 56 Marples Avenue, Mansfield Woodhouse. We need to ask Jimmy Wade some questions about the death of Albie Jones at Warsop Main Colliery in March.'

'The roof fall that caused the massive head injury?'

'The very same. I'll fill you in on all the gory details on the way to Woodhouse. Chuck me the keys. I'll drive while you finish your sandwich.'

Rob threw Danny the car keys and said, 'Didn't Rachel speak to Jimmy Wade at the time we were looking into the death?'

'Yes, she did. If I remember rightly, he's the guy who gave her the creeps.'

'That's right. I remember her saying she thought he was laughing at her, like it was all a big game to him.'

'Well, let's see if he's still laughing today, shall we?'

Danny drove the CID car slowly out of the car park and headed for Mansfield Woodhouse.

86

Marples Avenue, Mansfield Woodhouse – December 14, 1984

Danny parked the car on Marples Avenue, a short distance from number 56, and paused before getting out.

'What are you thinking?' asked Rob.

'I'm thinking that I may have missed a massive opportunity. I could kick myself for not following Rachel's intuition about this Jimmy Wade character.'

'I wouldn't beat yourself up. It was so manic during the early days of the strike, we worked with what we'd got at the time. Without that little nugget from Smedley, how could we have known any different back then?'

'You're right. Come on, let's go and talk to Wade.'

As they approached the house, they saw an old Vauxhall Viva parked on the driveway. Danny walked alongside the car and noticed a baby seat in the back.

'I thought Wade lived here alone?'

'That's what it said in Rachel's report, but that was back in March, boss.'

'That's very true. I guess things could have changed since then.'

Danny knocked loudly on the door.

The door was answered quickly by a young woman in her mid-twenties with a small child in her arms. Danny showed the harassed woman his warrant card and said, 'Police. We need to speak to Jimmy Wade.'

The woman left them standing on the doorstep and shouted back into the house, 'There's a couple of your lot at the door, Ray!'

Seconds later, a man appeared at the door.

'Detective Inspector Flint! What are you doing here, sir?'

'It's PC Turner, isn't it?' said Danny.

'Yes, sir, Ray Turner. I transferred to Mansfield from Canning Circus just before the start of the strike. I'm sorry, where are my manners? Don't stand on the doorstep. It's freezing; step inside. You'll have to excuse the mess, but we haven't been here long. We're still unpacking.'

The two detectives stepped into the lounge over the toys strewn across the floor.

A clearly embarrassed Turner shouted to his wife, 'Bloody hell, Sandra! Don't these kids ever pick anything up?'

Sandra bustled into the room, quickly picking up the children's toys.

'Please sit down. Can I get either of you a hot drink?' she asked.

Declining the offer of a drink, Danny and Rob sat down on the settee. Ray sat opposite in the armchair.

'It's not every day the CID call. What's the problem, sir?' he asked.

'How long have you lived here?' said Danny.

'We only took possession of the keys on November 13. That's why we're still in a bit of a mess.'

'Who'd you buy the house from?'

'We bought it from a bloke named Wade. We were dead lucky. It was only on the market for a couple of weeks, and it was a real bargain. I only got it because I've got a mate who works in the estate agents Wade put it up for sale with. Anyway, my mate let me know that the house was for sale, fully furnished and at a rock-bottom price. Apparently, this bloke Wade wanted a quick sale.'

He continued, 'I asked my mate to take the details out of the estate agents' window until me and Sandra could have a look. Well, as soon as Sandra saw the house, that was it; she loved it straight away. We put an offer in that same day, and it was accepted.'

'Can you remember when you and Sandra viewed the house, Ray?'

Turner paused, attempting to recall the date. 'I think it was sometime back in October. I do remember there wasn't a chain because we were only renting, and Wade was leaving the UK. Everything went through pretty quickly. Sandra's dad's quite well off, and he gave us the cash for a deposit, so clinching the mortgage was easy.'

'Leaving the UK?' asked Rob.

'I'm sorry?' said Turner.

'You just said Wade wanted a quick sale, as he was leaving the UK?'

'Yeah, that's what he said, Sarge. He told me he was a miner and that he was pissed off with Thatcher. I'm not a hundred per cent sure, but I think he mentioned South Africa.'

'What did Wade look like?' asked Danny.

'I only saw him the once, when we had the viewing. Everything was done through the solicitors after that. From memory, I'd say he was about six feet tall, slim build with short blonde hair and probably mid to late twenties. Is there a problem, sir?'

'No, there isn't.'

'Thank God for that, sir. I was beginning to get worried. Sandra loves it here, and I know I submitted the general report requesting permission to live here; that all got signed through okay.'

Rob raised his hand to stop Turner talking. 'Ray, stop worrying. There really isn't a problem with the house.

'Can you remember the name of the solicitors Mr Wade used for the conveyancing?' asked Danny.

'Not off the top of my head, sir, but I'll have some paperwork here somewhere. I'll dig it out and give you a call, if that's okay. In fact, I'm on evening's tonight, so I'll be coming into work in a few hours' time anyway. Do you want me to drop the details off in your office?'

'That'll be great if you can, Ray. I think that's all I need for now, thanks. How are your new neighbours?'

'They're fine. I've got old couples either side. They love the kids, so it's all good.'

'It's a nice house, Ray. I hope you'll all be happy here.'

'Thanks, sir, me too. Is Jimmy Wade wanted or something?'

'No, we just need to ask him a few questions, that's all.'

Danny and Rob stood up; Ray also quickly stood to show the detectives out. At the front door, he said, 'If that's everything, then, sir?'

'That's everything. Sorry to have disturbed you.'

'No problem, sir.'

AS SOON AS Ray had shut the door, Danny strode over the open-plan garden and knocked on the neighbours' front door. Eventually, the door was answered by an elderly man, who said brusquely, 'No, thanks, whatever you're selling. I never buy anything at the door!'

'Just a second, sir, we're the police. I need to ask you a few questions. It won't take long.'

The man carefully studied the warrant card being held up as Danny said, 'It will only take a few minutes, I promise you.'

'Spit it out, then, man. What do you want to know?'

No offer of a hot drink here, then.

Danny indicated the house next door and said, 'I wanted to ask you about your next-door neighbour.'

'That noisy bloody lot? Screaming kids, marvellous; that's all we need at our time of life.'

'I meant your previous neighbour, Mr Wade.'

'Oh, Jimmy. He was a good lad, no trouble at all, not like this new bunch of howling banshees.'

'Do you know where Mr Wade's moved to?'

'He's gone abroad somewhere, Canada, I think. I'm sure he told me he'd got a job near Niagara Falls. That's in Canada, isn't it?'

'Yes, sir, that's definitely in Canada. Has Mr Wade gone over there for good?'

'How should I know? He didn't tell me everything, you know. Jimmy was really quiet, not like ...'

'Not like your new neighbours. I know, you said. Well, thank you very much, sir. You've been very helpful.'

The old man started to close the door. Just before it closed completely, Danny put his hand on the door.

'Sorry, sir, there's just one more question. We understand that Mr Wade worked at Warsop Main Colliery. I was just curious how he would get to work from here. Did Jimmy drive?'

'Of course he drove.'

Danny was beginning to see the bigger picture. Could the death of Jones be linked to the other murders?

He pressed on, 'What sort of car did he drive?'

'Jimmy had a lovely old car. A dark green Ford Cortina Mk 1. It was in mint condition, beautiful. They don't make cars like that anymore. The car was originally owned by his grandfather. I think it was Jimmy's pride and joy.'

'Sounds amazing. What's happened to the car now Jimmy's gone abroad?'

'He said something about selling it to a dealer down south; got top dollar for it as well, apparently. The only problem was, he had to sell the car a few weeks before he left. He came home one evening with some disgusting Jap crap motor he'd bought. It was bloody horrible – a shitty dark blue colour and noisy as hell.'

'Okay, thanks, that's very helpful. Don't let all the heat out of your house, will you?'

The two detectives walked slowly back to the car.

'Are you thinking what I'm thinking, Rob?'

'Oh yes! A dark green Ford Cortina is just way too much of a coincidence.'

'Let's get back to the station. I need to find out whether Jimmy Wade was working or on strike until he left the country. We already know that Sergeant Reynolds and his PSU were involved in escorting working miners into Warsop Main Colliery. If Wade was a scab and going into work, it's possible we've just found our connection.'

Mansfield – December 14, 1984

After returning from Wade's old house on Marples Avenue, Rob quickly ascertained that Jimmy Wade was on the list of working miners and had indeed been escorted into Warsop Main Colliery each day by the PSU commanded by Sergeant Mick Reynolds.

Rob's enquiries revealed that Wade was one of the first miners to break the strike. The first time he had been back into Warsop Main Colliery was on June 25.

Armed with that information, Rob immediately drove to Proteus Camp, where he spoke at length to PC Ken Drury, the driver of PSU Mike Alpha One Zero.

Danny knew that the sergeant of any PSU always sits in the front seat of the van next to the driver. Rob knew that if anybody had information on Reynolds, it would be Drury.

PC Drury explained to Rob that Sergeant Reynolds regularly held conversations with one of the working miners. These conversations happened daily and were always out of earshot of other officers or other miners. Drury described how the sergeant and the miner would talk, drink coffee and smoke cigarettes while waiting for the battle bus to arrive.

Drury described the miner as being six feet tall, mid to late twenties, with short blonde hair.

He also recalled how Reynolds had totally overreacted one day when a younger member of the PSU had jokingly commented about the sergeant's new best friend, the tall, blonde miner.

Drury explained that Reynolds had gone way over the top with the young officer and threatened to throw him off the PSU and send him back to Wembley Police Station that very night. After that incident, nobody paid any attention to the sergeant and the miner. Drury told Rob from that day onwards all the younger officers on the PSU referred to the pair of them as "the odd couple".

After speaking to PC Drury, Rob then drove straight to Warsop Main Colliery, where he established that Jimmy Wade had not been in to work at the pit since October 28, the same date Sergeant Reynolds had last been on duty.

From that date onwards, both men had effectively disappeared. At least, they had until the body of Sergeant Reynolds had been found at Newstead Abbey.

When PC Ray Turner came on duty that evening, Danny spoke to him and learned that the name of the solicitors used by Jimmy Wade for the conveyancing of the house was Shaftsbury, Morton and Spinks.

PC Turner had brought with him a letter from the solicitors. The signature on the bottom of the letter was that of Richard Morton, one of the partners of the firm.

Danny and Rob had left work at ten thirty, satisfied that there was now more than enough evidence to prove a link between Mick Reynolds and Jimmy Wade.

Danny felt vindicated that his theory about a second killer still being at large was now looking more likely.

· · ·

BEFORE LEAVING WORK THAT NIGHT, Danny called Dave Smedley. He needed to know if Smedley had any knowledge of Wade's current whereabouts. Smedley assured him that he hadn't seen Wade since the day he'd been seconded down to Wales, and that he definitely hadn't seen him recently.

Finally, Danny circulated Jimmy Wade on the Police National Computer. He was now officially wanted in connection with the suspicious death of Albie Jones at Warsop Main Colliery in March 1984.

Newark, Nottinghamshire – December 15, 1984

Danny and Rob walked into the reception of Shaftsbury, Morton and Spinks Solicitors firm in Newark. It was early, and there was nobody else in reception.

Danny looked at the receptionist, who was busy typing, and said, 'Good morning, we're here to see Richard Morton, please.'

The receptionist didn't bother to look up from her typewriter, but continued typing as she said, 'Do you gentlemen have an appointment?'

Her desk and typewriter were across the office from the small reception window, and Danny found himself raising his voice over the click-clack noise of her typewriter keys.

With more than a little note of irritation in his voice, he replied, 'No, we don't have an appointment, Miss, but this is an urgent police matter, and I would very much appreciate your cooperation.'

He held out his warrant card for her to see.

The secretary stopped typing and looked over at the warrant card, inspecting it thoroughly before saying, 'It's not Miss, it's Ms, and you really do need to make an appointment. Mr Morton's a partner of this law firm, and he doesn't see anybody without a prior appointment.'

There was a note of annoyance in her voice now.

'Yes, Ms, I understand he's a partner, and I'm a Detective Inspector investigating two murders. Now, do what you have to do and get us in to see Mr Richard Morton, NOW!' said a clearly agitated Danny.

Obviously irritated, the woman stood up sharply and marched across to the window. 'Who shall I say wants to see him?'

'I'm Detective Inspector Danny Flint, and this is Detective Sergeant Rob Buxton.'

The receptionist stared hard at the warrant cards again being held out by the two detectives. She quickly scribbled down the names on her notepad and stalked through a door that led off her office.

'What a Rottweiler,' said Rob.

Danny smiled and nodded in agreement.

After three minutes, the door opened, and the Rottweiler reappeared – only now, she was more like a poodle. All of a sudden, she couldn't have been more gracious.

'Mr Morton will see you immediately, Detective Inspector,' she purred. 'Can I get either of you refreshments? A cup of tea or coffee, perhaps?'

Danny looked at Rob with a hint of a smile before replying, 'No, thank you.'

In the broadest Yorkshire accent he could muster, Rob said brusquely, 'Coffee, white two sugars. Ta, luv!'

'No problem, Sergeant,' she said quietly, but through gritted teeth. 'I'll buzz you in, gentlemen. Mr Morton's office is the first door on the left. I'll bring your coffee through shortly, Detective Sergeant.'

'Thank you, Ms,' said Rob, emphasising the *Ms* so it sounded like *Mzzzzz*.

The door lock buzzed open, and they walked into the private offices of Shaftsbury, Morton and Spinks.

Richard Morton was waiting at his open office door.

Morton was sixty-three years old, small in stature, but slim and fit with a full head of slate grey hair. He was also impeccably smart in a charcoal grey pinstripe suit, a crisp white shirt with gold and black onyx cuff links, and a maroon paisley pattern tie that was held by a tie slide that matched the cuff links. His black brogue shoes were highly polished.

There was no smile of welcome. He just fixed both the detectives with a hard look from his cold grey eyes and asked, 'Which one of you is Detective Inspector Flint?'

'I am, Mr Morton. Thank you for seeing us without an appointment,' said Danny.

'Ms Faversham, my secretary, gave me the impression that I'd little choice in the matter,' he said, his face breaking into a grin for the first time.

'A formidable woman, your Ms Faversham,' said Danny, returning the smile.

'Oh, you caught her on a bad day, that's all. She's a lovely woman and a fantastic secretary.'

Morton waved the two detectives into his office, saying, 'Sit down, gentlemen, please.'

Just as they did, Ms Faversham came into the office carrying a cup of coffee on a small tray. Also on the tray was a small plateful of assorted biscuits, a milk jug and a sugar bowl containing a variety of white and brown sugar cubes. She placed the tray down on the coffee table in front of Rob and said quietly, 'There you are, Detective Sergeant. Please help yourself to milk, sugar and a biscuit.'

'Thank you very much,' said Rob with a smile.

Ms Faversham then beat a hasty retreat from the room.

Morton sat down behind the large walnut desk that dominated his office. The desk was positioned directly in front of the only window in the room. It was a large plate-glass window that almost took up the entire wall. Through the fine net curtains, Danny could see that the view from the window was spectacular, overlooking the ruins of Newark Castle at the side of the River Trent.

The walls were panelled with a dark-coloured wood similar to the large desk. One wall was made up of floor-to-ceiling bookshelves; the shelves were stacked with a huge collection of law books.

In one corner of the room stood a large freestanding safe, metallic blue in colour. On the front of the safe in brass lettering was the maker's name, Chubb. Beneath the name was a large brass handle and a black combination dial.

The only other furniture in the room was a large red leather chesterfield settee, which matched the red leather captain's chair that Morton had behind the desk. In front of the settee was a dark wood coffee table upon which sat the coffee and biscuits. Rob and Danny had sat at each end of the chesterfield, and Rob busily put milk and two spoons of sugar into his coffee.

Morton turned to Danny and said, 'What was so urgent that you had to see me today, Inspector?'

'I need to ask you some questions about a conveyancing job you undertook recently. My understanding is that you dealt with this matter personally.'

'As I thought, you want to speak to me about Jimmy Wade.'

'Yes, we do. How did you know that?'

'Years ago, when I was a very young boy, my family lived at Newstead village. My father was a pitman. To cut a long story short, Inspector, there was a connection between my family and the Wade family. So when Jimmy Wade came to the firm, requesting that we represent him for the conveyancing of his house sale, I overheard him talking to one of our juniors. I enquired as to whether he was related in any way to the Wade family from Newstead. When he informed me that he was the grandson, I offered to do the conveyancing myself.'

'That still doesn't explain how you knew we wanted to talk to you about him today, Mr Morton.'

'Patience, please, Inspector. I completed the conveyancing with the minimum of fuss, as you would expect; it was a very straightforward sale. When Jimmy Wade came into settle his reduced bill, he left something with me. His instructions were very clear. I must only hand it to you, Detective Inspector Flint – but he stipulated clearly that I was only to pass this on to you if you ever came to my office making enquiries about the house sale.'

Rob, who had been sipping his coffee quietly, now hurriedly placed the cup on its saucer and leaned forward. 'What was it he left with you?'

Morton waved his hand towards Rob in a dismissive gesture. 'I'm sorry, Sergeant, I mustn't talk to anyone about this except Detective Inspector Flint, as I'm bound by client confidentiality rules. If DI Flint has no objections about you staying here, then I'm able to talk about this matter in front of you, but I mustn't refer to you in any way. So, if you wish to stay in the room, I must ask you to respect this and stay silent.'

Rob bristled, clearly annoyed at the stinging rebuke, but Danny said, 'It's okay, Rob. That's a fair comment.'

He turned to Richard Morton and said, 'We both understand the law regarding the privilege between a solicitor and his client. However, I would like my detective sergeant to stay; he'll remain silent and just observe. Now, what exactly was it that Jimmy Wade left with you that he so clearly wanted me to have, Mr Morton?'

Morton stood up and walked over to the Chubb safe in the corner of the room. He quickly twisted the combination dial first one way and then the other. Finally, he yanked hard down on the brass handle and pulled open the safe door.

He removed a white A4-sized envelope from the centre shelf before closing the door, pulling the handle back up and spinning the combination dial.

He then walked over to Danny and handed him the envelope.

Danny took the envelope. 'Before I open this letter, Mr Morton, are you prepared to stand in a court of law, if necessary, and confirm that this envelope was given to you by Jimmy Wade?'

'No court would ever ask me to do that and violate my legal privilege, Inspector. At any subsequent court proceedings, that fact would never be contested. You may open the envelope.'

'Are you aware of the contents?'

'Definitely not, Inspector. It was sealed when he gave it to me. There are three signatures on the back over the seal. they are my own, Mr Wade's and Mr Travis's, a solicitor who works here at the firm.'

'Could I borrow the letter opener on your desk to open the envelope, please, Mr Morton?'

'Of course, Inspector.'

Morton handed Danny a thin-bladed silver letter opener that had a thistle motif on the handle.

Danny reached into his jacket pocket and retrieved a pair of latex forensic gloves.

After quickly putting on the gloves, Danny slid the thin blade into the envelope, opening it carefully.

Inside the envelope were two more envelopes, one small and brown, the other letter sized.

Danny opened the brown envelope and found a small key. He then opened the second envelope and found that it contained a handwritten note.

DETECTIVE INSPECTOR FLINT
 Your answers lie with the key.
 Lloyds Bank, Market Place Branch, Nottingham
 Safety Deposit Box 212

THE NOTE WAS UNSIGNED.

Danny read the note aloud and then said, 'Does that mean anything to you, Mr Morton?'

'That doesn't mean a thing to me, Detective.'

Danny stood up. Morton also stood and walked around from his desk.

'Thanks for seeing us today, Mr Morton.'

'No problem, Detective Inspector. I'm intrigued: Will you be able to let me know what's in the safety deposit box?'

'If it's anything you need to know about, Mr Morton, rest assured I'll be in touch.'

Morton held out his hand. Danny quickly removed the latex gloves and accepted the outstretched hand.

'You understand why it has to be this way, don't you, Inspector?'

Danny nodded. 'I do, legal privilege and all that. There's one last question, when exactly did Jimmy Wade come in to settle his bill?'

'He came to see me on the morning of November 13 and paid his bill in cash. He gave me the envelope and his instructions then.'

'Thanks, Mr Morton.'

The two detectives left the building and hurried to their car, Danny gripping the envelope.

They got in the car, and Rob started the engine.

As he drove out of the car park and across the bridge that spanned the River Trent, Rob asked, 'I take it we're going to Nottingham?'

'Just as fast as you can get us there!'

Nottingham City Centre – December 15, 1984

They parked the CID car at the back of the main Central Police Station in Nottingham city centre and walked briskly down onto the Old Market Square. The city centre was heaving with shoppers as they weaved their way across the bustling square and into the main branch of Lloyds Bank. Outside, it was crowded both with customers of the bank and with patrons of the Flying Horse pub next door.

Once inside the bank, Danny walked up to the first cashier who was free. Showing his warrant card, he said quietly, 'I need to see the branch manager straight away, please.'

The young cashier nodded, left her seat and made her way through a door into the private offices. She returned almost immediately, followed by Mr Frederick Spooner, the branch manager.

Mr Spooner asked to see the detectives' warrant cards

again before allowing them through the armoured door into the back of the bank.

Once out of earshot of any members of the public, Mr Spooner said, 'How can I help you, Detective Inspector?'

'I have a key for a safety deposit box that is stored at this branch. It's imperative that I inspect the contents immediately.'

Spooner was clearly troubled; this was a highly irregular request. In all his considerable years in banking, he'd never known the police to make such a request.

'I'm sorry, but don't you need a warrant or something, Inspector?'

'No, Mr Spooner, I don't. I was given the key and instructions to go with it from the solicitor who was acting on the instructions of the man who set up the safety deposit box.'

Spooner huffed, shrugging his world-weary shoulders.

'I don't know; this is all highly irregular!' he said.

'But all highly proper, Mr Spooner, so can we get on with this, please? Time really is of the essence here.'

The branch manager rubbed the area of his forehead that sat just above his nose; he then pinched the top of his nose and squeezed his eyes closed as though trying to alleviate a headache. Suddenly, he opened his eyes as though he had made a momentous decision.

'Very well, Inspector. What's the number of the box?'

Danny held up the key and said, 'The safety deposit box number is 212, and this is the key.'

'Follow me, please. We have to go down to the vaults.'

Danny and Rob followed Spooner down two flights of stone stairs and into the vaults. Once inside, Spooner opened a large metal door, revealing a room where the safety deposit boxes were stored.

The room was about twelve feet long and eight feet wide. Both of the longer walls contained floor-to-ceiling safety deposit boxes. In the centre of the room was a large table that was bolted to the floor. The room was lit with a single, very bright fluorescent tube strip light.

The boxes themselves were black and made of brushed steel. In both corners of the room at ceiling height were two closed-circuit security television cameras that were pointing at the opposite wall to the one they were mounted on. These cameras covered both banks of security boxes, but did not have any view of the table in the centre of the room. This was to ensure the privacy of clients who wished to use the table to inspect the contents of their individual boxes.

Spooner retrieved safety deposit box number 212 and placed it on the table. Using a key from his pocket, he unlocked the first of the two locks mounted on the top of the box.

'I'll leave you to inspect the contents in private, Inspector. I've unlocked my lock; you'll need to open the other lock with the key in your possession. I'll be outside the door if you need anything else. When you've finished, just call my name, and I'll escort you out of the bank.'

'One last thing, Mr Spooner: Do the CCTV cameras record?'

'They certainly do, but they're on a forty-eight-hour loop. The system will only store images for two days. After that, it automatically records over any previous recordings.'

'That's a shame, but thanks anyway.'

Spooner then walked out, leaving the detectives alone in the vault.

Danny and Rob each took a pair of latex gloves from their pockets and quickly put them on. Danny took the key from the envelope and put it in the lock. One quick twist of the key to the left and the lock opened.

The strong box itself was eighteen inches high by two feet wide and two feet in length. Slowly, Danny lifted the lid; he was breathless with anticipation. Inside, a white A4-size envelope sat on top of several bulkier items below. Printed on the front of the envelope, in black felt-tip pen, were the words

FAO – Detective Inspector Danny Flint

DANNY REMOVED the envelope and placed it on the table next to the box; then he carefully removed the contents one by one and also placed those on the long table. The safety deposit box contained a portable Olivetti typewriter, a long blonde-haired wig, a single police uniform epaulette that had sergeant's chevrons on, a length of black plastic tubing, a four-foot length of thin nylon cord and a set of Ford Cortina Mk 1 keys.

Danny picked up the envelope and opened it.

Inside was a single sheet of white A4 paper on which was a typed note. Danny removed the sheet of paper and read the note to Rob.

DETECTIVE INSPECTOR DANNY Flint

I've enjoyed the chase and watching you doing your enlightening press appeals on the television. You've been a worthy adversary.

Just the fact that you're reading this letter proves that.

I had some fun with that oaf of a police sergeant, but he was a moron who wouldn't listen. We had our way with the two women, first at Forest Town and then again at Blidworth. We could have gone on and had many more if he hadn't been so stupid.

Oh well! That's all over and in the past now. I left the good sergeant hanging about for you to find near the abbey.

Hopefully you've found him by now.
We had a right laugh over 'The Coal Killer'.
Didn't you like the name?
I was disappointed you never gave the name to the press.
I've gone now, disappeared like a phantom. Don't bother looking because you'll never find me.
I'm far too clever for you to track me down, Inspector.
Is it South Africa, Canada or America? Ha ha ha!
Thank you for sending the lovely Rachel to see me about dear old Albie.
I really enjoyed my visit with her before I left.
A beautiful feisty woman, but she had to die too!
Sorry about that.
Not really!
Anyway, it's been fun, Detective.

THE COAL KILLER – aka Jimmy Wade – aka?

DANNY'S FACE was set like stone. He put the note down on the table next to the contents of the box.

He suddenly erupted and shouted, 'Bastard!' before hurling the now empty box across the room, clattering it into the opposite wall.

Turning to Rob, he said, 'It was this bastard all the time,, and he thinks he's killed Rachel.'

'I know, Danny. Look at the letter *c* on the note. This is obviously the typewriter they used, the blonde wig, the epaulette, the nylon cord, the keys for the car. He thinks it's all a bloody game.'

'The question is, where is he now? We've got to find him because he'll do this again and again until he's stopped!'

'Where do we start, boss? He's well and truly covered his

tracks. He's obviously not Jimmy Wade anymore. Somehow he's managed a change of identity.'

'It's hard to know where to start, but we've got to try to find him. Get the local CID to come down here and get this lot bagged and tagged. I haven't given up on catching this bastard yet.'

Mansfield Police Station – December 16, 1984

Danny knocked on the door of Superintendent Jackson's office.

He was waiting outside, holding clear evidence bags that contained the car keys, the epaulette, the nylon cord, the blonde wig and a clear plastic wallet that contained the typewritten note from Jimmy Wade.

Jackson's voice boomed out from within the office, 'Enter!'

Danny walked in and placed the articles recovered from the safety deposit box on the desk.

'What's all this?' asked a bemused Jackson.

'Read the note,' said Danny tersely.

Danny handed him the typewritten note.

Jackson slowly read the note, glancing up every now and then to look at the individual articles on the desk.

'Where's this Jimmy Wade character now?' he said.

'I don't know, but this bastard has killed a miner, two

women, and a police sergeant. He also attacked a policewoman, leaving her for dead. We need to find him as a matter of urgency, sir.'

'And just how do you propose to do that?'

'I want to set up a small task force to follow any leads we can find. There are things we can do to trace him.'

'What exactly can you do? Exactly what leads have you got?'

'Well, we think he's left the UK. We can check the ports, the airports.'

'Looking for who? Do you have a name to check against passenger manifests?'

'No, not yet.'

'How, exactly, are you going to get that name, Danny?'

'I don't know, sir, but I can't give up looking. This man's a psychopath, a stone-cold killer, and wherever he does end up, he'll definitely kill again.'

Ken Jackson was silent for a full five minutes while he thought over the information that Danny had given him. During that time, he occasionally picked up various items that had been placed on his desk as if trying to obtain inspiration from the inanimate objects.

Finally, he leaned back in his chair and said, 'This is what's going to happen, Inspector. You'll draft a report of your findings, everything you have on this individual Jimmy Wade. Description, age, medical history, dental records, anything you can get. You'll then write up a full synopsis of all the crimes he's suspected of committing here in the UK. I'll then ensure that this is passed on to every other police force in the world via Interpol.'

'Is that it, sir?'

'That's it. I can't afford to waste manpower on chasing a shadow, however abhorrent the monster is who casts that shadow.'

Slowly, Danny shook his head, then picked up all the

exhibits from the desk. He turned and walked out of the office without saying a word.

In all his career, he had never felt so bad.

He was having serious doubts about carrying on, he felt so low. He was struggling to accept the fact that his enquiries had been hampered from the start by cost and budgets.

The decision not to pursue the 'second killer' theory had been plain wrong and had almost cost Rachel Moore her life: When the toxicology report had finally come through for the post-mortem of Mick Reynolds, it had shown substantial traces of chloroform in the lungs and liver. Had Jackson bothered to wait, it would have shown categorically that Reynolds's death had not been suicide. Danny knew only too well that no senior officer would ever be taken to task over that wrong decision.

The chief officers at headquarters would simply hide behind their mantra of budget restraints and manpower shortages.

As he approached the CID office, he could hear hooting and hollering and happy laughing voices. The mood from within the office was completely at odds with how he felt.

Wondering what was happening, he opened the door.

Rob, smiling broadly, gripped Danny's shoulders and said, 'Fantastic news, Danny. We've just had a message from Joe at the hospital. It's Rachel, she's finally come out of the coma.'

'That's brilliant news, Rob.'

'It gets better, Danny. Rachel's already sitting up and talking. She can't remember a thing about that night, but Joe's told us the doctors think she'll go on to make a full recovery.'

'That really is the best news I could've heard today, Rob.'

Rob picked up on the muted response to the great news.

'Is everything okay?' he asked quietly.

'I've just come from Jackson's office. He isn't going to allow us to follow up on Jimmy Wade. I know it would've been a difficult, nigh on impossible task to track the bastard down, but all Jackson wants me to do is write a fucking report and pass it on.'

'Bloody hell, no wonder you're feeling down.'

'I just feel like that bastard Wade has got away with murder.'

Rob put his arm around Danny's shoulder. 'Come on, forget all that for now. We'll make a start on the report tomorrow. We can do it together and curse that wanker Jackson under our breath as we're writing it.'

Danny grinned and said, 'Don't let that wanker Jackson hear you calling him a wanker! It could seriously jeopardise your chances of promotion!'

'That's more like it! Come on, we're all going to the Railway to celebrate Rachel's recovery. Joe's meeting us there in half an hour. Come on, let's get shitfaced tonight! We can worry about all this other shit tomorrow.'

'I'll come for a drink, Rob — we do need to celebrate Rachel's recovery — but I just want to get home to Sue tonight. I've got some serious thinking to do.'

'Serious thinking about what, exactly?'

'I need to reassess my future. At this moment in time, I don't know if I even want to carry on doing this job anymore. Being told what I can and can't investigate properly, depending on how much it's going to fucking cost. I'm sick of the penny-pinching!'

'Danny, don't be daft. You'd chased Wade down, and he knew you were closing in behind him and would get him eventually; that's why he's fucked off out of it. You were right all along; your intuition was spot on. You can't quit. This is what you do; this is what you're bloody good at.'

'We'll see, Rob, we'll see. Come on, let's get to the pub and celebrate the good news.'

91

Singleton, New South Wales, Australia – December 31, 1984

The new tenant looked around the spacious living room. He had rented the second-floor apartment above Randall's Hardware shop on Main Street, Singleton, New South Wales.

Walking over to the window, he looked down over the busy street and watched people rushing home, ready to celebrate New Year's Eve with their loved ones. In the distance, he could see the orange hues of the rapidly setting sun glistening off the still waters of the vast Lake St Clair.

Singleton was picturesque, nothing like the grey drab mining towns he had left back in the UK.

The pretty town was just over a hundred kilometres from Sydney and lay on the banks of the Hunter River.

From the very first moment he'd arrived in the town, he knew immediately this would be where he settled.

He'd only rented this apartment for a couple of months.

He wanted a base he could settle into before starting work at the Beltana Mine.

The huge mine was nineteen kilometres from Singleton.

It was nothing like the antiquated mine he had been used to back in the UK. Beltana Mine was modern and vast, and it employed almost five thousand men.

After arriving at the town and renting the apartment, he'd spent a week at the mine getting used to where everything was and being introduced to his new workmates.

A lot of the other miners were also British. They, too, had emigrated to Australia, intent on starting a new life after becoming disillusioned with the UK mining industry following the long, bitter strike.

He was due to start his first working shift on 1 January 1985. He felt it was poetic: a new year, a new job, a new life, a new identity.

He walked to the large refrigerator and took out a cold can of Castlemaine beer. Flicking open the ring pull, he opened the ice-cold can and took a long drink. The cold lager burned his throat as he swallowed. The sun had now dipped below the horizon. Below his flat, street lights were beginning to come on.

As he looked out of the window, he reflected on the journey he'd taken, as well as the careful preparations he'd made that enabled him to arrive here.

The whole idea had come to him as a result of seeing an advert in the *Sunday Telegraph*. He'd read the paper after spending the morning in the Warsop Miners Welfare, listening to other miners moaning about the state of the coal industry in the UK.

The advert he saw had been placed by the Baluga Coal Management Company. They were specifically advertising for British mineworkers to move out to Australia to help develop the new mine at Beltana, which had opened in June 1983.

The very next day, he'd travelled to a country church in

North Yorkshire and searched until he found a gravestone that marked the death of a male infant named Lee Chivers.

Chivers had been born the same year as he had, but had died aged only three months. He went into the small church and checked the parish register. He soon found the entry relating to the death of Lee Chivers. He made a note of the names and details of the dead infants' parents.

Using these details, he had applied for and received a duplicate birth certificate in the name of the dead infant.

He then completed a passport application also in the name of Lee Chivers. He forged the signatures of the countersigners and posted off the passport application and the duplicate birth certificate, not really sure if it would work.

Much to his surprise, his new passport arrived shortly after.

He had then made the decision to go back to work as a scab. There, it took him almost two weeks before an opportunity arose that allowed him to get into the personnel office and remove his own file.

Taking the file home, he painstakingly copied and forged references in his new name of Lee Chivers. He then sent these forged and copied documents, together with a copy of his new passport, off with the job application.

Again, he had been very pleasantly surprised when the letter had arrived offering him a job at the Beltana Mine in New South Wales, Australia.

He had travelled down to Canberra House in London for the day to undergo a medical. He passed the medical easily and was granted a twelve-month visa. The visa was issued with an option to apply for dual citizenship at a later date.

After obtaining the visa and passing the medical, he immediately placed his house on the market for a ridiculous amount of money.

The house was quickly sold, almost too quickly; he was

forced to ask his solicitor to slow things down a little so he could complete everything else he needed to do.

As soon as the house was sold and the money had been cleared into his bank account at the NatWest Bank, he immediately went into the bank and withdrew all the money from his account. The next stop was a travel agent, where he purchased a one-way ticket to Australia, in his new name of Lee Chivers.

His flight left Heathrow airport in London at eleven o'clock on the morning of 15 November. He'd abandoned the blue Datsun Cherry car in the long-stay car park at the airport.

Arriving in Australia, he enjoyed Sydney for a week before travelling on the overland coach out to Singleton.

After arriving at Singleton, he rented the apartment and took his driving test with the Australian police. Having passed the driving test easily, he was granted an Australian driving licence in the name of Lee Chivers.

He then purchased a second-hand Holden hatchback car.

Armed with an Australian driving licence and a new passport to confirm his identity, he opened a bank account at the First National Bank of Australia.

Before leaving England, he had converted the money from the sale of 56 Marples Avenue into Australian dollars. He had hidden the Australian banknotes in the lining of one of his large suitcases. It was a risk bringing cash into the country, but it had proved to be a worthwhile gamble.

As soon as the customs officer at Sydney airport saw the twelve-month work visa and the letter confirming the job offer, he had waved him straight through customs.

He was now sitting pretty with over fifty thousand dollars in the bank, a new job at the mine, a new car and a nice apartment.

Later in the new year he intended to look for a bigger house to settle down in.

He took another long pull on the ice-cold lager and again

looked down from his window. The street below was full of people bustling along, getting on with their lives.

He reflected on the fact that getting to this point had been no easy task. It had taken months of careful planning.

As Jimmy Wade, he had easily outwitted the police in England. He was always one step ahead and had managed to get away with murder time after time.

Now reinvented as Lee Chivers, he felt confident, invisible and untouchable. He'd learned many lessons from the insane Mick Reynolds and now felt even better equipped to outwit law enforcement.

He would be patient and take three or four months to establish and orient himself. After killing Reynolds, he now realised he no longer had to rely on the urges to guide him. He was now the master of his own destiny. When he killed and whom he killed was completely a matter of his own choosing.

He knew the time would come soon enough for Australia to witness the arrival of Lee Chivers. There was nothing to stand in his way. The killing would soon begin again.

EPILOGUE

Beltana Mine, New South Wales – April 20, 1985

Dave Smedley was now a very happy man. The depression he had felt back in England now seemed a dim and distant memory. After arriving in Australia, he'd started his new job at the Beltana Mine, right on schedule on the first of March. He felt it was apt that he'd started his new job and effectively his new life on St David's day.

His wife, Louise, quickly settled in to her new surroundings and soon found them a lovely home just outside Singleton.

The pay from the mine was very good, and his new employers were extremely happy with his work.

They had quickly settled into their beautiful new home, and life could not be better for Dave Smedley.

It was now approaching ten o'clock at night, and Dave was reflecting on a hard afternoon shift as he walked across the large floodlit car park at the Beltana mine.

He was walking with Jeff Evans, another of the mine's supervisors. Jeff was a born-and-bred Australian and had been one of the first people Dave became friends with after his move down under. The two men walked slowly across the car park towards their respective cars.

As they walked across the huge car park, Dave saw a group of men approaching them.

His eyes were immediately drawn to a tall, blonde-haired man at the centre of the group, who was laughing.

Dave quickly looked away as he passed the group of men, who were heading in for the night shift.

Turning to Jeff, he asked, 'Did you see that tall, blonde guy who just walked past?'

Jeff quickly glanced over his shoulder, then replied, 'Yeah, he's another Pom like you, mate. He started back in January, just after the new year.'

'Do you know his name, Jeff?'

'Why, do you know him from back home?'

'I think I do, yeah.'

'Let me think. Yeah, I've got it, mate. His name's Lee Chivers. I reckon he lives near you, over in Singleton somewhere.'

Dave was totally shocked. He knew exactly who the tall, blonde-haired miner was, and it definitely wasn't Lee Chivers.

'Tell you what, Dave, the shift I've just had was a proper bastard. Do you fancy a couple of cold ones on the way home?' asked Jeff.

'I'd love to, mate, but there's something I've got to do urgently tonight. You okay to have that beer tomorrow?'

'Of course; no worries. See you tomorrow.'

Dave Smedley jumped in his car and raced out of the car park. As he drove his car along the twisting roads from the Beltana Mine to his house in Singleton, he was desperately trying to remember a name. As he pulled onto the driveway of his house, the name suddenly came into his head.

He ran straight into the house.

'Louise, love, what time is it in England?'

'What time is it now?' she shouted from upstairs.

'It's about half past ten, love.'

'Well then, it's about half past nine in the morning over there. Why?'

'Never mind, love, I'll be up in a minute. I just need to make a quick call.'

He dialled the operator. After a short wait, the operator came on the line.

'I'd like to be put through to Mansfield Police Station, Mansfield, Nottinghamshire, England. Thanks,' said Dave quietly.

A minute or so went by. All Dave could hear were clicks and other strange noises.

Patiently, he waited.

Suddenly, a voice came on the line: 'Hello, Mansfield Police, how can I help?'

'I need to speak to Detective Inspector Flint, please.'

'Just a second; I'll put you through to the CID.'

Another delay, then a voice answered, 'Detective Inspector Flint, how can I help you?'

'DI Flint, it's Dave Smedley.'

'What can I do for you, Mr Smedley?'

'I don't know if you remember me, Inspector, but I came to see you about the death of Albie Jones.'

'I remember you, Mr Smedley.'

'Inspector, I'm living in Australia now, at a small town called Singleton, not far from Sydney. I thought you'd want to know; I've just seen Jimmy Wade at the Beltana Mine!'

WE HOPE YOU ENJOYED THIS BOOK

If you could spend a moment to write an honest review on Amazon, no matter how short, we would be extremely grateful. They really do help readers discover new authors.

ALSO BY TREVOR NEGUS

EVIL IN MIND

(Book 1 in the DCI Flint series)

DEAD AND GONE

(Book 2 in the DCI Flint series)

A COLD GRAVE

(Book 3 in the DCI Flint series)

TAKEN TO DIE

(Book 4 in the DCI Flint series)

KILL FOR YOU

(Book 5 in the DCI Flint series)

ONE DEADLY LIE

(Book 6 in the DCI Flint series)

A SWEET REVENGE

(Book 7 in the DCI Flint series)

THE DEVIL'S BREATH

(Book 8 in the DCI Flint series)

I AM NUMBER FOUR

(Book 9 in the DCI Flint series)

TIED IN DEATH

(Book 10 in the DCI Flint series)

A FATAL OBSESSION

(Book 11 in the DCI Flint series)

THE FIRST CUT

(Book 12 in the DCI Flint series)

DCI DANNY FLINT BOX SET (Books 1 - 4)

Published by Inkubator Books
www.inkubatorbooks.com

Copyright © 2021 by Trevor Negus

Trevor Negus has asserted his right to be identified as the author of this work.

EVIL IN MIND is a work of fiction. People, places, events, and situations are the product of the author's imagination. Any resemblance to actual persons, living or dead is entirely coincidental.

No part of this book may be reproduced, stored in any retrieval system, or transmitted by any means without the prior written permission of the publisher.

Printed in Great Britain
by Amazon